BRIAN MORELAND

TOMB OF GODS

This is a **FLAME TREE PRESS** book

Text copyright © 2020 Brian Moreland

FLAME TREE PRESS
6 Melbray Mews, London, SW6 3NS, UK
flametreepress.com

US sales, distribution and warehouse:
Simon & Schuster
100 Front Street, Riverside, NJ 08075
www.simonandschuster.com

Thanks to the Flame Tree Press team, including:
Taylor Bentley, Frances Bodiam, Federica Ciaravella, Don D'Auria,
Chris Herbert, Josie Karani, Molly Rosevear, Mike Spender,
Cat Taylor, Maria Tissot, Nick Wells, Gillian Whitaker.

The cover is created by Flame Tree Studio with
thanks to Nik Keevil and Shutterstock.com.
The font families used are Avenir and Bembo.

Flame Tree Press is an imprint of Flame Tree Publishing Ltd
flametreepublishing.com

A copy of the CIP data for this book is available from the British Library
and the Library of Congress.

HB ISBN: 978-1-78758-414-3
PB ISBN: 978-1-78758-412-9
ebook ISBN: 978-1-78758-415-0

Printed and bound in Great Britain by Clays Ltd, Elcograf S.p.A.

BRIAN MORELAND

TOMB OF GODS

FLAME TREE PRESS
London & New York

'Homage to you, Osiris, Lord of eternity, King of the gods, whose names are manifold, whose forms are holy, you being of hidden form in the temples, whose Ka is holy.'
The Papyrus of Ani – Egyptian Book of the Dead
Translated by Sir E.A. Wallis Budge in 1895

PROLOGUE

Egypt, 1250 BC

Commander Tarik turned his back to the sandstorm and struggled to breathe. "Hurry," he shouted. Each man and woman grasped a thick cable to keep from being lost in the whirling sand. Nubian slaves balanced a wooden sarcophagus on their shoulders. Tarik led his soldiers and servants down an earthen ramp between brick walls and through a stone doorway cut into the mountain.

Inside the tomb, the passage narrowed and torches pushed back the darkness. The funeral procession followed Tarik through the tunnel. Their footsteps echoed off stone walls etched with hieroglyphs. As they entered the subterranean chapel, a serdab statue of the deceased watched in silence. Tarik ordered the slaves to set the sarcophagus on a platform. All of the chosen ones gathered around it for the rushed ceremony. The female servants, dressed identically for the burial in white gowns and beetle-green eye makeup, lowered to their knees. The others bowed their heads.

Tarik observed their solemn faces as the priest spoke the prayers for Nebenteru to complete his journey into the afterlife. The dead high priest had been King Ramses II's spiritual advisor. Tarik had overseen the mummification and all the treasures that would be entombed with the mummy. He had wondered about one silver object in particular, placed in the sarcophagus by the pharaoh himself, but then the coffin had been sealed with an order by the king that it never be opened again.

The kites – mourning women in gray dresses – joined their voices to sing the 'Lamentation of Isis and Nephthys'. The sorrowful notes rose and fell, traveling beyond the torchlight.

Tarik led the procession down a rock staircase, deep into the cave, to the burial chamber. One of the servant girls stumbled and had to be helped to her feet. Tarik saw terror in her eyes. Even his soldiers looked nervous. He needed to hurry. Fear was a contagion.

After the sarcophagus was sealed behind a wall, Tarik led the others into their own chamber. Next came the part of the ceremony everyone had been dreading. The priest knelt first, accepting his sacrificial death. Tarik braced himself, then drove his blade into the old man's chest and twisted. Tarik gave the order for his men to kill the slaves and royal servants. The commander made himself watch as his men's blades slit throats, and one by one bodies fell to the stone floor. The kites died singing. One slave panicked and fled deeper into the tomb.

Two soldiers started after him.

"Leave him," Tarik ordered. "We must seal the tomb."

Tarik and his soldiers hurried back to the entrance. Outside, the angry wind whirled sand so thick it was hard to see the dying sun. The storm had already done its work, burying most of the exterior masonry. Only the doorway remained. Following the orders of the pharaoh, the soldiers stacked mud bricks at the entrance. The howling wind grew muffled as the last brick closed off the outside world, forever imprisoning Tarik and his men inside the tomb. This cave was the pharaoh's greatest secret; all who built or visited it had been put to death.

After returning to the crypt where the others lay dead, Tarik studied the faces of the dozen men who awaited his order. He had led them into battle more times than he could count. "Each of you has fought bravely by my side. I am grateful for your loyalty and honored that the pharaoh has chosen us to journey together with the high priest to the Field of Reeds. May our hearts weigh light as feathers before Osiris."

Each man slammed a fist against his own chest. The emotion in their eyes wrenched Tarik's heart. For a moment, he allowed himself to wonder whether their deaths truly served anyone. Courage and loyalty were hard found in this life. To sacrifice his men seemed a horrible waste.

It was not for Tarik to question the gods.

He gave the nod. His men stabbed one another. Several collapsed, dead before they struck the earthen floor. Others lingered, their wounds mortal but slow to bleed. Anen and Khamet, his two best soldiers, brothers who had grown up as farmers in the Nile Valley, held one another as their blades twisted. Anen died first. Khamet hung on. He looked up at Tarik with tearful eyes, his mouth filling with blood. Tarik put a hand on the younger man's shoulder. "We will be together soon. Go peacefully." He slit Khamet's throat. Tarik then mercifully finished off his wounded brethren until he was the last one standing. He would remain in the crypt alone among the slaughtered. His death and journey to the afterlife would come later. He'd promised to guard the crypt until his last breath ran out.

A man's voice howled from deep within the tomb.

Tarik had forgotten about the escaped slave. Now he would have to hunt the man down himself. If anyone outlived the commander, Tarik would dishonor his king and gods and suffer in the underworld.

Tarik charged down another narrow staircase. His torch barely lit the darkness. The deeper he went, passage after passage, the more he began to wonder about the pharaoh's secret tomb and the peculiar metal object sealed with the mummy. What had the king used it for? The mummy's crypt was only part of a labyrinth of intersecting cave tunnels. Who had carved the descending staircases out of rock, creating a cavernous maze that seemed endless? On the tunnel walls, columns upon columns of prayer spells from previous dynasties merged with pictorial etchings he could not read. These reliefs covered the walls in ornate spiral patterns. Who had engraved these walls so deep in the earth? And why?

Tarik silenced his mind. His duty was to carry out the pharaoh's orders.

He listened for the slave but heard only the sound of flames as his torch stabbed at the darkness. He entered a chamber that reeked of fresh slaughter. His sandals slipped in warm liquid. He raised his torch. The floor, walls, and ceiling were spattered with blood.

Tarik's heart surged with alarm. He hurried to the far corner of the chamber. The slave's ravaged body lay crumpled in a heap. The corpse, riddled with bite marks, appeared half eaten.

A scraping sound echoed from the dark end of the chamber. Something hissed behind him.

Tarik whirled with his torch, sword raised.

Heavy breathing sounded from the dark.

"Who's there?" he called out.

Raspy voices circled Tarik. Dim shapes appeared just beyond the reach of the light. With them, came a sickly smell – fungus mixed with sweat. Misshapen shadows moved across the rock wall.

He swung his sword. "Stay away!"

Something struck his arm and batted his weapon away. A fiery pain erupted up Tarik's arm. Blood poured from a gash in his hand. He lunged with his torch at the shifting dark. The fire diminished to a small, clinging flame. As the darkness closed in, so did the things moving within it. When the last of the light winked out, Tarik found himself blind in a realm of endless black. Then came the pain of a hundred sticking blades as sharp teeth and claws dug into him, tearing flesh from his bones.

PART ONE
THE EXPEDITION

CHAPTER ONE

Egypt, 1935

The caves moaned like a chorus of lost souls, beckoning the team of British archaeologists as they scaled the mountain. When the eight men reached a cliff plateau lined with craggy fissures, Dr. Harlan Riley examined the entrance to the central-most cave and smiled. After unrolling a photo of a papyrus scroll, he compared the hieroglyphs with the symbols etched in the rock. Harlan found the crescent marking, then an image of Horus holding an ankh. The falcon-headed god was barely visible after centuries of winds had eroded the stone.

"We can thank the ancient Greeks and Romans for leaving us accounts of their expeditions," Harlan told his team. "This is the entrance they used."

Throughout the centuries, countless explorers had searched in vain to find the tomb of Nebenteru, where King Ramses II supposedly sealed his royal secrets. The Greeks and Romans had scribed tales of a series of caves known as Kahf Alssulta. Men of every devotion – soldiers and monks, scientists and thieves – had entered the caves, never to return from the endless honeycombed labyrinth. Knowledge of the mountain and its entombed mysteries eventually faded into myths buried in libraries and ghost stories told around nomadic campfires. Modern archaeology had turned its interests to more popular curiosities, like Tut's tomb in Thebes and all the enigmas surrounding the pyramids of Giza.

For Dr. Harlan Riley, the secrets within Nebenteru's tomb had become his Holy Grail. Whether the Greco-Roman tales were fact or fiction, he didn't fully know. But the piece of Ani's papyrus scroll he had pilfered from a tomb in the Valley of the Kings was authentic. It had been written as if intended only for the eyes of a pharaoh. Coded within the text was a subtext that alluded to a hidden gateway. Somewhere in cavernous darkness, revelations lay waiting to be discovered.

When he'd compared the scroll to the fourth-century writings of a Roman explorer searching for this cave, Harlan pinpointed the tomb's location east of the Nile. Two decades of searching Egypt's desert mountains had brought him to this moment. As his heart swelled and his eyes glistened with moisture, he thought of his granddaughter, Imogen, back home in London. He wished she could be here to share this victory.

Just three men of Harlan's group knew the full extent of what the scroll suggested they would find. Chalmers looked ashen as he peered into the cave's black maw. Benson thought only of the wealth and fame that would be theirs once they returned to England. Harlan had made a pact with his colleagues to maintain secrecy until they discovered the truth for themselves. The assistants and porters knew only what was needed to do their jobs.

Harlan switched on the lamp of his caving helmet and aimed the beam into the cave. Something deep within was calling him to enter.

"We are standing at the threshold of one of life's great mysteries," Harlan told his team. He entered the tunnel first. The others followed as the cave swallowed the Riley team whole.

London Herald
JULY 15, 1936

BRITISH ARCHAEOLOGIST FOUND ALIVE IN EGYPT, RETURNS TO ENGLAND

After being missing for one year, Dr. Harlan Riley, lead archaeologist of the Nebenteru Expedition for the British Museum of London, was discovered three weeks ago wandering the desert southeast of Cairo. Nomads found him nearly dead from dehydration. Dr. Riley has spent two weeks in hospital in Cairo. According to sources, Dr. Riley has been unable to explain what happened to the rest of his team — two archaeologists, one assistant, the group's Egyptian translator, and three porters — all are still missing and presumed dead after exploring a cave somewhere in the Eastern Desert mountains a year ago.

"What happened to Dr. Riley's team is a tragedy," stated Dr. Nathan Trummel, fellow archaeologist with the British Museum. "We have lost some of the greatest minds in the field of archaeology." Further, Dr. Trummel vowed to the Crown to do everything in his power to continue Dr. Riley's research and get to the truth of what happened in Egypt. Dr. Riley was recently transported to Hanwell Mental Hospital, London County for treatment. Mysterious scars covering his head and body have doctors and scientists perplexed. His speech is reportedly incoherent, and he remains on suicide watch.

CHAPTER TWO

October 15, 1936
Hanwell Mental Hospital
London, England

Every time Imogen Riley visited Hanwell, she clung to the hope that this time would be her last. As she pulled up to the gate's stone archway, she took a deep breath and braced herself for what lay ahead. A guard checked her papers, then opened the wrought iron gate. Imogen drove down a driveway bordered with leafless trees. Bruised gray clouds hovered over the old Victorian insane asylum, and a light mist dampened its high walls. A clock tower loomed over the main building's entrance. She parked out front and gave her keys to the front door attendant. Imogen felt someone watching her. Movement in a second-story window caught her eye. A pale shape quickly slipped out of sight.

Inside, a tall, heavyset orderly escorted Imogen down a long hallway. The hospital was agitated with constant noise. Mental patients gabbered. A few cried out. From somewhere nearby came the sound of metal striking metal. Crackling from above made Imogen look up. A caged light bulb, secured to the ceiling, flickered and went out, casting the hall in gloom.

"Bloody lights. They've been going on and off all morning," the orderly muttered. He led Imogen through a gated doorway and past the guard's post. In the farthest wing, the halls echoed with patients howling from their padded cells. The smell of body odor and sickness clung in the air. Through a door's square window, a grinning man with crooked brown teeth leered at Imogen. His eyes followed her as she walked by. She shuddered and turned a corner where a team of doctors and nurses were gathered. They fell quiet when they noticed Imogen approaching.

"Welcome back, Miss Riley," Dr. Fetter, a short, ginger-headed man in a white coat, greeted Imogen.

"Thank you, Doctor. How is he?" she asked.

"Having a good day, no outbursts. You're welcome to visit him."

"Has he improved?"

"He's making slow progress, I'm afraid. But he's been calm today, so that gives us hope."

Imogen's spirits lifted. Any day she was allowed to visit Grandfather was a good day. She'd been coming to the hospital a few days a week for the past three months. She often visited him in the morning before going to work at the museum. On Saturdays, she stayed and sat with Grandfather and read him a book or newspaper until the staff made her leave.

Taking a deep breath, she followed Dr. Fetter down another hallway. The light bulbs along the ceiling all flickered.

"Is that from the storm?" Imogen asked.

"Electrical system's been on the blink lately," Dr. Fetter said. "It's turning this place into a madhouse." He chuckled at his own joke.

The hall ended at a closed metal door. Light flickered from the gaps in the doorframe, more erratic than in the hallway. Dr. Fetter unlocked the door. When he opened it, the bulb on the ceiling buzzed and returned to normal, illuminating the sparse visitation room with its scratched-up walls, small wooden table, and two chairs.

Imogen followed the doctor inside the room. Grandfather stood in the far corner, whispering to the walls. He wore white hospital-issue pajamas. What little gray hair he had left grew in patches of stubble. The strange scars that covered his head and body still unnerved her. She barely recognized the man who had raised her. It was harder still to imagine that this poor creature had once been the highly intelligent archaeologist and professor who had led expeditions for the British Museum for decades.

Dr. Fetter approached him cautiously. "Harlan, you have a visitor."

Grandfather kept his back to them, mumbling phrases of the strange language that he had spoken since his time in the caves.

Dr. Fetter motioned for Imogen to take a seat at the table. Then he gently took Grandfather's arm. "Come sit with your granddaughter." The doctor guided him and sat him down across the table from Imogen.

"Hello, Grandfather." She touched his arm. "It's me."

His eyes darted about the room, looked everywhere but at her. It broke her heart to see him so frail. He trembled as he mumbled to himself.

Her temper flared and she shot Dr. Fetter a disapproving look. "You said you were going to reduce his medication."

"We tried. He became violent, so we had to up his dosage. For now, at least." He gave Imogen a weak smile, then glanced at his pocket watch. "If you'll excuse me, I have rounds to make." Dr. Fetter left her alone with Grandfather. The orderly sat in a chair just outside the open door.

Imogen opened her handbag and removed a newspaper, wrapped pastries, and a thermos of Earl Grey tea. "I brought you the *London Herald* and breakfast from J. Lyons. An English muffin spread thick with raspberry jam, just like you like it." She set the items on the table, hoping the familiar things would jar his memories and bring him back. Before his last expedition, Imogen and Grandfather had met for breakfast at J. Lyons and Co. every Saturday, a tradition they had maintained for years. They enjoyed doing crossword puzzles together, chatting about their shared work, or just sitting in companionable silence. They were the only family either of them had left in the world.

Imogen opened the newspaper to the puzzle page. Grandfather paid no attention to the paper or his muffin. His gaze flitted around her, like he was watching a fly buzzing about the room, but the windowless room had no flies. The light bulb crackled and blinked a few times. Suddenly, for the first time in weeks, Grandfather looked directly at Imogen. His gaze seemed to register her presence. "Immy…"

Tears welled in her eyes at the sound of her name, after so long. "Yes, Grandfather, I'm here."

He reached for her hand. "I'll be so sorry to leave you, but I don't have much time left."

"Of course you do. The doctors say you're in good health. You just need to rest here until you get back to normal."

"I will never be normal again. Not after what I've seen."

"What *did* you see?" She desperately wanted to know what had happened to him and his team in those caves. Where had he spent the past year? And how did he get all these peculiar scars that covered nearly every inch of his skin? Her fingers traced the raised welts on his right forearm. The symbols looked akin to a mixture of hieroglyphs and Sanskrit, only older perhaps. Anthropologists at the British Museum had been at the task since Grandfather returned from the caves of Kahf Alssulta. Apart from a few symbols – the all-seeing Eye of Horus carved into Grandfather's forehead and an ankh and scepter into each cheek – none of the writings matched any known language. The way the symbols covered his head and back, it was clear the markings had not been self-inflicted. Someone had done this to him.

"Grandfather, please…tell me what you discovered in the tomb."

"The only way to understand is to go there." Grandfather took her hands in his and looked at her deeply. "Dr. Trummel will take a team next month. You must go with them, Immy. Promise me."

For months, she had requested that the British Museum's board of trustees let her lead a return expedition. They had said no, citing safety concerns. *Would they really back Trummel?* After Grandfather was found wandering the desert and taken to a hospital in Egypt, Trummel, who had been working a dig near Cairo, had brought Grandfather safely back to London. For that, she was grateful. But she and Trummel were competitors too, both vying for the museum's strained resources, both interested in the same site. To make matters more complicated, not long ago they had been lovers in a secret affair, and she was reluctant to work with Trummel ever again.

Grandfather dropped his voice to a whisper. "I am leaving you something. Use it to secure a spot on Trummel's team."

"It should be *our* expedition, yours and mine." She desperately wanted to believe he could recover and they could work together again. "You're getting well. We'll have more adventures in Egypt. Like before."

"I would love that too." He gave her a tired smile. "If I were only able. But we must be honest with each other. I won't be returning to the desert. Go with Trummel. I need to know that you will carry on my work. Promise!"

"Of course. I'll go whether Trummel bloody likes it or not."

"That's my girl." He gripped her hands tight. "Go forth, Immy, but be wary like the rabbit, always alert of face."

"What do you mean?" she asked, not understanding his cryptic warning.

But before he could answer, the awareness left his eyes.

In seconds, he was gone. He crossed the room and resumed the strange whispering.

CHAPTER THREE

The madhouse peaked to a frenzy whenever Harlan Riley conversed with the gods. Patients shouted up and down the hallways, banging on steel doors with tiny windows.

Voices spoke to Harlan in tongues, gibbering from the rends in the white padded walls of his cell where he had tried to claw his way out, searching for tunnels that would lead him back to the tomb.

The voices spun around the walls and whispered into his head. Harlan nodded, understanding their urgent commands. They were calling him back. He grinned at the thought of finally being free. "Yes, I will do that," he said to the walls, talking with rapid movements of his hands. "I will, I will." From a hiding place beneath his mattress, he pulled out a small, leather-bound journal and fountain pen that Trummel had secretly given him. The black ink had run dry, so Harlan pressed the pen's sharp nib into a vein in his left arm. Using his own blood, he wrote furious passages into his journal.

I have walked in the footsteps of the pharaohs, seen relics beyond imagining. I have embodied the wisdom of the gods.

Harlan studied the myriad scars covering his arms – lines and dots, crosses and spirals. He felt the welts stitched across his face, fingertips reading the symbols like Braille. He understood every hieroglyph, every scripture. He knew if he turned his skin inside out, the writing would be there too, a text more ancient than the first Sumerian tablet. And if he were to peel his flesh from his skeleton, he'd find totems of faces scrimshawed into his bones.

He was a walking codex, yet his explanations only earned him blank stares. His doctors, believing him a lunatic, insisted on keeping him sedated.

Harlan felt fresh scorpion stings of pain each time he stabbed the pen into his wound. He needed ink, needed to tell his story. *Friends have abandoned me. Only two visit – my granddaughter, Imogen, and devout colleague, Nathan Trummel. And of course the ghosts of my team who surrendered their lives in the caves. I still hear their madding cries.*

A loud banging interrupted his thoughts.

Outside the cell, orderlies pounded on the door. The face of Dr. McCabe, head of the psych ward, filled a tiny window stained with a red handprint. "Harlan, remove the damn chair!"

The chair, propped against the doorknob, gave way a quarter inch at a time as the orderlies slammed their bodies against the door. On the floor lay the unconscious body of Harlan's psychiatrist, Dr. Fetter, his head bleeding from the unexpected blow.

Harlan's pen scribbled rapidly across the journal's page. Tears filled his eyes as he thought of his granddaughter. *Upon my death, I bequeath this book to you, Imogen Riley. I beg you to believe me. I have written herein only a fraction of what happened to me and my team, but there's more. So much more.* Harlan's shaky hand shifted from English to a rapid staccato of symbols, the codex speaking through him.

Bodies continued to slam against the door. The metal chair slid another inch, threatening to buckle.

Harlan's mind cleared, allowing him precious seconds of lucidity. He hastily drew a crude map. The door burst open. The metal chair clanged against the bed. Two orderlies rushed Harlan with Dr. McCabe behind them wielding a needle.

Harlan backed into a corner. Before they could grab him, he jammed the pen into his throat, opening his jugular.

CHAPTER FOUR

Highgate Cemetery
London

A cold October dampness clung to the headstones and crosses and dripped from the ivy that enveloped the surrounding crypts and trees. As the chill seeped through his suit, Dr. Nathan Trummel felt mixed emotions. He mourned the loss of the man who had been his mentor and friend. Had their opposing views not divided them in recent years, perhaps Trummel might have shed a tear for Dr. Harlan Riley. Over a hundred people had come to honor and mourn him, including board members, curators and staff of the British Museum, as well as colleagues and former students from Oxford.

The museum's board of trustees had spared no expense. Harlan's final resting place was a free-standing tomb in Highgate Cemetery's prestigious section called West Cemetery, in view of the gateway of Egyptian Avenue. His coffin, engraved with Egyptian gods and hieroglyphs, looked fit for a pharaoh. Centered on the casket's lid was the ibis-headed god, Thoth.

Sir George Harington gave the eulogy. "It is with enormous sadness in our hearts that we say goodbye to Dr. Harlan Riley, one of the greatest scientists of our age, who discovered and amassed an astounding collection of historical treasures for the British Museum while at the same time teaching and mentoring the next generation of explorers and archaeologists. It is a rare individual who can manage both..."

Trummel found Imogen Riley in the crowd. She stood nearest the coffin. He could tell by her posture that Harlan's thirty-two-year-old granddaughter was crying. Even in mourning, dressed all in black, her hair pinned beneath a pillbox hat and small veil, Imogen was a beauty. Beside him Bonnie seemed to sense that his attention had drifted. She glanced at him, then at Imogen.

Does Bonnie know? Trummel studied his wife's expression. She held her gaze straight ahead, her features purposely blank.

★   ★   ★

After the final prayer, Imogen placed a bouquet of white lilies on her grandfather's coffin. Then pallbearers carried the casket into the tomb.

An hour later most of the mourners had left the cemetery to attend a reception at the museum. Imogen stayed behind to be with Grandfather. A dozen bouquets adorned his tomb. The floral fragrance combined with the mossy dampness of the ancient stone made her think of home and the garden pond where Grandfather used to read her books. She still couldn't believe the man who'd raised her, who'd been her whole world, was suddenly, impossibly, gone.

Her grandfather had been the last of her family. Imogen hadn't felt this much sorrow since she'd lost her parents when she was eleven. It was as if her chest had been hollowed out.

Grandfather had been a kind man. He'd done his best to fill the void. Only as an adult was she beginning to understand all that the middle-aged widower had taken on when his young granddaughter appeared on his doorstep. He'd proven himself up to the task, though. He'd taken extra care to make sure she knew how much he loved her, to make it clear she belonged with him. *I am yours and you are mine.* Grandfather had said that every night when he'd tucked her into bed. Imogen had traveled with him all over North Africa and Asia. She had rarely felt alone. Until now.

From her purse, she pulled out the leather journal he'd written in during his months in the asylum. Most of the pages were scrawled with black ink and made little sense. There were many peculiar sketches among them, some of ancient Egyptian symbols, others too bizarre to comprehend. The final pages he'd written in his own blood were an even bigger mystery.

Still, Imogen treasured the strange book; it contained Grandfather's last words to her.

Immy, when you lost your mum and dad, I did my best to be there for you. Perhaps, not in the way a child needs a proper parent. The memories I cherish most are of the expeditions when you came along as my sidekick. You seemed as excited about the treasure hunt as I. Whatever you choose to do in this world, my precious girl, know that your grandfather loves you.

She thought about his life's work, his endless quest to find Nebenteru's tomb. Imogen never believed, as others did, that her grandfather's claims were gibberish, babblings of a departed mind. She still meant to prove that what he had witnessed in the cave tomb was real, that the symbols etched into his body were indeed, as he swore, "superior knowledge beyond man's understanding."

Imogen leaned into the crypt, pressing her hand to the coffin. "Grandfather," she whispered. "Whatever it takes, I promise to see your work finished."

"I echo that promise."

Imogen turned, surprised. Nathan Trummel stood behind her with his wife.

Bonnie stepped closer and put a hand on Imogen's arm. "I am deeply sorry. I lost my mum last year, and I still miss her. If you need to take some time away from the museum, I'll make sure my father approves it. A week, a month, however long you need. And you're welcome to stay at our country cottage in Cornwall. No one is there this time of year."

"Thank you, that's very kind." Imogen had trouble looking Trummel's wife in the eye.

Bonnie smiled. One corner of her mouth quivered. *She knows,* Imogen suddenly understood. Bonnie hugged her tight, then turned to her husband. "I'll wait for you in the car."

Neither Trummel nor Imogen spoke until Bonnie passed beyond a row of crypts and out of sight. Alone for the first time in months, neither seemed to know what to say. The last time they were together, he had told her how much he missed her and tried to convince her to meet him at their favorite hotel. While Imogen had missed him too, she turned him down. They had quarreled and parted ways. He had barely spoken to her since.

"I'm here to pay my respects," he finally said. "I owe so much to your grandfather."

Imogen tried to read Trummel's face. The archaeologist, who always wore khaki, looked out of place in a black suit and tie. The knot was slightly crooked. He'd slicked his dark hair back with too much Brylcreem. He had keen eyes, a commanding presence, and he lived solely for his passions – his beliefs, his work. For a short time he'd been passionate about her. Standing next to him stirred up buried feelings.

"I'm really sorry, Im," Trummel continued. "I know how much he meant to you." He opened his arms and she stepped into them.

"I feel so lost." She was glad to share the burden of her grief with someone. But their embrace wasn't the same. His body felt rigid; he held her at a distance. Nathan Trummel was unavailable, and not because he was married. His feelings for Bonnie posed the least of his barriers.

Imogen still believed that no two people were more right for each other than she and Nathan. They had split finally because he wouldn't leave his wife. *"You have to understand, divorcing Harington's daughter would be suicide for my career."* Trummel had once confessed this in bed while Imogen lay with her head on his chest.

Since Imogen had refused to continue their affair, Trummel had been cold to her. Now she realized that he was here with an agenda. She pulled away. "What do you want, Nathan?"

"You know." He nodded at the journal in her hands.

"I told you I won't part with it."

"Imogen, be reasonable. Some of what your grandfather wrote could be useful to the museum. There might be answers in the journal that help us understand what happened to him and his team."

"I've combed through the book," she said. "Most of it is indecipherable."

Trummel placed a hand on her shoulder, softer now, a lover's touch. "Think about it, Im; somewhere in Egypt's Eastern Desert sits a mountain riddled with caves." His tone had changed; now he spoke with the same charming enthusiasm as when they lay in bed together and he shared his ambitions. "In one of those caves rests a mummy's tomb that King Ramses II secretly had buried and sealed away. Finding that tomb would be a great discovery for the museum. We must find it before the Yanks, the Egyptians, or bloody Hitler's Reich claims it. You want to honor your grandfather by finishing his life's work. So do I."

"And you're convinced that his journal is the key."

"I'm willing to stake my entire career on it," Trummel said. "Hell, I gave my word to the Crown and all of England."

Imogen remembered his bold statement in the *London Herald*. She held the journal tight, unsure if she could trust him. "I couldn't bear to lose this."

"At least give me the last page," Trummel insisted. "The map he drew in blood."

She cocked her head. "What are you going to do with it?"

He sighed. "I told the board that Harlan's map could potentially lead us to where his team disappeared and from there we will find Nebenteru's tomb. They've agreed to fund another expedition."

It still infuriated her that Trummel had not included her in the meeting. She tempered her anger. The last thing she wanted was to get into a row in front of Grandfather's tomb.

She opened the journal and flipped to the last page. "It's only a partial map. He didn't finish it."

"It's a start," Trummel said. "Give me the map and I'll set out to find the tomb. When I do, I'll send for you to join me. This will be *our* expedition. Whatever we find, we'll share equal credit."

"The credit should be Grandfather's."

"Of course. We'll call it the Trummel-Riley Expedition. Harlan's name will be included with ours. What do you say?"

Imogen broke Trummel's gaze and stared at Grandfather's tomb. The epitaph engraved on his vault's plaque read:

DR. HARLAN ALDRIDGE RILEY
BEYOND THE MYSTERIES OF MAN AND GODS
AN EXPLORER'S QUEST NEVER ENDS

Teaming up with Trummel would allow her to carry on Grandfather's work and hopefully learn what he had discovered. She recalled a passage in his diary: *I have witnessed miracles. Nightmares. Forgotten realms. If I could but make you believe. They lie in Egypt, in Nebenteru's tomb. Seek its knowledge for yourself.*

CHAPTER FIVE

Five months later, March 1937
Eastern Desert, Egypt

Shimmering heat rose from the dunes, creating a series of mirages. Imogen swore giant stick figures walked along the edge of the world, like ghostly nomads from another age. As she drew closer, the giants disassembled, collapsing into the sand.

Only days ago she'd been in London, working in the dark basement of the museum, preparing Mesopotamian artifacts for the summer exhibit when she received a surprise telegram from Trummel.

Imogen, I've found what we seek! Pack your bags and your grandfather's diary and hop on the next plane to Cairo. I'll have Bakari waiting for you at the airport. This changes everything.

Now she rode atop a camel on her way to whatever it was that Trummel had discovered. Imogen and her Egyptian guide, Bakari Neseem, had traveled for four days across the desert on three overloaded camels. They were now somewhere southeast of Cairo. The city behind them had long since melted into the horizon.

Bakari quietly led the way. He was a bear of a man with a thick beard, sun-darkened skin, and a black turban covering his broad head. Only his eyes peeked through the narrow opening of his headdress. He rode armed with a sickle-shaped Khopesh sword sheathed on his hip and a pistol fitted in a holster. Imogen had tried to make conversation, but Bakari remained mostly silent, apparently preferring his own thoughts. During long stretches when the desert was flat and seemed to go on for eternity, he read a book while the camel carried him along.

Imogen used the solitude to think about all that she'd left behind – the museum project she'd abandoned, the emotional chaos she'd endured in the past several months. Her frenetic thoughts eventually slowed to the peaceful rhythm of camels' hooves crossing the sand.

At times when she and Bakari crossed over mountains, the Red Sea became visible in the distance. The view was spectacular, the sea bejeweled with diamonds of light as the rippling water reflected the sun.

The desert nights were just as beautiful. Last night they had camped on a mountain summit beneath a million stars. Speaking Arabic, Imogen had prodded Bakari with questions — did he have a wife and children? what were some of his favorite books? — only to get stone silence in return as his attention remained firmly focused on the book in his hand. The only words he'd spoken that night were "eat" after handing her some bread and ripe dates, and "sleep" when he closed his book and lay down on the other side of the fire.

In the morning they descended into a valley where the rocky terrain gave way to an undulating landscape of endless dunes. Imogen always felt a great sense of adventure and freedom when she rode atop a camel.

The first time she'd ridden one she had been twelve, traveling with Grandfather to visit the pyramids of Giza. To a girl who'd spent her whole life in the wet, green region of England, the African desert was a wondrous place — wide open, rich with earthy smells and textures, and so many new experiences. When the three giant pyramids and the Sphinx came into view, Imogen and her grandfather had raced their camels to see who could reach the ruins first. She still could recall the sound of his laughter carried on the wind.

She and Grandfather had joined a dig already in progress. The other archaeologists welcomed Imogen, giving her a brush and trowel and a spot in the sand to dig. The men discovered a new passage leading beneath one of the pyramids. Her grandfather, carrying a candle, had led her down the narrow tunnel to the burial chamber. The underground maze had worried young Imogen. "We could be lost down here," she whispered. "Perhaps never see sunlight again."

"There's always a way out," Grandfather said. "You just have to trust your instincts."

Wide-eyed with fear and wonder, Imogen had not once let go of Grandfather's hand. Eventually she had grown comfortable facing the dark unknown. She had loved exploring tombs with him, searching for lost treasure. She remembered his youthful grin, the sparkle in his eyes when he unearthed a new relic for the museum. Once, after finding an ancient scroll, he had grabbed Imogen's hands, danced with her in a circle, and sang 'My Hat's on the Side of My Head'.

Like a mirage, all her fond memories collapsed on themselves when she thought of how sad and lonely she'd felt the past months since Grandfather's death. Maybe this trip would be a fresh start, a chance to rediscover the adventurous young woman who had once traversed the ruins of Angkor and climbed Kala Patthar mountain in the Nepalese Himalayas.

The sun slowly arced above their caravan of camels. A black kite hawk flew overhead, its shadow gliding over the ground. At the crest of each dune, a new mirage danced on the horizon, playing tricks with her eyes.

Bakari looked over his shoulder at her. "Drink." He motioned with his hand.

She tilted her pith helmet, wiped sweat from her brow, and drank from her canteen. The trio of camels walked along the spine of a dune at a steady pace. Ahead, more shimmering figures moved at the base of a mountain. This illusion turned more solid as she drew near.

The excavation site was a network of tents around a freshly unearthed tomb. Egyptian workers, all in turbans, toiled in the sweltering heat, digging in the sand, hauling tools and supplies, as British soldiers in desert uniforms stood watch. Several of the men gaped at Imogen, surprised to see a woman enter camp.

Trummel waved as he approached the camels. His skin was tan again. He wore his prized pith helmet, faded and scuffed from years of digs, and his khaki field uniform.

Imogen's camel lowered to the ground. Stiff from hours of riding, she half climbed, half fell out of the saddle.

Trummel caught her in an embrace. "Easy, girl, you've got saddle legs."

"I'm fine, really." Imogen pulled away and started to retrieve her suitcases from the porter's camel.

"Let Bakari get those." Trummel snapped his fingers and the stout man took her luggage. "Take Miss Riley's things to her tent." Trummel looked back at her. "So good to see you. A hell of a sandstorm blew through this morning and tore away three tents. I was worried you wouldn't make it."

"It would take more than a storm to stop me," Imogen said.

"There's that spark I've always adored. Glad to see it back." His eyes twinkled when he smiled. For a brief second, she saw past the professional exterior that was 'Dr. Trummel', and he was just Nathan, the charming lover who used to playfully pull her into bed.

She glanced at his left hand. He'd taken off his wedding ring. "How's Bonnie?" she asked.

He shrugged. "Same as always, I expect. We haven't spoken since I left Cairo a month ago. How have you been getting along, Im?"

"Better now that I'm here. Traveling by camel suits me."

A pair of soldiers walked past them. Nathan's professional mask slipped back into place. "We can catch up later," he said. "I'm sure you're exhausted and ready to retire to your tent."

"I couldn't possibly sleep. I'm eager to see what you've discovered."

"That's my girl." Trummel's voice dropped to a whisper. "Did you bring the diary?"

Imogen patted the small satchel she carried over her shoulder. "Do you need it now?"

"Later. In private. I don't want anyone else to know it exists." Trummel started walking. "Follow me."

Imogen hurried after him, balancing on boards that had been placed over the hot sand. Workers rolled wheelbarrows full of rocks and dirt past them. The sounds of picks and shovels striking the packed earth echoed off the mountain. Working among the laborers were archaeologists and a few college kids. Trummel always brought along some of his Oxford students as assistants.

"We've been digging here for two months." Trummel talked as they walked. "This mountain has the most complex cave system I've ever seen." He pointed up to a dozen caves that riddled the overhanging cliffs. "The tomb we unearthed may well be the greatest find of the century." At the base of the mountain, an earthen ramp descended several feet between two retaining walls made of stacked mud bricks. At the bottom of the ramp, a soldier guarded an open doorway to a natural cave.

Most Egyptian tombs Imogen had visited were single-story, flat-roofed *mastabas* or multilevel pyramids. This appeared to be a rock-cut tomb, which made use of a naturally occurring cave system, like those at Gebel al-Mawta, 'the Mountain of the Dead'.

Scattered along the retaining walls, a few archaeologists and assistants brushed sediment from the ancient brick, allowing the tomb's façade to once again worship the sun after so many centuries.

Trummel nodded at the progress. "When we first arrived, only a few stones were visible. The rest were buried beneath the sand. The entrance to the cave was completely bricked over. The relics we've found inside date back to 1250 BC, when King Ramses II reigned."

"Nineteenth dynasty." Imogen smiled, feeling Trummel's excitement. "And you believe this is the tomb my grandfather found?"

"The very one. Others found the entrance, but Harlan believed his team was the first to enter the burial chamber since the mummy was entombed. Nothing appears to have been pillaged. The tomb is filled with priceless artifacts. Beyond the burial chamber, we found a stairway that leads down to an even older tomb that appears to date back to 3150 BC. Over five thousand years old. And there are walled-off passageways that could lead to even older crypts."

The monumental impact of such a discovery astounded Imogen. To be a part of such a significant dig was every archaeologist's dream. "How much have you explored?"

"We've just scratched the surface. There are more levels below the first one. How many, we're not sure."

"Can I have a look inside?" she asked.

"It isn't safe. We're still tunneling out the blocked passages, and we've had cave-ins. But come this way. You won't believe what we've found."

CHAPTER SIX

In the deepest part of the tomb, Sergeant Dan Vickers was beginning to regret taking this job. He despised caves. Too many tight places. Not being able to see an exit made him antsy. Whenever he pulled watchdog duty inside the tomb, Vickers spent half the time looking over his shoulder. He hated patrolling in the dark where he couldn't see who might be sneaking up behind him.

A hand goosed him, causing Vickers to flinch and curse.

His mate, Corporal Teddy Quig, sprung from the gloom and doubled over laughing. "You should see your face, Vick. White as an Englishman's arse."

Vickers punched his shoulder. "Cut it out."

Quig was always pulling pranks. There was a lot of tension around camp, especially since the disappearances started happening. Quig did his best to keep everybody entertained. Most of the soldiers laughed at his jokes. Sometimes, though, he took his pranks too far.

"Keep it up, me mate, and one day you're gonna get your head blown off."

"Last time, Vick, promise." Quig offered his best gold-toothed grin. On some of the previous digs he'd worked, he'd been paid in gold pieces. He had them made into caps for four of his front teeth. "My mouth is worth more than my savings," he liked to brag. Vickers believed him, because every pound Teddy Quig earned bought him pints at the Lamb and Flag.

Quig leaned against the rock wall. He lit two cigs and handed one to Vickers. The two soldiers smoked as they watched the Egyptian workers slam picks against a rock wall that blocked a passage to whatever the hell was on the other side. Probably another chamber. More dusty bones and relics. The tomb was full of junk – broken pottery and creepy dolls tangled in ancient webs. Some objects glittered with gold or colored gemstones. Vickers would be more excited if he got a cut of the find, but it all went to the museum. The archaeologists logged every piece. Once, when he and Quig were guarding one of the storage tents,

Vickers suggested they steal a little treasure for themselves. He had run his hand through a pile of gold scarab beetles patterned with emerald stones. "Bet they wouldn't miss a few."

"Gosswick will have your bollocks if you so much as think about it," Quig had said.

Vickers had dropped the scarabs, feeling guilty. Quig was such a do-gooder. It made Vickers wonder how they ended up mates.

He didn't really need to steal from their boss. The mercenaries were paid fair enough to protect Dr. Trummel's team and guard the booty coming out of the caves. They didn't earn enough to retire rich, mind you, but enough to live damned good for a few months and buy some fun nights with the whores back in Brixton. Vickers might even do some traveling after this job. He'd heard the Greek isles were filled with exotic women who swam naked in crystal waters. Now that was Vickers's idea of heaven on earth. Quig went on about how much he missed his mother's cooking and his gal back home. Doris in her knickers and Mum's cottage pie were Quig's versions of heaven.

The workers stopped hammering and began conversing in Arabic. At the center of the wall made of neatly masoned stones, a large hole began to form. Vickers tossed his cigarette. "Time to see what's on the other side." He whistled and yelled at the workers to move aside. He pulled a torch off the wall, climbed up a mound of rubble, and shone it through the craggy hole.

"See any more mummies?" Quig asked.

"Nah, just another bloody passage. Tighter than this one."

The tunnel beyond the wall curved slightly and vanished into the deepest blackness Vickers had ever seen. His neck bristled as he stared into it. A chill pressed against his face and seemed to seep into his skull. He called over the strongest worker in the group. "Musa. Go have a look." He handed the big man the torch.

Musa scaled the rock wall. He squeezed through the hole and jumped down on the other side. The light from his flame illuminated a hallway with decorative walls.

"Find out how far it goes," Vickers ordered. He wanted to make sure there was something worth finding. If this was a dead end, there were plenty of other blocked passages to clear.

Musa's rippling torchlight moved farther and farther away until it disappeared around the curve. Moments later, the man screamed.

CHAPTER SEVEN

Imogen and Trummel took refuge from the sun beneath a tarp. A young man in an olive green safari hat stood behind a tripod-mounted camera. He was photographing a grouping of artifacts. Using archival cotton gloves, he turned the relics to capture another angle.

When the photographer noticed he had company, he smiled at Imogen. "Well, you're a lovely surprise."

Trummel said, "Miss Riley, meet Caleb Beckett, my personal photographer."

"Actually, I'm on assignment from *National Geographic*," Caleb corrected.

"Assigned to document *my* discoveries," Trummel said.

Caleb's three-day stubble was in need of a shave, but he was handsome enough, especially his crystal blue eyes. He gazed at Imogen for several seconds, making her self-conscious.

Trummel cleared his throat and put a hand on her shoulder. "Imogen Riley is the curator I told you about from the British Museum, an expert in Egyptian mythology."

"I also do the dirty work to get our relics through customs," she said.

The photographer stepped from behind the camera and removed his gloves to shake her hand. "It's a pleasure to meet you, Miss Riley."

"So, how did you get involved with this lot?" she asked.

"This expedition is the most exciting thing happening right now. It's a privilege being the first to capture the tomb and all its treasures on film. I bet I've taken a hundred photos so far." Caleb's voice was deep and self-assured. He seemed very well educated.

"Your accent sounds American," she said. "Let me guess... New York."

"Chicago, actually," Caleb said. "Born and raised."

"Rather far from home, aren't you?"

"Home is wherever the magazine sends me. Say, I'm expanding my article to include your involvement in this expedition. Now that you're here, perhaps later we can sit down for an interview."

"Is that really necessary?" Trummel said. "Shouldn't you be focused on the dig?"

"Of course," Caleb said, obliging Trummel's ego. "But since Miss Riley's name is shared with yours on this expedition, it would be nice to get her perspective."

"I'd be happy to, Mr. Beckett," Imogen said, settling the matter. She observed the subject of his photograph: a set of four limestone burial jars with the heads of gods. "Canopic jars," she said, thrilled by this new discovery. "Absolute pristine condition. The hieroglyphs are still readable." She turned to explain. "During mummification, the ancient Egyptians used these containers to store the deceased's internal organs. The heads on the lids represent—"

"The four sons of Horus," Caleb interrupted. "Imsety watches over the liver. Hapy guards the lungs. Duamutef guards the stomach and upper intestines and Qebehsenuef, the lower intestines."

"You know your funerary deities." Imogen was pleasantly surprised.

"This isn't my first expedition." Caleb arched an eyebrow, inviting her to test his knowledge.

Trummel's hand tugged her arm. "Let's leave Mr. Beckett to his work."

Caleb tipped his hat. "Good day, Miss Riley."

When they were out of earshot, Trummel whispered to Imogen, "Pay no mind to the Yank. He's a womanizer. Back in London, I saw him drinking with two tarts at the hotel bar and later he took them up to his room."

Imogen grinned, amused that Trummel was being territorial. He led her into a tent. Relics were stacked on tables and cluttered the earth floor like the storage warehouse of a museum. The artifacts smelled of things long buried. Imogen and Trummel passed a table covered with several dozen shabti dolls, hand-carved stone figurines of mummies that represented the deceased's workers in the afterlife. She picked up one of the dolls, admired its intricate design. "Absolutely wonderful," she declared.

Imogen marveled at the treasures that had been removed from the tomb. The thought of bringing all this back to the museum elated her. She could already imagine the exhibit she would create to tell the tomb's story.

Around the table of dolls, crates stood filled with bones. Skulls perched atop stacks of femurs. The sight, which would have repelled most of her school chums, thrilled Imogen.

"Servant bones," Trummel said.

She grew excited. "Does this mean you found him?"

Of course, Trummel wouldn't answer right away. He loved to tease. He was a master at making people curious, then holding back details for dramatic effect; it was how he'd tantalized the museum's board into funding expeditions.

She followed him to the back of the tent's storage area. He ran a hand along a wooden sarcophagus. "We found this in the burial chamber."

The sarcophagus featured a likeness of a priest's face with a long chin beard and royal headdress. Its exterior was covered in colorful glyphs and etched paintings of a pharaoh communing with gods. The deity represented most was Anubis, the jackal-headed god who had taught the ancient Egyptians about mummification and guided the dying into the afterlife. Imogen leaned closer, deciphering what she could of the glyphs. The coffin texts, or funerary spells, were common for the dynasties dating from the Middle Kingdom onward.

"You'll be delighted to see what's inside." Trummel lifted the lid, revealing a remarkably well-preserved mummy. "I give you Nebenteru himself."

Imogen's smile widened.

The top section of bandages had fallen away, exposing most of the mummy's face and part of its sunken chest and bone-thin arms. After all these centuries, the mummy's teeth were still intact and its skin looked smooth as clay. One eyelid was sealed shut. The other had partially opened to reveal an iris painted on pads of linen that filled the cavity. The face, for the most part, was well preserved.

"The board members are going to love this," she said.

Very little was known about Nebenteru, a high priest from Ramses II's royal council. She felt a mix of joy and sadness standing among the relics. Her grandfather should have lived to share this moment with her.

She looked at Trummel in amazement. "I can't believe you've found it."

"Harlan's partial map helped. It still took a few months to find the right mountain and the tomb's entrance. The coffin text confirms this is Nebenteru. We've found over two dozen servants and soldiers, who were buried with him."

Imogen studied the unwrapped portion of the high priest's mummy. Something about its condition seemed odd. She gestured to the hands, gathered at the chest inches beneath the jaw. "This area looks less deteriorated than the rest of the body." She leaned closer. "There's a circular impression on the chest with peculiar markings."

Trummel grinned. "I have one more thing to show you."

In a second storage tent crammed with more relics and a British Army lorry parked near the back, Imogen followed Trummel past a guard to a metal trunk where the most important relics were kept. Using a key tied around his neck, Trummel unlocked the trunk and removed an object wrapped in cloth. "This is our greatest find thus far." He unwrapped the cloth and a silver disk fell into his palm. It was about the size of a teacup saucer, but thicker at the center where a round quartz crystal was embedded. The silver was shiny and polished.

"It looks brand new," Imogen said.

"That's exactly how we found it," Trummel said. "Not only had the metal not tarnished, but everything within three feet in diameter had less deterioration, including the mummy's flesh, as you so astutely noticed. I'm guessing the phenomenon has something to do with the crystal."

The embedded crystal should have been cool to the touch. Instead it was warm. Imogen was surprised by the disk's light weight. On the reverse side, she felt something etched across its surface. She flipped it over and recognized the strange markings that circled around the disk. They matched the scars that had disfigured her grandfather's face and body.

"I was speechless too when I first found the relic," Trummel said. "Your grandfather told me he held it briefly then placed it back inside the sarcophagus."

Imogen remembered her visits to the asylum. Whatever had happened to Grandfather here seemed to have scrambled his mind. His diary, a catalogue of strange symbols broken here and there by scribbled words, was equally incoherent.

"Grandfather never mentioned finding a silver disk, but he talked of others who showed him incredible things," she said. "There's a confounding passage in his diary: *'They inscribed me and filled my head with more knowledge than the human mind can handle.'* Did Grandfather ever tell you *who* he encountered in the caves?"

"I could never get that out of him," Trummel said. "Only that he was blessed with wisdom so astounding he didn't think I was ready for it." He seemed about to say something else, but then looked away from her.

"You know more than you're telling me," she said.

"I know as little as you do, probably less, since I've yet to read the diary."

Trummel was clearly holding something back but Imogen let it go for now. She turned her attention back to the silver disk. "What do you suppose this is?"

He shrugged. "I haven't a clue. I found the disk sealed in the coffin. Nebenteru's mummy held it to his chest."

As she leaned closer, Imogen had the disconcerting sense that the gemstone was an eye. That it studied her just as she studied it. She tried to shake off the thought, but it wouldn't leave her.

"Those markings aren't Egyptian," Imogen said. "Could they have gotten this from the Akkadians?"

"It doesn't match their cuneiform either, or any other cultures' in the region. The fact that it was buried with a high priest tells me it was important." Trummel took the disk back. "We're going to have to smuggle this out. When we leave for England, can I count on you to make sure it slips through the cracks?"

Imogen nodded. Smuggling for the museum was the only part of the job she disliked. She used special crates with secret compartments to transport the most important relics.

She wanted more time to study the patterns of the strange etchings, but Trummel locked the disk up again. "May I have the diary?" he said.

Imogen removed the small, worn leather book from her satchel. She felt reluctant to let it go. "I want this back intact."

"Of course, you have my word as a gentleman."

She handed the journal to him.

He flipped to the final pages written in blood. "Have you been able to decipher the codes?"

"I've tried to make sense of it..." she said. "These symbols are beyond my understanding. I met with a symbologist and he couldn't figure out their meaning either."

"There might be clues in here that we've missed," Trummel said. "During my visits, when Harlan was lucid, he shared things with me. I'm hoping the diary will fill in some of the gaps." Trummel locked up the book in the trunk. "For safekeeping."

As they walked out of the tent, he said, "Don't discuss the journal with anyone. I have reason to believe the Cairo Museum has inserted a spy among the workers."

Aiden Gosswick approached. A former captain in the British Army, he worked as Trummel's personal bodyguard. He led the team of mercenary soldiers charged with protecting the staff on foreign digs and guarding the treasures Trummel discovered.

Sporting his usual shaved head and handlebar mustache, Gosswick grinned at Imogen. "Well, sugar on a biscuit. Look who the wind blew in." He put a muscled arm around her, half strangling her in a hug. "Been a while, eh, Blondie?" She bristled at his pet name for her, one he'd given her when she was twenty and Gosswick still had hair. "Good to have you back on the team."

"Nice to see you too, Goss." Imogen shrugged out of the man's embrace. Gosswick's display of friendliness was all for show. She was fairly certain he hated all women, but intelligent ones, whom he was required to treat with respect, were a particular misery. On a previous expedition, she'd overheard the captain complaining to Trummel that she was a distraction to his men. Trummel relied on him, though, so she would have to ignore her feelings and find a way to get along.

"Excuse us a moment." Gosswick pulled Trummel aside and whispered in his ear.

Trummel frowned, then spoke to Imogen. "I need to see about something. Why don't you get settled in? Help yourself to the mess tent if you're hungry."

Trummel and Gosswick headed off toward the tomb's entrance.

CHAPTER EIGHT

As they crossed camp, an image of an earlier accident surfaced in Trummel's mind – a worker crushed beneath several tons of stones, the casualty of a cave-in, Gosswick had assured him. Trummel had heard whispers, though. The other workers spoke of the man having triggered an ancient booby trap inside the tomb.

The laborers had stopped working and were now gathered outside the entrance in a nervous clot. They looked petrified.

Spineless goats, Trummel thought. When the dig had started, his workforce had been fifty strong. Now he had half that. A few men had somehow gotten separated from the others inside the cave and disappeared. Others had quit. Then there was the mysterious case of Corporal Aleister. He'd been mapping out the tunnel system, when he suddenly went mad with panic. He swore he'd seen a face staring at him from the darkness of a tunnel. A voice had spoken inside his head. The next day Aleister shot himself. His suicide note read, "Damned are we who enter the abyss."

The huddle of workers dispersed as Trummel and Gosswick walked past and entered the tomb. The two turned on their electric torches and navigated a narrow passage and descended a flight of stairs. At the end of a long tunnel, they scaled a pile of rubble and stepped through a hole where rocks had been removed after a cave-in. In a chamber at the far side of the cave, two soldiers stood near puddles of blood.

Shit, not another one. Trummel felt a tightness in his stomach. "What the hell happened?"

"We don't know," Sergeant Vickers answered, sounding nervous.

"Tell Dr. Trummel what you told me," Captain Gosswick ordered.

"After we broke through," the soldier said, "we sent a worker in to explore what was in here. We'd just lost sight of him when the man started screaming. Quig and I entered and found all this." His electric torch shone over dark splatters on the wall. Large blood droplets on the floor led to a circular opening cut in the wall.

Quig pointed to it. "He must've gone down that shaft."

Trummel aimed the beam of his torch past the opening down a vertical cave tunnel, deep as a well. He couldn't see the bottom. He sighed in frustration. It was maddening trying to manage an expedition riddled with problems – workers disappearing, archaeologists falling ill, constant delays. The guards had begun complaining that strange noises escaped from the dark corridors inside the tomb. Workers were threatening to leave because they believed this mountain was haunted. On several nights, Trummel had heard moans from the cliff's high caves, but it was only the wind. As if it wasn't enough to deal with superstitions and fears, the more he pressed his team to dig into this tomb, the more he risked their lives. Now Trummel had another fatality on his hands.

"Did the others see this?" he asked.

"No, we evacuated the workers before finding the blood," said Vickers. "All they heard was the man screaming."

"What do you think killed him?" Gosswick said.

The two soldiers shrugged.

"Probably busted his head on a rock." Trummel pointed to a red-stained section of the tunnel where the ceiling hung low. "The blood loss caused delirium and he fell down the shaft." That would be the official story anyway. He studied the blood spatters on the walls and the thick pool of it on the floor and knew it wasn't true. The worker had bled too much for his injury to be a single cut.

Trummel stared hard at his soldiers. "This stays between us. Are we clear?"

Vickers and Quig nodded.

Gosswick gave orders for his soldiers to clean up the mess. When Trummel and the captain returned to the upper level, Gosswick lowered his voice. "Sir, the workers are shit-scared of this tomb. I'm concerned they'll quit. Maybe it's a good idea to cut our losses. We've found the mummy and plenty of gold—"

"We're not quitting," Trummel said. "Not until I've found what I came for. We need to work faster. How quickly can your crew dig out the next blockages?"

"Two to three days, I'm guessing."

"You've got less than twenty-four hours."

Gosswick frowned. "Sir, the men are working as fast as humanly possible."

"Work through the night, if need be. We can't waste another day."

CHAPTER NINE

While Trummel held a private meeting, Imogen went into the dining tent to quench her thirst with a cup of tea. There was a long table offering a buffet of canned sardines, pickled herring, sausage slices, cheese, and crackers. She nibbled on a piece of sausage, then poured herself a cup of Earl Grey.

At one of the foldout dinner tables sat a peculiar man with shoulder-length, dark hair and a thick beard. Imogen smiled but got no response. The man's eyes stared at nothing, the pupils hidden behind gray cataracts. A blind man. His hands laid out a large deck of cards as if he were playing solitaire.

Curious, Imogen walked over and watched him.

"You know, it's not polite to stare," the blind man said in a deep Scottish accent.

"Sorry. I was just looking at your cards. What kind of deck is that? I've never seen those symbols."

"It's an oracle deck. The cards give me insights. Sometimes glimpses of the past or future. Would you like a reading?"

"No, thank you."

"A skeptic." The blind man nodded. He waved his hand, as if touching the air between himself and Imogen. "You have a cloudy aura about you. It's as though you hide behind a veil. You don't trust strangers, especially not charlatans like me, eh?" He grinned.

Charlatan was exactly what Imogen had been thinking. She took a step back.

The Scotsman let out a hoarse laugh. "There's nothing to be afraid of, lass. A friendly card reading is all I'm offering." He shuffled his cards, fast like a magician. His desert-colored robes made him appear monk-like, but his rosy cheeks suggested the spirits he worshipped might come in a bottle. The long-haired blind man with the street-beggar's appearance seemed out of place among the rest of Dr. Trummel's staff.

"May I ask who you are?" Imogen said.

He smiled and touched his chest in a dramatic gesture. "I am Dyfan, personal psychic to Dr. Trummel. Do you believe in clairvoyance?"

"I believe what I see."

Dyfan held out his hands. "Allow me to make a believer of you. A quick reading?"

Imogen hesitated.

"There's no harm. You'll enjoy it, I promise. Have a seat."

She looked out the tent's doorway toward the tomb. Trummel and Gosswick had yet to return. She lowered herself into the chair opposite the blind man.

"Good, now let's have a bit of fun." He shuffled the cards. "Cut the deck anywhere you like."

Imogen split the deck into three piles. Dyfan restacked the cards and began turning them over. The first was a symbol of a Gordian knot. The second looked like the sun. The third, a horned devil with goat legs, made Imogen cringe. She didn't recognize the cards that followed, but they seemed inspired by pagan folklore. She was knowledgeable about Middle Eastern hieroglyphs but had never taken interest in the ancient Celtic symbols of her British ancestors.

Dyfan's head tilted as he stared past Imogen. "You're full of contradictions. Skeptical of all things spiritual. Yet you desire something to believe in." He smiled knowingly. "I'm seeing through your veil, aren't I?"

She didn't respond. While she had shunned religious dogma years ago, she had never been drawn toward mysticism. Instead she had found solace in science. It rendered the world concrete, believable.

"Books are your sanctuary," he continued. "You keep your secrets locked away. You trust few people. Your parents and grandparents are deceased. No close family. Oh, my." His face filled with concern as his fingers glided over one of the cards – a woman standing in a bonfire. "The tragedy of losing your mum and dad so early in childhood closed your heart to God."

Dyfan's reading called forth painful images...a blazing fire...screams of those caught on the wrong side of it. Imogen quickly pushed the memory to the darkest recess of her mind, where all the ghosts of her past were safely locked away.

"I prefer we not talk about my childhood."

"My apologies. Sometimes the cards pull up the dark things we hold down." Dyfan turned over an upside-down pair of lovers. "You're in love with a man you cannot possess."

Nathan's face flashed in her mind. They had worked side by side on expeditions for many years. Too many times Imogen had slept with him, foolishly believing that Nathan felt something more for her than lust.

Dyfan flipped over a new card. It looked like ivy, with three red blooms. "The card of tangled vines. There is another who keeps you from being with this man. Your lover has a wife. You keep hoping he'll leave her."

Imogen was surprised at the psychic's accuracy, but said nothing. The last thing she needed was Trummel thinking she was going to distract him from his work with emotional drama.

"The two cards together offer a warning. Trust your instincts over your lover's words."

Just then Trummel entered the tent along with Gosswick and a group of archaeologists.

Trummel grinned. "Imogen, I see you've met Dyfan. If it weren't for our psychic, we wouldn't be digging here."

He introduced her to the other archaeologists who worked with him at Oxford. Trummel's personal assistant was a pretty college-aged girl named Piper. She glanced at Imogen curiously with a hint of cattiness in her narrowed eyes, then quickly looked down at her notebook. Piper was most likely used to being the only female in camp. Imogen simply rolled her eyes and returned her attention to the group of men discussing their next big task.

Everyone gathered around Trummel as he unrolled a map across a table, revealing a sketch of the tomb. It looked like a three-level crypt with several joining tunnels that branched off in a dozen different directions. The cave entrance led into the top level.

Trummel said, "So far we've explored two levels. The chapel is on Level One. Level Two is the mummy's burial chamber. This morning, thanks to Dyfan, a new stairway was discovered here." He tapped the map, pointing to the branches on the second level. "As soon as enough rocks are cleared away, I'll be leading an expedition team down to Level

Three, which appears to be much older than the mummy's chamber. Miss Riley will be joining us."

She grew excited. What Dr. Trummel's team had unearthed could very well be the greatest discovery since Tutankhamun's tomb. And Imogen was here to witness it.

CHAPTER TEN

Two days later, clearing the blocked tunnel was proving to be a difficult task for the overworked crew. Somehow the ancient Egyptians had sealed off the third-level tunnel with one brick wall after another. The delays made Trummel irritable and Imogen restless. Since her arrival, he'd insisted she "take things easy." He ignored her protests when she said she felt fine to work. He had put her up in one of the nicest tents, across from his, with servants looking after her. She would have been just as happy sleeping on a cot in a storage tent.

If Trummel still had feelings for her, he didn't show it. There were always other team members present. He remained strictly professional, addressing her as 'Miss Riley'. She honored the rule he'd once given her, to address him as 'Dr. Trummel' around the team, never by his first name. She'd slipped once, calling him 'Nathan' at the dinner table. The mistake had earned her a hard look.

Imogen wasn't certain if the others knew about the affair, but Gosswick knew. He'd seen her leaving Trummel's tent in the middle of the night on the previous expedition. Gosswick still gave her disapproving looks.

With the third day winding to a close, Imogen was too anxious to sit in her tent and do nothing. She wanted to get her hands dirty. Most of all, she wanted to get her first look inside the tomb.

At dusk, she walked down the hill toward the cave. The setting sun cast long shadows on the ground. The red rock mountain was bathed in hues of orange light. She admired the ancient mud bricks of the two retaining walls that had been dug up. She didn't see any sign of Trummel or the other archaeologists. *They must be inside the tomb.* They might get upset if she showed up uninvited, but it seemed worth the risk.

She followed the sandy ramp that descended between the walls for about twenty feet. She passed a few Egyptian workers pushing wheelbarrows of rocks. Their clothes and turbans were covered in grime. At the cave's entrance stood a burly, blunt-faced guard named Corporal Rex Sykes. He was armed with a submachine gun.

Imogen suddenly felt repulsed as she remembered Sykes from previous expeditions. Last time she'd encountered him was at a hangar in Cairo. She had been doing inventory of the supplies that had arrived by plane. Corporal Sykes had unpacked wooden crates and handed out various guns and ammunition to the other mercenaries.

Sykes had kept ogling her and tried to impress her. "Ey Blondie, ever seen one of these?" He had held up his own submachine gun that reminded her of a gangster's gun. "This meat chopper is a Finnish Suomi KP/3-1." He patted its round magazine. "The drum mag holds seventy-one rounds. The gun spits 'em out in rapid fire. Can turn a man into Swiss cheese in seconds. Care to hold it?"

"Thanks, I'll pass." She saw up close that the gun's wooden stock was covered with numerous skulls and spears etched into it. "You decorate that yourself?"

"That's my number of kills," Sykes said proudly. "Eight in the Congo. Ten in Sudan. Twenty in Kenya. If you really want to see something nifty, I'll show you my Kikuyu finger necklace." He had started to reach into his shirt, but Imogen stopped him, not wanting to see his gruesome battle trophies.

The tall mercenary had made her nervous then and did so now as his gaze watched her approach the cave tomb. When she tried to enter, Sykes stepped in front of her. "No one goes in, Blondie."

"You're letting everybody else enter." She referred to a steady stream of workers who walked in and out of the doorway.

Sykes said, "They've got a job to do."

"So do I. I'm Dr. Trummel's partner on this dig. And from now on you'll properly address me as Miss Riley."

"I don't care if you're the queen herself. You aren't going in without permission."

The nerve of this soldier. "Maybe I'll have a word with Captain Gosswick about your rude behavior."

Sykes's flint-gray eyes didn't show an ounce of worry. "I'm only following orders. You want a tour, miss, come back with the boss."

"I am the boss!"

"Sorry, Miss Riley." He stood rigid, blocking the entrance.

On previous digs, Imogen had been able to go wherever she pleased. As she stomped up the ramp, she spotted the journalist, Caleb Beckett, leaning against the brick wall. He wore an amused expression as he watched her ascend the ramp.

"What's so funny?" she asked.

"You behave like a woman used to getting her way."

"Were you spying?"

Caleb raised a cigarette. "Just having a smoke."

"I don't see why we need a guard at the entrance. When my grandfather ran digs, I had full access to the tombs."

Although she extended no invitation, Caleb walked alongside her toward camp. "There've been disappearances," he said. "A few workers have gone missing in the caves. And one of the storage tents was vandalized. Security clamped down after that. Haven't you heard?"

"No." It bothered her that Trummel was keeping things from her.

"The incidents have made everyone anxious. I'm only granted access when Dr. Trummel takes me in for a photo shoot." A camera hung from a strap around Caleb's neck.

"Do you take that thing everywhere?" she asked.

"Even to bed with me." He chuckled. "Actually, the story I'm doing requires a few scenic shots – dunes, camels, the mountain. Dawn and dusk provide the best light. Among photographers, it's called God's light."

Ahead, the sun was sinking below the horizon. It looked like a shimmering golden ball. He stopped abruptly. "Whoa, stay right there."

"What is it?"

"The light on your face. It's perfect." Caleb touched her cheek to brush something from it. "Don't move." He sighted into his Rolleiflex and snapped a photo. "Turn your head just slightly to the right. That's it."

"Do I smile?"

"No, I don't care for forced expressions."

Imogen was still tense from her ordeal with the guard, and the wind was strong. She could barely keep her hair off her face. Finally she gave up and let the wind take it.

Caleb studied her through the lens. "Yes, just like that." He raised the camera. "I never miss the chance to capture beauty."

The compliment made her smile, just a little.

He snapped a picture. "I'm referring to the sunset, of course." He winked.

Caught off guard by his remark, a small laugh escaped her.

Caleb snapped another picture. "There's what I was hoping to see."

"Imogen!" Trummel crested a dune and hurried toward them, his boots kicking up sand. "There you are. I've been looking all over for you." He eyed Caleb. "What are you two doing out here?"

"Miss Riley was graciously posing for the magazine," Caleb said.

"I see," Trummel said. "Well, I need to steal her away. Dinner is served in the mess tent, and Miss Riley and I have business to discuss."

"Would you care to join us, Mr. Beckett?" Imogen asked.

"I'm sure he's got some film to develop," Trummel said.

"Yes," Caleb said. "I'll catch up with you later."

CHAPTER ELEVEN

After dinner that evening, the team sat by a campfire and passed around a bottle of Beefeater while Trummel told tales of his wild adventures. "It is the winter of 1932. Dr. Harlan Riley, Imogen, Goss, and I, along with a few Sherpas, are camped out at some ancient fort ruins in the Himalayas, when a torrential blizzard rolls in, the likes of which none of us has ever seen."

Imogen felt a chill as she recalled the snowstorm. She'd almost frozen to death.

Trummel paced around the campfire, making grand gestures with his arms. "The squall is hitting us with all its might. The Sherpas are frightened. Something other than the storm has them spooked. A relentless wind scours the stone ruins. Half our equipment blows away. Our team runs outside, trying to salvage what we can. That's when I see it...." He paused for dramatic effect. "A yeti," Trummel said, dead serious. "The abominable snowman."

His students gasped. A few let out nervous chuckles. Piper wore an enamored expression that Imogen had seen before on the faces of Trummel's female students.

He waited for silence, then continued, "The beast stood eight feet, a mountain of muscle covered in white fur. The worst ape stink that ever struck your nose. Its monstrous face had gray skin. A mouth full of sharp teeth. Black eyes stared at me like it wanted to rip me apart. Then it roared."

"What did you do?" asked Piper.

Trummel smirked. "I did what any sensible chap would do. Ran like hell."

The others laughed. Imogen made eye contact with Trummel and shook her head.

He sat back down. "Miss Riley doesn't believe the yeti legend. But she didn't see one."

"The blizzard made it impossible to see *anything*," Imogen shot back.

"You heard the beast roar," Trummel challenged.

"Or the wind howl," she countered.

"Well, I know what I saw." Trummel looked around at his team. "There are still places on this earth that remain shrouded in mystery. Every ancient wall I've studied is carved with mythical creatures. The dragon-headed Sirrush at the Ishtar Gate of Babylon. The winged Anunnaki at Sumer." He stared directly at Imogen. "Who's to argue that some of the ancient gods and monsters didn't exist? Our ancestors certainly believed in them. Which reminds me of a jungle expedition at the ruins of Angkor…"

Having heard most of Trummel's embellished stories, Imogen excused herself. She liked to take night walks at the various excavation sites. She loved the quiet, the flick and snap of tarpaulins, the call of camels from their pens, distant voices of the nightshift workers. The sounds faded behind her as she walked straight out into the night. She climbed several dunes, then sat down in the sand. The stars were bright tonight, the moon a thin crescent that offered barely enough light. Imogen removed her shoes, dug her toes in the sand. The wind died down to a peaceful quiet that could only be enjoyed far out in the desert.

She heard him first, his sure, unhurried step. *Has Nathan finally come to be alone with me?* She took a deep breath, bracing herself for the encounter. *No matter what he says, don't do anything foolish.*

The man crested a dune and disappeared again. He reappeared a minute later. With the starry night as a backdrop, the silhouette of a man wearing a safari hat loomed over her. It was just the journalist, Caleb Beckett.

"This isn't a good place for you, Miss Riley. It's not safe."

Imogen bristled. "Because I'm a girl."

"You're a woman, not a girl, and I'd warn a man just the same." Caleb wore a holstered pistol that she hadn't noticed earlier.

Imogen stared up at his shadowed face. "During dinner, I asked Dr. Trummel about the disappearances. He told me some of the workers have walked off the job. Provisions had been stolen from one of the tents. That's normal, believe me."

"There's nothing normal about this tomb. Trummel downplays the problems we've had lately. I take them more seriously."

Imogen didn't respond.

"I've made photographs," Caleb said. "A few times when workers disappeared in the cave there was blood. Quite a lot of it. Someone doesn't want us digging here."

"If you're trying to scare me, Mr. Beckett, it won't work."

"I'm merely informing you about the dangers. You should think twice about venturing away from camp without an escort."

"I'll be more careful," Imogen conceded finally. "But I'm not ready to go back to camp just yet."

"Would you mind company?"

"I suppose there's room on this dune for two."

Caleb dropped down beside her. They sat in silence a moment, staring up at the stars. Sounds of the night workers echoed in the distance.

"Dr. Trummel says this tomb is an enigma," Caleb said, "although he won't explain further. I imagine it has something to do with the location, a mummy entombed so far from civilization. What's your expert opinion?"

Imogen considered. "Most tombs were built along the Nile or near a city, areas inhabited by people. My only guess is this was once near an oasis and five thousand years of migrating sand has covered up any trace of a nearby village."

"Maybe there's an entire complex buried beneath these dunes, like the tombs the Met archaeologists found near Luxor."

She stiffened. "I suppose that's possible, if Trummel's map is correct, and there are, in fact, more than two levels beneath us. I find it interesting that you bring up the Met. Have you worked for them?"

"I traveled to Luxor last year and did a story on their find." He was quiet for a moment. "Judging from your tone, you suspect me of something. What is it?"

"You Yanks take a less sportsmanlike approach to archaeology. A few years ago, the Met sank so low as to implant a spy on one of my grandfather's expeditions. It's not a huge leap to imagine they would plant a man disguised as a journalist."

"I'm interested in discoveries that impact our understanding of history, not helping one museum outdo another. I'll leave the competition to you tomb raiders. And, despite your assumptions, I have dozens of published articles to prove that I am, in fact, a *real* journalist."

"I've clearly insulted you. I apologize, Mr. Beckett."

Caleb barely let her finish. "You're forgiven." He removed cigarettes and a lighter from a shirt pocket and held open the silver case toward Imogen. "Got these in Cairo. Would you like a smoke?"

"I don't usually...but yes, I'll have one." She leaned forward as he lit her cigarette. He left the lighter burning a beat longer than necessary. Why *had* Caleb followed her out here? If not to spy, then what?

"So, how about that interview, Miss Riley?"

She had forgotten that she had promised him one. "Of course, ask away. Just don't try to pry the museum's dirt out of me. I've sworn an oath of secrecy."

"A challenge. I like that." She heard Caleb rummaging in his satchel. He turned on an electric torch. The light bounced off the page of a worn notebook. "How long have you worked with Dr. Trummel?"

"A little over ten years. I first took some of his courses at Oxford. He came to work for the museum and teamed up with my grandfather on numerous expeditions. After I graduated, they both helped me get a job at the museum."

"As a curator?"

"Actually, I started out at entry level, logging artifacts in the basement. Eventually I was promoted to curator."

"And you accompany archaeologists on expeditions."

"Growing up, I traveled everywhere with my grandfather. By the time I was twenty-five, I had worked digs in Egypt, French Indochina, Iraq, and the Himalayas. Now I only join archaeologists when they find something of interest to the museum."

"I knew your grandfather. Met him on a dig in Saqqara. A remarkable man." Caleb asked sharp, pointed questions. Did Grandfather believe the theories he raised in his book, that the pharaohs were linked to a race that predated the first Egyptian dynasty? What drove her grandfather to spend twenty years in search of Nebenteru's tomb? Was the British Museum's board withholding information about the failed expedition?

Imogen offered what little she knew. "Grandfather had always been secretive about what he was searching for. It had something to do with the piece of Ani scroll he'd found in the Valley of the Kings." She explained that in his early years, before she was born, Harlan Riley had apprenticed under renowned Egyptologist Sir E.A. Wallis Budge.

Budge, who passed away in 1934, had written many books and made numerous contributions to Egyptology and the British Museum, most notably obtaining the over-seventy-foot Papyrus of Ani from the Egyptian government back in 1888. He brought the papyrus scroll back to the museum in London where it was currently stored. When Caleb inquired about the Papyrus of Ani, Imogen explained that it had been created in 1250 BC with cursive hieroglyphs and decorated with colorful paintings of people, animals, and gods throughout. "It contains prayer spells that make up the Egyptian Book of the Dead. I've had the privilege of studying the original version on numerous occasions.

"Years ago, when Grandfather found a new piece of the scroll that clearly matched the one in the museum, Sir Wallis Budge helped him translate it. They discovered, hidden within the text, a mention of Nebenteru's tomb and concluded that it was concealed within a mountain." She nodded toward the one that loomed over them. "By that time, Budge had been too old to travel to Egypt and was nearing retirement, so Grandfather made a pact with his mentor to find Nebenteru's tomb for England. That's all I know."

She left out that she suspected the museum's board members were withholding secrets. She was relieved when Caleb paused to write notes.

"My turn to ask you questions," she said.

He gave her a curious smile. "Okay. Shoot."

"Earlier, when Dr. Trummel introduced you as his 'personal photographer' you seemed uncomfortable. Why?"

"We disagree as to my role here. My assignment is to shadow him and take photographs when he makes discoveries."

"Where's the discrepancy?"

"He thinks I work for him. When I'm on assignment, I'm my own boss. I don't take orders."

"I understand your frustration. I've butted heads with him for years."

Caleb nodded. "Dealing with Trummel's ego is a small price to pay for the chance to capture history in the making."

"Well, I'm glad you joined the expedition. Normally, I spend weeks in camp with men who drink too much and bathe too little. You strike me as different. I haven't completely ruled out spy, though."

He seemed amused. "You're still not sure about me?"

"I'm not sure of anyone." Her confessional tone embarrassed her.

"I once read that you were raised by your grandfather. Where were your parents?"

The question caught her off guard. "They were killed when I was eleven."

"I'm sorry. What happened?"

"It's still hard for me to talk about. After my parents' funeral, I was brought to my grandfather. We became inseparable. It took a while but he taught me to approach life as he did, seeing it as an adventure to be relished.

"He provided me with a string of tutors who traveled with us." Imogen laughed. "Several tried their best to discipline me, teach me manners, make me into a proper lady. I was ungovernable. In the end Grandfather would side with me and send the tutor packing. He gave me all the freedom I wanted. I guess becoming an orphan made me independent."

"You're making light. Losing both parents at such a tender age must have been devastating." He turned off the flashlight. "Tell me something real."

Something real. Imogen was used to joking and dodging having to articulate her feelings. As she thought back to her childhood, all the pain she had buried began to surface. She pushed it back down. "I'm sorry. I can't."

He nodded, as if understanding. "I lost both my parents a couple years back. Dad to a heart attack and Mom to cancer. Sometimes it helped to talk about them. Now, I just think of them as happy together in heaven."

"You really believe heaven exists?" Imogen said.

"Absolutely, don't you?"

"I don't believe in anything I can't see with my own eyes." Maybe she could be so honest because she couldn't see much of Caleb's face, just the shape of him in the night's gloom. "I question everything that's unexplainable."

"Does that include God?" he asked. "Do you question *Him* too?"

"Oh especially Him. Or gods, depending on your beliefs. Religion is all dogma and wishful thinking."

"That's harsh."

"Examine the ancient texts from a scientific perspective. Man began longing for a power greater than himself as soon as he could form the thought. He invented unseen gods to worship, placing them in the stars where he imagined an afterlife, preferably better than the present one." Imogen shook her head. "I've yet to witness anything to convince me that such fantasies exist."

"Ironic coming from a woman who specializes in Egyptian mythology. Their whole culture was based on worshipping gods."

"Just because the ancient Egyptians believed their myths doesn't mean I have to." She hated being probed by believers in the mystical. It made her feel closed-minded, which she wasn't. At least she didn't see herself that way.

"So you're an atheist." Caleb's tone sounded as if he disapproved.

"I'm a scientist. Science is provable, measurable." She looked across the dark sand toward the dig. "This tomb exists. It's tangible. I can explore it and measure it. The concept of anything spiritual is nothing more than blind hope that a supreme being is watching over us."

Caleb rested his hands on his knees. "Does that narrow viewpoint make you blind to miracles?"

Imogen smiled. She loved a heated debate. "And you've seen them – these miracles?"

"Every time I make a photograph. The camera has taught me many things, Miss Riley. Here's one – the world has many dimensions, many realities, but a mind, closed like an aperture, registers nothing."

"Well, I'm more complex than a camera. If you weren't so quick to judge, you'd see that."

When Caleb didn't respond, she knew what he wanted – *something real*. "I would like to see proof more than you know, Mr. Beckett. I suppose that's part of why I'm here."

"An agnostic then. We all question." There was a smile in his voice. She felt his body sit closer to hers.

The sudden intimacy made Imogen uncomfortable. "I should turn in for the night," she said. "We have an early morning."

"I'll go with you." Caleb stood and offered his hand.

She rose and brushed the sand from her khakis. She and Caleb hiked the dunes in silence. The pocked sand and shadows looked like another planet.

She stopped at the top of the last dune. It overlooked the site, which at this hour glowed with lantern light. Caleb stopped beside her. A cool wind blew across the desert. There were no other ruins in sight. Just endless dunes, surrounding mountains, and a vast night sky.

"Could you stay up a bit longer?" Caleb asked.

"I might."

"How would you like to see something fascinating?"

CHAPTER TWELVE

Trummel stared into the crackling campfire. His personal servant, Bakari, sat beside him, reading a book. The rest of the crew had turned in for the night. Trummel was too keyed up to sleep. He didn't need Dyfan's card reading to tell him that tomorrow was going to be momentous. Trummel could feel tingles in his palms, a sign he'd received before every major discovery. *I'm so close.*

As he went through Harlan's diary, jotting down notes, he thought back to his first of many visits to the asylum. Harlan had been an amazing thing to behold. *A human codex*, he'd called himself. Trummel had been fascinated by the markings welted across his colleague's flesh in spiral patterns. There was not an inch of his skin that had not been inscribed.

"What happened to you?" Trummel asked him.

Harlan looked up at the ceiling, head angled like a lizard's. He claimed to hear voices and spoke to unseen listeners. His mind was so scrambled from the trauma and the drugs the doctors were giving him that most of what he said sounded like gibberish. Sometimes he spoke in different languages. As far as Trummel knew, his friend only spoke English and enough rudimentary Arabic to communicate with his Egyptian workers. Now Trummel picked up bits of ancient Sumerian and Persian and a third language he'd never heard before. There were brief moments of lucidity, when Harlan recognized Trummel sitting in front of him. The older man managed to speak a few phrases that made sense. When he talked, his hands moved in odd gestures, as if he were drawing complex math equations in the air.

"Where's Imogen?" he asked, looking around for her.

"It's just me here," Trummel said.

"Oh…will she be visiting today?"

"I don't know." Trummel was growing impatient. "What happened in the cave, Harlan?" He asked the question a dozen times before he finally got an answer.

"The cave...oh yes, we found the path," he said excitedly, the old Harlan returning briefly.

"What do you mean? The path to what?"

"To them."

"Them, who?" Trummel almost got an answer, and then Harlan was up out of his chair, pacing the room. Again, he spoke to the ceiling in that strange language, pausing to listen, nodding as if he understood.

"They don't want me here. I shouldn't have come back." Harlan grabbed Trummel's wrists. "You have to get me out of here. The doctors...keep sticking me with needles. Please, get me out of here."

"I'm doing what I can, Harlan, but you have to get better first." He got his friend to settle back into his chair. "Here, I brought you something." Trummel pulled out a small leather diary and a pen. "I want you to journal what you know. It's very important we record your discoveries."

"I can't remember."

"Do your best and try to remember. Do it for the museum, for science. Hell, do it for me, your old friend. I want to find what you found." When this inspired no response, Trummel changed tactics. "If you can tell us what happened to you and your team in the caves, then maybe that will help you get well and the doctors will let you go home."

"Will you take me back to the caves?" he pleaded.

"Yes," Trummel said, unsure if that was possible. "If you'll tell me how to find the tomb. I'll take you back."

"Splendid." Harlan nodded, then slumped into an almost catatonic state.

Over the course of a few months, Trummel had made several visits to see Harlan and check the progress he'd made on his diary. There were ramblings of barely readable notes broken up with intricate symbols that matched his scars, and, strangely, mathematical equations and musical compositions, as if at times Harlan somehow embodied Einstein and Mozart. During Trummel's last visits, days before Harlan wrote the final passages in his own blood and killed himself, he had spoken coherently for a short time, sharing bits and pieces of what he and his team discovered in the cave complex beneath Nebenteru's tomb. Enough to propel Trummel to find the tomb for himself, no matter what the costs. Only he knew the secrets that had died with Harlan. With their discovery Trummel would rewrite history.

The campfire burst with crackling embers.

He snapped his head toward the sound of approaching voices. He reached into his satchel and gripped his pistol. Bakari put down his book and unsheathed his sword. They watched and waited as the voices drew closer.

Trummel couldn't help feeling that he had enemies within his crew. Any one of the workers could be spying for the Cairo Museum or the Egyptian government.

He trusted Bakari. Trummel's six-foot-four porter had served him on a previous expedition. He was a man of few words, but extremely loyal. Bakari would never betray him.

Trummel trusted Gosswick, too. The other soldiers, however, were greedy enough to sell their own mothers for the right price. Even Dyfan, whom Trummel relied on for his keen psychic ability, could know more than he was telling. Then there was the American journalist. Trummel had liked him at first. When they met in Cairo, Trummel and Beckett had swapped adventure tales over drinks and talked long into the night. Now he had an off feeling about the Yank. If it weren't for the importance of Beckett's piece for *National Geographic*, Trummel would have sent the journalist home weeks ago.

His hand around the pistol's grip, Trummel listened to the approaching voices, recognizing them as they got closer. Imogen was walking with Caleb in the gloom between the tents. The intimacy in their voices suggested they had become better acquainted.

What's she doing with him at this hour?

CHAPTER THIRTEEN

Imogen followed Caleb back to his work tent, a makeshift darkroom. The interior smelled strongly of developing fluid. At the far end of the tent, he'd strung twine overhead in rows. To the twine, he'd clamped photographs. Several were of Trummel and his team standing at the crypt's entrance. More pictured Trummel's discovery inside the tomb as he and the others gathered around the mummy's sarcophagus. Rows of images catalogued relics and the skeletons of those buried with the high priest.

"Do you believe in mummies' curses, Miss Riley?"

She stifled a laugh. "Of course not. The idea of a three-thousand-year-old curse is superstitious nonsense."

"What about the deaths that plagued Carter's team after they opened Tutankhamun's tomb?"

"Pure coincidence."

"And the inscription Carter found? 'They who enter this sacred tomb shall swift be visited by wings of death.'"

"Some newspaperman made up that rubbish. I know for a fact no warning or curse was found in Tutankhamun's tomb."

He stared at her unconvinced.

"Mr. Beckett, I have spent years preserving and restoring mummies. Neither I nor my staff have ever suffered any curses."

"Have you ever seen anything like this?" He handed her a stack of photos that captured the mummy from various angles. A close-up showed its bony hands holding the strange metal disk against its chest.

"Dr. Trummel showed me the disk earlier," Imogen said. "It's an unusual find."

"There's something even more peculiar." He gave her a photo of Trummel holding the disk. The crystal at the center seemed aglow, as if illuminated from within. It cast a bright light on Trummel's face, reflected in his eyes.

"Was the light caused by your flash?" she asked.

"I didn't use a flash. When Trummel pulled the disk from the mummy's hands, it began to glow."

"Glow how?"

"The light was blue, brilliant." After a moment he took the photo back. "Maybe I'm not supposed to be showing you this."

"I'm sure it's quite all right. I'll be the one to ensure this relic reaches England. Did you notice anything else?"

"The disk made a humming sound. We all took turns holding it. It felt warm as it vibrated. It remained that way for several minutes before the light and vibration dimmed and finally turned off." He placed the photographs in a folder. "You'll think this is nonsense too, but I had the feeling when it was happening that the crystal was reading me somehow. My hands tingled for days after. Everyone who handled the disk has experienced phantom sensations – headaches, dizzy spells – along with terrible nightmares. Some of the others fear we might have picked up radiation from the disk."

"Technology that emanates power would be too advanced for the ancient Egyptians," Imogen said.

"What about the Dendera light?" he challenged. "Couldn't that be proof?"

Imogen was amazed that he knew about the heavily debated theory among Egyptologists. "It's pure fantasy. Let me guess. Did Trummel drink too much and bend your ear about piezoelectricity and the pyramids being giant superconductors to outer space?"

"Actually, I made the connection on my own. Before I came here, I visited the temple complex near Dendera." He opened a folder and pulled out photos of the familiar ruins. "Inside the Hathor Temple is a wall with a relief that depicts what appears to be Egyptians holding a giant light bulb." He showed her a photograph he'd made of the wall that some pseudoscientist had nicknamed "the Dendera light."

Caleb looked at her with all seriousness. "Trummel believes the relief suggests the ancient Egyptians had access to electrical technology capable of generating light."

"As brilliant as he is, Trummel is among a fringe group of scientists who believe such outlandish theories. Most Egyptologists see the relief for what it is: a symbol of fertility." Imogen pointed to the photograph. "The tube the priest is holding is actually a lotus flower, and the coil inside it is a snake. The top end of the bulb is being propped up by a djed pillar, a symbol for the backbone of the god Osiris along with a set of outstretched human arms. The symbols were part of their mythology."

"Then how do you explain the silver disk lighting up?" Caleb asked.

"Hallucinations. There was no light. You merely imagined it."

"How could we have all imagined the same thing? And how do you explain our nightmares?"

"You opened the sarcophagus inside the tomb and inhaled embalming fluids that have been sealed up for centuries. I've experienced all the symptoms you described, as well as suffered hallucinations and vivid dreams on previous digs. The air inside a tomb can have strange effects on the mind. Don't worry, Mr. Beckett, the nightmares and headaches will eventually subside."

Doubt remained in his eyes. "I hope you're right. I could use a good night's sleep."

She smiled. "I recommend a cup of chamomile tea with a dash of bourbon."

He laughed. "I'm glad you arrived, Miss Riley. It had gotten rather gloomy around here."

As she helped Caleb put away his photos, Imogen admired one he had taken of her. Her shoulder-length blond hair blew wildly to one side, a few rebellious strands crossing her face. The setting sun was a ball of fire directly behind her.

"Wow, I've never seen a photo quite like this." The way the sun created a corona of light around her head gave the photograph an ethereal quality.

"Beautiful, isn't it?" He stood close. "You can keep it if you like."

"Thank you. I'll hang it in my study." After they put his photos away, Caleb escorted Imogen to her tent. "I've enjoyed getting to know you, Miss Riley."

"Please, call me Imogen."

"Only if you call me Caleb." He tipped his hat. "Good night, Imogen."

"'Night." She watched him walk to the far end of camp and disappear into his tent.

Dyfan was seated in a chair outside his tent, smoking a pipe. The blind man nodded. "I wonder what Dr. Trummel would think if he saw you leaving another man's tent at this hour?"

"It's none of his bloody business," she said. "Nor is it yours."

Who was *he* to judge her actions? She allowed the psychic one card reading and now he presumed some kind of moral authority over her. Perhaps he'd only been trying to warn her. When she entered her tent, she found Trummel waiting.

CHAPTER FOURTEEN

"None of my bloody business?" Trummel said angrily. "Everything that goes on with my team is my bloody business!"

"What are you doing in my tent?" Imogen asked.

"Waiting for you to get back. It's after midnight, for Christ's sake."

"I didn't know there was a curfew."

He lowered his voice. "Most everyone else is asleep. What were you doing out with my photographer at this hour?" Trummel's eyes roiled with jealousy. It was the most passion he had shown her in ages.

"He interviewed me for the magazine and showed me the photo he took earlier." She held it up. "Then he walked me back to my tent, like a gentleman."

"Nothing more happened?"

"Of course not. Why are you so concerned?"

His voice softened and suddenly he was Nathan again. "Because I've missed you, Im. I've missed *us*."

His unexpected affection triggered a rush of feelings she hadn't felt since they were lovers. He looked at her the way he did when he first seduced her in Cairo. They had just finished a three-month expedition at the pyramids of Giza. All the staff had been released, and it was just the two of them, staying in a two-bedroom suite at the Continental-Savoy. What was supposed to have been a single night's stay before flying home turned into two passion-filled weeks. Afterward, he returned home to Bonnie. Nathan described his marriage as hollow, loveless. He and Imogen had continued the affair a few more months, and then, feeling guilty for betraying Bonnie, Imogen broke it off.

Now as she absorbed Nathan's confession that he'd missed her, Imogen placed Caleb's photograph of her on a small table beside her cot. The windswept image stared back at her.

Nathan moved closer until she could feel the heat coming off his body. He caressed her shoulders. "Have you missed me too?"

"Of course," she whispered.

He pulled her into him and slowly kissed her forehead, her cheek, her lips. Imogen slipped from his arms and stepped away. "Nathan, I can't."

"What's the matter?"

"You're still married. I told you before, I can't be the other woman." She crossed her arms. "I won't."

He considered this a moment, then said, "I'm planning on leaving her."

The news came as a surprise. "When?"

"As soon as I return to England, I'm going to tell Bonnie I want a divorce."

"Her father will have you fired."

"I don't give a damn about Harington. After I bring back the relics from this tomb, the rest of the board will beg me to stay."

She thought of their amazing find, enough to fill an exhibit that would attract visitors from all over the world. Something he said bothered her. "By *relics*, you mean the silver disk you found with the mummy?"

"I mean what we're going to find deeper inside the tomb. We've only scratched the surface of this site."

"And what *do* you expect to find?" she prodded.

He winked at her. "In due time, Im."

"I don't like that you're keeping secrets. We're supposed to be equal partners."

"We are. I also know that there are spies in our camp." He nodded toward the tent's canvas walls and lowered his voice. "Someone could be eavesdropping even now." He moved in close again, whispered in her ear, "I promise that you and I will share credit for the expedition. And Bonnie will no longer come between us." He kissed her again. This time she kissed him back.

But when he fumbled with the buttons of her shirt, she caught his hand and stepped away. "Not until after you've left Bonnie. I don't want to cheat."

He reached for Imogen, persistent as always. "Come to bed."

It took all her will to deny him. "While we're working together, our relationship will be strictly professional." These were his rules after all.

Once he ended his marriage, she would give herself, heart and soul, to Nathan Trummel.

He studied her. "You expect me to restrain myself for weeks while working alongside you? That's bloody torture." He pulled back the blanket on her cot. "Come on, Im, let's go to bed."

"I care deeply about you. I want you. But not like this. It's been a long day and we've got an early morning." Imogen held her tent flap open, showing him the exit. He left angry.

CHAPTER FIFTEEN

That night, a fierce wind blew in, shaking Storage Tent 2. It whipped the canvas, blowing sand in through the front slit. The gritty taste in Private Joe Dunlap's mouth was a constant reminder he worked in purgatory.

He always got the shit jobs. That was his lot in life. He came from the poorest suburb in Liverpool, where generations of Dunlap men suffered for meager wages. Runt of the litter in a family of ten kids, "Little Joe" Dunlap had always been at the bottom of the pecking order, gotten the smallest pork chop at supper, and carried out the most dreadful chores. That curse followed him when he signed on to work as part of Captain Gosswick's crew. Ever since Dunlap had gotten here, he'd been stuck working the graveyard shift.

At least he wasn't pulling cave duty. For once, the fates had shown him mercy when he won a bet in a poker game – three lovely queens trumping a fool's bluff – and got to switch duties with Private Bigsby.

An hour into his shift, Nigel Bigsby stopped by Storage Tent 2 to bring Dunlap tea and biscuits, another perk from winning the bet. Bigsby was dusted from head to toe in sand. "It's a bloody tempest out there." He pushed his goggles up to his forehead and spoke in a mock old English voice. "'Alas, the storm is come again! My best way is to creep under his gabardine; there is no other shelter hereabouts.'"

"What's that from?" Dunlap asked, not understanding a single word of it.

"Shakespeare's *The Tempest*, of course." Bigsby was always quoting from his books. At supper he'd spouted off lines from *Don Quixote*. Now he gazed at Dunlap with eyes full of envy. "That chair looks mighty comfortable."

Dunlap leaned back. "It's heavenly."

Bigsby dug a hand in his pocket and pulled out some pound notes. "I'll pay you fifty quid to switch back to cave duty."

"You could offer me all the gold in Egypt, mate, and I wouldn't switch places." Dunlap poured a cup of tea from the thermos, dipped a biscuit in the steaming cup, happy to be away from the tomb.

Bigsby sighed. "I guess it's me and the cave ghosts then. 'Misery acquaints a man with strange bedfellows.'"

"The only bedfellows I want tonight are these ladies." Dunlap held up a pinup magazine.

"Better not get *too* carried away with that. Gosswick is lurking about." Bigsby pulled down his sand goggles and quoted Shakespeare again. "'Once more unto the breach, dear friends. Once more.'"

★   ★   ★

Nigel Bigsby made the harrowing march through the sandstorm to the cave. It was going to be a bugger of a night. He passed bleary-eyed workers as he descended the dirt ramp to the tomb's doorway.

Rex Sykes, who'd been guarding the entrance during the day shift, looked down at his watch. "'Bout damned time, Bigsby."

"Sorry, I was just—"

"Save your story, I'm off to bed." Sykes hurried up the ramp, leaving Bigsby alone at the gate. Twenty feet underground, at least he was out of the sandstorm.

An Egyptian worker singing in Arabic rolled a wheelbarrow past him and vanished in the gloom of the cave. The laborers were working deep in the tomb tonight, one level down. He could just make out the sound of their picks striking the stone walls.

Nothing to do now but pass the time till the bright eye of dawn winked in the morning. Bigsby flicked on an electric torch and opened a book that he'd brought. *The Lair of the White Worm.* He'd be spending the night with Bram Stoker. *Talk about a strange bedfellow.* Stoker's gothic writing got under Bigsby's skin and festered there – *like a nest of white worms.* He chuckled at the pun. Stoker was perfect reading to keep Bigsby awake all night.

He barely read half a page when he heard a scraping noise behind him. A stench of foul body odor caused his nose to twitch. The workers sweated all day and rarely bathed. Many stunk as bad as the camels. He turned, expecting another group of workers to emerge from the cave's bowels. No one came.

The scraping sounded again a moment later. Bigsby stepped a few feet into the cave, swishing his torch beam. A body pressed up against him from behind. Before he could cry out, a hand clamped around his mouth.

CHAPTER SIXTEEN

Outside, a sandstorm rattled the canvas walls of her tent. Inside, Imogen lay twisted in her sheets, unable to sleep. She could hardly believe what she'd done. Nathan had finally expressed his feelings and she'd denied him.

Before she could talk herself out of it, she was on her feet. She dressed and hurried out into the windswept night. She crossed the alley that ran between the tents. Nathan's tent was illuminated with faint lantern light. That had been their signal on previous digs. "I'll leave a light on after midnight when I want you to come to me," he had told her.

Imogen stopped and drew a deep breath. She entered his tent and crossed to the hanging sheet wall that shielded his cot. She would climb in beside him and show him she was sorry. Imogen unbuttoned her shirt and let it fall to the floor. Shadows moved on the other side of the sheet that hung as a divider. She heard a pleasured sigh, high-pitched, a woman's voice.

Peering around the sheet revealed Piper's bare back.

Imogen stifled a gasp.

Nathan opened his eyes.

Before he could respond, Imogen snatched her shirt off the floor and hurried from the tent.

She collapsed on her own cot, not believing what had just happened. Her chest ached. She kept hearing Piper's sigh. Imogen didn't bother fighting tears. She just let them fall.

CHAPTER SEVENTEEN

Dunlap sat alone, already missing Bigsby's company. The storage tent was overstuffed with statues and figurines. Their dead eyes seemed to stare right at Dunlap. He tried to ignore them. Instead he flipped through an issue of *Stolen Sweets*. The magazine had a nude blonde on the cover, sitting on a rock, shielding her privates. One nipple was partially exposed. The sight of her made him long to be with a girl. His thoughts were interrupted suddenly by a noise at the far end of the tent.

A *tearing* sound.

Dunlap jerked in his seat. He dropped the nudie mag, drew his pistol, and stood. "Who's there? Hello? Bigsby?"

When no one answered, he weaved through the crowd of statues, shining his torch into the gloom. "Quig, you better not be pulling a prank."

The tent flapped wildly. A gust of sand hit his face. At the very back of the tent, the fabric had been split with a rent as tall as he was. "Bugger."

Teddy Quig liked to spook him, but Dunlap didn't think he'd go so far as to damage a tent. Must've been the wind. Gosswick and Trummel were going to be pissed.

Something rattled behind him.

Dunlap panned his lights over the statues. One rocked sideways and righted itself. He shone the light around it. Nothing moved.

Just past the relics, one of the expedition's vehicles, a British Army flatbed lorry, was parked inside the tent. Something was making a racket on the other side of it.

"Quig, if that's you, this ain't funny. I've got my pistol drawn."

Dunlap slowly started around the truck toward the rattling sound. Something crashed to the floor.

Christ! He walked along the driver's side, his gun aimed nervously at the dark. He played the torchlight over the ground. The trunk where Trummel kept his most important relics was lying on its back, the wood badly scraped. Two of the drawers had been torn open, their contents strewn across the sandy floor.

Dunlap rushed to inspect it. Something sharp sliced the backs of his calves. He cried out in pain, discharging his pistol as he fell to the ground.

Under the truck something moved. A large body shrouded in darkness. Dunlap's light passed over a face that made him scream. He tried to crawl away. Claws dug into his wounded legs and dragged him beneath the truck.

CHAPTER EIGHTEEN

A burnt figure made of glowing orange cinders reaches for Imogen with fiery fingers. She backs away and tries to scream. She can't make a sound...

A noise outside her tent pulled Imogen from the dream. She sat up, groggy.

Men shouted. Echoing *cracks* sounded. Gunshots, Imogen realized.

She leapt off the cot and ran to the tent's door.

The camp was in chaos. The sandstorm blew tent flaps like ragged shrouds. Imogen wrapped a linen scarf over her head and shielded her face from the flying sand as she hurried toward the men's voices. She ran into someone. Lowered the wrap to see who it was. "Caleb."

He gripped her shoulders. "You okay?" he shouted.

She nodded. "What's going on?"

"A ruckus of some sort."

Screams sounded beyond the roiling sand. They were coming from the edge of camp.

Imogen and Caleb passed others running in the opposite direction. One crashed into Imogen, nearly knocking her to the ground. The fleeing figure cursed in Arabic and kept running.

Trummel appeared, his hair mussed, shirt untucked. Piper stood at the entrance to his tent, wearing only a robe. Trummel shouted for the workers to stop. They ignored him, ran straight for the camels, threw saddles on them, and rode off into the dark.

Trummel cursed. "What the devil is going on?"

Gosswick ran toward them. "Sir, there's been an attack."

CHAPTER NINETEEN

Imogen and Caleb gathered with Trummel, Piper, Bakari, and eight soldiers in the storage tent. Next to the truck, a young soldier named Dunlap lay on the ground, dead. His chest and rib cage had been sliced open in several places. Deep gashes bisected both calves. His hands were covered in blood. Three fingers were missing, severed at the knuckles. The young man's blank eyes stared up at them.

Piper gasped.

"What the hell?" Trummel asked, visibly shaken.

The soldiers looked scared. Most had been asleep during the melee.

Sergeant Vickers answered. "It was too dark to see, sir. We shot at *something...*" He shook his head in disbelief. "...but it moved fast. Like an animal. It escaped into the tomb."

"Bigsby's missing," Gosswick said with a grim expression. "We found blood at the entrance but no body."

Trummel paced, shaking his head. "No animal within a thousand miles could attack a man like this. What we have is a saboteur, someone hiding among us, trying to undermine the dig. If he can run us off, he can enter the cave alone and steal its treasures. Search the cave. Bakari and I will search the camp. Whoever did this will have blood on his hands and his clothes. Do it now before he has a chance to clean up."

"Aye, sir." Gosswick led his men out of the tent.

Imogen and Caleb remained with Trummel, Piper, and Bakari. Piper wouldn't meet Imogen's gaze. The girl looked so terrified Imogen almost felt sorry for her.

"Will you postpone the cave expedition?" Caleb said.

"Not a chance," Trummel said. "This makes resuming the dig all the more urgent. Christ, he got into my trunk." He began rummaging in the drawers. Books and documents lay scattered in the sand.

"Was Grandfather's diary stolen?" Imogen asked.

"No, fortunately I kept it and the disk in my tent." Trummel stood, abandoning the mess. He turned to Imogen, Caleb, and Piper. "I suggest you three go back to your tents. Bakari, escort them. I'll get this all sorted."

CHAPTER TWENTY

Inside the tomb, Captain Aiden Gosswick and four of his men followed a blood trail through the winding tunnels. Every few feet, red streaked the walls.

They reached a chamber where the trail ended in a large pool of blood. It looked like the floor of a slaughterhouse. The stench of offal assaulted Gosswick.

A pair of boots and part of a torn khaki uniform lay discarded near the blood.

"Shite, somebody got Bigsby," Quig said.

Gosswick cursed. He'd lost three of his men on this dig. First Aleister's suicide, then Dunlap, now the kid who quoted Shakespeare.

"What now, sir?" Sergeant Vickers asked.

"I want the bastard who did this." Gosswick spun around the chamber, jabbing the beam of his torch into every crag and crevice. The cave branched off into three deeper tunnels. Each one had traces of blood, as if Bigsby's body had been butchered into parts and carried off in three directions. Another thought struck Gosswick. They were dealing with a cunning killer, who bloodied each tunnel to throw them off his trail.

"Vickers, Quig, take the left tunnel," Gosswick ordered. "Sykes, Watters, take the right."

The soldiers split off. Gosswick explored the center tunnel alone. He had to get away from the abattoir smell. It drummed up horrid memories of Kenya that he'd rather keep buried.

The stench of slaughter followed Gosswick deeper into the tunnel. His heart pumped faster. Pressure pushed at his temples and skull until he felt his head might explode. "Shit," he whispered.

A sound echoed from the darkness up ahead. Laughter. Deep and hoarse.

Gun raised, Gosswick followed the blood trail through a passage that seemed to narrow as he ran. The grown man's laughter turned to childish snickers. When the tunnel finally opened into a circular chamber, the snickering voices went silent. The blood trail ended at a hole in a wall. He slowly approached the cavity and probed it with his torchlight. Another vertical shaft channeled downward to an unknown depth.

The giggles echoed all around him, hollow and high-pitched, like the sounds of children playing in some ghostly realm alongside ours.

Gosswick spun in a tight circle. The walls here were decorated with cave paintings that looked nothing like the Egyptian art he'd seen in other parts of the tomb. The ancient graffiti was crude and primitive, painted with red ochre. The scenes were of slaughtered children. Among the carnage in the painting stood a tall shadow figure.

The cries of children coming from the walls sent Gosswick running back the way he'd come.

CHAPTER TWENTY-ONE

Last night had been a disaster. Most of the workers had fled, taking every last camel. Only Bakari and another devoted porter remained. Neither had been found with blood on their hands. Whoever killed the two soldiers had either escaped with the workers or was hiding somewhere inside the tomb. The whole camp was on edge. Dyfan offered little help, complaining of a blackout he'd suffered while the attack transpired. Trummel had barely slept.

This morning, he stood shaving in front of his mirror when he heard the flaps of his tent open. The mirror reflected Imogen behind him. She didn't look pleased.

"What is it?" Trummel knew but was in no mood for a row.

"Goss just informed me that I'm to leave camp with the others."

"That's right."

Most of the archaeological staff and students, including Piper, were loading up three of the lorries, preparing to drive back to Cairo. Trummel wanted to minimize the risks. Only a handful of men would remain to accompany him into the tomb.

"There's no reason for you to be here now. It's too dangerous for a woman. Two men died last night, and God knows where the killer is. I won't risk you. Go home. Or stay in Cairo. I'll put you up at the Savoy, if you like."

"I'll do neither."

"Be reasonable. Is this really about you finding me in bed with Piper?"

"You betrayed me," Imogen said, sounding hurt. "How could you after everything you said...?"

Trummel ran the razor blade down his foamy neck as he stared at her reflection in the mirror. "What can I say? You turned me away."

"How long have you been sleeping with her?"

"Keep your voice down, for Christ's sake!" he whispered angrily.

"How long, Nathan?" she said in a softer voice.

He shrugged. "A few weeks. It's nothing. Not like you and me. I care about you, Im. That's why I want you to go back with the others where you'll be safe."

Outside, the driver honked the truck's horn.

"Go, before you miss your ride."

Imogen didn't raise her voice. "I'm half of this expedition. I can interpret hieroglyphs better than you, and I didn't come all this way to turn back just because you've taken a student half your age into your bed. You couldn't get me on that truck if you had the help of a dozen men. Oh, and we're through. From now on we are work partners, nothing more." She walked to his cot where earlier he had been reading Harlan's journal. Imogen picked it up and waved it at Trummel. "And Grandfather's diary stays with me." She took the damn book and stormed out before he could say another word.

CHAPTER TWENTY-TWO

After three lorries drove away loaded with artifacts and the departing members of Trummel's team, only a skeleton crew remained at camp. As she had promised, Imogen was among them. She had been relieved to watch Piper ride off with the others. The girl was a distraction Imogen didn't need.

At breakfast, one of the soldiers slopped watery porridge into bowls. Everyone seemed anxious. Most ate in silence. Even Gosswick looked out of sorts. Bakari sat by himself, as usual, his nose in a book.

Imogen poured herself a cup of strong-smelling coffee. She tried to push Nathan from her mind but it was hard. Images kept flashing through her mind – Nathan when they first slept together in Cairo… Bonnie's kindness at the funeral…Piper's naked back, the sounds she'd made in the throes of passion. They hadn't slept together once, but for weeks! How many other women had he slept with in secret? Thinking back, Imogen couldn't decipher the true things he'd told her from the lies.

I've been a fool. Her hand shook, spilling hot coffee on her khaki pants. She cursed as the stain spread. *Stop thinking about him. Concentrate on the dig.* Whenever her emotions got out of control, she reined them in by diving into work, being a scientist. She was much more comfortable being analytical than emotional. *To hell with Nathan.* She reminded herself why she had come here – to finish Grandfather's work and bring back what relics he originally discovered to the museum.

Her anger decreased to a simmer. She sat at a table with some of the other members of the team. Four of the soldiers, Vickers, Quig, Watters, and Sykes, were carrying on about how they were going to cut the bollocks off whoever killed their mates.

Imogen tuned them out and drank her coffee in silence. She opened her grandfather's journal and began flipping through the pages, examining all the strange symbols he'd drawn. She was trying to recall what he'd told her at the asylum, when she noticed Dyfan sitting by himself a few tables away. He appeared to be staring at her. Not just *at* her. *Into* her. For a moment, she felt that her mind was an open book and Dyfan was turning the pages, learning anything he wanted. The blind man smiled at her and nodded.

She tried to ignore the sensation.

Caleb took the empty seat next to her. "Good morning," he said with too much cheer. "Glad to see you stayed behind."

She nodded and stirred her porridge but didn't eat.

"Funny, I would have taken you for a morning person," he needled.

She gave him a half smile. "I normally am. I didn't sleep too well after last night's events."

"I barely slept myself," Caleb said. "But this morning's expedition has got me all excited." He opened a rucksack filled with photography gear. He pulled out a small camera and a hard-shell case that contained a dozen flashbulbs. As he installed the flash extension to the camera, he asked Imogen, "Are you packed and ready to explore the tomb?"

"Dr. Trummel pulled me off the expedition. He tried to make me leave camp with his students. I refused."

"Since you stayed, you'll have to come with us." Caleb frowned. "I'll have a word with Trummel."

"No, please, I don't want you to fight my battles."

"I wouldn't mind." He gave her a warm smile.

"You're very kind, but I'll deal with Trummel myself." Her attention turned to a young man with wire-rimmed glasses who sat across from her. He was drawing something strange on a sketchpad.

Caleb must have followed her gaze. "Imogen, this is Ely Platt."

Ely was no older than twenty, she guessed, one of the wide-eyed students who'd been enthralled by Trummel's yeti story last night.

"Ely's our mapmaker. He's detailing the tomb's cave system," Caleb explained. "He's also a gifted artist. You should see some of his comic book sketches."

"That's not a map you're drawing," she said, leaning nearer.

"It's something I dreamt last night." Ely turned the image so Imogen could see it. He had sketched himself running through a tunnel. A misshapen shadow loomed behind him.

"That was some dream," Imogen said.

"I've had the same nightmare ever since I arrived. Whatever that thing is, it keeps chasing me." Ely kept drawing, filling in the shadow that stalked him.

"I've been bothered by nightmares myself," Caleb said. "I don't remember much, only that I'm trapped underwater and can't breathe."

"It's the tomb," Ely said. "It's cursed."

"Curses are the stuff of pulp fiction," Imogen said.

Ely looked around at the others in the tent and whispered, "Those of us who've been here for months are convinced some unseen force affects our dreams. It's coming from the tomb."

She almost mentioned her own bad dream: the burnt figure reaching for her. It had disturbed her sleep three straight nights. She wasn't ready to admit she was suffering the same delirium as the others. The only way she could think to explain her dreams was that she had also touched the mummy's disk. Maybe it held some kind of power, as Caleb had feared. Not a curse but radiation of some sort. Could radiation infect their dreams with horrors?

She noticed Ely sketching symbols in a border around his drawing. The same strange glyphs she'd seen before. "What do you know about those?" she asked.

"I found them engraved on a wall in the deepest part of the tomb. They also appear in my dreams."

Imogen opened her grandfather's diary at the pages filled with the codes written in blood. Several of the symbols matched Ely's.

Caleb studied both texts. "What do they mean?" he asked.

"It's an unknown cuneiform," Imogen said. "I haven't been able to decipher the codes yet."

"May I have a try?" Ely asked. "I'm pretty good with puzzles."

She slid the book over to him. His eyes moved rapidly over Grandfather's crude drawings. He scanned the rows, flipping back and forth through the pages, stopping finally on a page crammed with words. He held the book open above his head, looking up at it, then set it flat on the table. His finger tapped his forehead as he scanned the pages. Then he returned to reviewing the codes at the back of the book. "Forty-two."

"What?" Imogen asked.

"There are forty-two rows of symbols. Twenty-one on each page." Ely flipped back to the middle of the book. "And on these two pages there are forty-two word sequences. Twenty-one on the left page and twenty-one on the right."

"Let me see." As Imogen studied the pages, Caleb leaned over her shoulder. The words at the center of the book, scrawled in black ink, were scribbled so wildly that she hadn't made sense of Grandfather's ramblings. She shook her head. "My grandfather wasn't well when he made these notes. I'm afraid they may be useless."

Ely turned the book around, then placed his hands flat on the pages, covering most of the words near the binding. "Look at it this way." The words at the edges of each page that he had left uncovered formed two lists of names: *Shadow-Eater, Blood-Drinker, He Who Comes from the*

Slaughter, Cave-Dweller, Pale One, Bone-Crusher, Eater of Worms...

Imogen drew closer. "They're demon names from the Book of the Dead."

"They correspond with the rows of the symbols," Ely said.

She turned to the back of the book, compared the rows of codes to the rows of names. They lined up almost perfectly. "Absolutely brilliant, Ely! I could kiss you."

The young man's cheeks reddened.

"What are the lists of names for?" Caleb asked.

"I'm not sure, but I think it's a kind of Rosetta stone," Imogen said. "It may allow us to translate the unknown cuneiform language."

Imogen could barely contain her excitement. This discovery could be the key to unlock another ancient culture. For centuries no one knew how to translate the Egyptian hieroglyphs. A major breakthrough occurred in 1799 when French soldiers in the small village of Rosetta, Egypt, discovered a black granodiorite rock carved with three ancient texts all saying the exact same thing in Greek, hieroglyphic, and demotic. In 1822, Jean-François Champollion deciphered the Rosetta stone, making it possible to translate Egyptian hieroglyphs.

With renewed enthusiasm for the expedition, Imogen spent the next half hour with Caleb and Ely writing the codes with their accompanying demon names on the same page at the back of the journal. Later, when she had more time, she would deconstruct the words, symbol by symbol, and attempt to make an alphabet.

Trummel entered the breakfast tent, looking cheerful. He clapped his hands and smiled. "Good morning, team. Who here is ready to make history?"

PART TWO
INTO THE ABYSS

CHAPTER TWENTY-THREE

The cave was a warren of intersecting tunnels. Beams of light from their mining helmets shone around the narrow walls of the passage. Twelve explorers wearing rucksacks and bedrolls on their backs walked single file. At the front of the group, Dyfan groped the walls, feeling the way with his fingertips. Rounding a bend, he vanished in the dark.

Behind Dyfan walked Gosswick and two soldiers, Sykes and Watters. They remained quiet, aiming their beams into crags and adjoining tunnels.

Imogen followed Trummel, keeping him squarely in the glow of her headlamp. Tight spaces didn't agree with her. As the walls narrowed, she fought panic. *Breathe*, she reminded herself. As the only woman on the expedition, the last thing she wanted was to be perceived as a hindrance. Each time side tunnels gaped open beside her the icy blackness threatened to undo her resolve.

Behind her, Caleb and Ely were sticking close. Bakari and another Egyptian porter, both loaded down with gear, walked next. Quig and Vickers brought up the rear.

Imogen thought of the two soldiers who had been murdered the night before. It was quite possible that the killer was still down here, hiding somewhere in the tunnels.

The cave grew darker and colder as the explorers put distance between themselves and the exit. Lengths of the walls had been painted or carved with glyphs. In an attempt to conceal the tomb from marauders, the branching tunnels had been engraved and embellished too, creating a maze of choices that looked very much the same. Imogen's vision swam when she thought how easily they could become lost. *Don't think. Breathe.*

The explorers entered the chapel. A stone offering table where food and drink would have been placed sat near the back of the chamber. An open area surrounded a platform where the mummy's coffin would have rested during a funeral ceremony. Engraved in the wall was a decorative false door. Found in most Egyptian tombs, the false door acted as a threshold between the living world and the realm of the dead. Imogen envied the ancient Egyptians' faith in the spirit realms. How at peace they must have felt, believing they were helped by unseen gods.

She peered through a square window cut into the rock – the serdab, a small chamber where a statue of the deceased stared back at her. The stone face, painted brown with black eyes and a gray chin beard, was a telling likeness of the high priest entombed here. According to the coffin texts that Trummel had translated, Nebenteru had been a royal oracle for King Ramses II. Imogen thought of the silver disk found with his mummy. She still could not imagine its use.

Caleb, who had stopped to photograph a wall painting, nudged Imogen. "We need to keep moving. Our tour guides are leaving."

Imogen smiled. "I could spend hours studying this one spot."

"There'll be time for that later. Let's see where these tunnels take us."

The front soldiers, Trummel, and Dyfan had already led the team past the chapel and into the far tunnel. Their headlamps were beginning to fade. Beyond the chapel another decorative hallway led to a large, square hole in the floor. A painted sign, hanging on a spike, read 'Level Two Shaft'. The near-vertical staircase descended to another level thirty feet below. Their party gripped ropes that acted as makeshift railings, as they climbed down small steps cut from the rock. Like the others, Imogen had to walk sideways to keep from falling. At the bottom, the cave tunnel led through a series of burial chambers that had been sectioned off with walls of stacked stones. Many of the walls had been broken through.

"This is where we found the bones of the servants and soldiers," Trummel said as they passed through one of the rooms. "This next chamber is where the mummy was entombed."

The flash from Caleb's camera bathed portions of the crypt in light.

Imogen slowly spun in a circle, admiring walls painted with faded murals of gods and goddesses.

Caleb said, "Osiris and his siblings."

Imogen pointed. "And Thoth, Khepri."

Their helmet lamps illuminated a giant mural of the jackal-headed god. Anubis stood over a sarcophagus, responsible for shepherding the soul of the departed into the afterlife.

"Him I know too well," Imogen said.

The rest of the team hurried past, barely noticing the paintings. Imogen and Caleb picked up their pace and followed another long tunnel, this one narrower and cruder than the previous ones. They scaled a hill of bricks and crossed through another broken wall. On the other side, a narrow passage curved.

Imogen stepped up beside Caleb, who was peering into a hole in the wall.

"What is it?" she asked.

"Another shaft."

"How far down does this tomb go?" Imogen wondered.

The shaft was a natural-cut fissure that led deep down into some other part of the cave. Instead of steps, there were only small holes in the wall that might have been footholds. A few feet down, Imogen's headlamp beam spotlighted dark stains.

"Dried blood?" Caleb asked.

"It's more likely striations of red jasper."

Caleb called out "Hello!" into the shaft. His voice echoed.

"Are you expecting someone to answer?" she asked.

Gosswick whistled. "Imogen, Flash. Keep moving."

"Flash?" she whispered to Caleb.

He shook his head. "The stupid nickname Gosswick gave me."

"He calls me Blondie."

"Blondie fits nicely," Caleb said.

"Don't you dare start using it," she warned.

As Imogen and Caleb caught up with the others, the beam of Trummel's headlamp played across their bodies accusingly. "Keep up," he ordered.

A second staircase led down to Level Three. They followed another long passage through a series of brick walls that had been recently cleared. The hieroglyphs in this tunnel were much older than the others.

"The five-thousand-year-old tomb," Trummel announced.

"Any idea of its purpose?" Imogen asked, trying to read the walls. The glyphs had badly eroded. The etchings that were visible didn't match any of the ancient Egyptian symbols.

"This wall has me perplexed," Trummel admitted. "There's cuneiform here that could be Sumerian mixed with some other sort of ancient text."

"What would Sumerians be doing in an Egyptian cave?" Imogen asked.

"I've been asking myself the same question. They must have traveled here from Sumer long before the first Egyptian dynasty."

The tunnel ended at a wall with a mural of a goddess with her wings spread. The vibrant colors shimmered in the light. It was one of the most breathtaking pieces Imogen had ever seen.

"She looks strikingly similar to an angel," Caleb noted.

"It's Ma'at," Imogen said, "the goddess of balance, morality, truth, and justice. I've seen this recently." She opened the diary and flipped through the pages, stopping at an illustration that matched the one painted on the wall. "My grandfather was here."

As the group gathered, Trummel said, "No one in our team has been beyond this point. This marks the start of virgin territory."

Imogen didn't see any intersecting tunnels.

"It's a dead end," Gosswick said.

Ely reviewed a map he'd drawn. "There's supposed to be another tunnel round here."

"We're near it." Dyfan flattened his palms against the bricks. "The next passage is beyond this wall."

Trummel snapped at the soldiers. "Break through it."

Each soldier carried a miner's pick. As they approached the wall, Imogen stepped in front of them. "Wait. You can't destroy the mural. There has to be another way down."

Trummel looked annoyed. "It took weeks to reach this point. I'm not wasting more time looking for another route. Step aside."

The soldiers hefted their picks, and Trummel pulled Imogen out of the way. The ancient wall crumbled under the hammering blows, destroying the goddess one bit at a time. The wings first, then her lovely face.

Dust rained down from the ceiling.

Imogen hoped it didn't cave in.

"Mightn't this upset the gods?" Caleb asked.

"It's not the gods that worry me," Imogen said. "This is shabby science. My grandfather would be sick at the prospect of destroying this painting. He'd have never stood for it." She projected her voice so Trummel would hear. "There are protocols to follow. Since when do we condone the destruction of antiquities?"

Trummel pretended he didn't hear. She didn't understand his behavior. When they had worked together before, he had carefully preserved every inch of his sites. Now, he had an eager look in his eyes.

Within minutes, the soldiers had chipped away a window that opened into a hollow chamber.

Trummel poked his head through the crag, aiming his headlamp. "Amazing," he breathed.

He stepped aside to let Imogen have a look. She peered through the window. Her helmet beam passed over the heads of hundreds of small mummies. Unlike the high priest's mummy, laid to rest in a wooden sarcophagus, these smaller mummies had been entombed without coffins. They looked like bodies web-spun by a giant spider and stored for future feedings.

Imogen found a page in Grandfather's diary that depicted these, as well.

The soldiers continued chopping at the wall, cutting the small portal into a jagged doorway.

"From here on, we venture beyond the original map," Trummel said. "What lies beyond? I can't say, but I assure you this expedition is one of great importance. You were chosen because you are the best of my team." He scanned everyone's faces, purposefully avoiding eye contact with Imogen. "I expect whatever we discover will change all our lives."

"What do you expect to find?" she challenged.

"I'm not ready to share my hopes. I will say this…what I believe we'll find will rival any discovery before it. Those of you who remain loyal and endure whatever challenges lie ahead I plan to pay a handsome bonus of five thousand pounds each."

The soldiers smiled.

"We'll do whatever it takes," Gosswick said.

Imogen didn't care about the extra money. Hoping to find what her grandfather discovered prodded her forward. She looked to Caleb. If he was apprehensive, it didn't show.

"You in, Beckett?" Trummel asked.

Caleb gripped the camera hanging across his chest. "I didn't come all this way to miss your grand discovery."

Trummel nodded and stared hard at Imogen. "Miss Riley, are you done carping?"

"I don't agree with your methods. But I won't turn back."

"Then we're all set," Trummel said.

Imogen felt a rush of adrenaline as she followed the others into the sepulcher. The smell of dust and decay was strong in this crypt.

Caleb took pictures. His flashes lit up hundreds of small mummies that crowded the space. A narrow path cut through them. Imogen felt like a giant walking through a throng of worshipping dead. Many of the mummies stood erect at various heights, from shin high to knee high, propped up one beside the other like bandaged dolls.

Ely's face wore a worried expression. "Are these babies?"

Imogen knelt to get a closer inspection. "Cat mummies."

"Shit, I bleedin' hate cats." The blunt-faced soldier named Sykes kicked a mummy. It burst apart, raining dust and broken bones.

"Show some respect," Imogen scolded. "Cats were sacred to the Egyptians."

"Bleedin' pests is what they are," Sykes grumbled.

Imogen hoped Gosswick would reprimand his soldier. The captain only smirked.

Walking single file, the group panned their headlamps over the feline dead. The cats had been immortalized in every position – sitting, standing, lying on their side as if napping. Many had decomposed, leaving only bone and fur. Dander floated in the air, disturbed by the group passing through. Some cats had been bound into cylinders with decorative woven wrappings that looked like baskets. Others had been bandaged with all four legs and the tail free. The soldiers had no regard for the corpses. Boots crunched over the mortified remains of tails and paws. At the center of the chamber loomed a large black stone statue of a cat resting on its haunches.

"Bastet," Caleb whispered, "goddess of cats. She doesn't look pleased."

"Can you blame her?" Imogen whispered back.

The group followed a thin trail to a circular clearing around the statue. Its polished obsidian reflected their lights. Beyond the cat goddess, more rows of mummies stretched into the darkness. Caleb photographed Bastet and her bandaged litter.

"Why entomb so many cats with the high priest?" Caleb asked Imogen.

"Priests raised kittens in temples and then killed and mummified them as offerings to the gods. In fact cats were of such high importance to the Egyptians that they were often entombed, along with mice, rats, and bowls of milk to help the cats reach the afterlife. One of the largest discoveries was in the late 1800s. Eighty thousand mummified cats were found in the tombs of Beni Hassan. I explored it myself a few years ago and brought back trophies for the museum. In other tombs along the Nile, archaeologists have found whole menageries of mummified animals – dogs, birds, even baboons."

Caleb snapped another photo. The flash caught movement to their left. Something or someone dashed into a crag in the wall.

"What the hell was that?" one of the soldiers shouted.

The others raised their guns.

The burly soldier, Sykes, waded through the mummies and aimed his torch and pistol into the narrow crag. "Gone."

"Who else could be down here?" Ely asked nervously.

"Our saboteur must be following us," Trummel said. "Let's keep moving."

The soldiers returned to the head and rear of the group. Everyone stayed close together as they followed the path through the mummies to the far end of the crypt.

Trummel turned to Dyfan. "Are they here?"

The blind man held up his hands, as if seeing with his palms. "I sense them, yes. But not in this chamber."

"Where then?" Trummel snapped.

Dyfan knelt, placing both palms on the floor. "Below us, deeper in the mountain."

Trummel pulled out the crude map based on his psychic's vision. "We're already on Level Three. Are you saying there's a fourth level below this one?"

Dyfan nodded. "And a fifth. The levels seem endless."

CHAPTER TWENTY-FOUR

One by one, the twelve explorers descended a third stone stairway down to Level Four. Sergeant Dan Vickers felt sick to his stomach. Every passage and staircase seemed to be closing tighter and tighter around him. His right hand shook. He squeezed it into a fist.

Quig noticed. "You okay, mate?"

"Just dandy," Vickers joked, trying to hide his discomfort.

At the bottom of the stairs, the group gathered into a cramped chamber with three square holes carved into the walls. Each led in a different direction. Tight, horizontal stone passageways, the size of air vents, disappeared into cold blackness.

Dyfan stepped to the square at the back wall. "It's this one."

"Are you sure?" Trummel shined his light into the mouth of the passageway.

The blind man nodded. "Aye, the pull is strong from this one."

Vickers's heart seized at the sight of the narrow crawlspace. He hated tight places – a remnant of the torture he'd endured in childhood at the hands of Cyril, his vicious older brother. Sons of a mortician, they had grown up in a funeral home. Little Danny Vickers had often felt paralyzed with fear by dark, enclosed places. He remembered being trapped inside a casket, his massive brother sitting on top. He could hear Cyril's demanding voice. *"Stop crying like a little milksop. Grow some bollocks, Danny, or I'm gonna bury you in this."*

The other explorers climbed into the tunnel, crawling forward flat on their stomachs.

Vickers whispered to Quig, "I can't go in there."

"Sure you can. I'll be right in front of you. Just keep your light on me."

The two soldiers were the last to start into the tunnel. Light from Quig's headlamp somehow made the space seem smaller. "Nothing to it." Quig grinned, flashing his gold teeth. Then he climbed into the tunnel. "Reminds me of the sewer pipes I used to explore back home."

Soon Vickers stood alone in the box-shaped chamber. He had the urge to run back up the stairs and get the hell out of this cave. But his sense of duty to Captain Gosswick and the opportunity to earn a big bonus motivated Vickers to suffer the tight passage. He drew a deep breath and clambered into the tunnel. He had the sensation he was entering a long coffin that stretched to infinity. The walls hugged his shoulders. The low ceiling scraped his helmet. He pushed his pack and miner's pick ahead of him. It was slow going, every inch was torture. All he could see was a channel of stone and the soles of Quig's boots several yards ahead. His mate was inching away, moving at a faster pace.

Vickers struggled to breathe in the dusty air, his throat so dry he could barely swallow. He stopped and leaned his helmet against the wall and clamped his eyes closed.

Fear is only in your head, you spineless sod. More of Cyril's taunting. In his mind, Vickers was again a helpless boy stuffed inside a casket and fighting for breath.

"Let me out!" he had screamed, hitting his fists against the coffin's lid. "Cyril, please let me out!"

Vickers drew several deep breaths and fought the panic rising in him. When he opened his eyes, the stone walls seemed to have narrowed further. A couple of times, his elbows got stuck. The ceiling too was pressing down. The light from Quig's helmet danced in the tunnel far ahead, the black gulf between them growing fast.

"Quig, wait!"

His mate stopped twenty feet ahead. "What's wrong?"

"I can't do this."

"Sure you can. We're almost to the other end. The others are already out."

From the far end of the tunnel, Gosswick yelled, "Quig, Vickers, what's the holdup?"

"Be right there, Captain!" Quig yelled. "Vick, you gotta keep moving. I can't turn round."

A scratching sound issued *behind* Vickers. "Did you hear that?" He looked back over his shoulder, aiming the beam of his helmet past his legs. From where the tunnel swallowed his light came hollow scraping sounds.

"Danny…"

The voice sounded like Cyril's.

Impossible. His brother was dead. Vickers had killed the bastard on a hunting trip, made it look like an accident. He could still hear the sound of the shotgun blast echoing off the lake. A flock of ducks took flight as Cyril fell to the ground.

Now Cyril's angry voice taunted him from the darkness. "I'm coming for you, Milksop. And this time I ain't playing."

It's just my mind playing tricks. There's nothing there.

The stone vibrated beneath Vickers. Behind him, something heavy was moving toward him through the dark.

An ungodly shriek pierced his ears.

"What the hell was that?" Quig yelled.

Vickers pissed himself. "Someone's in the tunnel with us."

Behind him the darkness growled with animal rage.

"Hurry, Vick!" Quig took off, crawling fast.

Vickers pushed his pack and scrambled forward.

The scraping sounds behind him drew closer. A rotten smell filled his nostrils.

As he turned to look back, his light shone on cadaver hands. They gripped the backs of his ankles. Vickers kicked at them. Panned the light upward.

The thing behind him wore Cyril's face, the right side torn away by the shotgun's blast.

⋆　　⋆　　⋆

When Teddy Quig heard the animal shriek, a primal terror took over. His mind and body answered the survival instinct of prey fleeing a predator. He clawed his way to the end of the tunnel. It was only after Gosswick and Sykes pulled him out that Quig thought of his mate.

Vickers was still midway down the tunnel. He screamed. Then his body shot backward, the light of his headlamp growing smaller and smaller, as if some unseen force pulled him down the tunnel. His howls retreated, and then abruptly cut off.

"Vick!" Quig started back into the tunnel, but the others grabbed him and held him by the arms. "Vick!" Quig yelled again.

Only silence answered back.

CHAPTER TWENTY-FIVE

The soldiers were on edge as the team continued down a hallway with a low ceiling. Trummel believed their attacker wanted to sabotage his expedition. Caleb wasn't so sure. It seemed to him that their party was being hunted. He'd heard the shrieks from the killer that claimed Vickers and couldn't believe a man made that sound.

Caleb's assignments often came with risk. This felt different. He was grateful that his pistol was holstered to his hip.

"Let's continue to explore Level Four," Trummel announced.

A man is dead, Caleb thought.

To protest would accomplish nothing, except maybe allow their attacker to catch up.

Caleb followed the others down a naturally occurring passageway. The end of it opened up into a long, rectangular antechamber large enough for the group to spread out. More murals covered the brick walls – pharaohs, gods, and rows upon rows of hieroglyphs, none of which Caleb could decipher.

"Fascinating." Trummel ran his fingers along the symbols of ankhs, birds, snakes, and beetles. "This dates back to the first dynasty. It shows the pharaoh meeting with the god Djeheuty." Trummel looked at Caleb and explained, "The Greeks called him Thoth – the god of wisdom who passed down knowledge from the heavens."

⋆　⋆　⋆

Thoth was represented as having a man's body and the head of an ibis, a bird with a long, curved beak.

With his camera, Caleb framed Trummel examining the wall and pressed the shutter release. The archaeologist explained Thoth's importance to the knowledge of the ancient Egyptians, how he gave them writing, the hieroglyphs. "Thoth also scribed the Book of the

Dead. It contained funerary spells and rituals that helped guide the souls of the dead through the afterlife. And over here is one of the most worshipped gods of them all, Osiris."

In the painting, Anubis was standing before Osiris, who was seated on a throne.

"Why does Osiris have green skin?" Caleb asked.

"That is one of Egypt's greatest mysteries," Trummel answered. "Dr. Riley and I debated it for years. According to legend, before Egypt was civilized, its people practiced cannibalism. Osiris arrived and taught man to grow and eat vegetables and grains."

Imogen added, "The myths claim he civilized the early Egyptians, gave them laws and taught them to worship a variety of gods." She shone her light on a part of the wall that showed several dozen gods, each represented with a human body and different animal head. "Dr. Trummel takes the myths literally, as if Osiris really existed, while I see them as allegorical. Whoever wrote them depicted the god-king with green skin so people would believe in beings higher than themselves. But Osiris, like all mythological deities, was only a fictional character."

"I beg to differ," Trummel said. "I believe Osiris was the true first pharaoh of Egypt. He paved the way for future kings. The pharaohs who followed were all considered powerful, divine beings who communed with the gods. King Ramses II went so far as to state that he was a direct descendant, half mortal, half god. That is why he had his statue built among the gods."

"Or Ramses *made* himself one," Imogen countered, "because he was the pharaoh with the largest ego."

Trummel shook his head and looked at Caleb. "Miss Riley is so wed to logic she cannot see the true messages these walls are telling us: The pharaohs knew much more than they revealed to the masses."

"Dr. Trummel only sees what he wants to believe," Imogen shot back.

Trummel seemed ready for an argument but Imogen had already moved down the wall, her flashlight illuminating an extensive mural. "There's more over here." The mural contained several levels and stairways. On each level, Egyptian figures stood with various deities. "This entire wall depicts the Amduat."

Caleb asked how the word was spelled and scribbled the name into his journal, stepping clear of the wall for a better shot.

Imogen explained, "The Amduat is the sun god Ra's twelve-hour journey through the underworld. It is an allegory about death and the afterlife. Here at the bottom a man's soul is standing before a pantheon of gods in the Hall of Ma'at."

Thoth and Anubis were present, as well as a creature with a crocodile head and body of a hippo along with other gods who Caleb didn't recognize. The journalist in him wanted to understand all that the archaeologists knew. "Tell me more about Ma'at."

"It's the Hall of Judgment," Imogen said. "Ancient Egyptians believed that when they died, their souls journeyed through Duat, the underworld, and arrived at this hall where they were judged by the gods. Their hearts were weighed by Anubis on a scale against a feather. If their life had been full of good deeds, then their heart would be lighter than the feather. The pure soul would then be allowed to pass into the Kingdom of Osiris and spend eternity with the ancient gods in the Field of Reeds."

"Like getting into heaven," Caleb said. "Saint Peter decides if a soul is worthy of passing through the Pearly Gates or descending to hell."

"Something like that," Imogen said. "Duat also had its version of hell, and if a soul's heart weighed more than the feather—" she pointed to the creature with the crocodile head, "—then Ammit, Devourer of the Dead, ate the heart, and the soul was banished to suffer in an underworld of demons."

"Lovely," Caleb said.

Imogen remained serious, intent on reading the glyphs. "This representation of Duat is unusual. Here a pharaoh travels alone through the maze of stairways and tunnels." In the painting, the pharaoh carried a torch in one hand and a sword in the other.

"I've walked in the footsteps of the pharaohs," she muttered.

"What is that from?" Caleb asked.

"Something my grandfather wrote in his journal. He must have come here too."

"How would he have gotten here?" Caleb asked. "We had to knock through a stone wall to get to this level."

"The way we came in was not the only entrance," Trummel explained. "Harlan's team had entered a cave somewhere higher up on the mountain. He told me the entire cave system is a maze of tunnels. His team were able to reach Nebenteru's tomb from a back tunnel. It had caved in by the time we found it."

On the wall, her finger traced a familiar path through a hall of cats, down a flight of stairs, through the horizontal tunnel, to this very chamber. The levels and stairways continued down and down the wall to the floor.

Gosswick and his men approached. The captain said, "Sir, we've explored this entire level. It looks like we've reached a dead end."

Trummel pressed his hands against the wall. "There has to be a hidden passage." He led Dyfan to the wall, guiding the older man's palms to the mural.

Dyfan frowned but didn't take his palms from the wall. "There's more beyond this room," the psychic said finally. "I can feel it."

Trummel used his fingers to test the bricks beneath the painting. The others followed suit. Something sounded deep in the tunnel behind them. It raised the hairs on the back of Caleb's neck. He reached for the wall, his fingers moving faster.

The ginger-haired soldier named Watters went to the room's only doorway and shone his light down the passage. "Something's coming."

The long scraping sound came again, closer this time.

Watters backed away from the door.

"I think I've found something." Trummel pushed a brick inward, and it snapped into place several inches deeper than the rest.

The wall and floor began to shake.

Caleb pushed Imogen to the ground and shielded her body with his just as an avalanche of bricks broke loose and tumbled to the floor. Sand and rocks rained down around them, clunking off their helmets.

After several seconds the quaking stopped. Caleb waited while the cloud of dust settled before he finally helped Imogen to her feet. "Are you all right?"

She nodded, looking past him. "Dr. Trummel? Dyfan?"

Trummel got to his feet. A small cut near his eye was bleeding. Bakari stood also, dust covering his thick beard.

"Dyfan's not moving," Ely said.

The Scotsman had a bleeding head. Caleb checked his pulse. "He's alive."

The others slowly emerged from the rubble.

Caleb counted nine team members. There should have been eleven. "Who's missing?"

Gosswick looked at their party. "*Watters*." He ran to where the wall had caved in.

A soldier's bloody arm was visible among the rubble. Watters's head was somewhere beneath a huge brick. Gosswick released a string of curses.

Farther back, another crushed body was half-visible in the rocks. The second porter.

"Fadil," Bakari said. "He's dead too."

The dust settled, revealing a pile of giant stones, which now blocked the exit at the front end of the chamber.

"God, we're trapped." Quig scaled the mound, searching for a way out.

Everyone tried moving the stones. The rubble blocking the doorway was too heavy to clear.

"We must have sprung a booby trap," Trummel said.

"Shit!" Quig hurried back along the rubble toward them. "I just saw something." He aimed his beam at a small hole at the top of the rubble covering the doorway. "Something moved on the other side of the cave-in."

"What did it look like?" Trummel asked.

Quig shook his head. "I don't know. Not human."

"Why do you say that?" Caleb asked.

The soldier shook his head. "It didn't move like a man." Whatever it was, it had spooked Quig.

"You sure you didn't imagine it?" Gosswick said.

"Damn sure. I swear it's the thing that got Vickers. It's hunting us."

Caleb remembered the ungodly howl that had come from the tunnel just before Vickers vanished.

To Trummel, Caleb said, "Are you sure your saboteur is a man?"

He scoffed. "Of course. Please, tell me you're not giving in to Quig's bogeyman theories."

"There is a pattern of men disappearing in the caves," Caleb said. "What if someone or something inhabited the tunnels before we arrived?"

"Some sort of cave dweller?" Imogen said.

"Or someone from a previous expedition," Caleb said. "A man who's gone insane." He almost said like Dr. Harlan Riley, but caught himself.

"Speculation is getting us nowhere," Trummel said. "Now that we're blocked in, the saboteur is the least of my concern. Two of our own are dead and now we're bloody trapped."

"What do you suggest we do?" Gosswick asked.

Trummel thought a moment, examining the end of the chamber that wasn't covered in rubble. "There has to be a way through one of these walls."

★   ★   ★

They spent two hours searching the walls for a hidden door. Studying the mural on the wall, Imogen tried to decipher the Egyptian's map of the multilevel cave, but the half that might offer a way out was broken in the rubble. Trummel said a few parting words for Watters and Fadil, who had died from the cave-in. Quig added a heartfelt eulogy for his friend, Vickers.

Caleb and Ely tended to Dyfan, who had returned to consciousness. The Scotsman drank from a canteen, while Caleb bandaged a cut on his head. When he felt good enough to stand, they helped Dyfan to his feet.

"How you feeling, old chap?" Trummel asked.

Dyfan felt his bandage. "A bit woozy, but otherwise all right."

Trummel nodded. "Good, we need you to use that ability of yours to find a way out of this crypt."

"Give me a moment while I tap into this place." The blind man closed his eyes. He raised his palms and spun around. He walked the thirty-foot-long chamber to the far end and stopped before a giant mural on the back wall, which featured the all-seeing eye of Horus. The psychic held out a hand, his palm inches from the stone. Silence fell over the group.

Dyfan knelt, following his hand, which groped the air downward until it reached a spot on the floor. He brushed sand and rocks. Something metal glinted in the stone floor.

Trummel knelt beside Dyfan, sweeping the last of the sand away. "Great work, old chap."

Caleb peered over their shoulders at a circular bronze disk. It resembled a manhole cover. Only this one was larger, five feet in diameter and engraved with symbols.

Imogen crouched to get a better look. "The Egyptian glyphs say, 'No man or woman is allowed beyond this point except the pharaoh.'"

"Remove it," Trummel said.

"What if it's another trap?" Caleb said.

"This appears to be our only way out," Trummel said.

Two small loops jutted from opposite sides of the bronze disk.

"Give me a hand," Gosswick barked at his two remaining soldiers.

Sykes and Quig stuck picks through the loops and yanked upward. The metal cover was several inches thick.

Caleb braced for another cave-in. The walls remained still. The soldiers hoisted the portal cover and dragged it to one side. Stone steps descended into the floor, beyond which lay the blackest hole Caleb had ever seen.

CHAPTER TWENTY-SIX

The group gathered around the opening. Several feet down, the darkness absorbed the beams from their headlamps. Each step was a chiseled ledge too small for human feet. The descending staircase was so steep that looking down gave Imogen vertigo. An odor escaped from the hole, damp and earthy, like a creek after a storm.

Trummel lit a torch and dropped it down the staircase. The torch kept falling, down and down. At last the flames snuffed out.

Quig chattered nervously.

Trummel hushed him. "Listen…"

Hollow sounds echoed from somewhere deep within the shaft.

The blind man nodded. "We're very close. Yes, yes. Do you feel that, everyone?"

Imogen's body tingled. A strange vibration emanated from below. It rose up her boots, her legs, reverberating in her chest. "A rhythmic pulse of some sort."

Quig held up his shaking hand. "Bloody hell. I'm vibrating like a tuning fork."

Trummel grinned. "It's powerful. All that energy stored for centuries."

"Kahf Alssulta," Imogen said. "Grandfather wrote that the Greeks and Romans called this cave system 'the Cave of Power.'"

"It contains a source that men have been seeking for ages." Trummel's eyes were alight.

"Is that what you're after then?" she asked. "Power?"

"I'm here for the same reason as you. To succeed where your grandfather failed." Trummel waited to see that his insult had stung.

"You're here because I was kind enough to lend you *his* map."

Trummel knew better than to argue. Imogen always had the last word. He looked at his watch. "We've burned over half a day. We need to conserve batteries. Everyone except Goss and me, turn your headlamps off."

After seven people shut off their helmet lamps and electric torches, the group remained silent.

Trummel turned to Gosswick. "Rig up the climbing rope."

★   ★   ★

Once the rope was secured with a pulley system, Trummel looked at his team. "We need a volunteer to make the first descent."

No one spoke.

"I'll go first." Caleb looked past the steep staircase into the black void. Whatever lay beyond that darkness, he wanted to be the first to see it. He switched on his helmet lamp, but the beam only lit up a dozen more steps that led deeper down the cave's throat.

"Are you sure you've got the climbing skills for this?" Trummel asked.

"I've rock climbed before." This was true. Only it had been outside, in broad daylight, scaling mountains. This was like descending into a bottomless well. The narrow steps would offer purchase but not much. "When I finally reach bottom, how do I signal you?"

"Tug on the rope a few times," Gosswick said.

"Here take this with you." Trummel handed Caleb a small Union Jack flag the size of a kerchief. "If there's enough passage to continue down there then stay at the bottom. Tie this flag to the rope and send it back up. We'll join you as quickly as we can get everybody down."

Caleb nodded and tucked the flag kerchief in his pocket.

Gosswick wrapped climbing rope around Caleb's waist. "You've got bollocks, Flash. Don't break your neck."

Quig and Sykes worked together, lowering Caleb into the hole. Cool, clammy air struck the back of his neck. He kicked off the steps to guide himself down, leaping a few feet at a time. The light above diminished as the circle where the others stood grew smaller and farther away.

The tube's walls were engraved with alien symbols. Caleb's hand traced the etchings as he passed them on his way down.

A hundred feet down, the staircase disappeared into a dark silver pool. Its surface mirrored his reflection.

"Hold up!" Caleb called. He grabbed on to the side of the stairwell. The rope tightened. Using the rock steps for guidance, he lowered himself until his hand reached the pool's watery surface.

Only it wasn't water. Its texture felt dry, like running his fingers through liquid mercury. The reflective surface rippled when he touched it. He couldn't see what lay beyond.

Trummel called down, his voice reverberating. "Are you at the bottom yet?"

"I'm not sure," Caleb responded. "I seem to have reached a spot that defies the laws of physics."

He slowly stuck his entire arm through the pool. The surface yielded and a texture, like tiny mercury beads, formed around his bicep. This sensation only happened for a few inches. Then on the other side, he felt air that was slightly cooler than the air in the stairwell. Other than that, his outstretched fingers touched nothing. When he pulled his hand back out, it was completely dry.

CHAPTER TWENTY-SEVEN

At the top of the hole, Imogen had nervously watched Caleb shrink as he dropped deeper, until he became very small. His light bounced off the walls of the staircase where he had stopped. Every sound he made traveled up to them with a ghostly echo.

Imogen felt something was wrong. A cold rash of fear sprouted gooseflesh across her arms. She didn't know why she was suddenly afraid. She'd explored many tombs without issue.

The first time Imogen had entered a tomb, she was twelve, working as Grandfather's apprentice. She had followed him into a crypt. He had lifted the lid of a sarcophagus, showing Imogen her first mummy. The sight of it had filled her with a mix of terror and wonder. She had been afraid then that they were doing something wrong, upsetting the dead.

"What if we're not supposed to be here?" she had asked her grandfather. "Won't the dead be mad?" She'd passed her torch over the mummy's gray face.

"The man who was mummified is nothing but bones. His spirit has moved on. This crypt is now ours to explore so we can understand his people's history and learn from them."

"Then why was the tomb sealed?" she'd asked with little girl logic.

"So no one would find it but us," Grandfather had said with a grin.

This vertical tunnel seemed different. What if the Egyptians had sealed off this staircase and buried the seal for a reason? *No man or woman is allowed beyond this point except the pharaoh.* As much as her curiosity made her want to discover what lay beyond it, her instincts prickled. Maybe in this instance it would be better *not* to know.

Imogen wanted the men to pull Caleb back up, but what if this was the only way out?

"I can't tell how far the stairway goes beyond this barrier," Caleb called up.

"Can you keep going?" Trummel shouted down.

There was a long hesitation, and then Caleb called back up, "I'm going to explore a little farther, see what's beyond this."

"Hang on. We'll lower you."

The rope slackened, and when Caleb went down a few more feet, he vanished.

CHAPTER TWENTY-EIGHT

The instant Caleb crossed through the liquid mercury pool, the stairway ended and he stepped off a ledge. He fell several feet. His stomach leapt into his chest. Then the rope went taut, strangling his rib cage. He hung in midair. His legs kicked at nothing. His light beam found no rock walls in any direction. The voices from above had gone silent. He looked up and could no longer see the others. Again, his light reflected off that dark silvery pool; only now he was on the other side of it.

Caleb tilted his headlamp down. A sheer drop fell away into a black abyss. It was as though he had reached the end of the earth and what lay beyond was infinite nothingness.

There was only madness down here. He wanted to return to the others, but the rope continued taking him downward. He gripped the line, spinning. "You're all right," Caleb said aloud. "Just breathe. *Breathe.*"

The mantra he'd learned from a deep-sea diver helped him keep his sanity a few years back. Caleb had once experienced a nightmare in a watery chasm that had taken him to the edge of fear. Now, alone in pitch darkness, he was going beyond that edge. His mind kept playing tricks on him. The black nothing that surrounded him became a black sea. Bodies in dive suits floated. Skeletal faces stared accusingly from beneath the glass of their metal helmets.

Bony hands tugged at his ankles.

The inkiness threatened to swallow him.

Caleb kicked, panicking.

He looked down. Nothing there.

Just breathe.

He drew shaky breaths as he continued downward. Slowly his breathing became more regular until finally he was able to think more clearly.

He shone his headlamp down. There had to be a bottom.

Somewhere below was the trickling of water. The lower he

descended, the stronger he could hear water growing nearer. At last he landed in a shallow pool, his feet touching bottom. The water came up to his thighs. Real water, this time. Around the pool his headlamp shone over damp cavern walls covered in fungus. The rock shimmered. Panning his light around the pool, he saw a vast cavern that continued deep into the darkness. He unfastened the rope, tied on the Union Jack flag, and gave the rope a tug. It ascended, disappearing in the dark.

While waiting for the next person to come down, Caleb climbed the rocky bank. A few feet from the pool, the shale turned to a porous white rock floor. Sharp stalactites hung from the ceiling like the teeth of some prehistoric beast. He walked thirty yards from the pool. His boots crunched over something. He shone his headlamp downward, exposing a human rib cage.

He jumped away from it, crushing more bones beneath his boots. This stirred an avalanche, causing a tall mound of bones to slide down around his feet. As his beam passed over them, countless skulls gawked through hollow sockets. The cavern was filled with hills upon hills of white bones.

CHAPTER TWENTY-NINE

Moments later, the soldiers pulled the rope with the flag out of the hole.

Trummel offered it to Imogen. "Want to go next?"

She could tell by his smug expression that he was challenging her.

"Of course." She switched on her helmet lamp and stared down the steep tunnel.

Gosswick and Sykes secured her with the rope. As they lowered her down, her abseiling skills came back. She kicked off the walls with ease. Midway down she stopped to run her fingers across the unusual glyphs carved into the walls. *These must predate the Pharaonic period.* That meant this stairwell was over five thousand years old.

She reached the mirrored pool that Caleb had disappeared through. Right above it, tucked inside a nook, sat a stone figure. She leaned in to inspect it. Seated with its knees bent, the statue had the body of a man and head of a cobra. Its surface had eroded badly. One arm had broken off. The snake head stared menacingly at her, a forked tongue protruding from its open mouth.

She returned her attention to the pool. She tentatively touched its dark silver surface. Her reflection rippled, then returned to being smooth as glass. Behind her she could see the lights from two of the others shining down.

"I'm crossing through," she announced.

Imogen held her breath, kicked off the stairwell, and leapt through the portal of liquid air. The moment she crossed through, light, tiny beads formed around her head. She saw flashes of her life – her mum tucking her into bed singing a lullaby, a raging fire, a funeral among a field of tombstones, Grandfather's scar-covered face – then absolute darkness. She had expected her boots to connect with more stairs on the other side. The initial freefall caught her by surprise. Then came the violent snap of the rope as it went taut.

She felt disoriented, unable to grasp anything but the rope. As the men above continued to lower her, she descended through the silent darkness.

Where was this taking her? What happened to Caleb?

A light winked up at her from a hundred feet below. Caleb stood at the edge of a pool. "How you doing up there?" His voice reverberated off the cavern walls.

"That was one hell of a ride." She spun on the line as she drew closer to the bottom.

Caleb waded out into the center of the pool and helped her out of the rope. "How about that leap through the portal? First step is a doozy."

She laughed. "I literally felt my heart in my throat."

"You won't believe what's down here."

He led her out of the pool and through a cavern that expanded into a wide-open darkness. A pan of her light revealed many hills of bones.

"It's a mass grave." She studied the hills like a scientist. "The skulls are both human and a variety of animals." The beam from her headlamp played over a large, horned creature. "Looks like a bull."

"The death toll must have been in the thousands," Caleb said. "Why would so many be entombed here?"

"Maybe this was a burial ground of plague victims." She imagined a scourge sweeping Egypt, killing countless numbers. Their diseased bodies might have been dropped into the pit, and the hole sealed shut to trap the virus. "Don't touch the bones with your bare hands."

It didn't comfort her that they were breathing in centuries of entombed death. She could feel the foul air dusting her lungs.

Imogen checked her compass. The needle spun crazily, unable to find north. She could hear trickling up ahead.

Caleb started down a path that snaked between the mounds.

"We shouldn't go far," she said, following him. "The others will be down soon."

"We'll just have a quick look around," he said.

The crushed bones that made up the foot trail appeared trampled. *Others have walked here before us.* That thought unsettled Imogen's nerves. Trespassing over the remains of the dead was a thing she had never gotten completely used to.

She and Caleb found the source of the trickling sound. An aquifer coursed from a cleft in the rock, widening into a channel, which stretched thirty feet across. The far bank was laden with bones. "It's like the mythical river Styx, isn't it?"

Caleb nodded. "I was thinking the same. Didn't the Styx separate Earth from the underworld?"

Imogen nodded. "Charon ferried lost souls across it into Hades."

"Comforting," Caleb said.

Both heard the noise at once. It sounded like footfalls, crunching over the bones behind them.

They both whirled around.

"What was that?" Imogen whispered. Her heart beat heavy in her chest. She couldn't see beyond the ring of their headlamps, but the noise, which had resounded off the curved limestone walls, was unmistakable. Something crept behind the mounds.

Caleb stepped between Imogen and the noise. Both remained silent for a long moment.

"It must have been a tumbling rock," Imogen said.

"Look." He pointed up. "Another of our party is coming."

Light glinted in the air high above the pool. The shape was lowering fast.

They hurried back to the shallow pool.

Trummel fell toward them with a big grin on his face. "Amazing!" A skilled mountain climber, he dropped to the pool easily and unfastened his rope.

"We think we heard something moving over there," Caleb said.

Trummel shone his light where Caleb had pointed. "Probably bats."

"We've left the tomb," Imogen said. "So what is this place?"

"You wouldn't believe me, if I told you," Trummel said.

"Try."

"Your grandfather and I held a theory that the underworld described in the Amduat was based on a real place. I believe the pharaohs journeyed through these caves as a secret rite of passage before ruling Egypt."

"Like a shaman's vision quest," Caleb said.

"Exactly. According to the section of Ani scroll that Harlan found, the knowledge of this place ended with Ramses II, who sealed the tomb and buried his secrets with Nebenteru's mummy."

"You believe that Duat actually exists?" To Imogen, the idea seemed ludicrous.

Trummel aimed his light on the mounds of bones. "That's what I'm hoping to prove."

CHAPTER THIRTY

An hour later, Gosswick, an experienced caver, was the last to abseil down to the cavern floor. All nine explorers stood in a circle with their rucksacks and supplies.

"We've entered what appears to be an old burial pit." Trummel climbed up one of the bone piles. "This right here is the kind of discovery archaeologists live for. And we've found it!" His excitement echoed in the cavern.

Ely nudged Imogen. "I've dreamed of this place too." He flipped through his pad of black sketches to show her one that matched the subterranean charnel house.

The vibration they had all felt earlier now coursed through Imogen, as if resonating from somewhere nearby. "The pulsing is stronger down here."

"Maybe it's all the bones giving off the vibration," Ely said. "Maybe it's their ghosts we're feeling."

The blind man shook his head. "No," Dyfan said. "The vibration has another source."

"Can you identify it?" Trummel asked his psychic.

Dyfan shook his head. "My clairvoyance is foggy down here. But I sense we're getting close to your relics. In that direction." He pointed toward the hills of bones.

Trummel started walking. "Onward then."

Imogen felt a rush of adrenaline as she and the others followed Trummel's lead. A trail wound through the mounds of broken skeletons. She guessed the number of dead was in the thousands. A noise like tumbling stones echoed off to the right. Everyone turned toward the sound, headlamps illuminating the white hills. Bones slid from the top of one of the mounds.

The soldiers aimed their pistols.

Ely backed up to the center of the group. "What's disturbing the bones?"

"Probably the vibration of our footsteps," Trummel said.

More rustling sounds came from behind the team. Other hills moved, releasing small avalanches. A human skull rolled onto the path between Quig's feet.

"We're standing still now," the soldier said, panic creeping into his voice. "Why are the bones moving?"

Trummel picked up the pace. "Keep walking."

The group moved with a sense of urgency. The mounds ended at a wall of bone that towered high above them.

This pit is more than just a burial ground, Imogen realized with a mix of wonder and horror. The hills of bones were stores of human bricks for a necropolis.

Everyone followed the wall, keeping their lights trained on the white mounds to their left. Imogen sensed they were being watched.

The soldiers kept their guns drawn, ready to fire. At last the group reached an archway made of human skulls. At the top, the centermost skull had the horns of a massive bull and a long upper jaw.

Sykes and Quig stepped through the archway first, shining their lights around. The rest of the explorers filed through one at a time. Beyond the entrance, a passage meandered through a bone labyrinth. The masonry matched nothing Imogen had seen before in Egyptian architecture. If the Egyptians didn't build this, who did?

Lights probed the latticework of rib cages, and thatched walls built of humerus and femur bones twined together with clavicles and vertebrae. Every so often her light passed over bizarre patterns, like a skull embedded in a spider's web of finger bones. In several places, tanned hides stretched across doorways. On closer inspection, Imogen saw that some of the skins suggested human anatomy. One bore a tattoo.

Everyone remained silent as they twisted through the maze.

As the beam of her headlamp pierced the slatted walls, Imogen couldn't shake the feeling that something on the other side watched her.

With a gasp Trummel stepped through another bone archway. The group followed.

"It looks like some kind of museum," Caleb said.

The square chamber was crowded with sculptures. Someone had erected skeletons in various stances. They were clad in decayed clothes and long-tarnished armor. *Warriors*. Several wore helmets, and had swords and shields tethered to their hands. Some warriors stood as though frozen in battle, their swords clashing.

"An exhibit of antiquities," Imogen said, admiring a skeleton holding an Egyptian sword.

"These are Roman legionary soldiers," Caleb said excitedly as he walked through a platoon of the dead. They wore silver helmets and shoulder plates with groin protection and wielded gladius swords and shields.

"This unit is Greek." Trummel played his torch over another group of skeletons. These wore bronze Corinthian face helmets and carried spears. Others Trummel identified as Akkadian, Persian, and Sumerian, all arranged in chronological order according to when their civilizations had flourished.

"A display of changing war technologies?" Imogen said.

"No," Trummel said. "These are the explorers who came before us." He turned to Imogen. "Your grandfather came across numerous accounts of explorers through the ages, who entered these caves in search of its source. Most never returned. I thought they were myths."

"I'm not sure I like what happens to those who succeed," Caleb said.

"They've all been marked." Imogen showed the others where the bones of a skeleton had been carved. The intricate designs were similar to art she'd seen scrimshawed on ivory. Only these etchings matched the indecipherable welts across her grandfather's body. "Who built this place?" she said.

Trummel shook his head. "I haven't the foggiest. This is just another one of the great mysteries of Kahf Alssulta."

At the far end of the subterranean museum, in an alcove, they gathered around a stone pedestal where a giant two-legged skeleton towered over eight feet tall.

"Holy shit!" Ely said.

"What the hell is that?" Quig asked.

"Astonishing." Trummel's light traced the dead creature's long bones and massive rib cage. An enormous skull, shaped like a prehistoric wildcat, had incisors that would put a tiger to shame.

"Bugger," Gosswick muttered as he examined bony hands that fanned out like rakes. "Claws must be six inches."

"Any idea what this beast was?" Caleb asked.

"A marvel. None of its kind has ever been discovered," Trummel said, grinning. "Until now."

"Perhaps it was assembled from the bones of other creatures to represent a deity," Imogen offered.

Trummel frowned. "Of course, you'd try to debunk it. Look at the length of those femurs, the size of its teeth. Those aren't assembled parts."

She ignored his condescension. "We're standing at an altar." Her light shone across decorative human skulls that had been left on the pedestal at the skeleton's enormous feet. "These look like offerings." Broken skullcaps, made into bowls, contained thick, lichen-covered liquids that smelled like mud and fungus.

Trummel told the others to step aside while he posed in front of the giant skeleton. "Beckett, take my photo. This is definitely one for your magazine."

Caleb snapped a shot with his camera. The flash caused the monstrous skull to burn like a ghost in Imogen's mind. Before she could begin to speculate what species this thing belonged to, or why the contents in the offering bowls looked fresh, Trummel was on the move again.

CHAPTER THIRTY-ONE

The back of the chamber had two exits that tunneled in opposite directions. Dyfan chose the one on the right. They continued down another stretch of twisting hallways.

Gosswick carried his .455 Webley service revolver, his finger close to the trigger. He thought he heard the snickers of children coming from beyond the maze walls. He glanced back at Sykes. "Did you hear anything?"

"Nothin', Captain. Quiet as a graveyard." Sykes chuckled at his own joke. No one else found it funny.

Gosswick, who'd worked enough missions with Rex Sykes to know his gallows humor, nodded and kept walking. Dyfan continued to guide them through endless passages and small chambers with bones that had been bound together in grim designs. Remarkable if art made from broken skeletons was your cup of tea. It wasn't Gosswick's.

He passed a wall made entirely of small human skulls. Again, he swore he heard children's laughter. The pressure inside the back of his head was building. This goddamned winding maze. The slatted walls reminded him of the tribal huts he'd walked through in Kenya. A dark memory tried to surface. Flies clotting the eyes of black corpses. The winged insects buzzed inside Gosswick's head, forming into children's faces. *Think of something else. Anything but that!*

He distracted his mind with thoughts of finding the relics Trummel was seeking. Gosswick imagined all the things he'd do with his cut of the treasures. Retire to Paris where money could buy the most beautiful women. Picturing himself in a silk bed full of French whores made the flies in Gosswick's head retreat. He smiled and kept walking.

★   ★   ★

At every juncture, Dyfan looked more confused and took longer to decide which route to follow. Trummel hoped his psychic wasn't getting them lost. The maze grew darker, too. The lattice walls of aged white bones became stained dark bone corridors where black mold bloomed. Above them hung an infinite blackness, like a sky devoid of moon or stars.

The air grew foul as the passage widened into a large square chamber. Eight stone slabs dominated the room, their scratched surfaces mottled with crimson stains. The room looked like some kind of abattoir. At the head of each table, stone channels flowed down to troughs. The sticky floor was littered with broken bits of bone and hair. On one wall hung a dozen archaic knives, hooks, and gouges.

"This might have been a mummification chamber." Trummel pulled a long hook off the wall. "These were used to pull the brain out through the corpse's nose."

"What are these for?" Caleb asked. His torch illuminated instruments with strange twisting blades.

"I've never seen anything like them," Trummel said. "Or these." A set of giant, four-foot-long triangular blades hung from the ceiling. Clay canisters stood in one corner. Trummel removed the lid of one and was assaulted by a stench of congealed liquid.

"Blood and marrow," Sykes said. "I spent me childhood working in a slaughterhouse. I knows a butchering room when I sees one." The soldier pulled down one of the giant cleavers. "It'd take a mighty strong bloke to heft one of these."

Trummel tried not to imagine the slaughters that took place here. A dark thought struck him: had Harlan Riley's team endured suffering in this chamber?

Sykes opened another clay jar. "This blood is fresh."

"Oh, God…" Quig picked up the scraps of a bloodstained uniform. 'BIGSBY' was stenciled inside the collar.

"Who could've done this?" Sykes asked.

"This ain't right," Quig said, his voice rising. "We shouldn't be down here!" He felt his way along a wall, searching for a doorway. "Where the fuck is the exit?"

"Calm down, soldier," Gosswick ordered.

A strange vibration began to pulse from the ground into the soles of Trummel's boots. It grew stronger with every second.

The group began to chatter in panic.

"*Quiet*," Trummel said.

When everyone went silent, there came a distant drumming, sticks against sticks, or bones against bones. The floor shook with the sound. It grew louder, closer.

Trummel drew his pistol. There was no place to run. The beating was coming from every direction. The others huddled in the center of the abattoir.

The drumming sticks now sounded just beyond the four walls. Through the slats, the team's headlamps spotlighted the movement of chittering things with albino skin. They screeched and howled. Hundreds of long, pale fingers with claws poked through the cracks. The bone walls shook and rattled, threatening to break apart.

The soldiers panicked and fired their guns. The screeches rose to a pitch that pierced Trummel's eardrums. He covered his ears. Beside him, Dyfan fell to his knees.

The air became hot and acrid with gun smoke and the reek of animal stench.

Every pistol boom battered Trummel's eardrums.

"Stop shooting!" Bakari yelled.

Gosswick and Sykes stopped. Quig kept shooting, his face riddled with terror.

"Stop! Stop!" Bakari pushed Quig's arm down. "You'll only anger them more."

Trummel tried to make sense of the scene. Bakari, his Egyptian porter, barely spoke. Now he was taking charge of the group, urging them not to panic. "Nobody move." Bakari faced one of the shaking walls. From his pack, he pulled out a curved goat horn and blew into it. The horn issued a low, throaty sound. The things behind the walls lowered their screeching voices. The walls stopped shaking.

Bakari turned and blew his horn in the opposite direction. On all four sides of the chamber, claw-tipped fingers withdrew from the slats. Bakari blew his bugle a third time. The nightmarish drumming and chittering retreated, fading to silence.

Trummel stared at his servant. "What the hell, Bakari?"

"We need to leave quickly." Bakari struck a match and lit a flame on the end of his torch. "Follow me."

CHAPTER THIRTY-TWO

Everyone remained silent as they twisted through the bone labyrinth, following Bakari's lead. Imogen kept to the center of the passage. She heard scraping and clumping sounds beyond the lattice walls. Ahead, Quig jerked with his light and gun at every noise. The soldier looked on the verge of panic.

Imogen couldn't shake the feeling that they were being followed. What were those creatures that had clawed at the walls? And where was Bakari taking them?

He finally led them through a ten-foot-high archway and back into a dark cavern. Imogen released a sigh of relief. Beyond stretched more white hills of shattered skeletons. At first she wondered if their guide might have brought them back to where they started, but the trail was wider than before, heavily trampled, and littered with ancient carts filled with bones and chopping tools. *We must have come out another side of the maze,* Imogen thought.

Footfalls skittered off to her right. A pan of lights briefly lit a pale blur that moved between the mounds. The soldiers fired off shots at the creature. The thing vanished into a hole that burrowed beneath a bone pile. What sounded like a roving pack of hungry predators growled from the darkness.

"Come, hurry." Bakari led the team down a hill to the underground river and stepped onto a dock. He unfastened the rope of a long boat. "Get in." The guide took Imogen's hand and helped her onto the boat. Caleb sat on a bench beside her. Dyfan and Ely squeezed in behind them.

Trummel and his soldiers waited on the dock. Sykes and Quig kept their guns trained on the darkness beyond the riverbank.

"Where are you taking us?" Trummel demanded.

"Out of their territory," Bakari said. "We'll all die if we stay longer."

"Whose territory?" Gosswick asked.

"No time to explain. Get in the boat."

The growls drew closer.

Trummel and the soldiers hopped into the boat. Bakari pushed off from the dock and grabbed a pair of oars fastened to rigging at the back of the boat. He paddled out to the center of the wide underground river. Snarls followed them along the banks until the boat went under a low-hanging rock ceiling. The banks rose, becoming cavern walls. The horrid sounds of the creatures trailed off behind them.

Imogen looked over her shoulder at Bakari. How had he known his way out of the maze? Or that a boat waited at the riverbank? The Egyptian remained stone-faced while he worked the oars with his thick arms.

The long wooden boat creaked as it followed the gentle current of the river. It reminded Imogen of the legendary night boat, or Mesektet boat, that the sun god Ra used to sail through the underworld at night. His death and voyage as Auf, which meant 'corpse', had symbolized rebirth.

Ely trailed his fingers in the water.

"Take your hand out of the water," Bakari ordered. "Unless you wish to lose an arm."

Just then something large splashed a few feet from the boat. Imogen's light found only rings of waves and bubbles. "Are there crocodiles down here?" she asked.

Bakari whispered, "No talking."

The boat came out from beneath the low-hanging ceiling and passed through a channel with cliff walls. High above, cut in the rock, cave dwellings loomed over them. Trummel and Gosswick aimed their beams at hollow windows and doorways. The walls had been carved with peculiar designs, similar to the artwork found on the skeletons in the maze. The number of dwellings was far too many to count. The river cut through several islands of rock. Hanging bridges crossed over the water, from island to island, to more cave dwellings on the other side. Imogen thought she saw movement in one of the upper windows; it may have been the play of shadows on the stone. But something was out there. Screeches fell from the upper levels. Creatures hissed at them from the shadows as Bakari rowed past. Occasionally something issued a low, throaty growl. Whatever inhabited this subterranean village wasn't pleased at their being here.

Imogen scooted closer to Caleb on the wooden bench.

A dark bipedal form scuttled across one of the hanging bridges. The movement caused the rickety bridge to sway.

The soldiers' guns clacked as their barrels aimed upward.

"Don't shoot," Bakari commanded.

Quig chattered nervously. Gosswick shushed him. The captain chewed on a matchstick as he surveyed the gaping doorways of the cave dwellings.

Caleb tapped Imogen's arm and pointed to one of the rock islands. A large amphibious creature that had been resting on the banks slid to the water's edge and disappeared beneath its surface. It had moved too fast for her to make out what it was. Judging by its length and the way it moved, her first thought was *crocodile*, but this creature had sleek spotted skin and too many legs. She'd counted eight, instead of four.

Imogen watched the flowing dark water, the intricately woven bridges, and the looming landmasses as the boat passed between islands, and she thought of Grandfather. *It's another world down here. No wonder you wanted to return.*

There were many totems carved into the rock. Some had human faces, some animal. Some Imogen believed were gods. The human faces worried her. They seemed trapped in a world that wasn't theirs.

Beyond the islands, the high cliffs tapered off as the river channel opened up. The angry howls eventually died down. Bakari continued to paddle another half hour. Then the river grew shallow and the boat ran aground.

"Everyone out and follow me." Bakari tied the boat to a stalagmite, then headed for shore. Trummel and the soldiers eyed one another suspiciously, not sure whether their guide could be trusted. Trummel finally gave the nod and the others hopped out and followed Bakari through a channel.

After ten minutes of hiking through ankle-deep water, Bakari led them to an entrance cut in the stone. He ducked under the low doorway and entered another natural cavern. Unusual stalactite formations hung from the high ceiling like giant wasp nests. Large albino insects slithered across them like silverfish and disappeared into holes.

No one had spoken a word since leaving the boat. Exhausted and scared, the group followed the Egyptian guide through a forest of stalagmites. He didn't stop until they reached an alcove with a dry floor padded with gray dirt. At its center, a ring of rocks circled a fire pit filled with ash and chunks of coal. Just past the pit was a clear pool beneath overhanging rock. The dome-shaped alcove was cozy, a cave within a cave.

"We camp here," Bakari told them.

Imogen dropped her pack and sat on the soft ground next to Caleb and Ely. All three exchanged looks but none spoke.

Trummel stared hard at his porter. "Bakari, explain yourself."

When the porter didn't answer, Trummel stepped closer. "How do you know your way round down here?"

"I think we're looking at our goddamn saboteur." Gosswick aimed his gun at Bakari. Quig and Sykes pointed their guns, as well.

"Did you kill Dunlap and Bigsby last night?" Gosswick asked Bakari.

"No. It was *them*." He nodded toward the darkness outside the alcove.

Quig's gun hand tremored. "Those *things*...they got Vickers, too?"

"What are they?" Trummel demanded.

"We must talk later." Bakari said. "First, we must build a fire. We won't be safe until we have its protection. Everyone, shine your lights at the entrance," Bakari ordered. "The brightness hurts their eyes. Ely, Imogen, come give me a hand."

She and Ely followed Bakari to the alcove's back wall. He pushed a large stone sideways, revealing a hidden chamber that stored coal, clay pots filled with a sludge that looked like tar pitch, and torches made from long bones. Imogen wondered how Bakari knew all this was here as he handed her and Ely pieces of coal and ordered them to put them in the fire pit.

Using some of the tar pitch and pages from his book for kindling, Bakari knelt at the fire pit and attempted to light the coals. They were slow to catch flame. Outside, the cave echoed with the clumping of feet over rocks.

"Shit, they've found us," Quig said.

"Keep shining your lights at the entrance," Bakari ordered. The group kept their headlamp beams trained on the darkness that pressed against the cave's opening. Imogen tensed. Something growled from the dark. Would their headlamps be enough to keep whatever was out there from coming in?

At last Bakari had a large fire going in the pit. The smoke billowed up a hole in the rock ceiling that acted as a flue. He then reached into a crevice and pulled out four torches. He lit each one and stuck them into the dirt on the camp's perimeter.

Outside, creatures growled in protest. The sounds of hooves running over rocks trailed off.

"They won't come near fire," Bakari assured them.

Quig lowered his pistol and wiped sweat off his brow.

The torches and campfire offered enough light for them to turn off their helmet lamps and spare their batteries. The others watched Bakari warily as he sat by the campfire. The anger and fear in the air was palpable. Gosswick, chewing hard on his matchstick, still kept his gun trained on Bakari. Quig's knee bounced and he kept glancing at the cave's entrance. Sykes's cold lizard stare was unreadable. Imogen worried that the soldiers would turn violent.

Trummel's anger was more controlled. "Bakari, you've been keeping secrets from me. Now, I demand answers. What were those creatures?"

"Demons of darkness," the Egyptian said.

Quig let out a burst of nervous laughter. "Are you saying we've all died and gone to hell?"

"Nonsense. Demons don't exist." Imogen reached for a scientific explanation. The pale-skinned animals, which had moved beyond the bone walls, walked on two legs. It was an unusual attribute in nonhumans. Perhaps cut off from outside, an undiscovered species had evolved separately in caves where survival and procreation depended on different factors.

"Demons exist in these caves," Bakari said. "The ones we saw are called 'bone keepers.' They are the builders of the maze. They aren't nearly as dangerous as their masters, Slaughterers Who Drink the Blood. I wanted to make sure we were gone before they arrived."

"You've known about all this? This whole time?" Betrayal sounded in Trummel's voice. "While members of my crew have disappeared?"

Bakari nodded.

"Why the hell didn't you tell me?" Trummel's raised voice bounced off the cave walls. "Christ, you could have warned us."

Bakari remained calm. "I am forbidden to speak of *them* or this place while aboveground. To do so would shame my ancestors and my god, Osiris."

"Do you think I give a fuck about your bloody ancestors?" Gosswick said. "You've put our lives at stake."

"You took the risks upon yourselves by coming here," Bakari said. "As much as I wanted to help you all aboveground, I have sworn an oath to remain quiet. Only when people cross through a portal into the Dark Realm am I allowed to help."

"How many times have you been down here?" Caleb said.

"Too many." Bakari stirred the glowing coals of the fire. "For thousands of years my ancestors have guided explorers through these caves. It is what I was born to do." He opened the top of his shirt, showing them a labyrinth of scars. "A map was carved into me by my father and grandfather when I was a boy. They taught me the ways of the realm and my role as its guide."

"Why keep this place secret?" Imogen said.

"The caves are sacred, meant to remain secret until man discovers them. From every part of the world explorers, like yourselves, have been drawn to the Dark Realm in search of its source. What they don't understand is they did not choose to make this journey; the source called them here."

Imogen thought of the burning desire she had felt to take over her grandfather's work. Like him, she had left behind everything to answer some inner calling.

"It is far from an easy journey, however," Bakari continued. "Some reach the source that beckons them. Others fall victim to the caves' demons. As a guide, I can only lead people from the maze through the river channel and leave them to their fates."

"Well, aren't you a bloody help?" Gosswick said.

"I do what I'm permitted," Bakari said. "I cannot do more."

"Did you know my grandfather?" Imogen asked.

Bakari nodded. "I guided his team."

"What happened to them?" she asked.

"Some were slaughtered." He looked at Imogen. "Your grandfather and two others made it to the next gate. I don't know what happened beyond that point. I can only guide so far."

"Is this the underworld the Egyptians wrote about?" Trummel asked, the gleam returned to his eye. "Have we truly crossed into Duat?"

"That is one name for it. This realm lies between the living and the dead. It connects to all continents through caves that contain secret portals. Every civilization has written legends about their version of the underworld."

Imogen began to feel a tingling sensation as everything that her grandfather ever taught her began to piece together like a cosmic puzzle. The various mythologies he had read to her as a child, describing hidden realms, gods, and monsters. "I see a pattern in all the ancient writings," Grandfather once told her. "The Egyptians, the Hindus, the Maya, the Sumerians…it's as if they were all writing about some hidden truth. One day, my dear granddaughter, I'm going to discover that truth for myself."

Imogen stared at Bakari as the puzzle pieces in her mind fell into place. "The Book of Gates and the Amduat describe the underworld as a soul's journey through twelve gates to reach the afterlife. If what you're saying is true, then when we crossed through that portal, we entered the first gate into a dimension that is no longer our world."

Bakari nodded. "Yes, but Duat, as the ancient Egyptians described it, is based on the limited experiences of a few Egyptians who visited this dimension. The twelve gates they wrote about are only a fraction of the Dark Realm. An infinite number of levels and gates surround us. You could spend the rest of your days exploring. If you were lucky enough to survive." He scanned each of their faces. "There are dangers and obstacles ahead. Demons to encounter. Malevolent spirits to whisper you off course. The darkness itself is a conscious entity that can drive a man to madness. It knows your fears, your darkest secrets, the heavy burdens you carry in your hearts. This realm will do everything it can to stop you."

Imogen stared beyond the torches and felt the darkness staring back.

"So," Quig said, "where's the nearest exit?" He let out another burst of nervous laughter.

"Some gates lead back to the caves of the mountain," said Bakari. "But you must choose the right ones. Other gates only take you deeper."

"We need to get to the higher realms," Trummel said to Bakari. "Will you guide my team safely through the gates?"

"I wish that I could. I am just a lower realm guide and not permitted beyond the next gate."

"How will we know which to choose?" Imogen asked.

"That you will have to decide for yourself. Every soul's journey is different. Once I leave you at the next gate, you will have to rely on your instincts and wit to find your way."

"Where will you go then?" Imogen asked. "Certainly not back the way we came."

"I will wander the tunnels until a portal presents itself."

"Can Dyfan and I go with you?" Ely asked. "He shouldn't make this journey, and I'm none too keen myself."

"Take me too," Quig said. "I've had enough of these caves. I want the hell out of here."

Bakari shook his head. "I'm sorry. The path I take is the way of my ancestors. Only my kind can travel it."

"What if those of us who want to leave set out on our own?" Ely asked.

"Your chances of survival would be extremely slim," Bakari said. "If the *shemayu* don't slaughter you, something else out there will. It's best you stick together."

"There will be no more talk of abandoning the team," Trummel said, staring hard at Ely and Quig. "We're going to keep crossing through the gates until we find what the last expedition discovered."

A silence fell over the group.

"I suggest we all eat and then get some sleep," Bakari said. "Tomorrow's journey will challenge your limits."

PART THREE
THE GATES

CHAPTER THIRTY-THREE

The alcove had enough space that Trummel's team could just spread their bedrolls around the campfire. With the curved rock wall to their backs and a ring of torches guarding the entrance, they were cocooned in firelight. Everyone remained silent as they ate from small tins of canned meat, each brooding on his or her own thoughts. Bakari brewed a pot of tea, which Imogen welcomed to calm her nerves.

She didn't know how she would ever sleep that night. She worried the fires wouldn't be enough to protect them. Her mind kept conjuring images of creatures moving behind the lattice walls. She imagined being taken in her sleep, bound to the stone slab for slaughter. Would her skull be placed on the altar at the giant's feet? Or would her bones be carved, then put on display in the museum of the dead?

Stop thinking about it, she told herself.

She needed something to occupy her mind. She spotted Dyfan sitting off by himself amid a cluster of stalagmites. He seemed abandoned there. When Trummel wasn't pressing the psychic for information, he ignored the blind man.

Imogen poured a cup of tea and carried it to Dyfan. "Thought you might be thirsty."

"Thanks, lass." His blind eyes looking past her, he held out his hands, and she gently set the cup in them.

Imogen sat down beside him. "How are you?"

"Tired is all. I'm not in the shape I used to be." He opened a flask and poured liquor into his tea. "Fancy a nip? It's Irish whiskey."

"No, thanks. I'm more of a wine drinker."

"Can't do anything about that," he said. "All I carry's the strong stuff."
Blood trickled from a cut on his forearm.

"You're hurt," Imogen said.

Dyfan raised his wounded hand. "Just a scrape. I'm fine."

"That needs to be cleaned before it gets infected. Here, let me patch
you up." She poured canteen water over his hand to clean the cut. Then
she retrieved a first aid kit from her pack. As she dressed the wound, she
noticed a gold band etched with a Gaelic pattern on his left ring finger.
"You're married?"

"Only in spirit," he said. "My Gwendolyn passed years ago." Dyfan's
face softened when he said his wife's name.

"I'm sorry." Imogen squeezed his arm.

"She still watches over me." He touched the air above him. "I can
feel her presence all the time, even down here."

Talking about spirits made Imogen uncomfortable. "So," she said,
"I've been wondering…how did you end up with Trummel?"

"You mean how does a blind charlatan come to work as part of an
archaeology team?"

"I didn't say that."

"You sound skeptical."

"Sorry, I've known some dodgy fortunetellers. My mum never
planned anything without consulting a tarot reader. Even as a kid, it was
obvious to me – the woman was filling Mum's head with blind hope
while swindling her out of her money."

"The psychic failed to predict your parents' deaths," Dyfan
said. "That's why you're angry. It's why you distrust any who
claim clairvoyance."

It was true. Her mum had gotten a reading the day before she died.
The psychic had said there were good things on the horizon. "I'm sorry.
I'm being rude. You've been nothing but kind, and I'll admit uncannily
spot on."

He patted her hand. "I'm used to being lumped with con artists and
frauds. I was born without the use of my eyes, but I've always been able
to see into people. Intuition is available to any who learn to open their
third eye." He tapped the center of his forehead.

"Afraid I've only got two." She chuckled nervously.

"I've gone and made you uncomfortable again. You asked how I ended up here, a member of Trummel's team. The answer is we met at a séance a year ago in London. Society friends of his wanted a peek beyond the veil. I saw it then that Trummel was about to make an important discovery. I saw a mountain in the desert, an Egyptian tomb. Most shun my advice. He offered to hire me, and I said yes. The answer surprised us both. I'm too old to make such an arduous journey and I didn't need the money."

"Why did you agree to join us?"

"I answered a calling of my soul, that's the nearest I can come to describing what brought me here. My soul was hungry to explore this place."

Imogen knew the feeling. She finished bandaging his arm, taping the gauze. "There."

"Thank you, lass. It's been ages since a woman looked after me."

"Now, I'd better get some sleep. Good night, Dyfan."

"Sweet dreams, child."

As Imogen walked back to the campfire, she noticed that Ely and Quig had already climbed into their sleeping bags and turned in for the night. Twenty feet from the fire, Caleb sat quietly against a cave wall, with his eyes closed. He was meditating with a wooden cross and rosary beads in his hands.

Trummel and Gosswick were off in the shadows having another private meeting. Beside the campfire, Bakari worked with a peculiar ivory tool along his arm, the needle at the end of it injecting ink into his skin. He registered her beside him. "How can I help you?" he asked.

Imogen knelt, examining the tattoo. The fresh ink was bloody. "What does it say?" she whispered.

"The markings represent all the people I've guided through the Dark Realm." Bakari rolled up his sleeve farther. Small inked lines banded his arm from wrist to bicep. "This is your group." Beside the new lines on his wrist was the year, 1937. Other groupings were marked 1935, 1906, 1882, 1796, 1630…all the way back to 1500 AD.

With few wrinkles and only a scattering of white hairs in his thick black beard, Bakari could pass for forty.

"How old are you?" she asked.

He smiled. "Too old to be guiding much longer." He rolled up his other sleeve and showed her a tattoo of a circular shield. Inside it were constellations of dots and lines. He said with deep emotion, "The names of my family." He touched each marking. "My eldest son, Toku; my middle son, Benyi; my youngest daughter, Niri; and my wife, Neesha."

"You miss them."

He nodded. "Very much. But not for long. Your group will be my last. Then I'll return home to pass the legacy onto my sons."

When Gosswick and Trummel approached the fire, Bakari rolled his sleeves down, covering the tattoos.

"I suggest we all get some sleep," Trummel said. "We'll stand guard in shifts."

CHAPTER THIRTY-FOUR

Scorching heat. Imogen, trapped inside a little girl's body, runs through a cloud of smoke. Somewhere in the house a baby cries. Men and women shout. In other rooms, the house begins to collapse. People scream in the haze behind her. A giant serpent of fire slithers across the ceiling above. The little girl keeps running, coughing from all the smoke. Ahead stands a woman ensconced in flames. Her fiery arms reach for the girl. "Come to Mum, Immy."

Imogen woke up gasping.

★   ★   ★

While the others slept on bedrolls around the fire, Caleb took watch duty at four a.m. He sat near the alcove's entrance, just a few feet behind the torches. The darkness beyond was quiet, but still it thrummed with energy. He sensed movement out there. At times he thought he saw the air ripple with bubbles. Shapes floated just beyond the firelight, like bodies drifting at the bottom of a black sea. When he blinked, they were gone. But a familiar pain awakened at the core of Caleb's chest, old wounds reopening.

Will I ever get over what happened? he thought.

He began to ponder why he'd been so strongly drawn to this expedition, into the depths of these caves. At first he thought he'd come here to write about Dr. Trummel's discovery of a hidden tomb. The thrill of adventure drew him. But after crossing through the gate and learning about what this place was, Caleb began to wonder if he had been drawn here for a different reason. He remembered a quote from St. John of the Cross. "If a man wishes to be sure of the road he's traveling on, then he must close his eyes and travel in the dark."

Caleb stared at the infinite blackness beyond the burning torches. *God, is this my "Dark Night of the Soul"?*

Footsteps approaching from behind startled him. He looked through the stalagmites toward the campfire. Imogen climbed up the slight incline and sat beside him, leaning against a rock outcropping. Her skin shone pale in the torchlight. Her eyes scanned the dark, more cautious than afraid.

"Can't you sleep?" he asked.

"I got a few winks. How's the watch?"

"I was on the verge of boredom until you showed up."

She gripped a gold necklace. He'd seen her reaching for it several times before.

"What's that you're wearing?"

She opened her hand. A half-heart pendant lay in her palm.

"Does someone own the other half?" he asked.

She nodded.

Of course, a woman this fascinating would have a man in her life. He felt his heart drop. He had enjoyed the sparks he felt between them. He had secretly hoped getting to know her might lead to something more.

She said, "You wear a necklace too, I've noticed."

Caleb pulled the silver chain out of his shirt.

She lifted the pendant from his skin. "Saint Michael, the archangel. It's beautiful."

"When I turned twelve, a nun in Chicago gave this to me. She said I had angels all around me. She could see them watching over me."

Imogen smiled. "So you've hung out with nuns, have you?"

He released a small laugh. "Quite a bit, in fact. I attended a private Catholic school and later went to a seminary. I was studying to be a priest."

She looked at him sideways. "*You*, a priest?"

"Does that seem impossible?"

"A little."

"That was a lifetime ago."

She leaned forward, resting her arms on her bent knees. "What made you want to become a man of the cloth?"

"At the Catholic school, priests and nuns were my teachers. I admired their devotion. When I turned twenty, the priesthood seemed like my calling."

"What changed your mind?"

"Celibacy didn't agree with me. I couldn't imagine my life without a woman in it."

"Do you have a girlfriend then, or a wife, waiting for you somewhere?"

Caleb smiled and shook his head. "I travel too much to settle down. Marriage can come later, when I'm older." He squeezed the St. Michael pendant and dropped it in his shirt again.

A sound, like an animal scuttling over rocks, echoed outside the cave. Imogen and Caleb looked toward the darkness beyond the torches. They listened for a moment. A long silence, and then the footfall seemed farther away.

"Have you seen anything moving out there?" Imogen asked.

"Nothing like we saw in the maze. I've seen other things, though." He hesitated.

"Go on."

"A memory. It almost seemed like the dark pulled it from my mind."

"What kind of memory?"

"A bad one. An incident that happened three years ago while I was researching a story for *National Geographic*." His feelings of guilt returned as he told her what happened. "I had gone deep-sea diving in a cave with a team of marine explorers in Egypt's Blue Hole. It's north of Cairo, near the city of Dahab. It was my first true dive after a day of training. I chartered a boat from an Egyptian skipper named Ahmad and paid two Greek divers, Nicolai and Christoph, to take me down with them so I could capture their dive on film for the magazine. We wore these heavy copper Siebe Gorman helmets and full bodysuits that inflated with air. The helmet, which fitted over my entire head, made me feel claustrophobic. My vision was reduced to small circular windows on the front and sides. I remember being confused as Ahmad's hollow voice began speaking into my ear. The skipper turned me around and showed me how his telephone box had lines that connected to our helmets for two-way communication with him. Our breathing hoses tethered us to the boat. The crew made jokes about me as I stood at the edge of the deck in this awkward suit, staring into that blue water. As air pumped into my helmet and suit, I had a brief moment of fear seize me; then Nicolai tapped my shoulder and signaled to climb down the ladder."

A chill washed over Caleb as he remembered that day. He, Nicolai, and Christoph had plunged deep into the vertical cave. They'd planned to dive no more than sixty feet to study coral fish. After Caleb took a few photos in the sunlit waters with a bulky underwater camera, he noticed something intriguing farther below. He asked the skipper to drop him deeper. Christoph objected, waving his arms in protest. But Caleb was adamant. What mattered most in that moment was gathering research and photos for his story. He spoke through his helmet's phone with the skipper up top and offered to pay everyone more if they let him dive deeper. Ahmad and the Greeks finally agreed, and the lines dropped the divers lower.

Deep below the natural arch, where the sunlight faded into gloom, they found a watery grave. Skeletons floated one against the other, so many it was impossible to guess their numbers. Fish had eaten the flesh from their bones. Some skeletons still wore fins; free divers, Caleb guessed. They must have ventured so deep their lungs had burst. The underwater cemetery was exactly the kind of discovery that would get him a feature story in *National Geographic*.

Christoph wanted to leave and tapped his wristwatch. Caleb signaled to wait till he got a few more photos. Nicolai posed for pictures with the dead. Christoph pulled out his knife and cut off a finger of one of the corpses. He wanted the gold band. Some of the skeletons broke apart as the Greeks swam through them. A skull covered in plankton floated toward Caleb. He batted it away.

Suddenly something began to go wrong with the air in Caleb's suit. He felt pain in his joints and bones, knotting around his shoulders. His skin began to itch, as if insects were crawling all over him. He gasped for air, became disoriented and terrified. This was decompression sickness. That knowledge brought a fresh jolt of adrenaline.

Caleb let go of his camera. It sank and dangled from a tether below his feet. Nicolai and Christoph began to panic. They jerked violently as if they were also getting decompression sickness. Their movements caused the skeletons to drift closer, crowding the divers. Bubbles clouded the water around them. Caleb searched through the chaos for the others.

The Greeks' air hoses had gotten tangled. Caleb reached them. The two men were struggling to unravel themselves. Ahmad's voice was screaming through Caleb's helmet speaker, asking what was happening. In an act that could have only been spurred by delirium, Christoph severed Nicolai's air hose with his knife. Nicolai's suit, releasing air like a balloon, shot off into a cavern wall, then sank, vanishing into the wide black hole.

Caleb tried to go after him, but his air hose locked at this depth. He watched the dark abyss in shock. He'd never witnessed anyone die. Suffering from stomach cramps and ringing in his ears, Caleb feared he was seconds from death.

Christoph flailed his arms in a cloud of bubbles. Caleb tried to calm him, but the man jerked and kicked, then went limp in his arms. Blood covered the glass of Christoph's faceplate as his eyes and nose hemorrhaged. Then Caleb, shaking badly from the bends, found himself alone among the floating dead. He was down there for what felt like an eternity until the crew on the boat pulled him and Christoph's body to the surface.

Retelling the story caused all the guilt and pain to fully surface. "Had I not pushed them to take me deeper, Nicolai and Christoph would still be alive."

"They were experienced divers," Imogen said. "They were responsible for their mistakes."

"I'd been warned that diving past a hundred feet increased the danger of getting the bends. At the time, I had thought I was invincible. After I surfaced, I spent several hours confined inside a hyperbaric chamber shaped like a coffin. It cured most of my symptoms. I still occasionally suffer from vertigo. But it's the guilt that never leaves me. I've been carrying the weight of their deaths in my heart ever since." They both fell silent for a moment, and then Caleb said, "There's something else you should know.... When I first crossed through the portal earlier, I saw skeletons floating around me as if I were back in the Blue Hole. A diver grabbed my ankle. It was so real. He looked so much like Christoph, even the bloodstained faceplate. For me, it was reliving the worst moment of my life."

"It's this place," Imogen said. "If you stare into the darkness long enough…"

"Bakari said it knows our darkest secrets. I think it somehow projects them."

She pondered this a moment with an inward gaze. "According to the Amduat, the underworld is a place for a person to confront oneself on the way to the afterlife. The soul is tested before it reaches the Hall of Judgment."

"Like coming face-to-face with your sins in purgatory," Caleb said.

"I feel better after sharing mine with you. What secrets have you been holding on to?"

Imogen never talked about her childhood with anyone. Grandfather had tried a child therapist once, but Imogen had refused to talk with him. She couldn't bear to relive the nightmare of what had happened to her family, even in her mind. "I'd rather keep my secrets to myself."

"Are you sure?" Caleb prodded. "Perhaps, sharing them lessens their power."

"Maybe another time, Father Beckett," she joked. "Not tonight."

Quig approached, rubbing sleep from his eyes. "My turn. See anything moving out there?"

Caleb shook his head. "Stare into the dark long enough, though. You'll know we're not alone."

Imogen walked with Caleb back to where the others were sleeping. He added more coals to the fire. She went to the pool of clear water and washed her face. As the ripples on the water's surface smoothed out, she stared at her shadowy reflection. Constant dread had frayed her nerves ever since she'd learned they weren't alone down here. Now, as she considered that the spiritual laws the early Egyptians had believed in might be true, she feared more than dying. Her whole life, her scientific mind had believed death was an end to consciousness. The moment her brain and body died, so would her awareness. In a strange way, she had found that comforting. Not having to think anymore. But what if she had been wrong? What if there was an afterlife and it offered two possibilities: ascension or descending into darker realms? According to early Egyptian texts, the souls who failed to prove their spiritual worthiness suffered among the demons and lost souls of Duat. *Is that what's in store for me if I die down here?* The thought filled her with dread.

Imogen returned to the campfire, where Caleb was getting ready for bed. "Do you mind if I lay my bedroll next to yours?" she asked. "I might actually sleep."

He nodded.

She dropped hers a short distance from Caleb's. Lying on her side, Imogen closed her eyes.

Something skittered outside the cave. She inched closer to Caleb and finally fell asleep.

CHAPTER THIRTY-FIVE

Whenever Teddy Quig got scared, his teeth chattered. The constant banging of his metal caps hurt the nerves in his gums. He bit down on a knuckle to get the chattering to stop. He felt devastated about what happened to Vickers back in the tunnel. His distant screams still echoed in Quig's head. *I abandoned him.* Guilt snaked through his gut and nested there. Worse than the guilt was the relentless fear of the horrors he'd seen in the maze. They were out there, lurking beyond the torchlight. He could feel them, watching. Could smell the animal stink of them. A couple of times, he heard something skitter. Whatever it was had set rocks tumbling. With each noise, he jerked around, aiming his gun into the dark. Then all would settle quiet again, except for the incessant clacking of his teeth.

To take his mind off his fears, he thought of Doris, his girl back in London. From his chest pocket he pulled out a small photograph of her standing by the River Thames with Tower Bridge behind her. God, he missed her. She was nineteen and full of sunshine, an artist who had turned Quig's gray world into a place of bright colors. More than anything she wanted to become Mrs. Teddy Quig. Before he left for Egypt, they had promised to marry when he returned. He'd finally have the money to fulfill their dreams. They would move to the seaside town of Margate in Kent. Doris would paint seascapes and he'd get work on a local charter boat. They'd have a couple of wee kids and spend their weekends at the beach. That was heaven on earth to Quig.

A cold breath dampened his face. All thoughts of Doris fled.

The flames of the torches flickered sideways, threatening to go out.

A chill coursed through him, and the shivers started again.

A familiar voice whispered Quig's name from the darkness. It sounded like Vickers.

"Vick? Is that you?" *It couldn't be.*

"You left me for dead."

The sound of his mate's voice shook Quig to his core.

"You fled like a coward and left me to be butchered."

The snake of guilt in Quig's belly slithered up into his chest and coiled. He couldn't breathe.

He heard something heavy being dragged over the rocks. It echoed outside the alcove. Then the stench of animal musk struck his nose.

He looked back at the sleepers to see if any had awoken. No one around the campfire stirred. Quig tried to shout a warning, but his throat closed so tight he couldn't utter a sound. Then his teeth began chattering again.

The scraping noises drew closer.

Quig whirled around. Just beyond the edge of the firelight, the darkness formed into a chaos of moving bodies. It sounded like an overcrowded herd of animals fighting for space, climbing over one another. Out of this writhing bedlam, Vickers's voice sounded again. "We've found you."

CHAPTER THIRTY-SIX

Imogen awoke to the madness of someone yelling.

Gosswick cursed as he walked the border of the torches. "Quig! …
Fuck's sake, Quig, get back here!"

Imogen, Caleb, and the others pulled on their boots and joined the
captain at the alcove's entrance.

"What's happening?" Trummel asked.

Gosswick looked frantic. "Quig's gone missing. Anyone see him
last night?"

"Imogen and I did," Caleb said. "He relieved my watch at four a.m."

"He was leaning against that rock when I went to sleep," she said.

"The demons lured him," Bakari said.

"Christ!" Gosswick grabbed a burning torch and walked out of the
alcove. Sykes followed him.

Bakari, Trummel, and Caleb grabbed torches. Imogen followed
them into the dark. They called for Quig but got no answer.

Bakari caught up to Trummel. "Let me lead. Everyone, stay close.
Whatever you see in the dark, don't fire your weapons unless I say."

The search party stayed in a tight half circle as they climbed down an
incline of loose shale. Firelight pushing back the darkness, they entered a
crater. The stone had been cut into circular bands that gradually spiraled
in tiers like a primitive amphitheater. At the bottom, on a round stage
surrounded by towers of stacked rocks, something white, atop a pedestal,
reflected their light. It was a miner's helmet, the headlamp cracked.
Gosswick picked it up. Beneath the helmet lay several bloody teeth, a
few of them gold-capped.

Gosswick shouted at the surrounding dark, challenging Quig's
murderers to show themselves.

Imogen and Caleb traded worried glances. "Take this." Caleb
handed her his torch, then aimed his pistol at the blackness beyond the
stone towers.

A few rocks tumbled into the crater. Beyond the group's ring of light echoed scuffles and animal grunts. The air grew foul with the scent of musk and excrement. On the rock cliffs above, dozens of red eyes reflected the lights.

Gosswick aimed and shot his pistol.

"Stop, you'll anger them!" Bakari shouted.

Beasts cried out, retreating deeper into the gloom. Angry screeches and yowls filled the circular cavern. The cacophony was maddening.

The soldiers shouted back, firing more shots into the dark. The thundering blasts rang in Imogen's ears.

Bones flew at them from the dark, striking the ground at their feet. A skull with hair still partially attached. A gnawed leg bone, still red with morsels of meat. Something hard thunked Imogen's helmet. It was a severed hand, the fingers picked clean of flesh.

Shielding Imogen with his body, Caleb shouted, "Run! Go!"

She ran with the others, retreating to the alcove. The mortar of bones landed on the cave floor behind them.

Ely had stayed behind with Dyfan. They huddled by the dwindling campfire.

"What's happening?" Ely asked.

"The demons are furious thanks to Gosswick," Bakari said.

Gosswick squared off with the Egyptian. "*They* killed my soldiers."

Trummel stepped between them. "Calm down, both of you. We need solutions, not squabbling."

Snarls echoed just beyond the torchlight at the edge of the alcove. Dark shapes moved in flickering blurs. A frenzy of claws swiped at the flames. The sounds the creatures made were deafening. *There must be hundreds out there*, Imogen thought.

"We're trapped." Sykes took cover behind a stalagmite, gun aimed. Gosswick did the same. The others retreated to the back of the cave.

Trummel turned to Bakari. "What are our options?"

"They won't cross the fire."

"We can't stay here," Caleb said. "All those things have to do is wait until our fires burn out."

"How do we reach the next gate?" Imogen asked.

Bakari pointed to the cave's only exit. "Through them."

"Blow your horn again," Caleb said. "Won't that ward them off?"

Bakari seemed conflicted. "The horn is supposed to grant safe passage through the maze and down the river. The bone keepers are highly religious and respect the horn as the voice of their god. The demons that I fear have followed us here are the more vicious *shemayu*, the wanderers. They have no beliefs to guide them, only hunger. The horn hurts their ears and confuses them. The sound also enrages them, makes them want to rip their prey apart."

"Sounds to me like they're already enraged," Caleb said. "Blow the horn loud enough to hurt their ears. While they scatter, we'll run."

Bakari frowned. "The horn will buy minutes. Once we're out there, our only protection will be our fires and our lights."

"We have guns," Gosswick said, joining the group.

"You can't shoot them all," Bakari said. "We are horribly outnumbered."

"I say we take our chances with the horn," Caleb said.

"What other option do we have, Bakari?" Trummel asked.

"We could stay here and hope the *shemayu* leave before our fire and batteries run out. It could take days. They are relentless hunters once they've discovered prey."

"We don't have that kind of time," Trummel said.

"It's a risk either way," Caleb said. "Right now we're rabbits trapped in a hole."

"Rabbits with guns." Gosswick's bravado sounded thin. "I say we fire a barrage of shots. See if we can scare them off."

Bakari shook his head. "Killing a few would only ensure the rest never leave. I promise you, you don't want to be here when the fires die out."

Trummel weighed his options. "Everyone, grab up your gear. Bakari, when we're ready, you blow that horn until their eardrums burst."

As they quickly packed up their bedrolls and rucksacks, Bakari poured extra tar pitch into a white membrane pouch that bloated like a rubber hot-water bottle.

When Imogen asked what the container was made from, he told her, "It was a *shemayu* stomach," then he capped it with a stopper and hung the pouch's strap over his shoulder. "The pitch will help us keep the torches lit."

Imogen took a deep breath as she pulled on her pack. The creatures' constant screeching made it impossible to think.

When their party had gathered near the entrance, Bakari pulled the curved and ribbed horn from his pack and blew. The acoustics of the alcove made the horn bellow louder, low and resonant, like a foghorn. Outside, the angry howls and screeches turned to sounds of panic. The rumble of trampling feet echoed farther and farther away. The howls faded but not far enough to make Imogen feel out of danger.

Bakari pulled the torches out of the ground and passed them to the others. Then the group followed their underworld guide into the void.

CHAPTER THIRTY-SEVEN

The eight explorers hurried through the cavern, carrying five burning torches. The beams of their headlamps cut a swath through the darkness. Ely tried to stay in the middle of the pack. He wished he had a gun. His only protection was the barrier the lights provided. The creatures had stopped screeching. But their footsteps sounded close. Their musky odor was a constant presence. They followed the group, like nocturnal predators stalking a herd, waiting for a straggler.

Ely hurried alongside Dyfan. Since the psychic had gotten confused in the maze and seemed to have lost his sense of direction, Trummel had relieved Dyfan of his duties as guide. Ely looked after the blind man, making sure he didn't fall behind. "Watch your head." Ely put a hand over Dyfan's helmet as they walked under low-hanging rock.

"Thanks, lad."

"Stick with me, sir. I'll be your eyes."

"Be my feet too, would you? My blisters are screaming."

Ely liked the Scottish mystic. Dyfan had traveled all over Wales, Ireland, and Scotland and had an encyclopedic knowledge of stories about haunted moors and mystical creatures. When he received psychic guidance for a place, he said it was like watching the ghostly light of the will-o'-the-wisp floating out in front of him. That was how he knew which direction to go.

"Have you seen the will-o'-the-wisp lately?" Ely asked.

"Unfortunately, no. It seems the deeper we go the foggier my mind gets. I don't know what's ahead any more than you do."

The rocky terrain flattened as they stepped into the river basin. The dirt was damp and spongy with a few shallow pools. Several sets of footprints pockmarked the mud. Others had followed this route before them. The strange bare footprints were marked with a sixth toe. That and the pointed shape – decidedly not human – unnerved Ely. The prints were left by the *shemayu* or some other species of demon.

Ely's heavy rucksack was becoming a burden. Since some of the other men had been killed, Dr. Trummel had made Ely carry supplies. He felt like a pack mule. He didn't complain, though, just gritted his teeth and willed himself to keep walking. The group seemed to be making good progress. They'd hiked more than an hour without incident.

"How much farther to the gate?" Trummel asked.

"It's just ahead," said Bakari. "Remember, liquid doors are yours to pass through. Solid doors require a code."

"What sort of code?" Imogen asked.

"Each sealed door is encoded with a cipher and watched over by a guardian. The key to each door is a word or words, which must be discovered by any travelers who wish to gain entry."

A gunshot sounded, startling everyone.

Sykes stood with his submachine gun aimed off to the right. "One of those things was creeping up on us." The soldier's headlamp shone in the dark. Fifteen feet away a stripe-skinned creature with jutting bones lay dead. "Got the bugger." Black liquid spread from the hole in its chest.

Howls erupted behind them. The creatures were close.

"You shouldn't have killed it!" Bakari yelled. "Now we'll have war. *Run!*"

A dry river channel stretched ahead of them, disappearing beyond the beams of their headlamps. The heavy pack bounced against Ely's back as he ran. The stitch in his side hurt so badly it felt like his belly might split. He kept a hold of Dyfan's arm and ran.

Screeches echoed behind him.

Dyfan stumbled over the uneven shale floor. Ely caught the old man before he went down. "You've got to keep running."

Caleb slowed beside them, grabbing Dyfan's other arm. Ely panned his flashlight over the demons' faces with their strange zebra-striped markings. The creatures shrieked as the light hit their eyes. They jerked away but didn't retreat far.

Bakari and the soldiers stepped past Ely, jabbing their torches at snarling shapes that scuttled over one another.

"Keep moving," Caleb urged Ely and Dyfan. Then he ran to the others at the edge of the fighting.

Ely heard shots fired behind him as he helped Dyfan up a short incline. "The others are just ahead."

CHAPTER THIRTY-EIGHT

The dry riverbed merged into a tunnel masoned of bricks. Another fifty yards in, the tunnel dead-ended into a wall with a solid slate door. A nook above the archway held a stone guardian with the body of a man and head of a gazelle. Its narrow legs were folded against its chest, its hoofed feet exposed.

"The next gate!" Trummel pressed his hands against stone, trying to move it.

Imogen trained her light on the door.

Gunshots sounded behind them. The demons' constant shrieking made it impossible to think.

On the wall to the left of the door, each of the small bricks was engraved with a hieroglyph. Imogen wiped a layer of dust from the codex, revealing faint dots and lines.

The gazelle-headed guardian stared down at them blankly.

Ely arrived at the gate with Dyfan.

Trummel began randomly pushing the stones inward. The door remained solid, but the tile floor trembled and a strip of stones fell away. Imogen trained her light over the gap made by the missing tiles. A dark chasm yawned beneath them.

"Stop!" Imogen shouted.

But it was too late. The ground shuddered again and another strip of floor fell inward. The stones seemed to drop quietly for several seconds. Then there came a distant clattering far below.

"The door is booby-trapped," Imogen said. "Press the codex in the wrong sequence and we'll lose more floor."

Caleb and the others fought twenty yards away, holding off the demons. The men were losing ground, drawing closer.

"Get to the gate!" Bakari yelled. "There are too many of them."

Imogen heard the men retreating toward her as she stooped in front of the codex. The brick walls rose on either side of the giant door, blocking any other means of escape.

Trummel reached past her, pressing bricks inward. Another strip of floor crumbled away.

Bakari, Caleb, and the soldiers leapt over the gap and landed on a platform where the others crowded at the doorway. The men held up their torches and shot at anything that got too close. Just beyond their lights reflective eyes glared. The horde massed together, clogging the tunnel from wall to wall.

"Bloody hell," Gosswick said, shoving his torch into the dark. The smell of burning flesh filled the air. "They don't give up, do they?"

Imogen handed Ely her torch, then dug the journal from her satchel. She flipped to the pages lined with rows of illustrated glyphs alongside the demon names. The codes must have been designed to solve the gate's cryptograms. She ran her finger down the list.

Imogen eyed the statue of the gatekeeper and thought, *I've seen the gate guardians on the Papyrus of Ani*. In the legend of Duat, the way through a gate was to guess the demon's name and speak it. She studied the stone buttons beside the door, then scanned the pages of codes. "Grandfather already solved half the riddle by providing the list of demons. All I have to do is match the code that translates to this demon's name."

"Hurry," Trummel urged.

Through trial and error, Imogen found the first two characters – the half-moon and ankh. Pressing them caused the gazelle demon's ears to flap back and forth. It must have been a clue that she had solved part of the puzzle. She punched in the first demon name on Grandfather's list that began with those two characters. "Biter of Heads." Her voice echoed in the tunnel.

More flooring fell away. This riled up the *shemayu* even more.

Caleb and the soldiers fired into the demons. Some fell into the gap. Others growled at the edge of the drop. Something rained down on the group. Wet and sticky. Two of the torches sputtered and went out. Caleb touched the wet spot on his shoulder before the scent hit him. *Excrement.*

Gosswick's pistol clicked without firing. He'd run out of bullets. "Cover me!" he shouted. Caleb could hear him slotting bullets into the cylinder.

Another volley of the thick shit porridge struck them. Another torch fizzled and went out. Only two remained lit. The headlamps helped their party see but weren't bright enough to hold the demons at bay. The creatures pressed forward. The air was thick with their putrid scent. They chattered and shrieked, their devil faces leering from the darkness.

Caleb held his camera up and snapped blindly. The flash lit up the crowd, assaulting the demons with bright white light. The creatures shielded their eyes and retreated several yards, their bodies smoldering. Caleb tossed the used flashbulb and hurried to mount another atop his camera.

"Great thinking, Flash," Gosswick said. "Keep hitting the buggers with light."

While Imogen searched the codes, the growling *shemayu* screeched in the dark. Only a twenty-foot half circle of light protected the group from being overtaken.

Bakari pulled off his pouch of tar pitch and worked to get his torch relit. Only Trummel's torch offered protection. One creature lunged into the firelight. Caleb blinded it with his flash. Smoke drifted from its face. Gosswick fired his gun multiple times, filling the demon's chest and head with holes. It fell to the ground amid heaps of others.

"They're getting bolder," Caleb said.

"Imogen, how are you coming with the codes?" Trummel shouted.

"I've found nine that begin with half-moon and ankh." She punched in a long set of glyphs beside the door and called out another name. "Bone-Crusher."

The doorkeeper statue shook its head.

Gosswick cursed as more floor stones fell away. Caleb looked over the edge and couldn't see the bottom. They had three, maybe four, tries before the platform they stood on broke apart, dropping them all into the gulf.

It took precious seconds for the stones above the gate to reset.

A rock was hurled from the darkness. Then another. One struck Imogen's rucksack. As Caleb was attaching a flashbulb, a stone shattered it.

The *shemayu* returned to the edge, shielding their eyes against the light.

A rock struck Sykes in the shoulder. He cursed and fired off more shots.

Another attempt by Imogen failed. The shrinking floor forced everyone into a tighter space.

A demon with ram horns loped from the dark. Trummel fired, hitting the creature in the chest.

"Six codes left," Imogen yelled. The next one she tried didn't work, leaving them with less than eight feet of platform.

A couple of the demons attempted to jump across. Both missed and fell shrieking into the dark. Several climbed onto one another's shoulders.

"What are they doing?" Trummel shouted.

"Forming a bridge," Caleb said. He ran closer and tripped his shutter, firing another flash. The creatures shrieked and shut their eyes against the light but didn't retreat. The first group fell forward like a ladder across the divide. One creature gripped the edge of the platform. Others started across the bridge from the other side. Gosswick held a torch to the nearest creature's head. Its flesh caught fire. The demon tried to hold on but eventually lost its grip, sending the whole chain of bodies shrieking into the gap. Any attempt to hold the demons off would be temporary. There were just too many of them. Trummel's team would eventually be overtaken.

Bakari blew his horn.

The creatures retreated.

"Take this." Bakari tossed his pouch containing the tar pitch to Trummel, then drew out a large curved sword.

Caleb watched in awe as Bakari leapt over the wide chasm and landed on the other side. He swung his sword at the demons so fast his arm became a blur, slashing throats, severing limbs.

Imogen punched another set of symbols. The wrong code caused the gap in the floor to widen. Dyfan lost his balance and almost fell, but Caleb grabbed him and pulled him closer to the door. Everyone gathered in a tight knot at the gate.

"We're running out of floor," Trummel told Imogen.

"I've almost got it. The guardian is the key." Her frantic fingers pushed another set of symbols.

"Look." Caleb pointed up to the statue. Blood was dripping down the sides of its mouth.

"Another clue." Imogen punched in another code and shouted, "Blood-Drinker!"

The horned guardian above kicked its hooves against its perch. The slate door turned to shimmering liquid.

Trummel pushed Imogen through and followed along with Ely and Dyfan. Gosswick and Sykes crossed through next.

Caleb stopped at the gate and looked back. "Bakari, come with us!"

"Go!" he shouted and fought to hold off the crowd. "As long as the portal remains open, the demons can cross through."

The flames of Bakari's torch snuffed out and the darkness swallowed him. Caleb knew he should retreat through the door but he couldn't look away. Suddenly a bright blue light flashed. Bakari began to glow with a phosphorescent aura. He had removed his shirt. His back, chest, arms, and face were alight with strange markings. He faced the growling horde and blew his horn again. Another sonorous bugle cry reverberated off the tunnel walls. Instead of retreating, this time the demons attacked.

Shadows lurched from all directions, biting into his chest, back, and arms. The big man collapsed beneath a feeding frenzy. The blue light of Bakari's skin faded until there was only darkness and the sound of predators growling.

A large horned demon charged out of the darkness. It leapt over the gap just as Caleb dove through the gate.

CHAPTER THIRTY-NINE

Imogen huddled with Trummel, Ely, and Dyfan. Caleb burst through the liquid door and stumbled toward the others. The soldiers backed away and positioned themselves for battle. Caleb joined them. All three men stood with their guns aimed at the door.

A pair of hands clawed at the watery doorway, long fingers reaching through. The demon's screeches and growls were muted. Sound didn't travel well from one realm to the next. The liquid door sparked with electricity. The fingers snapped back, disappearing. The rippling door began to solidify until it hardened back into slate.

"What happened to Bakari?" Imogen asked.

"He stayed back to hold them off," Caleb said.

"Will he reach the portal that takes him to his family?" she asked.

Caleb shook his head. "Bakari let the demons devour him so we could get away."

Grief gripped Imogen's heart. Their mysterious guide had devoted his life to guiding humans through these caves. That he'd sacrificed himself to save their party made her feel sick. "We should say some parting words for Bakari," she suggested.

"We've no time to dally." Trummel seemed to have no remorse for the loss of his porter. "Dyfan, can you get a read on this place?"

"Sorry, no."

"Try, damn it!" Trummel yelled.

"I'm doing all I can." Dyfan pressed his fingers to his head. "Something in the caves blocks my ability."

"Then use your cards."

"The cards are silent too."

Trummel rounded on the blind man. "If you can't lead us to the relics, what use are you? You're a liability, that's what. Old. Blind. Ely practically carried you through that last bit."

"Don't talk to him that way!" Imogen snapped.

"I'll talk any way I please."

★   ★   ★

Caleb hated Trummel in that moment. Caleb wandered a little away from the group, Bakari's body still glowing with blue light in his mind. He mounted a flashbulb and fired it into the dark. Something glinted on the ground a dozen yards away. He hurried forward, training his headlamp on the cave floor.

"There's a path!" he shouted. He shone his headlamp over a muddy trail carved into the creek bank. Water trickled close by. "The creek continues this side of the portal. I say we follow it." While he waited for the others to reach him, he cast his light along the riverbank. By the time Imogen reached him, he had found the strange relic – a bare human footprint. The first they'd seen since entering the caves.

CHAPTER FORTY

To conserve batteries, they turned off most of the headlamps again, relying on the light from four flame torches and Trummel's and Gosswick's helmets to carve a path through the gloom. The trail of footprints led into a thicket of blackthorn briars. The group questioned how a swamp forest could grow in a place without sunlight. No one had an explanation. Trummel kept his theories to himself.

We discovered the path to them.

Harlan Riley's cryptic words drove Trummel forward with a surer step than the others. He wondered what else Riley's team had encountered in this strange and treacherous dimension before making the ultimate discovery.

"Duat claimed all members of my team," Harlan had confessed in his final days. "They were not mentally strong enough to finish the journey. Only I crossed through the highest gate and witnessed the revelations hidden at the heart of the Dark Realm."

Trummel wondered who among his own team would make it through the last gate. He knew before entering the cave that his party was embarking on a soul's quest, and there would be casualties.

Harlan had been devastated by the loss of his team. "My fellow explorers died because of me," he had said, teary-eyed. "Had I not been so compelled to find the heart of the tomb..."

Harlan had a soft spot for those working beneath him. Trummel worried less. He left the fates of others to the gods.

After passing through the second gate, the seven explorers walked for an hour through a forest of twisting briars. Occasionally branches crackled in the distance as if something were moving out there. Trummel had the sense they were being followed.

A black void that bordered the thicket stretched to infinity in all directions. Infinity bothered some. Not Trummel.

Show me everything. Trummel mentally sent the request into the darkness, knowing it was intelligent and could read his thoughts. *I want to see Duat in all its glory, no matter the costs. Take any soul you wish, but please spare me as you would a pharaoh.*

Ely walked beside Dyfan, lugging his pack, steering him. *Doting*, Trummel thought angrily. The lad had been an eager student at Oxford, a hand-raiser, willing with the extracurricular work to assist his professor. Trummel didn't respect arse kissers, but idolatry had its uses.

Now when they stopped for a drink and a short rest, Trummel sipped lukewarm tea from a thermos and stared into the dark. The track of footprints vanished as the spongy terrain turned into shin-deep black water. It filled his boots, making them heavy as he slogged through the mud. A humid fog seeped between the thorn branches. Trummel had the sensation he was no longer in a cave, but walking through a swamp forest. And he would never admit this to anyone, but he suddenly worried that they were lost.

As if by some miracle, or perhaps Duat showing Trummel the glory he requested, a small light appeared in the darkness ahead. He halted the group.

"What is it?" Gosswick came to his side, gun drawn.

"Hold your fire," Trummel whispered.

A glowing white orb, slightly larger than a billiard ball, floated toward them. The others watched warily as the sphere buzzed around them.

"Amazing." As Imogen stepped closer, its radiance illuminated her face and reflected twin spheres in her eyes.

"Careful," Gosswick warned.

"It seems friendly." She reached up to touch it, and the orb flew backward like a startled insect.

It stopped a few feet in front of Trummel. The light inside constantly shifted from solid to partially transparent. Imogen was right. The energy vibrating from it seemed benign. The orb made a small circle in the air, a come-hither motion. Then it meandered through an opening in the trees.

"I believe it wants us to follow," Trummel said.

"You sure that's a good idea?" Gosswick asked.

"Can you think of a better one?" Trummel responded, eyebrow raised. Not waiting for an answer, he followed the glowing sphere as it floated ahead of them, occasionally slowing to allow the group to work their way through the brambles. Once it stopped to allow a large black water snake to slither its way through the trees ahead. This made Trummel uneasy. He hated snakes.

The Amduat and pyramid paintings depicted many snakes in Duat, including a giant serpent god, Apophis, also known as Apep. Trummel remembered one painting of the underworld that pictured a snake longer than several men. He kept a wary eye on the tall reeds and thick brush where such a creature could be lying in wait for a meal to pass by.

Vulnerable from all sides, the explorers raked their lights across the surrounding trees. Trummel almost thought there was nothing but snakes and the orb in this maze of thorny branches, until a quicksilver shape shot past his light. He jerked his beam, spotlighting a piece of white fabric floating in the water ten feet away. The sight made his heart stop.

As Trummel approached, the fabric shot away like a frightened fish. A splash followed and he swore he glimpsed a pair of kicking feet.

Beyond the torchlight, branches snapped.

The group huddled together.

Gosswick jerked around and cocked his pistol.

"See something?" Trummel asked.

The captain's face had gone pale. "I hear children. Laughing." He wiped sweat from his forehead. "Don't you hear them?"

Trummel eyed the others. "Anyone else hear children?"

They all shook their heads.

"I hear something disturbing the branches," Caleb said.

Imogen nodded. "I do too."

The branches shivered again. The cracking sound was distant, like a breeze whispering through the thicket.

"Shut up! Shut up!" Gosswick shouted.

Trummel turned to his captain. "Hold it together, Goss."

Ahead the white orb floated in place, waiting.

"Let's keep moving." Trummel walked toward the orb. It bobbed once and resumed leading them through the briars.

They sloshed through the water another few hundred yards, a distant snapping and splashes following them. Whatever was out there, it didn't seem to mind that they heard. Ely and Imogen began to talk of seeing things moving in the dark.

"We're safe as long as we stay within our lights," Trummel said, hoping it was true. Were all demons afraid of fire and light as the bone keepers and *shemayu* had been? He didn't know. Now that Bakari was gone there was no one to ask.

The ball of light brightened as it stopped. A massive ancient tree towered above the forest like a god. With its knobby, wrinkled bark, the tree had a familiar and unnerving shape to it. The top came to a jagged, leafless crown. Branches jutted from its trunk like deformed arms. At its base, tentacles of roots rose partially out of the water in humps. Trummel approached the wide trunk. Carved into the bark was a single word:

JARVI

Trummel stumbled backward, bumping into the others.

"Are you all right?" Imogen asked.

No, I'm not bloody all right. He couldn't remember feeling so shaken. When he shone his light back in the direction of the crudely carved word, it was no longer there. A chill coursed through his bones. The tree had changed too, now thin and thorny like all the others in this infinite forest. Confused, he spun in a circle but couldn't find the ancient tree anywhere. Had he imagined it?

"What did you find?" Caleb asked.

Trummel shook his head. "Must have been a trick of the light."

"How long till we rest?" Ely asked.

"When we find dry land." Trummel continued wading through the water, weaving through tangles of branches that seemed to have no end.

A girl's voice whispered from the dark. "Let's play hide-and-seek," she called.

Trummel turned his light to where the giggle had sounded. "Did you hear that?"

The others stood silent, watching him as if he'd gone mad.

Gosswick mirrored his paranoia. "You believe me now about the kids?"

Trummel mopped sweat from his brow. "It's this place. It's testing our will. Don't let it get to you."

As he sloshed through the water, he heard the familiar giggles of a young girl. His mind returned to the Finnish swamp forest of his youth. He was ten, running. And she was there, his twin sister, Nell. Gray light and mist had filtered through the spiny, leafless trees that rose from the black water.

Running along a muddy trail, young Nathan and Nell were two explorers searching for Viking treasure, while their father and mother, both archaeologists, worked a nearby dig of Nordic ruins.

Nathan and his sister had been inseparable since the day they'd left their mother's womb. Nell had been born one minute earlier and boasted of being the oldest, while Nathan claimed that spending extra time in Mum's womb had developed his brain more, making him the smartest. They'd challenged one another in playful competition, but no one, not even their parents, could ever come between them.

"Bet you the last of the lemon drops I can beat you to that tree," Nell challenged, holding up the bag of sweets their father had given them.

"You're on," Nathan said.

The twins raced a hundred yards to a tall pine. Nathan was easily beating her, but slowed at the last second to let her win. They leaned against the pine's massive trunk and laughed, out of breath.

"Told you I was faster," Nell bragged.

"Too quick for me," Nathan conceded. They both knew the truth.

"Here." She shared the remaining sweets with him anyway.

Nathan popped a lemon drop in his mouth and pressed his forehead to his sister's. They looked into each other's eyes, a staring contest, willing each other to blink, until they both broke out laughing.

Nell was a fearless girl with flowing dark hair and an infectious laugh. Nathan could be in the worst of moods and his sister would put her arm around him, give him a nudge, and suddenly everything would be all right again. He remembered her clearest on that day in Finland he most wanted to forget. September fourth of 1903. One minute she was walking hand in hand with him, the next pushing him away and yelling, "Let's play hide-and-seek!" Nell ran through the trees. "Bet you'll never find me."

Nathan pressed his head against a tree, eyes closed, and counted, "One potato, two potato..." When he got to twenty, he opened his eyes and ran looking for her. At first he felt the thrill of the hunt as he searched behind trees and logs. He whistled a few times, his signal for her to whistle back and give him a clue. Each time she whistled, she sounded farther away. They were only supposed to stay within a few hundred yards of where their parents were working. Nathan got mad that his sister had ventured deeper into the forest.

After a half hour passed since she last whistled back, he grew very concerned. "Nell!" His voice echoed across the swamp. "You win! Come out. Now!"

No matter how many times he called, she didn't come. Then she whistled from somewhere beyond the pines. Something felt terribly off. The psychic connection he'd always felt with her, like an invisible line that tethered them together, was gone. He couldn't *feel* her.

He wandered farther into the woods to an area overgrown with thorn briars and trees with sharp branches. Among her small shoeprints in the mud were bigger prints made from work boots. Soon her tracks disappeared at the base of a giant leafless tree with deformed branches and a jagged crown. The word *JARVI* had been etched into the bark. Nathan found Nell's white stockings and shoes spotted with blood, tucked under one of the tree's exposed roots.

Frantic, he followed the boot prints along a ribbon of mud that stretched between two swamps of black water. "Nell! *Nell!*" he shouted over and over.

A flock of storks startled and took flight.

He spotted Nell's white dress drifting several yards from the shore, where the land disappeared into stagnant water. She was still in it, floating facedown.

The memory of his sister's death still tore at deep wounds in Trummel's heart.

After his parents notified the police, a search party found an old shack deep in the swamp where a recluse named Göran Järvi lived. He had kept Nell's knickers and the last of the sweets. Nathan, who had been waiting with his parents for the search party to return, could still see the killer's mangy bearded face and wild eyes as the police escorted Järvi out of the woods. The man's arms were cuffed behind his back. He had looked right at Nathan with a grin and whistled the same signal Nathan had heard in the woods.

Now, a singsong whistle sounded from the dark woods followed by the crackle of branches. With a shudder, Trummel wondered who was tempting him into the thicket, his sister or Järvi?

It's not real, he tried to convince himself. Nell lay in Highgate Cemetery in England where their mum's relatives were buried, and Göran Järvi had been shot by a firing squad in 1918.

The crackling branches and taunting whistles continued until the group reached a small island of mud and jutting stones.

The swamp fell silent.

The white orb guided them through an old cemetery. They walked among crooked tombstones covered in grime and lichen. Trummel remained in morbid silence as he came upon a large gravestone. It wasn't Egyptian. The curved gray rock tombstone belonged in an English graveyard. The angel's face protruding from the stone made Trummel's skin prickle. He wiped moss from the surface until the words etched in the stone were clear. As he read the epitaph, he fell to his knees and touched the name.

HERE LIES

NELL TRUMMEL

A BELOVED DAUGHTER AND SISTER

WHO DIED MUCH TOO SOON

1893–1903

CHAPTER FORTY-ONE

Captain Gosswick surveyed the many graves, finding his soldiers' names etched on several: Dan Vickers, Theodore Quig, Joe Dunlap, Nigel Bigsby. As much as it saddened Gosswick that he'd lost so many of his men, it was the other graves that gutted him most.

Dozens of dirt mounds covered the island with barely a thin wooden cross to mark each one. He recognized them as Kikuyu graves, the dead tribal people who'd been buried by Christian missionaries. He didn't need epitaphs to know who was buried here. Many graves were under swamp water, with only the rickety crosses visible. Gosswick's heart shuddered as he stepped between smaller dirt mounds. Twenty of them. From their crosses dangled trinkets – a bead necklace, a doll, a tiny pair of shoes.

Sykes walked up beside him. "Does this look familiar to you too?"

Gosswick uttered one word, "Kenya."

Three years ago a dark period of his life had branded permanent scars on Aiden Gosswick's soul. He'd been between expeditions, so he and a few of his soldiers had signed on to do mercenary work for a gold mining company near the town of Kakamega. It was the heart of the Kakamega gold rush, and because of the Great Depression, men from all over the world had flocked to this armpit of western Kenya in hopes of finding glittering rocks in the mines and rivers.

Gosswick and his crew protected the mines controlled by Skinner Mining Company. The company's owner, Lachlan Skinner, rewarded his soldiers with bonuses of gold for doing his dirty work. Gosswick and his men, having come from the slums of England, were happy to oblige.

The mine's black workers, mostly men and lads from the Kikuyu tribe, feared Skinner. He was a brutal disciplinarian, and many of his workers had whip scars lashed on their backs by Skinner himself. He'd made enemies too. One was Abu Khan, an underground Kikuyu rebel who lived like a ghost among the tribe. Several of Skinner's laborers were discovered smuggling gold, and rumor had it "the Black Ghost" was using the gold to buy guns. After years of growing tension between the Kikuyu and the white European settlers, it was feared that Abu Khan was planning an uprising to take over the mines.

Skinner paid Gosswick handsomely to flex his military muscle, subdue the local tribes, and do all he could to smoke out their Black Ghost. "I want Khan's head," Skinner demanded. He intended to place the rebel leader's head on a pike above the mine entrance to remind the workers who they should be loyal to.

Gosswick painted his face red to match one of the Kikuyu demons. Then he set off on a witch hunt with a squad of three mercenary soldiers – Sykes, Quig, and Vickers – and thirty lethal Maasai warriors who had been given rifles. During a raid, they had driven huge gun-mounted lorries through the villages in a brigade that sent the Kikuyu scattering for their huts. Skinny black children playing in the dirt road stopped and stared until their parents scooped them up and ran.

Gosswick and his crew got out and walked the villages, holding guns and machetes. The trigger-happy Maasai shot their rifles toward the sky, mostly to terrorize their long-standing enemies. The rivalry between Kikuyus and Maasai went back hundreds of years. Gosswick tasted the tension of war in the air as he spoke to the chiefs of the surrounding villages and demanded they turn over Abu Khan. When the chiefs acted as if he didn't exist, the mercenaries stormed their huts. They found caches of gold and hidden guns – and took them.

Over the next few weeks, Gosswick's squad made more raids into the villages and skirmished with bands of Khan's men. Standing behind a mounted machine gun on the back of one lorry, Gosswick rattled off continuous shots, mowing down rebels fighting from ditches in a field. Sykes helmed the second gun, his bullets ripping holes through hut walls. Bodies of the slain rebels were then tied to the backs of the bumpers and dragged through the village to send a message.

Nicknamed *Moto Nyoka*, which translated to 'Fire Snake' in Swahili, the brigade with the red-faced demon soldier shooting from the back of a truck became a legend in those parts.

Gosswick got so used to the bloodshed it numbed him. He'd lost count of how many days he'd walked past corpses bleeding on the roads. His men shot at village dogs that fed on the dead. What got to Gosswick were the kids peering through the wooden bars of their huts as he and his men lined up their fathers and executed them. Children lost their mothers, too, when the women foolishly tried to protect their husbands.

After six months of senseless killing, Gosswick began to question if the Black Ghost ever existed. Perhaps he was only a figment conjured by a corrupt businessman who feared his own shadow.

On his days off, Gosswick drove into the Kakamega town and drank the horrors away at a bar. Across the street was an orphanage. There were always kids giggling and playing in the streets, reminding him of his sins. If there'd been anywhere else to go, he would have. He recognized some of the children, whose parents he'd killed. They didn't seem to recognize him without his war paint. Still guilt began to eat at Gosswick like a cancer. He brought the children sweets. Excited, they would crowd around him, patting his pockets for treats. He played hopscotch and stickball, even secretly donated some of his pay to the orphanage.

Until one day Skinner's spies made a horrible discovery – Khan's rebels were running the orphanage, hiding guns there and possibly the Black Ghost himself. Skinner ordered Gosswick and his men to raid the building. When their brigade of trucks rolled into town, Gosswick's crew faced twenty small boys and girls who could barely lift the pistols and rifles they'd been given. The children lined up on the sidewalk in front of their building like miniature soldiers. Not one was older than twelve and a few were as young as five. The sight was so absurd that Sykes cracked a joke about Khan recruiting pygmies. The other soldiers chuckled.

Standing behind his mounted Lewis gun, sweat beading on his forehead in the dry heat, Gosswick yelled for Abu Khan to come out. No one answered. He studied the dirt-crusted windows of the two-story building, and then his gaze returned to its young sentries. One of the little girls rubbed her eyes as if ready for a nap. The other children watched the brigade, some squinting into the sun, a few straining to hold their guns upright.

Gosswick hadn't wanted to fight them. He'd even tried talking them into dropping their weapons.

But one of the nervous orphan boys fired a shot. It may even have been a mistake. Gosswick would never know. The bullet pinged off the barrel of his machine gun and something in him came alive, a soldier's reflex. Gosswick unleashed the Lewis gun. When it was over, he had slaughtered all twenty-two children.

The Black Ghost was never found.

Every night the dead children haunted Gosswick's dreams. They giggled, tossed the ball with him, felt his pockets for treats.

Now, standing on this impossible island of graves, he feared he might be going mad. He heard the Kikuyu children giggling in the dark. Out in the swamp, beyond the ring of their lights, the giggles turned to screams. The staccato sounds of machine-gun fire rattled in a long burst. Gosswick clamped his hands over his ears.

No one else seemed to hear anything – the children or gunfire. The others quietly explored the vast graveyard, lost in their own thoughts.

The machine-gun fire ended abruptly. Gosswick strained his eyes back at the swamp forest. The spiky trees began to spin in circles around the island. He knelt on one of the mounds. His fingers touched a bony leg, and he recoiled. He stared at his trembling hand.

Sykes put a hand on his shoulder. "You all right, Captain?"

"Do you remember what we did to the Kikuyu?"

His most loyal soldier looked at all the graves and nodded. His face remained as hard and stoic as ever.

"How does it not get to you?" Gosswick asked.

Sykes faced him and stared with cold eyes. "Killing's just part of the job."

★   ★   ★

Ely walked with Dyfan through the garden of tombstones.

"I see the will-o'-the-wisp," the psychic whispered. He hurried to a tombstone and stroked the engraved words, his fingers pausing over each letter. "It's hers, isn't it?"

Ely wiped away lichen, revealing Celtic designs and an epitaph. "Gwendolyn Arwen Penrose, 1895–1930. Maker of divine music. A goddess who loved a mortal."

Dyfan closed his eyes and smiled. "When my wife used to play her violin, her music took me to faraway, enchanted places." He tilted his head. "Do you hear that?"

The blind man stood and faced the water. "My Gwendolyn's out there. I can hear her bow caressing the strings." Tears fell as he moved his head in time to an imaginary concerto.

Ely listened. He heard nothing beyond the occasional crackle of branches. Then he swore he heard someone calling his name, only it wasn't a woman but a man with a heavy smoker's voice that he recognized. "Ely..."

The hairs rose at the nape of his neck. Ely slowly turned and began walking toward the voice. At the center of the graveyard he came upon a long wooden box filled with soil. The moist dirt moved with pale worms.

Impossible.

The sight of the box took Ely back to a terrible time in his childhood, when he spent a summer near Monk Lakes, living and working at Mr. Garrick's worm farm. Behind the farmer's house stretched a long, one-story structure with a curved roof and rock walls covered in dead vines. The only light came from several broken windows, holes in the arched ceiling, and a few light bulbs hanging twenty feet apart. The cavernous interior, which had once housed barrels of wine, was now lined with long, open wooden boxes filled with soil and every kind of species of earthworm and grub. Ely had fed the worms, made sure their dirt bedding stayed moist, and captured them for the local fishermen who bought them as bait. Sometimes, when Ely took a break to read a comic book, Mr. Garrick would get onto him. "You need to feed the worms, boy!" Then he'd roll up the comic book and hit Ely on the head. "Back to work."

The heavy-smoking farmer had always stunk of tobacco and sweat. He worked hard during the day and drank hard at night. He took great pride in his worm farm. "Got the largest assortment of worms in the whole of England," he often boasted to customers. "European night crawlers, red wigglers.... If they squirm, I got 'em."

At the very back, he had one special dirt box filled with white worms that fascinated Ely. These were longer and fatter than the brown earthworms. Valuable, too, because Mr. Garrick imported them from India. When he found out Ely wasn't selling the white worms, the farmer whipped him with a garden hose. Ely had suffered so many bruises he could barely sleep for days.

A scrawny lad who had been raised by a single mother, Ely had been impressionable and eager to have a father figure. At first, he believed he deserved to be disciplined. He had looked up to Mr. Garrick and desperately wanted to please him. The farmer took advantage of this and more than once beat Ely. "Every boy needs discipline. Sufferin' a bit of pain will make a man outta you."

The hose whippings became more frequent and severe. One day, while Mr. Garrick was getting drunk, Ely shoveled out several worms and stomped on them. Mr. Garrick saw the mess and chased him through the compost barn. "I'll kill you, you little shit!"

Ely tried to get away, but the man was faster and stronger. He pinned the boy down and stuffed dirt and worms into his mouth. As Ely choked, Mr. Garrick got up and started to walk away. Ely, crying and spitting dirt and bits of worm, grabbed a shovel and struck the bastard on the side of the head. His boss fell to the ground. Blood covering his ear, Mr. Garrick tried to crawl away. A rage Ely didn't know he had in him took over, and he brought down the shovel, over and over, and smashed the farmer's head in, killing him. Afraid of what would happen if anyone found out, Ely buried the body in the crate with the white worms. Then he ran away and caught a train to Dartford, where his mother lived. Months later, the newspaper reported that Mr. Garrick's skeleton had been found buried with hundreds of fat white worms. There was brief mention of a teen who had worked for Garrick, but none of the customers knew Ely's last name or where he might have gone. Thankfully his boss had run a dodgy business and paid Ely only in cash. The farmer had been deep in debt with mobsters, so police decided hit men must have killed him.

Memories of that traumatic summer had stayed with Ely. Now, he trembled as he stared down at the lidless, wooden crate filled with soil and squirming white worms. Somehow it had manifested in this cemetery. He kicked the frame to make sure it wasn't an illusion. His boot struck solid wood.

"Ely Platt..." the smoker's voice rasped again. The dirt in the box shifted. A mouth that no longer had lips said, "You can't escape me, boy..."

★   ★   ★

For Imogen, crossing the island's graveyard made her heart ache. Sobs rose in her throat for several tombstones she discovered, each marked with the names from her childhood: the dozen staff members who had worked at her parents' house, among them her favorites – Mr. Kent; Mr. Edwin; young Rory; the cook, Miss Beatrix, and her helper, Mabel; nanny, Miss Emily – and at last her parents, William and Cora Riley. All the people Imogen had abandoned in the fire.

Guilt and grief filled her heart until she could barely breathe. She knelt between her mum's and dad's graves, side by side, just like at the cemetery back home. Somehow it was replicated here, mixed in with graves that others in the group recognized.

Caleb found Imogen. He read her parents' epitaphs and knelt beside her. His quiet presence reassured her.

"Did you find your family here too?" she asked.

"Not mine," was all he said, but she could tell something had bothered him deeply.

★   ★   ★

The group gathered finally at the center of the island where the orb hung suspended, the only benevolent entity in this godforsaken realm. Caleb assumed the illuminated sphere must be an angel sent to guide them through the valley of death.

Caleb had no explanation for the existence of this impossible graveyard. He was still disturbed by the two headstones he'd found etched with familiar Greek names: Nikolai and Christoph, the deep-sea divers he'd watched die in the Blue Hole. How could they be buried here among Imogen's family, Trummel's sister, Dyfan's wife? Gosswick and Sykes claimed to be responsible for a large number of the graves. A realization suddenly dawned on Caleb. This cemetery wasn't a resting place for loved ones who'd passed. It was a repository for the sins Caleb and the others had committed.

In Catholic school, he'd learned about purgatory. Father Victor, the school's headmaster, had told the students, "Nothing unclean shall enter the kingdom of heaven. After you die, your soul must purge its sins."

The surrounding branches shook. A drifting fog shrouded parts of the swamp. Pale faces appeared in the mist, just beyond the branches. There must have been fifty or more dead souls out there. As the fog began to roll across the island, swallowing crosses and tombstones, the dead came with it.

CHAPTER FORTY-TWO

Trummel searched for a way to retreat, but the haze disoriented him. The glowing orb floated above them, a passive observer. Had it guided them here to suffer among the dead? Was this the end of their journey?

"Nathan…" The voice was thin, girlish.

Trummel turned. Nell had risen from the swamp. She wore the same white dress from the day she'd been murdered. The soaked fabric clung to her body. Blood stained the bodice. She stood just yards from Trummel, her feet planted in the dark water. "Let's play hide-and-seek," she called. Water dribbled from her mouth with each word. But the voice was Nell's.

From the trees behind her came a singsong whistle. Trummel felt an icy coldness at his core as if he were still a boy traumatized by seeing his sister's killer. Göran Järvi, thick-bearded and wild-eyed, stepped from the mist and placed his dirty hands on Nell's shoulders. Then the fog covered their ghosts.

Trummel turned to the orb. "Take me out of here!"

As if understanding, the ball of light flew to the water's edge and started into the swamp. Trummel chased after it.

★ ★ ★

Lost in the fog, separated from the others, Ely worked his way through the cemetery. Where had everybody gone? He called out their names, but no one responded. A winding path led him into an arched rock structure covered in brown, leafless vines.

"Hello, anybody in here?" His voice reverberated off ancient stone walls. The deep interior stretched far beyond the beam of his light. A pungent smell of mildew and damp earth filled his nose. What he'd thought were the ruins of a crypt now resembled a familiar place straight from his nightmares. His mouth hanging open in shock and disbelief, he walked among several open wooden boxes filled with dirt. They stretched the length of the compost barn.

The smooth soil began to wriggle with earthworms. Ely's muscles and joints locked up as he gasped. The mere sight of worms terrified him after what he'd experienced as a lad. The night crawlers poking out their eyeless heads seemed to know he was there, turning toward him as if controlled by one mind.

In the box to his right, the dirt tremored and cracked. A pair of bony hands broke the surface and gripped the sides of the box. Mr. Garrick's corpse rose out of the soil. Dirt and white worms tumbled off his foul-smelling body. Damp clothing hung on his bones in tatters.

Ely remained petrified as a shameful warmth trickled down his leg.

Mr. Garrick's corpse stepped out of the box and lumbered toward him with a lurching gait, flogging his own thigh with a three-foot length of rubber garden hose. "Come suffer your lashings, you little shit..."

Ely yelped and turned to run. The nozzle of the hose struck his shoulder. He cried out. The second lash crossed his back. The fiery stings awakened old scars. He tried to get away. He stumbled between the pine boxes, enduring an agony of whips across his neck, spine, and lower back. Ely's feet slid in the mud. He fell hard on his side. Mr. Garrick jumped onto his chest, pinning him to the ground. "You need to feed the worms, boy..." A cluster of slimy white tongues extended from Mr. Garrick's mouth and brushed Ely's face. The feelers took hold, biting his cheeks like leeches.

Screaming, he pushed his boss's rotten head away with the sound of cracking neck bone. He wriggled out from under the farmer's corpse and scrambled to his feet. The blood-sucking worms still clung to Ely's face. He ripped them off, tearing skin. He ran toward the doorway, feeling a burn on his cheeks where bite wounds beaded with blood. Only when he was out of the worm barn and back into the field of headstones did he dare look back. Mr. Garrick stood twenty yards away, his head hanging crooked on his neck. "You can't escape what you did, boy. Run all you want. I'll find you."

Ely burst into a sprint. He had to find the others. Had to get far away from here. The mist cleared for a few feet near the water's edge. He found Dyfan wandering aimlessly knee-deep in the swamp. Behind a veil of fog, a dead woman emerged from the thorny trees and was walking toward Dyfan with the same stiff gait as Mr. Garrick.

She spoke something in a language that might have been Scottish Gaelic.

"Gwyn, is that you, love?" Dyfan called.

Ely charged into the water and grabbed the blind man before the woman could reach him. "Come with me." Ely dragged his friend back to shore.

Dyfan fought against him. "I must be with my wife."

"It's not her," Ely said, seeing other stiff figures materializing from the fog. Mr. Garrick joined them, whipping his thigh with the hose.

Ely pulled Dyfan. "More of the dead are coming. Let's go!"

Together, they walked fast through the cemetery, toward a beacon of light up ahead.

★   ★   ★

On the far side of the island, Captain Gosswick and Corporal Sykes found themselves wandering out of the cemetery and into a tribal village of thatch-roof huts shrouded in the mist. The very sight of the slat-walled structures filled Gosswick with dread. At the center of the village loomed a post where Gosswick's men had tied the Kikuyu chief and executed him in front of his tribe. The elder's eye sockets were black hollows after crows had plucked out his eyes.

Sykes stared up at him. "How can we be back in Kenya?"

Gosswick shook his head, too shocked to speak.

The chief raised his skull and shouted a war cry. More voices cried out from the darkness. As the fog thinned just beyond the huts, thirty or more dark-skinned Kikuyu emerged from all directions. The men carried spears and shields. Their bullet-riddled faces exposed teeth and bone. The bald women wore bloodstained skirts and bead necklaces. The tribe ranged around the village in a loose formation, but the outer reaches were tightening, encircling the soldiers. Gosswick and Sykes stood back to back, guns raised.

The chief cried out again and the tribe of dead Kikuyu howled with him. A spear flew through the air and narrowly missed Gosswick's shoulder. He and Sykes ran in opposite directions. Gosswick hid behind a hut as more spears struck the walls and ground.

The slow-moving dead ambled toward him on rotten limbs. Every walking corpse opened its jaws and released the screams of dying men and women. A thick wall of fog rolled in and engulfed the village. Short bursts of machine-gun fire echoed all around. Gosswick watched as horrific scenes played within the whirling smoke…shadow figures of British mercenaries and Maasai warriors raced through the huts shooting and hacking every Kikuyu man and woman who fought back. Crying children ran in the chaos. A bald soldier with red face paint jumped out of the smoke and charged toward Gosswick. He stumbled backward and fell into a deep pit. The stench of rotting death burned his nostrils. Gosswick's headlamp had gone out, casting his world into gloom. All he could see was swirling fog overhead, half lit by an unseen moon. He hit his caving helmet until the lamp's beam split the darkness. He was sitting in a large mass grave of black corpses. The aftermath of his death squad's bloodiest slaughter lay in twisted heaps all around him. At least fifty dead. Swarms of flies dotted the decaying flesh. Amid jutting limbs and broken rib cages were lifeless faces with gray eyes rolled back and jaws hanging open.

Standing at the edge of the pit, Gosswick's red-faced double stared down at him. The maniacal soldier he'd run away from, had drunk countless whiskeys to forget, grinned with a murderous gleam in his eyes. Gosswick aimed a shaky pistol at his former self.

The devil-faced mercenary raised his machine gun and shouted, "*Shetani mekundu!*" Then he raced off into the fog. The gunfire and screams faded away.

Gosswick couldn't stop trembling. Where was Sykes? He called the soldier's name. Only gibbering moans answered back. The dead began to writhe beneath him. Hands clawed at his arms and legs, groped his head. Gosswick screamed and fought to break loose, but the corpses clung to him. He felt himself sinking beneath them.

"Sykes! Help!"

A Kikuyu warrior with all his teeth exposed crawled over a pile of bodies toward Gosswick. He kicked the skeletal chest to keep the dead man at bay. The warrior raised a knife. His skull exploded with the boom of a gunshot. The body toppled over beside Gosswick.

Sykes jumped down into the pit. He smashed a few more skulls with the butt of his submachine gun as he made his way to where crawling corpses half buried Gosswick. The burly soldier kicked several aside and helped Gosswick to his feet. Together they shot at the dead rising around them. Bullets tore through flesh, chipped bone off exposed skulls. Bodies fell left and right. Gosswick and his best soldier cleared a path, crushing bones and human muck with their boots as they ran over a floor of moving corpses.

Gosswick reached the edge of the pit first. "Give me a boost."

Sykes helped him climb out. The fog began to brighten. The ball of light floated up above Gosswick. A welcome sight, the orb signaled to follow and then drifted over the trees.

As he turned to help Sykes out of the pit, the soldier cried out. A spear stabbed through his right leg. All around the grave mangled bodies stood.

Sykes cursed. "Help! Get me out of here!"

Gosswick tried to shoot the encroaching dead, but his gun clicked empty. More spears skewered Sykes, piercing his stomach and shoulder. In seconds the horde inside the pit swarmed him from all sides. Wild-eyed with terror, he shrieked for Gosswick to pull him out. The captain watched helplessly from the edge of the grave as the dead Kikuyu crowded on top of Sykes.

God, they're eating him alive. As Sykes's screams were replaced by the sounds of teeth chomping flesh, Gosswick fled to save himself. He ran into the center of the village and froze. Twenty dead Kikuyu children stepped out of the huts, giggling.

Gosswick backed away, shaking. Something touched him from behind. He spun around to find an emaciated child. Dirt caked the boy's eye sockets and smudged his cheeks, but his dark skin was smooth, except for the scar by his left ear. This was Matu, the boy Gosswick had saved from the bullies in the market at Kakamega. One of the first to fall when Gosswick gunned down the orphans.

Now the slaughtered children clicked their teeth. They started closing in, begging, "Treats, treats." Their little hands reached for Gosswick.

He stumbled backward, away from Matu and the crowd of other children. He turned and ran toward the glowing orb, weaving through a field of wooden crosses as more in the ground awakened.

★   ★   ★

In the chaos of the fog and phantoms, Caleb and Imogen hurried across the cemetery, searching for the others. Sounds of feet squishing through mud echoed in the haze to their left. Caleb glimpsed corpses with burnt faces, still smoking as if they'd stepped fresh from a fire. They were coming for Imogen.

She stood paralyzed. "Daddy..." Her voice broke.

A well-dressed man with a half-scorched skull stepped around a tombstone, slowly walking toward her.

Caleb pushed Imogen to run. She resisted.

"None of this is real," Caleb told her. "It's some kind of test."

She nodded absently, still watching the burnt corpse.

"We have to keep moving," Caleb urged.

She nodded again, but this time she took Caleb's arm and ran with him down the center of the cemetery. The island tapered into a thin strip of land that stretched through the swamp. On either side, the mist closed in, bringing its undead horrors with it.

Ahead, the orb shone bright through the trees. Caleb saw Trummel reach it first, then Ely, Dyfan, and Gosswick. Imogen and Caleb arrived last. No one spoke as they gathered. The orb seemed to count their number. Then it started off again. The explorers waded into the water and worked their way through a tangled channel of mangroves. Branches crackled all around. Swishing helmet lights spotlighted pale faces just beyond the thicket of trees.

At the rear of the group, Caleb ignored the hollow moans behind him as he waded through waist-deep water. He weaved through cloying branches, wishing he had a machete. He heard splashing behind him. Fog covered the island now and drifted through the channel. Rotted bodies walked stiff-limbed into the water after them.

Bubbles formed in the water close to Caleb. He backed away, but they followed. Then two men in deep-sea diving suits rose from the water. Caleb shone his light over the round faceplates of their helmets. The bloated decomposing faces of Christoph and Nicolai stared blankly back at him.

Caleb kicked backward, fighting against the water and clawing branches of the mangroves. He pushed a floating log between himself and the undead divers, then hurried into the mangroves to catch up with the others.

Imogen had waited for him. "Hurry!" She held up a large overhanging branch.

Caleb hurried beneath it, dropping the branch behind them. Together, they moved driftwood, creating a barrier between them and the dead. Caleb and Imogen slogged through an obstacle course of mud, logs, and crisscrossing branches.

At the end of the channel, the trees opened onto a wider body of water with only a few trees spaced apart. The orb shot across the lake, lighting the way to another shore a hundred yards out.

They started across through hip-deep water, passing bone-white trees that stood like sentinels. Caleb stumbled and fell into a hole, sinking, the mud pulling him underwater. Imogen turned back, found his arm in the murk, and pulled with more force than he would've thought possible.

They were the last to reach shore, collapsing onto solid land beside the others. Caleb gripped Imogen's hand. Dyfan stared forward, trembling. Ely was crying. Trummel looked shell-shocked. Gosswick had turned pale and struggled to light a cigarette. And Sykes was missing. Only six of their team had made it through the swamp.

In the distance, echoed whispers and moans. Branches shook from the other side of the fog, but the dead remained within the briar woods.

CHAPTER FORTY-THREE

Shining as brightly as the North Star, the white orb led them up a hill to a giant round door embedded in a cliff wall. Like the previous gate, this one was sealed. A nook on the left side housed another seated stone guardian. This demon statue had the body of a man with the head of a rabbit. Like the previous gazelle-headed statue, the rabbit guardian's legs were bent at the knees and pulled close to its chest. A codex key of stone buttons lined the wall beneath its perch.

Imogen searched the codes written at the back of the diary. She studied the sequences, translating them.

Caleb leaned close. "You've found something."

"Maybe. The codes seem to align with drawings of the gate guardians from the Papyrus of Ani. Grandfather made small drawings of them in his journal. Each has the first three letters of code beneath it." She showed Caleb the drawings of various Egyptian demons seated with their knees bent.

Imogen shook her head, amazed. "They're clues to the gates' puzzles but not the whole answer. Opening each gate is still a guessing game, but his hints will narrow the choices."

"Can you open this one?" Trummel sounded impatient.

Imogen studied the cipher on the wall, then flipped through the pages until she found a drawing of the rabbit guardian. She memorized the three symbols beneath, then flipped back to the pages filled with codes and searched for a match. Six names started with the same three symbols. She guessed at the first sequence and then braced herself for a booby trap. Nothing happened. Her fingers shook as she entered a second sequence. Still nothing. She pictured Grandfather standing at this door, his brow furrowed as he tried to solve the riddle. *Which one is it, Grandfather?* It would have helped immensely if he'd drawn all the guardians together with the codes and names, but had the diary fallen into other hands, he would have given some stranger the key to Duat.

Instead he'd left the information in a riddle that he thought Imogen could solve. She studied the rest of the options. A smile tugged at the corners of her mouth as she recognized one of the names. Grandfather had said something like it when she saw him last. *"Go forth, Immy, but be wary like the rabbit, always alert of face."* She'd thought it strange at the time. But there was a lot strange about Grandfather after the Nebenteru Expedition, so she'd let it go. She pushed in the stones that matched the fourth set of symbols and called out the name "One Who Is Alert of Face." The stone rabbit's head nodded, and then the gate's door turned to liquid.

"Well done," Caleb said.

The white orb, reflecting in the gate's mirror, glowed bright as if pleased. Then it flew across the swamp like a shooting star and disappeared.

"I guess we're on our own," Imogen said.

On the other side of the gate, a long circular passage burrowed through the rock. While Imogen waited for everyone to step through the portal and regroup, she emptied water out of her hiking boots.

Ely did the same. "My feet felt like bricks were tied to them." His face was still red from crying. He sniffled and wiped his nose.

"Are you okay?" Imogen asked.

"Shaken up, actually. What I saw back there..." The student shuddered. "I think this place is making me crazy."

"You aren't alone," Imogen said. "I think we're all going a bit nuts."

This brought a smile to Ely's face.

"All right, teatime's over," Gosswick barked. Those were the first words he'd spoken since losing Sykes. Gosswick had walked off by himself and smoked a cigarette, then returned with a hardened expression. Despite their differences, Imogen felt sorry for Gosswick. He'd lost every one of his soldiers.

Carrying fire torches, Gosswick and Trummel took the lead. Following Caleb, Imogen fell in line with the others. Ely, who still looked after Dyfan, brought up the rear. This new cave they crossed through was tube-shaped. It reminded Imogen of the London Underground. She could almost imagine a train bearing down.

"Where do you think this leads?" Ely asked.

Imogen shrugged. "At least it's a straight shot for a change."

Gosswick and Trummel, who never once stopped to rest, walked fifty yards ahead. It was mostly dark in the tunnel, since they were saving their batteries. The flames from their torches rippled light on the curved walls. That they hadn't encountered any threat allowed Imogen to relax a little. Condensation beaded the ceiling and plinked into tiny pools. Cool drops fell on her helmet and shoulders. Soon everybody's boots were splashing through ankle-deep water, and the tube seemed more like a sewer channel. They'd already walked about a kilometer without seeing any offshoots.

With nowhere to go but forward, the group walked at their own pace for a long stretch. Imogen, Dyfan, and Ely occasionally chatted to fill the time. Caleb, who'd grown quiet, walked a few feet ahead. Imogen wondered what he might be thinking about, but didn't pry.

Sloshing through the shallow water, she thought she heard rustling noises coming from above. She stopped and looked back at Dyfan and Ely. "Do you hear something in the walls?"

Ely held his torch up and Imogen switched on her helmet light. Holes pocked the rock walls and ceiling. At first she saw nothing, just heard crackling sounds coming from the walls. Then pale worms emerged from the holes. Their segmented bodies stretched out from the walls and ceiling like feelers. One touched the back of Ely's neck.

"Oh, God," he cried out and slapped the thing away.

Splashing sounds echoed all around. Worms poured out of the holes by the dozen, as if the walls were hemorrhaging their entrails.

Walking backward, Ely switched on his headlamp. He played his light over a writhing mound that had formed in the tunnel behind them. "What the hell is that?" The mass of worms grew quickly as more sloughed off the walls and attached to it.

Ely pushed Dyfan and Imogen. "*Move! Move!*"

The three of them raced through a gauntlet of feelers that slowed them down. White worms continued to disgorge from the tunnel walls, splashing in piles beside Imogen's feet. Some were a foot long and resembled eyeless albino snakes. Something thumped onto her helmet and roped onto her shoulders. She pulled off a handful of the slimy creatures and slung them against a wall, but not before she felt a sharp sting on her palm. "They bite."

A long worm dropped on Ely's arm. By the time he ripped it off it had left a bloody welt. "Christ, they've got teeth."

The tunnel's pocked holes continued to fill up like maggoty wounds. Soon the squirming mound behind them was taller than Ely. It moved toward them through the water. Imogen and Dyfan fled as fast as they could. The tunnel floor, now cluttered with fleshy ropes, dragged at their ankles. Imogen had to stop several times to pull worms off her legs. Caleb arrived and helped her and Dyfan. Feelers reached toward them from all around, moving like curious snake heads.

Caleb stabbed his torch at the walls. The worms hissed.

"Help!" Ely's voice sounded behind them.

Imogen turned back to help. Ely was knee-deep in the squirming mass. "They're biting me!" he cried. "They're eating my legs!"

More worms roped down from the ceiling, covering Ely's head, his shoulders.

"What can I do?" Dyfan groped blindly.

Imogen tried to scrape the creatures off Ely but they clung as though bound. "Grab a hand," she told Dyfan. "Help me pull him free."

As they worked to free Ely, the mound of white worms behind him towered nearly to the ceiling. The horror drifted closer. Several of its tangles flicked out like tongues.

Caleb helped Imogen and Dyfan. They tugged in unison, the worms biting them as they worked to free Ely. Imogen's neck, shoulders, and hands were on fire. Her beam spotlighted the mound looming over Ely. In the middle, the worms parted, revealing a man's slime-covered face. He called out, "Feed the worms, boy..."

Looking over his shoulder, Ely yelped and swung his torch, trying to burn the man inside the mass. Several tentacles shot out from the mound and wrapped around Ely's arms and head. His torch fell onto the squirming floor and sputtered out. He began wailing.

"What's happening?" Dyfan cried.

Imogen watched helplessly as the writhing mass pulled Ely into it. He howled in pain, kicking and fighting to break free.

Caleb grabbed Dyfan and Imogen, pulling them away. "We can't save him."

Ely's blood splattered the white mass as the worms devoured him. He'd stopped fighting. The man inside the hill of worms pulled Ely deeper into it. Feeding sounds echoed in the tunnel. Ely's lifeless face came to the surface once – bloody welts crisscrossed his cheeks, his eyelids – then he vanished in the tangles.

All around them the worms retreated, slinking back into holes. The towering mass backed away and disappeared into the dark tunnel.

Imogen stood frozen. Dyfan wept soundlessly. Caleb tugged both of their arms. "He's gone. We have to go!"

Trummel and Gosswick were splashes of light on water far up the tunnel. Imogen and Caleb each took one of Dyfan's arms, and walked quickly. In the tunnel ahead, the torches of the others winked out all at once.

"Where did they go?" Caleb said.

Imogen was too exhausted to think. The beam of her headlamp bounced over the shin-deep water and up the walls. Thankfully all the worms had left. She hurt all over. The bites throbbed. Dyfan was heavy and her side ached, but she kept walking at a brisk pace.

A wall rose ahead in her beam, blocking the tunnel. It glinted, light on water, their reflections drawing nearer. "It's a liquid door," she shouted. "That's where the others went."

Passing through the door felt like running beneath an icy waterfall. On the other side, they stepped onto a rocky bank that glistened with drips of water. A shallow stream trickled nearby. Beyond that was more cavernous dark.

At least they were out of the worm tunnel and seemed safe for the moment.

Everyone but Trummel and Gosswick was bleeding from small bites.

Imogen shot the two men a glare. "Thanks for helping us back there."

"We were too far ahead," Trummel said. "Had you all kept up—"

"Don't say it," Imogen said, cutting him off. "Just don't."

Trummel clamped his mouth shut and looked away, his jaw tight.

While the five of them sat on boulders by the stream, washing wounds and drinking from canteens, they took a moment to mourn the loss of Ely. Dyfan said a prayer for him. After a short rest, Trummel had them moving again. On the other side of the stream, he led the way along a narrow path that wove between tall stalagmites. At the top of each of them, stone branches connected to a spiky ceiling covered in white webs.

Dyfan halted. "Wait! I feel a terrible menace in this realm. We should turn back."

"There's no other way but to follow this path forward," Trummel said. He shone his light into Dyfan's cataract gray eyes. "Unless you want to go back through that tunnel and end up worm food, like Ely, I suggest you move your damn legs."

"How can you be so callous?" Imogen asked Trummel.

"I have no patience with stragglers. Anyone who slows us down is putting us all at risk."

"Logic would say there's more danger in moving too hastily."

"There's little point in debating with you, Imogen. No matter what, you always have to have the last word."

"Only because you're too thickheaded to listen."

Trummel turned and forged ahead. He and Gosswick walked at a brisk pace, expecting the others to keep up.

Imogen let out an exasperated growl. The others abandoned Dyfan. Without Ely to guide him, the blind man seemed lost. "Stay with me, Dyfan. I'll look after you." She placed his hand on her shoulder and walked in front of him. She felt him shivering as he stayed close, matching her every step.

"What are you sensing?" she asked.

"I can't get a clear vision of it," Dyfan said. "But I feel a sadness knotting my chest. Deep grief. I haven't felt this way since…"

Caleb paused. "Am I going crazy, or do I hear music?"

"I hear it too," Imogen said.

"It's coming from back in there." Twenty paces ahead, Trummel stopped too and shined his light into the dark forest of rocky spires. Everyone paused and listened. A sad and haunting concerto seemed to come from a single violin.

"It's the damnedest thing," Gosswick muttered.

Dyfan's eyes teared up. "It's Chopin's 'Nocturne'."

"What's it coming from?" Imogen asked.

"Gwendolyn!" Dyfan broke away from her and stepped off the path. Feeling his way through the stalagmites, he hurried toward the source of the music.

"No, come back here." Imogen started after him, meandering through the clustered poles of rock. Several times she had to turn sideways to squeeze through some narrow places. For a small blind man, Dyfan moved fast, desperately calling out his wife's name. As they combed their way through this cave forest, the violin music seemed to speed up, the bow dragging harshly across the strings and creating sharp, violent chords.

Imogen reached a clearing covered in spiderwebs. The ground was so white it looked blanketed with cotton. As Dyfan walked across it, toward the music, the webbing that stretched between the stalagmites vibrated.

"Dyfan, stop!" She rushed across the clearing. Just as she grabbed his arm, he stepped on a soft patch of ground that gave way. He fell into a dark hole, pulling Imogen down with him.

CHAPTER FORTY-FOUR

Imogen and Dyfan dropped twelve feet and landed on a soft, padded floor. The impact was hard enough to knock the wind out of her. Dyfan lay beside her, cursing. "Are you okay?" he asked.

"Nothing broken." The sudden drop had startled her more than it hurt. "How about you?"

"Fine, I guess," Dyfan said, "except for these bloody webs."

Everything they touched clung to them in sticky strands.

"Spiders!" Dyfan began to hyperventilate and slap at invisible spiders. "Get them off me! Get them off!"

Imogen gripped his arms. "Calm down. I don't see any spiders. Just cobwebs."

Wheezing, he sucked in deep breaths and finally slowed his breathing. It was during a moment of silence that Imogen realized that the music had stopped. Had the web itself lured them here? She looked up at the glittering white, webbed funnel they'd fallen through.

From above, beams spotlighted them. The others gathered around the top of the hole. Caleb called down, asking if they were okay.

"We're both fine," Imogen said. "Just took a bit of a tumble."

"Can you climb out of there?" Trummel asked.

"I don't know. I'll give it a go." Imogen tried climbing, but the cotton-candy wall just ripped away. "I don't see any way to climb back up."

"Stay put then," Gosswick yelled. "I'll have a rope down in a jiff."

Caleb leaned over the hole. "What's down there?"

Imogen's beam panned out across a cavernous tunnel woven in white webs. Only it wasn't a natural cave. "Oh my…I must be hallucinating. It seems like we've fallen into a sitting room of a house. I see an antique sofa, coffee table, a small dinner table and chairs, a fireplace, windows with curtains."

Everything was covered with gossamer threads that glittered.

Dyfan reached out and touched a rocking chair. It squeaked as it rocked. "I don't think you're hallucinating."

As he and Imogen walked about the room, a wood floor creaked beneath their boots. A section of it was covered with a faded rug.

Dyfan felt his way around the velvet-textured furniture. "This feels strangely familiar."

Imogen wiped cobwebs off a framed photo. Her heart nearly stopped. "Dyfan, there's a picture here of you and a woman."

"Impossible."

"I swear it's you. You're dressed in a brown plaid suit and bowler hat. Your beard and hair are shorter, but there's no question that's your face."

"Describe the woman to me."

"She's thin and beautiful with long, wavy hair and lots of freckles on her face. She's wearing a dark velvet dress and holding a violin."

Dyfan gasped and took the picture from her. "I recognize this frame. The corner has a nick from when I dropped it." His eyes grew moist as his fingers caressed the photo. "This was taken in Edinburgh at the night of my wife's last concert. When Gwendolyn played her violin, there was not a dry eye in the house."

The sad music began playing again, so hauntingly beautiful that it stirred up the grief in Imogen's chest. It was coming from another part of the house.

"She's here." Dyfan dropped the picture and started down a hallway.

"Wait." Imogen gripped his shoulder.

"I have to go to her. Gwendolyn's not well. She needs me."

"No, we should stay near the hole."

"I was called back to my house for a reason," he argued. "I won't go any further until I know her spirit is at rest."

Imogen grabbed a log poker from the fireplace. "Let me lead then."

With Dyfan following, Imogen crept down a long hallway. She passed two closed doors. The music seemed to be playing in a room at the end of the hall. More framed photos hung on the walls.

"I see pictures of you and Gwendolyn on your wedding day," Imogen told him. "And one out in the country of you posing with a gray Scottish deerhound."

"That was Calla," Dyfan said fondly. "She was a good dog. Had her fifteen years. Calla died not long after Gwendolyn."

"I don't know how it's possible we're in a house with your photos."

Dyfan felt the plaster walls. "It's definitely my old home. I knew every crack and creak of this place." Halfway down the hall, he pushed open a door that smelled strongly of dried flowers. "This room was my herb room."

Her light shone across shelves of dusty jars. Bushels of dried sage hung from the ceiling. Imogen was about to ask what he used this room for, when the hypnotic music coming from the far room turned into short, harsh chords. The bow strokes quickened as Imogen and Dyfan moved toward the sound. Cobwebs covered the open doorway. As they got within a foot of the door, the music stopped mid-chord. Imogen pushed aside the webs with her poker.

They entered a master bedroom that was covered in silky white threads. What she saw next caused her heart to skip a beat. On a queen bed, propped against pillows and a headboard, sat a frail woman in a nightgown. She looked as if she had died ages ago and had mummified. Spider webs cocooned her legs, enshrouded her torso and arms, and veiled her face like a corpse bride. Her cheeks and throat somehow still had a thick layer of dry flesh. Her eye sockets looked filled with cotton. Wispy red hair dangled around her skull and shoulders. The bedridden woman lay still with her violin propped across her lap.

"Gwen, my love. It's me."

Imogen remained at the foot of the bed, gripping her log poker. "Don't go any closer."

Ignoring her, Dyfan knelt at the side of the bed and took the woman's bony hand. Her head turned slowly to face him. She stared at him for a tense moment.

Dyfan teared up. "I've missed you, too." He behaved as if he was listening, then shook his head. "No, love, I tried my best. I tried everything."

"What's she saying?" Imogen asked.

"She blames me. She won't forgive me unless I lie down with her. Says I belong here with her. You must go, Imogen, while you can. Gwendolyn says to hurry."

"That's complete rubbish, Dyfan." She couldn't bear to leave him behind. "You must finish the expedition with us."

He lowered his head. "I'm not deserving. Gwen says her spirit won't rest until I suffer with her."

A red tear rolled down the webs covering the woman's cheek. *Is she crying blood?* Imogen leaned over the bed for a closer look. No, it wasn't a blood tear but a tiny red spider. It hopped off the woman's face and scurried along her shoulder toward Dyfan.

"Step away from her," Imogen pleaded. "It's a trap. It's not Gwen. It's something pretending to be her."

The woman's corpse pointed her violin bow at Imogen.

"She warned you to get out," Dyfan said. "She warned you."

A ripping sound came from behind Imogen. She turned the beam of her headlamp until it found the source of the noise. Along one wall, several giant round egg sacs hung from the ceiling. They glowed when her light hit them. Hundreds of spindly red legs pressed against the swollen, translucent walls. The tearing sounds were the egg sacs splitting open. Tiny red spiders began to crawl out.

"We need to get out of here *now!*" When Imogen turned back toward the bed, Dyfan's wife was strangling him. He was on his knees, choking, his eyes rolled back to the whites. A horde of spiders spilled from the woman's mouth. They crawled on Dyfan's arms and chest. He jerked his body in terror.

Imogen slammed the iron poker across the corpse's arm, snapping bones.

Dyfan fell to the floor, screaming and slapping the spiders. She helped swat them off with her free hand. A bony hand grabbed her arm. The dead woman's jawbone unhinged and larger spiders dropped out of her throat with hundreds of smaller ones, as if she were regurgitating organs and blood.

Imogen swung the log poker and smacked the skull sideways. The hand released her. She helped Dyfan to his feet. As they bolted for the door, several egg sacs ruptured. Fat crimson spiders scurried out and jumped on her. Dozens of legs moved across her back.

"Shit." Imogen slammed her body against a wall, crushing them. She then pulled Dyfan down the hall with more spiders jumping at their heels. In the sitting room, she tipped over chairs to block the swarm. She didn't stop until she and Dyfan were under the hole where a rope was being lowered down.

"Where did you go?" Caleb asked.

"Never mind. We have to hurry." She quickly wrapped the rope's loop around Dyfan. "Pull him up!"

As Caleb, Trummel, and Gosswick began pulling the blind man up, Imogen heard the clicking of legs behind her. An army of spiders crawled along the floor and walls, coming toward her in red waves.

"Throw me a torch!"

Caleb tossed down his. It landed at her feet. She picked it up and jabbed the fiery end at the creatures that skittered nearest her. The first row of them caught fire and squealed as they died.

The rope dropped through the hole again. She grabbed for it, set the torch on the ground, and started to climb. Hand over hand. Her shoulders strained as she pulled herself up. Caleb was leaning over the mouth of the hole, arm outstretched. She nearly reached him when the rope slipped, dropping her several feet. She dangled over the den, hearing the spiders skitter below.

"What's happening up there?" she called.

Before anyone could answer, she felt the rope go slack. She hit the floor hard.

"Shit, stalagmite broke," Gosswick called. "I'll find another place to tie off."

"Hurry, damn it!" Caleb yelled.

Imogen grabbed the torch off the ground. Now hundreds of spiders crawled on the floor, furniture, and walls of the den. They looked like widows, only solid red with eight white eyes. Amid tiny tick-like ones were some big buggers with bulbous backs the size of her fist. She turned in circles, burning those that got too close, crushing others with her boots. "Please hurry!"

Someone fell through the hole and dropped beside Imogen. She shone her light that way. It was Caleb with a rope around his waist.

The webs covering the furniture began to bounce. The white threaded walls moved like plucked harp strings.

Imogen gripped Caleb. "Did you feel that? Something's coming!"

"You first." He helped her into the loop, then cinched it around her.

Imogen gave Caleb back his torch. "Hurry up after me."

He nodded and yelled, "Pull her up!" Caleb gave Imogen a boost, pushing her up until she was over his head. As Gosswick and Trummel pulled her upward the rest of the way, spiders crawled up the web tunnel walls. One leapt on her chest, crawling toward her neck. She batted it away.

After reaching the top, she rolled over the edge of the opening, gasping for air. Gosswick worked quickly to pull the rope off her. She looked back down into the hole, but all she saw were spiders.

★   ★   ★

Caleb stomped on the damned things and burned several others with his torch. When they scattered, a woman rasped from down the hall. Her web-covered corpse, crawling on bent arms, dragged the lower half of her body across the wood floor. She began to shake violently. Eight red legs pushed out of her cocooned torso and lifted her off the floor.

"Oh, shit!" Caleb took a step back, holding out his torch. From his pocket, he fished out a small bottle of Dyfan's whiskey. Caleb lobbed it at the floor in front of the hallway. The bottle broke, splashing the floorboards and walls. With his torch, he ignited the whiskey and backed away. Fire bloomed in the den, rippling up the walls. On the other side of the flames, the spider woman screeched and backed up in the hallway. The fire spread quicker than expected, burning the sofa. Framed pictures fell of walls.

Caleb coughed as the smoke hit his lungs. He crouched low to the floor where the air was still breathable. All the furniture in the den caught fire. Flames consumed curtains that hung around dusty windows. In all the chaos, a thousand spiders scurried over one another to get away from the spreading inferno. Many of them curled into charred crisps. Some crawled up Caleb's legs. He swatted them off with his hand and burned them with his torch. The wall of heat pressing against him was becoming unbearable.

Precious seconds had passed since Imogen got out. *Where's the damn rope?*

Caleb coughed again. Smoke stung his eyes. If he didn't get out soon, he was going to be consumed by the blaze. To his relief, the rope dropped down. He grabbed it and was about to step into the loop when a god-awful shriek sounded behind him. The woman with spider legs was crawling across the ceiling.

"Christ!" He fell back against the wall and jutted out his torch.

Eight, long skinny legs clicked as the creature moved around the flames. Silk shot out of the spinnerets of its backside, adding more web streamers to the fire. The thing dropped to the floor. The body of it was arachnid, but the head, shoulders, and front arms were shaped like a woman. Singed red hair covered her skull in wisps. At the top of her face, several beady eyes stared at him with hunger.

The creature reared back on its hind legs, exposing white markings on its abdomen. Caleb lunged with the torch and burned its belly. She squealed and retreated. Flames from the burning den scorched her back. The spider woman cried out and leapt toward Caleb. As he fell backward, her abdomen landed impaled on his torch. Her legs clicked around him. She screamed in pain, her mandibles snapping inches from his face.

Caleb jammed the torch deeper into its guts and shoved the creature off. The spider woman writhed on its back as flames burned its innards.

The heat became unbearable. Glowing smoke blinded Caleb. His hands found the rope, and he climbed up it as fast as he could. The others pulled Caleb to the opening. Below his feet, fire was rising up the funnel. When he reached the top, Imogen grabbed his belt and helped roll him away from the smoking hole just as a burst of flames shot out of it. Embers rained down all around.

Caleb sucked fresh air into his lungs.

Imogen knelt beside him and put a hand to his cheek. "I thought we'd lost you."

Caleb coughed and rasped. "Water."

She put a canteen to his lips and he drank a few gulps. Fiery smoke billowed from the hole beside them.

"We have to get away from here," Imogen said. As she helped Caleb to his feet, Dyfan cried out. He'd backed into a giant web that stretched between stalagmites. He shouted, flailing his arms and getting more tangled. Gosswick and Trummel were struggling to pull Dyfan free when a huge red spider, the size of Dyfan's head, shot from the corner of its web straight for them.

Trummel grabbed a knife from a sheath on his hip and stabbed the spider inches from Dyfan's face. The arachnid's spiny legs wriggled on the end of the knife. Trummel slung it to the ground and stepped on it.

Its plump back burst like a melon beneath his boot. Gosswick sawed at the threads to cut Dyfan loose.

Chittering sounds echoed from above. Caleb looked up. "Holy shit!" Thousands more spiders were crawling along the mesh that covered the cave's ceiling. Several were even bigger than the one Trummel had just killed. They dropped from spindles and scurried down stalagmites.

Everyone started running. The group raced a hundred yards back to the path. They followed a wide gully that curved through the cavern forest. Caleb tugged Dyfan forward. Gosswick fired shots at hog-sized creatures that scuttled between the rock poles. Glancing back down the path, Caleb saw nothing but a red moving carpet of clicking legs.

"The gate's just ahead!" Trummel shouted.

They reached another solid stone door. Imogen tore away the webs covering the threshold, revealing an arch with hieroglyphs engraved in the bricks. In a nook sat a cobweb-covered statue of a baboon demon.

"Get it open!" Trummel yelled.

She scanned the pages of codes in her grandfather's journal to work out the riddle.

Dyfan hovered next to her, trembling.

Trummel and Caleb held the growing mass of spiders at bay with two sputtering torches. Gosswick shot one of the hog-sized spiders, sending it rolling backward. More shrieking creatures charged through the dark forest.

Imogen punched in the keys and called out, "Savage-Faced."

By a stroke of luck, the door turned liquid.

"Go! Go!" Caleb ushered the others through the gate. Spiders leapt toward him as he fell backward through the portal.

CHAPTER FORTY-FIVE

Caleb landed beside Trummel. Nothing else attempted to cross the threshold as it turned solid. While the others took a moment to catch their breath, Trummel and Gosswick panned their beams. They had entered a small, domed chamber with smooth stone walls. Four sealed doors led in opposite directions.

"Looks like some kind of juncture between realms," Gosswick said.

The air was warm and dry.

Trummel studied the weary faces of his team's four survivors – Gosswick, Dyfan, Imogen, and Caleb. Trummel said, "That was a close one, but we're safe now. And one realm closer to what we came here for."

"Is that all you can think about?" Dyfan said.

The question angered Trummel. "We have to stay focused on our mission. If we don't, we'll all go mad down here."

"I'm not ready to enter another realm," Imogen said. "Not after what we've just been through."

Dyfan's cataract gray eyes stared in Trummel's direction. "My intuition never warned me we would encounter a realm of spiders. The buggers terrify me." He shuddered.

"Have they always?" Caleb asked.

"Since I was a wee lad. When I was six, I walked into a large web crawling with baby spiders. I got bit a few times on the face. After that I developed a phobia."

Caleb said, "I don't think it's a coincidence that Dyfan has a fear of spiders and we've just traversed a spiders' den."

"What's your point?" Trummel said.

"Duat somehow mimics our most dreaded fears," Caleb said. "Before we began this expedition, Ely showed me a drawing. It resembled the writhing mass of worms that killed him in the tunnel. He said he drew it from his nightmares."

Dyfan said, "Ely told me that when he was a lad, he had worked at a worm farm and the man who ran it had beat him. You're saying the worms in that tunnel were pulled from Ely's memory?"

"Not just his memory," Caleb said. "A deep-rooted fear in his psyche or a traumatic event he experienced. Same with you and the spiders. I've also encountered horrors that are personal to me. These realms turn the things from our nightmares into physical forms."

"Or drag us down to hell," Gosswick muttered. "Years ago Sykes, Quig, Vickers, and I did mercenary work in Kenya. We were at war with the Kikuyu tribe. I lost count how many we killed – men, women, and children. It was a very dark time in my life. Back at the cemetery in the swamp forest, I saw dead Kikuyu rising from their graves." The captain's face shook. "They tore Sykes apart."

"That swamp we crossed through," Trummel said. "It was the very swamp in Finland where my sister died."

"Nell," Imogen said.

Trummel nodded. He had shared his memories of Nell when he and Imogen were close. That forest had haunted his dreams since childhood, but inside Duat it had become a physical reality. "I saw the very spot in the swamp where Nell was murdered. Duat conjured every last detail – her bloodstained dress, the whistle we used to call each other, even the tree where her killer had carved his name into the trunk. That's where I'd found Nell's bloody stockings and shoes. At the cemetery, my sister and her killer were among all the dead who attacked us." Nell and Järvi had not been ghosts here, but undead flesh and bone. It still disturbed Trummel as more suppressed memories surfaced.

After Nell was buried, Nathan's parents had shut down emotionally, focusing on their work and sending him off to boarding school. For the next year, Nathan suffered unbearable heartbreak and night terrors. Göran Järvi became a bogeyman who stalked Nathan in his dreams. The child killer showed him that there were evils in the world. Nell's tragic loss and his parents' abandonment taught Nathan that caring about others made him vulnerable to those evils, and susceptible to excruciating pain. So he closed off his heart and found solace in developing his intellect. Already a bright kid who excelled above his fellow students, he became consumed with his studies and seeking greater knowledge. People no longer mattered. The more knowledge he'd gained, the more powerful he'd felt and eventually the nightmares and grief ended. Trummel's heart became so callous that he forgot what it felt like to have a twin sister. He had thought she was long buried in the recesses of his mind, but seeing her ghost in the swamp had brought back his heartbreak. Trummel would never show weakness to the others, but inside he felt deeply shaken.

"I saw my family too," Imogen said. "Everyone who died in the fire."

"What if it wasn't some higher calling that drew us here?" Dyfan asked. "What if it was our mistakes or past traumas we never dealt with? That last realm re-created my house down to the pictures on the walls. Gwendolyn was there, playing her music. She wanted me to suffer. And truth be told, I deserve whatever punishment Duat has in store for me."

"What happened to your wife?" Imogen asked.

"She married a stubborn fool, is what," Dyfan said. "We lived out in the country near Glasgow. We lived a happy life until one day Gwendolyn fell ill and wanted to go to hospital. I didn't believe in modern medicine to the point I was vehemently against it. I was raised to be a healer in the old way, like my mother. I had inherited all her herbs and elixirs." He shook his head. "No matter what remedy I tried, Gwendolyn grew sicker. I swore I could save her, not some damned doctor. Within a week, my wife was dead. My ego killed her."

Imogen touched his shoulder.

"When I was talking to my dead wife in the spider den, she said that I am finally facing my demons, just as each of us will face their own." Dyfan took a nip from his flask.

"Would you mind sharing some of that?" Trummel asked.

Dyfan handed him the flask. Trummel took a chest-burning gulp, then passed the flask around along with a tin of biscuits.

Imogen and Caleb shared a canteen. Trummel's jaw tightened at the sight of the two getting closer. When the journalist had first joined the team, Trummel had enjoyed his company, even admired his womanizing back at the hotel in London. Those feelings had changed after Imogen arrived, and the Yank made her his target. When Caleb had been down in that hole with the fire, Trummel had secretly hoped he would meet his demise.

You should be grateful he survived. You need the journalist.

I don't, actually. All I need are his photographs. Another journalist can write the story. Hell, once I return to England with the relics, journalists will be lining up for the chance to write my story.

Trummel looked at Caleb's camera bag. "Do you still have the rolls of film you've taken?"

"Don't worry. I've captured plenty of pictures of you, so far."

"Let me have the finished rolls then."

Caleb looked at him sideways. "What do you need them for?"

"Safekeeping."

"They're plenty safe with me."

Trummel scoffed. "You've fallen behind more than once, and we almost lost you in the spiders' den. I can't risk you losing my film. Those photos are too valuable." He held out his hand. "I insist you hand them over."

"The negatives are the property of *National Geographic*. After we return, I'll be sure to make you photographs."

Trummel and Caleb stared each other down.

"Enough," Imogen said, breaking the silence. "The photographs are the least of our worries. We should figure out where to go from here."

Trummel looked at her and nodded. "Right."

After a short rest, his team had recharged enough to get moving again. They just had to figure out which direction to go. Trummel studied the four doorways, all solid with coded tiles beside the archways and seated doorkeepers with demon heads – a baboon, one with a head of flames, a body with a head of two entwined snakes, and one with a hooded head and blades for fingers. They could eliminate the door they'd just come through, the one guarded by the baboon demon. That left three.

"Imogen, I need you to figure out which gate to take next," Trummel said.

"I already have." She looked up from the diary where she had been writing notes. "If Dyfan is right and we're facing our demons here, I know where Duat will lead me." She stepped before the second door and looked up at the demon statue with the head of flames. On the gate's side panel, she pressed the tiles corresponding to a sequence of symbols from the diary, then said, "Fiery One." The door turned to liquid.

Trummel gathered his satchel and started for the door. "Let's be ready for anything."

Crossing through the gate felt like stepping into a furnace. Stretching before them was a hellish landscape of twisted black rock surrounding roiling pools of oil. Flames danced across their surfaces. Gases shot up from vents in the angry, molten rock.

"We've arrived in hell," Caleb said.

"Lakes of fire." Imogen tensed and took a step back. "They're described in the Amduat."

Trummel wiped sweat off his brow with a handkerchief. The blistering heat was hotter than a steel smelter. The way through was to cross over an outcropping of black rock that rose between two fiery pools. The next gate was visible on the other side.

"We can make it," Trummel said.

"We'll burn to a crisp," Caleb said.

"Not if we move fast," Trummel said. "Beckett, you're welcome to lead. Or stay behind, if you don't have the bollocks."

Imogen was shaking her head.

Trummel glared at her. "You said you wouldn't hold me back."

"I draw the line at burning alive." There was real fear in her eyes.

Trummel knew about what had happened to her family. "Duat is offering you a chance to confront your past. I faced mine and survived."

"The others haven't fared so well. What about Ely, Quig, and Sykes?" she challenged.

"They were weak," Trummel said. "I expect more from you. Fuck's sake, Imogen, I say we chance it."

"Look." Gosswick pointed toward the rock bridge. Charred bodies covered in flames had begun to crawl out of the lakes. One was a woman holding a crying baby. Another woman and a man came to the edge of the bridge.

Imogen gasped. "They're my mum and dad."

Over a dozen burning people blocked the way to the other side.

"You sure you want to go through them?" Gosswick asked Trummel.

The burning corpses' wails echoed off the surrounding rock walls.

Imogen backed away. "I can't. I'm sorry." She ran back to the gate. Caleb took Dyfan's arm and followed her.

Trummel eyed Gosswick. "I guess we abort."

Back inside the junction chamber, Trummel watched Caleb consoling Imogen, and his resentment of the younger man grew.

"We need to press on," Trummel insisted.

"Just give her a moment," Caleb snapped.

It took all of Trummel's restraint not to deck the Yank. Trummel never handled matters with his fists. He had Gosswick for that. "Let's keep one thing straight, Beckett. I give the orders on this expedition," Trummel barked. "Imogen, pass me the journal."

She handed it over without protest.

Only two doors remained. Trummel chose one at random. Above the gate, a twin-headed snake statue stared down at him. "Let's try this one." Trummel flipped to the back of the book where Imogen had matched the gate codes with corresponding demon names. Several were checked off, which narrowed down their choices. Going down the list and punching sequences on the door's panel, he solved the code in three attempts. He called out, "One Who Is Repulsive of Face." The snake heads untwisted and the portal opened.

Trummel gripped his torch. "Goss and I will explore the realm first. The rest of you wait here until we return." He and the captain stepped through the portal.

On the other side, an ancient tile floor stretched away from the portal. Pools of water reminded Trummel of a Roman bathhouse. A low ceiling was painted with a mural of a giant coiled serpent.

Gosswick craned his neck and whistled.

"The snake god Apep," Trummel said. "He battled the sun god Ra during his journey through Duat."

"I hate snakes," Gosswick said.

Then perhaps we're in the right place, Trummel thought.

Columns decorated with broken frescos surrounded the baths. Serpents wound around them from floor to ceiling.

Before venturing too far from the gate, Trummel paused and eyed his soldier.

"What is it, sir?" Gosswick asked.

"I need to know if I can count on you."

"Of course. Have I not proven my loyalty?"

Trummel remembered meeting the captain back in 1922 at a pub where washed-up veterans gathered. Aiden Gosswick had been getting piss drunk after being discharged from the army. England was between wars and no longer had a use for him. Broke, homeless, with no family, he'd had nowhere else to turn. Trummel had needed mercenary soldiers to protect his team on an expedition in French Indochina, so he offered Gosswick a job. They had traveled together on many expeditions over the past fifteen years. "We're a long way from the Wolfhound Pub, aren't we, Goss?"

"If you hadn't pulled me out of the shithole, I'd still be there drinking or dead. I'll always be indebted, sir."

Gosswick was a sentimental man. He also had a weakness for gambling and whores and owed a lot of people money.

"If you help me achieve what I'm after, I'll pay off your debts and make you a very rich man."

Gosswick grinned. "I'm all in, sir."

"I don't trust Beckett. I may need you to dispatch the problem for me at some point."

Gosswick considered, but not for long. "It'd be my pleasure. What about Imogen?" Goss's eyes sometimes had a gleam that Trummel found disturbing.

"Don't lay a hand on Imogen. I've got other plans for her."

CHAPTER FORTY-SIX

"My whole world shattered when I was eleven," Imogen said.

Caleb and Dyfan waited, giving her time to share what she had been holding in since that horrific night.

"I was a kid during the Great War, back in 1915. Half our country was off fighting over in Germany. In England, we lived in fear of air raids and bombings from Zeppelin airships. I remember there being a lot of tension at home. My father's business had been in German imports. He bought fine-crafted musical instruments and sold them at his music shops in London and Surrey. Before the war, my family made yearly trips to Frankfurt. Dad had made a lot of friends there, mostly instrument makers. When the war broke out, he was put in a difficult spot. A married couple, who'd become like a family to us, Heinrich and Olga Müller, fled to England with their newborn baby. My parents took them in. I remember a few fun nights of Heinrich playing violin while Dad played cello. Mum would sing. She had the most lovely voice. Olga baked and let me help with the baby. At the time, I didn't see anything wrong with the Müllers staying with us. They were so kind and did not support the war, nor did my parents.

"We had a full staff of English servants at our manor in Surrey, and several of them despised the Müllers. Our housemaster, Geoffrey, quit. According to him, we were housing the enemy. He returned with an angry mob, who protested outside our house. They called my father a German sympathizer and a traitor. Father's response was to lock all the doors, shutter the downstairs windows, and wait for the mob to leave. Then we would escape to our manor in the country. But Geoffrey's mob wouldn't stop their shouting and throwing things at the house. I can still hear the banging at the front door and objects hitting the shutters. Olga's baby crying. I couldn't take it anymore."

Imogen shook her head. Once again, anger and guilt weighed heavy in her heart. "I was a headstrong girl who had hated Geoffrey with a passion. I couldn't stand by and let him and his protestors threaten my family. While my parents and the Müllers were discussing what to do, I snuck off to my parents' bedroom and got my father's pistol. He had taught me how to shoot it. I opened an upstairs window and fired the gun. I aimed at the drive, not intending to hit anyone. I just wanted to scare the crowd so they would leave us alone. But the bullet ricocheted off the pavement and struck Geoffrey's leg. He swore vengeance as his followers carried him off.

"My father took the gun away from me. He was so angry and scared he was shaking. My mother was worried that I'd done more harm than good.

"Later that night while we were packing to leave, someone chained all the doors and...set fire to our house." Her mind filled with screams. "We were all trapped inside, fifteen of us. The fire spread fast. My father, along with the Müllers and several servants, died fighting the flames." Imogen could feel the heat burning her skin, the smoke filling her lungs. She recalled how a bright orange fire had engulfed the ceiling. "Mum helped me out a window. It was too small for her. When I got outside, I promised her I'd run round to the front of the house and open the door. But I couldn't get the chains off. In my nightmares, I still hear my family screaming in the fire."

Caleb took her hand.

"You wonder how I lost my faith in God. It was the fire. When death took my parents and everyone dear to me, it did more than end my happy childhood. It changed me."

"How?" Caleb said.

"Before, I believed in magic, angels, the unseen. I spent long summer days exploring the woods and heather fields near my home. I was an only child but never lonely. I felt spirits with me in the woods. I pretended lightning bugs were fairies. Those strange magical days were the best of my childhood. The fire burned all my magical thoughts to ash and took my faith too."

She wiped her eyes. "It helps to have said it out loud, but it doesn't change what happened." She admired the way Caleb listened. "You would've made a fine priest."

He released her hand. "No, I would make a very compromised priest."

"We won't let this place get to us," she said. "If you see something else, we'll talk about it. Okay?"

He nodded. "You too. You can tell me anything. When I saw the men who died because of me, I felt terrified myself."

"We've all been humbled by this place," Dyfan said. "It is pure evil and means to draw us into our own personal hells."

"I don't see it that way," Caleb said. "I believe we're in some sort of purgatory. It offers a chance to face our sins and forgive ourselves for the wrongs we have committed. The existence of this place only deepens my faith."

"You think faith is going to save you here?" Imogen said. "All I've seen so far is people dying without mercy."

"She's got a point there," Dyfan said.

Caleb said, "A nun named Sister Maya once told me, 'When you find yourself in complete darkness, faith, even blind faith, will be the guiding light back to God.'"

"I hope you're right," Imogen said. "Because I have never been more in the dark."

★   ★   ★

Beyond the bathhouse, Trummel and Gosswick carved the gloom with their lights. The chamber echoed with the sounds of their boots crossing the tile floor. An infinite number of paths wove through a forest of columns.

"Another bloody maze," Gosswick said. "Perhaps, we should—"

"Shhh." Trummel held up his hand at the sound of running feet. From the corner of his eye, he caught a flash of white disappear behind a column. Then he felt a connection that he hadn't felt since he'd shared his days with his twin. "Nell?"

His ten-year-old sister stepped into the beam of his headlamp.

Trummel could only stare.

"What is it?" Gosswick asked.

"Right over there. Do you see her?"

"All I see is a shadow of something. Must be a trick."

Nell looked very much alive, the same as the day he last saw her. Her lacy white dress was clean, and she was wearing white stockings with her favorite black shoes. She smiled the way she always did when she was grateful to see him. "Nate, I've missed you so much."

Hearing her voice brought back all the pain of losing her. His chest grew heavy and his eyes watered. His logical mind argued that she was dead, but the Nell who stood before him was so real, the connection between them as strong as ever. He had missed the feeling of his sister, as if a part of him had been cut away. He now felt as if that severed part was being healed, becoming whole again.

Harlan had spoken of witnessing miracles inside Duat. *"I saw my wife, Julia, there, and we spent a glorious time together. It was my reward for making it to the higher realms."* What if Trummel had passed some sort of spiritual test and the gods were returning her to him?

"I've missed you too, Nell." He ventured a step toward her.

"I want us to be together again," she said, "forever and ever."

"As do I."

"Let's play hide-and-seek." She dashed off into the dark.

"Wait, come back!" Trummel ran after her. He searched behind column after column. "Where are you?"

Her whistle echoed up ahead.

Gosswick called for him from behind, but Trummel kept searching. He descended a set of steps into a pitch-black pit. His headlamp spotlighted Nell standing twenty feet away.

"Found me; now you gotta catch me." She wiggled her finger for him to come to her. The invisible tether that connected them pulled him toward her. She held open her arms for him to hug her.

"Dr. Trummel, stop!" Gosswick shouted from the top of the steps.

Hissing echoed all around.

The hairs stood on Trummel's neck. A swish of his torch revealed he was standing in a pit filled with snakes. Stacked in piles, slithering over one another. Dozens of them moved toward Nell until there was barely a footpath between brother and sister.

Trummel froze.

Snakes of every color coiled around Nell's legs. "Brother, you've become so selfish and cold-hearted. You belong among the snakes with us."

Behind Nell appeared Göran Järvi, carrying a python around his neck. From the shadows, half a dozen cobras rose up in striking stances, flaring their hoods. Nell and Järvi turned from solid to transparent, flickered like projected film images, and then disappeared.

Trummel's chest felt a sting of betrayal. He'd been fooled and led into a trap. While seeing Nell alive must have been a trick of the mind, the snakes that infested this realm looked real enough to kill him.

He slowly backed away. One of the king cobras attacked. A gunshot fired and the cobra's head exploded. Trummel hurried up the steps as Gosswick unleashed several more shots into the pit, killing the snakes that snapped at Trummel's heels. This only riled up a hundred others.

Nell's giggles echoed in the chamber.

Trummel ran with Gosswick back through the columns with sounds of hissing behind them. In the bathhouse, the pools were writhing with black water snakes. They slid their heads up the side walls. Nell floated facedown in one of the pools, dead as the day he'd found her. Snakes slithered over her back.

In another pool, Järvi rose out of the water, covered in a slithering mass. He grinned and sounded a singsong whistle.

Ahead, the liquid gate whirled. Trummel and Gosswick crossed through it and returned to the junction room.

"Fucking hell," Gosswick cursed, breathing heavily.

Imogen, Caleb, and Dyfan stood.

"What did you see?" Caleb asked.

"A realm full of snakes," Trummel said, catching his breath. Although he was shaken, he did his best to maintain his composure. He wanted nothing more than to get far away from Nell's ghost and her killer. Had Duat's omniscient darkness conjured them from his memories? Whether hallucinations or real ghosts, they terrified him. "We need to keep moving. Let's try the last gate."

Imogen punched in several glyph combinations on the final door. It took her a moment to solve the riddle. Then she punched a code and called out the name, "She Who Shows the Way."

The hooded demon scraped its finger blades together and the gate opened.

CHAPTER FORTY-SEVEN

Imogen followed the others up a winding staircase. Colorful crystals embedded in the curved walls illuminated as they passed. The more she walked, the better she felt. Talking about what happened to her family had lifted some of the burden from her chest.

After a hundred steps, the spiral staircase led into a chamber with smooth alabaster walls. Archways and curved tunnels tapered off into the gloom in three directions. They looked more like hallways of an ancient building than a natural cave. The acoustics were so fine-tuned that the group's footsteps and voices echoed. They entered a great hall with a vast ceiling.

The group walked between two rows of giant white statues carved into granite walls. The animal faces represented the Egyptian gods and goddesses. A few had human faces, like Isis and Nephthys. The two rows, facing one another, reminded Imogen of the temple of Ramses II at Abu Simbel, only there was no sign of Ramses among these. Evidently here the self-idolizing pharaoh was not allowed to sit among the gods. At one end sat Amun-Ra, the king of the gods, the one who originally traveled through Duat. At the opposite end towered Osiris, ruler of the underworld.

Imogen felt tiny in their presence. Of all the ruins she had ever explored, this pantheon of statues was by far the most spectacular. Caleb looked as amazed as she was.

"Just imagine," she said, "if the legend on that wall back in Nebenteru's tomb is true, a pharaoh doing his rite of passage might have passed through this very chamber."

I have walked in the footsteps of the pharaohs, her grandfather had written.

Caleb snapped photos of the statues. "I can't wait to show these to my editor. Hey, Blondie, how about modeling for the magazine?"

"I told you not to call me that, Flash." She posed next to Ra's enormous stone feet.

He took her photo. "Now, that's one for my personal collection."

"Save your flashbulbs for the shots that matter," Trummel barked. "Let's keep moving."

Beyond the giant statues, the passage opened to a chamber with another stairway that spiraled down. Trummel started descending the steps.

"Don't go down there!" Dyfan said frantically.

"Why not? What's below?"

"I don't know but I sense it's very bad."

Trummel backed away from the staircase. "So all of a sudden you've got psychic abilities again?"

"It must come and go," Dyfan said. "All I know is it's imperative that we keep moving forward, not down. Whatever waits below would mean death for all of us."

Trummel nodded. "Let's keep going forward then."

Imogen was glad to pass the spiral staircase. After traveling through the bone maze and swamp, she had descended as far as she wanted to go.

Beyond the staircase, they entered a chamber with quartz walls that glittered when their lights passed over them. The energy here was invigorating. She felt an incredible lightness as all her previous anxieties fell away. She wondered if this was what mystics felt when they claimed to feel a connection to God.

"Come see this," Gosswick called from an adjoining room.

The others followed his voice. The wide chamber shimmered with gold, silver, and colored gemstones. Imogen looked around amazed as their lights panned across multiarmed goddess statues with jewelry hanging from their arms and fingers. Among dozens of necklaces hung twines tied to amulets, rings, and watches.

Trummel ran his palm through the streamers of gold and silver chains. "There's enough here to make us all rich as kings."

More trinkets bejeweled the walls in nooks with tiny ledges. These were human artifacts left behind by countless others who had ventured into the caves. Gosswick picked up a pair of dusty spectacles. Trummel thumbed through an old Bible.

While the other three explored intersecting rooms, Imogen walked with Caleb between the multiarmed statues adorned with necklaces.

"Pretty incredible, don't you think?" he said.

"It's magical," she admitted, feeling as if she had stepped into the vault at the Tower of London where the crown jewels were kept. Something familiar caught her eye. From a statue's finger hung a gold necklace with a half-heart pendant.

"It can't be…" Tears dampened her eyes as she pulled it down.

"What is it?" Caleb asked.

"This was Grandfather's." She pulled out the pendant she wore around her neck, showing him how the two broken halves made one gold heart. "I thought it was lost forever." Imogen fumbled with the clasp, but she was all thumbs and jumbled nerves.

"Let me." Caleb opened the catch. Standing close behind her, he fastened Grandfather's necklace around her neck. The two halves of the heart pendant now hung against her chest.

"What do the broken hearts mean?" he asked.

"Isn't it obvious?"

"Perhaps, but I want to know what they mean to you." He turned her so she was facing him. "Tell me something real." His gaze held hers as he waited.

She drew a deep breath and then exhaled. "Right after my parents died I was lost. More than just sad, I was angry. Angry at God, angry at myself for not being able to save them. I felt so abandoned. There I was a confused eleven-year-old girl without her mum and dad. I didn't want to live any longer." She shook her head, remembering what she'd almost done. "In our country house, my grandfather's study has this giant fireplace. I remember one day standing in front of a blazing fire in the hearth. I seriously thought of walking into the flames. I wanted to burn to ashes and blow away to wherever my parents went. Whether it was heaven or nothingness, I didn't care. I just wanted the pain and emptiness to end. I was readying myself to step into the fire, when I heard Grandfather calling my name." She could hear his voice in her head as he ran up the stairs, yelling, "Immy! Where are you, darling girl?"

"He sounded so excited. He'd been away shopping and had no idea what I was contemplating. Grandfather entered his study with the biggest grin and surprised me with a gift." Telling Caleb the story brought up the memory as real and emotional as the day she'd experienced it.

Grandfather had opened a long velvet case. Inside were two gold necklaces, the halves of the heart pendant conjoined. On the back sides he'd made an inscription. One half read *Yours*. The other half read *Mine*.

Grandfather had knelt in front of her. "I know that your mum and dad are gone. I miss them too, very much. But you and I stayed behind for a reason. We must carry on and live more adventures. No matter what hardships we face, we will always have each other." He separated the heart pendant and placed one necklace around her neck, the other around his. "Always remember, Immy, I am yours and you are mine."

"He saved me from myself that day, and many other dark days during my teens when my sadness became unbearable. A couple of times I stood on a bridge overlooking the Thames and came close to jumping. But grasping Grandfather's necklace gave me strength to go on another day."

As she told the story to Caleb, a heavy pain in her heart lifted. "I never told him that I had considered suicide. Never told anyone."

Caleb pulled her against his chest and held her for several moments. When she pulled away, sniffing, she looked down at the heart pendant. "This doesn't feel right, taking his necklace. I've got a strong feeling Grandfather left this here as an offering." She took off both necklaces and hung them together on the statue's finger. The two heart pieces spun in a circle. Now, strangely, she felt whole again.

"You think that's what this chamber is?" Caleb asked. "A place to leave offerings to something divine?"

Imogen looked around at all the jewelry, watches, and other personal effects left behind by bygone explorers. "I think it is."

Caleb nodded and closed his eyes. His hand drew a holy cross from his forehead to chest, shoulder to shoulder. He stayed quiet for a moment. When he opened his eyes again, he removed his silver St. Michael necklace, kissed it, and hung it on the statue's wrist.

Imogen smiled inwardly. For the first time in months, she felt at peace about her grandfather's death. He'd come here because he had been called to find a deeper meaning in his life. Somehow he had left completely transformed. She believed now that he came home to tell her about this magical realm. When he died in that asylum, she wondered if his spirit might have returned here somehow. Imogen couldn't explain how, but she felt his presence here. It comforted her to think that he'd been watching over her this entire time.

Imogen realized she and Caleb had been separated from the group for quite a while. The others had ventured on into the vast rooms of altars and treasures. When she started for the exit, Caleb took her hand. "Imogen, I don't know if I'm going to get another chance to do this."

Before she knew it, he pulled her into his arms. Caleb kissed her with a passion she had never felt before. She kissed him briefly, then caught herself and quickly pulled away, feeling a bit dizzy.

He looked embarrassed. "I'm sorry, I don't know what came over me."

"It's okay, just caught me by surprise. I had no idea…"

"I have a confession to make," Caleb said. "I've known about you a couple years now, since I interviewed your grandfather. The way he described you intrigued me, so I did some research and read an article about you in an archaeology magazine. I was amazed by your accomplishments. Then when I finally met you, I felt instantly drawn to you, as if I had found a kindred spirit. I've wanted to kiss you since the night I walked you to your tent."

Imogen was speechless. No man, especially not Nathan Trummel, had ever expressed this much affection toward her.

Caleb looked vulnerable as he said, "I wasn't sure if you might already have someone."

"I did. I was…I mean, it's over now, but it's too soon to start…" She stepped away from him. "Sorry, but I'm just not in the right place to…"

"No need to explain. I understand." Caleb's tone didn't hide his disappointment.

She felt bad. Truth was she liked the way the feeling of his kiss lingered on her lips. But her broken heart was still mending. The idea of getting emotionally involved with another man so soon…. She didn't think her heart could handle it.

An awkward silence fell between her and Caleb. She looked toward the doorway to the next chamber. "Trummel will send Goss looking for us."

"Let's get back to them then." Caleb walked past her, clearly bothered by her rejection.

CHAPTER FORTY-EIGHT

Caleb and Imogen didn't say another word as they weaved through the statues. He had made an utter fool of himself, assuming that the attraction he felt toward her was mutual. For two years his curiosity about her had grown into an infatuation. The romantic woman he had imagined her to be was nothing but fantasy. In reality, Imogen was a complicated woman whose heart was entombed behind thick walls. After that botched kiss, Caleb was grateful to return to the group and distract his mind.

In the next room, they found an even greater collection of treasures left on altars at the feet of statues – amulets, rings, daggers in gold and silver sheaths. Many of the relics looked to date back thousands of years.

Trummel picked up a gold crown with a cobra. "This could have been left by an Egyptian from the Middle Kingdom."

"One of the pharaohs?" Caleb asked.

"The entrance to Duat was kept so secret that I imagine there weren't many common Egyptian explorers before Ramses II. These look like treasures left by kings."

"Are these the relics you've been searching for?" Imogen asked.

"No, these are an unexpected bonus." Trummel grinned, looking around the room. "The museum will pay us a fortune for these. Everyone, load up your packs."

Trummel and Gosswick began to stuff their rucksacks.

"I don't think we should take these," Imogen said.

"Why the hell not?" Trummel said.

"This chamber feels sacred."

"She's right." Dyfan grimaced and clutched his chest. "I'm getting a bad feeling about this. Please, stop."

"I don't need to hear any moral protests," Trummel said. "Imogen, unless you want me to have a word with the museum's board about your unwillingness to help, I suggest you load every pocket you can fill."

She crossed her arms. "Tell the board what you like. I won't be a part of this."

Trummel's face reddened. "You have done nothing but disappoint me. Whenever we get out of here, I'll see to it you lose your job. As to the bonus money – the rest of you can keep Imogen's share."

"You can have my share too," Caleb said.

"And mine," Dyfan said.

"Suit yourselves."

Gosswick grinned. "More for us."

A sound like women shrieking in a crazy house echoed from the corridors.

Everyone backed to the center of the ring of statues.

From the chamber's back arched doorway, four beings in red robes glided into the room.

Trummel and Gosswick raised their guns. Caleb stood protectively in front of Imogen, uncertain what sort of beings these were. They looked like nuns in red habits. Solid veils covered their eyes. The bottom halves of their faces were exposed, revealing albino white skin and feminine lips. Three of them were young, and one had a deeply wrinkled face. Every inch of their visible flesh was scarred with alien markings. Their arms remained folded at the midsections of their robes, pale hands with scrimshaw designs and long fingers clasped across their abdomens. The four nuns hovered inches above the ground at the edge of the group's circle.

No one moved for several tense seconds.

The scar-faced women didn't seem to fear the firelight. They didn't so much as flinch when Gosswick cocked his gun.

"Nobody shoot," Dyfan warned. He tilted his head. "They're speaking to me."

The nuns remained silent, their lips perfectly still. Dyfan nodded and murmured, as if having some internal conversation.

"They're telling me we have angered the Supreme Ones. They will spare our lives if we leave behind what we've taken."

"And what if we refuse?" Gosswick said.

The eldest nun lashed out her hand. Gosswick flew back against the wall and floated six feet off the floor, his arms spread like Jesus on the cross. The other nuns raised their hands. Several daggers rose from the altars and shot across the room, stopping inches from Gosswick's face and body. Wide-eyed, he trembled before the mercy of the blades.

"Okay, okay," Trummel said. "Put him down."

The nuns lowered their hands and the captain fell to the floor, gasping. In one quick motion, the knives returned to their altars.

Trummel pulled the pilfered treasures from his pack. "Goss, put back what you took."

The two thieves begrudgingly placed a couple of dozen relics on the altars.

"All of it," Dyfan said.

The women's heads snapped in the direction of Trummel. He dug at the bottom of his pack and pulled out the gold Egyptian crown.

When everything was back on the altars, three of the red nuns floated backward and vanished into unseen chambers. The youngest drifted toward one of the dark doorways and motioned for the group to follow.

"What the hell is she?" Trummel asked.

Her head snapped back at him, then turned to Dyfan. "She's a *naturu*, a realm guide," he said. "Like Bakari's race, who guides people through the lower realms, she's part of a more advanced race that guides explorers through the middle realms. We've entered a sacred sanctuary that lies between the gates. She insists we follow her."

"I don't trust her," Trummel said.

"I'm afraid you have no choice." Dyfan started after her receding figure.

The *naturu* led them out of the treasure chamber and down a corridor partially lit by torches. There were no sounds except for the echo of their footsteps on flagstones and the rippling of torch flames. As they walked past another stone spiral staircase that led down to yet another level, Caleb spotted a group of red-robed figures drifting into the bowels below. In unison, all their heads snapped up in his direction. He sensed that, even with veiled eyes, the women could *see* him.

Can they read my mind too? Caleb did his best to control his thoughts. Something he had gotten good at. Two years of seminary school had not been for nothing. He meditated on the positive, prayed to his guiding angel. The nuns below looked away and continued their descent.

Caleb still wasn't certain if these beings served God or something evil. He hoped their realm guide had no intention of taking the group downstairs. There could be a dungeon with demon monks preparing for their inquisition.

Their guide led the explorers past the staircase, through a doorway to a courtyard. Ancient brick structures with flat rooftops and hollow, glassless windows rose on either side. Across the courtyard loomed a monolithic building with bell towers and spires. A cathedral, perhaps, but there was nothing Catholic about this subterranean convent.

For a sanctuary, the exterior was gloomy and devoid of life. No gardens, no sunlight. Just deep shadows and giant gray statues at every turn. Some resembled Egyptian gods. Others looked Sumerian, like the winged Anunnaki gods Caleb had seen carved into the ruins at the ancient city of Ur. Other sculptures here were idolized beings with similar alien markings to the nuns.

The guide led them toward the edge of the convent to another gate. The stone guardian was a demon with a head of a vulture. The *naturu* waved her hand over the symbols engraved at the threshold. The vulture flapped its wings and the gate opened. Their guide floated through first.

As Caleb passed through the gate, a chill seeped into his bones.

The group followed their guide across a stone platform. The nun stopped at a stone bridge that crossed over absolute nothingness. She pointed a long white finger, directing them to go.

"She says we must cross the Canyon of the Lost," Dyfan said.

Caleb leaned over the edge. Hollow voices, as if from lost souls, cried out from far beneath the bridge. He couldn't see them, though. The void below was just as black as the void above. The narrow stone bridge stretched to infinity and tapered off into the dark.

"Where does it lead?" Trummel asked.

"She says we'll find out on the other side," Dyfan said.

"Looks like the darkest reaches of hell," Trummel said. He hesitated, calculating the risks. "How do we know she's not sending us to be damned?"

"She's growing impatient." Dyfan sounded agitated. "We must hurry. The bridge won't be here much longer."

Trummel said, "Tell her to show us another gate."

A dozen more red nuns floated through the portal and formed a menacing wall, blocking the way back.

Caleb said, "I think we've worn out our welcome."

Trummel glared. Gosswick, hand on his gun, looked ready to unleash violence. Trummel shook his head. "Let's go." He started down the bridge with his soldier in tow.

Dyfan paused, silently thanking the nun who had shown them the way. Then he started over the bridge, using one of the low walls as a guide.

Caleb had learned in South Africa that sometimes territorial respect was the best way to stay alive. He put his palms together and bowed to the nuns with a gesture of gratitude. Then he followed Imogen onto the bridge.

CHAPTER FORTY-NINE

The bridge was frightfully narrow. Imogen made slow progress at first, as if crossing a tightrope. The side barriers only reached to the middle of her thighs. Peering over the edge at the emptiness didn't help her balance. The frosty air, the moans of lost souls below made her shudder. She stopped after a few feet.

Caleb stepped up behind her. "You need me to help you?"

She shook her head. "I can do this."

"If you need me, I'm right here."

She willed herself to continue walking, step-by-step. *Don't look down.* She kept her gaze locked straight ahead. Dyfan and the other two were thin shapes far ahead of her.

From below, familiar voices began to call Imogen's name. She seized up. She stared over the edge. Her burning house was down there.

"What is it?" Caleb asked.

"I hear screaming. It sounds like everyone who died in my house. My parents, their servants."

"I don't hear anything."

The tortured cries of her family being burned alive were too much. Imogen shut her eyes. "I can't bear it."

"Imogen…" called her mother's voice. "Come join us. Jump!"

★　★　★

Caleb stopped when he noticed light glowing far below the bridge. In the sea of blackness was what looked like a tiny dollhouse caught on fire. Tiny people covered in flames stood in front of the house, waving their fiery arms. Caleb still couldn't hear any sounds. Whatever they were saying, it was for Imogen only. He had only taken his eyes off her for just a second. When he looked toward her, Imogen was standing on top of the bridge's narrow wall. She stared down, as if about to jump.

"Imogen!" Caleb called.

She didn't respond. Still looking down, she teetered forward.

Please don't fall! Caleb feared if he grabbed her, he'd push her over the edge. She had a catatonic expression, like a sleepwalker.

Caleb eased toward her. "Imogen, wake up."

She blinked and looked at him, confused. Then peered back down and seemed to realize she was standing on the ledge. "Oh my God." She wobbled and stretched out her arms to keep from falling.

"Please, come down."

"They want me to jump."

"Whatever you're hearing or seeing, it's not real," Caleb urged. "It's just this place pulling up your darkest memory. Don't let it get to you." He offered her his hand.

She took it and stepped down onto the center of the bridge. Clearly dizzy, she fell against his chest. "I don't know what came over me."

As Caleb held her, they both looked back down. The burning house was gone, replaced by the empty void.

A tremor shook the bridge. Behind them, a section broke off and fell into the gulf.

"Keep moving," he urged.

Imogen walked faster ahead of him. Caleb spotted Trummel's and Gosswick's lights fifty yards ahead. They had made it to the other side.

"Hurry!" Trummel called.

The bridge groaned. More tremors split the stone. Imogen and Caleb leapt over a crack and burst into a full run. The bridge grew brittle, like running on cracking ice. The stones fell away only feet behind them.

Ahead the others waited in a metal box attached to a flat rock wall. An elevator of some sort, like those found in mineshafts. Only this one was sleeker in design, like a large black cube open on one side. The track it was connected to ran up and down the wall.

Twenty more yards.

The walls along the bridge broke off and plummeted. Only a thin strip of stone still reached the elevator. Caleb stumbled over cracking rock. *Not gonna make it. Yes, you are!* As pieces fell away, he jumped forward. His boots found solid purchase. He kept running.

Ahead, Trummel and Gosswick leaned out of the cube and took Imogen's hands. They pulled her inside. As Caleb got within six feet, the bridge in front of him disintegrated. He came to a halt on an island of bridge that remained. He teetered at the edge, swinging his arms to keep from falling forward into the black nothingness below. He stepped back. Behind, the bridge was completely gone. The rock beneath his boots continued cracking. "Oh, shit."

The leap to reach the elevator seemed impossible without a good running start. Trummel and Gosswick stood at the entrance. "Come on, Caleb. You can make it."

Behind them, Imogen urged him to be careful.

Everything Caleb was carrying suddenly felt like a heavy burden. If he was going to make that jump, he needed to be as light as possible. He took off his backpack.

"Toss us your gear," Trummel said.

Caleb hurled the backpack across the gulch and they caught it. He then pulled off his camera bag and canteen and tossed them to Trummel and Goss.

More chunks of bridge fell away until he only had two feet of stone to stand on. And it was cracking and trembling beneath his boots.

"Give me some room, I'm going to jump!"

The others backed inside the cube. Caleb whispered a quick prayer, then leapt as far as he could, stretching out his arms. His hands missed the floor of the elevator and caught hold of a metal bar just beneath it. The undercarriage creaked. The lift rocked on its track as his body swung like a pendulum. His pistol fell out of its holster and clacked down the stone wall. Caleb hung by both arms. His legs dangled over dark emptiness.

Hanging beneath the elevator, he could no longer see the others.

"Caleb?" Imogen frantically called from above.

"I'm alive!"

She peered over the edge. "Take my hand." Her arm reached beneath the undercarriage for him. Caleb stretched up his hand, but their fingers barely touched.

"It's no use," Caleb said. "Get back inside before you fall out."

"Hang on, Caleb." Her arm withdrew.

"Wait, I see a ladder," he called. It ran up and down the wall next to the track. He let one hand go from the bar and stretched for the rungs. Too far away. Hanging by one arm, he swung his body toward the ladder and almost fell. He quickly gripped the bar with both hands. He struggled to hang on. His arms and shoulders ached, growing weak. In a matter of minutes, his exhausted hands would let go. His sweaty palms started slipping.

"Help!" Caleb shouted.

Gosswick reached down and offered his hand. "Grab on."

Both men had to stretch their arms. Their hands connected.

"Now, let go your other hand," Gosswick said. "I've got you."

As Caleb let go of the undercarriage, the weight of his body pulled Gosswick halfway over the edge. Caleb dangled by one arm as Gosswick gripped his wrist. Their hands held on to one another, both men straining. Then Gosswick's fingers released their grip. Caleb slipped loose, and the next thing he knew he was plummeting into darkness.

★   ★   ★

Trummel peered over the edge of the open elevator, along with Imogen. She screamed Caleb's name. His falling voice trailed off until there was only silence below. Imogen kept calling for him as if that would somehow bring him back. Dyfan, visibly shaking, fell back against a wall. He stared hard in Trummel's direction – the psychic knew.

Imogen leaned dangerously close to the edge, reaching toward the darkness.

"He's gone." Trummel pulled her back inside and held her. "I'm sorry, Im, we did all we could." As she cried on his chest, he met eyes with Gosswick and gave him an approving nod.

CHAPTER FIFTY

Falling…Air whooshed past Caleb as he fell for several seconds. His heart threatening to burst, he had never felt so much terror as he braced for impact. It came too fast. He plunged into deep water and blacked out.

When he came to, he was lying on a boat that bobbed up and down. It was sunny, the first glorious daylight he'd seen in days. Seagulls flew overhead, cawing in the wind. He smelled the saltiness of sea air. Waves splashed against the hull.

How did I get to the ocean? Have I died? Is this heaven?

A crew of hooded figures in slick gray fisherman coats was moving about the boat. Rubber boots stepped past his head. One boatman dropped an anchor. A second turned on a noisy piece of machinery that vibrated the floorboards. A third mariner approached Caleb, holding a large copper mask – the Siebe Gorman deep-sea diving helmet with round faceplates on the front and sides. The mere sight of it caused Caleb's throat to constrict. It was then he realized he was fully dressed in a diving suit. Tubes had already been hooked into his suit. He held up his gloved hands. "What's going on?"

The crewmen didn't speak as they went about the boat. The one holding the helmet had webbed hands with long fingers. Caleb turned to where the sun shined on the lower half of the crewman's face. He reeled at its hideousness. The boatman wasn't human. Its pale skin was spotted and slick, the lipless mouth sewn shut with fishhooks. Where a nose should have been, it had two air holes. Its eyes were hidden by the hood of the coat. The creature's ribbed throat breathed with gills. It stank of dead fish that had been left to dry in the wind.

Assaulted by the stench, Caleb jerked away from the strange being. *It's not real. I'm dreaming, suffering some sort of nightmare. Wake up! Wake up!* Nothing changed. The boat continued to float up and down, the sun bobbing with it. He felt seasick and rolled over and vomited. He tried to sit up in the bulky diving suit. His heavy weighted boots anchored his legs to the floor. Another boatman hurried over and held Caleb down.

"Let me go," he pleaded.

They put the heavy metal helmet over his head and locked it on. His world reduced to staring out of three small round faceplates, Caleb struggled to breathe. Claustrophobia kicked in, reminding him of the dreadful hours he'd spent inside a decompression chamber. He shook on the floor of the boat. "Get me out of this damned suit!"

Several boatmen helped him to his feet. The suit, attached to the air pump by a long hose, began to inflate with air. Caleb continued to scream, but the creatures ignored him. They switched on a light inside his helmet and a flashlight mounted on his shoulder. They walked him to the edge of the boat. He stared down at the dark blue water. He recognized the rock formations that curved around the boat. Egypt's Blue Hole. The place of his nightmares.

Caleb panicked and fought against the boatmen. They pushed him off the boat and he sank underwater. Like anchors tied to his feet, the heavy boots pulled him down, deeper and deeper, past cavern walls and coral fish. Sunlight faded to a cold, empty darkness. Two deep-sea divers emerged from the black and grabbed hold of Caleb. He couldn't see anything through their faceplates, but saw their names stenciled on their suits, Nikolai and Christoph, the Greeks he'd abandoned here. They pulled Caleb deeper into the abyss, to the underwater cemetery where skeletons drifted for eternity. Going mad, Caleb screamed inside his helmet.

★   ★   ★

Imogen remained lost in her own world as she sat on the floor in the corner of the lift. She couldn't believe Caleb was gone. Over the course of a few days, she'd grown to care about the American journalist. He'd risked his life for her more than once. He'd confided in her. His unyielding faith had been a source of hope in her darkest moment. He'd even kissed her. Although she had been confused at how to handle his sudden affection, she had felt more bonded to him since. Her heart now ached with a fresh wound to accompany many others. When she had set out on this journey, she never dreamed she would watch so many people die. She felt guilty for all of their deaths. Trummel, her partner in tragedy, seemed unaffected by Caleb's loss or any others. *All he cares about is finding bloody relics. How could I have ever loved such a callous man?* The foolish woman who had been seduced by him and carried on a sordid affair seemed so far away now.

Trummel felt no remorse over the loss of the Yank. In fact, it was good riddance. Caleb had been nothing but a thorn in Trummel's side. Now that his team had been reduced to the only three people he really needed for his mission, Trummel turned his focus on getting up to the next level.

He looked around the magnificent cube they were in. "This elevator, if that's what it is, seems impossible. Its technology and design are beyond anything I've ever seen," Trummel said excitedly. "Simply marvelous." The black metal walls embedded with tiny crystals and flecks of gold gave off a reflective sheen. In a multitude of perfectly square panels, circuitry lines networked with alien hieroglyphs, labyrinthine conduits, and octagonal buttons.

Gosswick touched an ankh symbol and frowned. "Don't tell me this lift was built during ancient Egyptian times. The technology looks more advanced than anything invented in our century."

"I'm not sure we're still on Earth in 1937," Trummel said. "When we crossed through the portal into Duat, I believe we left earth and time far behind. Harlan told me the higher he ascended through the gates, the greater the technologies he encountered."

"And who built these technologies?" Dyfan asked. "Have you considered that?"

"That's all I've thought about since Harlan came back covered in glyphs and speaking that strange tongue."

Imogen, who was still sitting in a corner, wallowing in grief, glared up at Trummel. "After all we've been through, the people we've lost, do we really want to ascend any higher? I'm frightened at what we might find."

"I'm feeling apprehensive myself," Dyfan admitted. "I vote we search for a portal that provides an exit."

"This is no time for losing sight of our purpose," Trummel said. "Besides, the bridge that got us here is gone. We already know what kinds of demons reside in the lower realms. The only way to go from here is *up*." He pulled a lever multiple times, but the lift wouldn't budge.

"Just our bloody luck," Gosswick grumbled. "We're trapped in a box on the side of a cliff."

"This lift was clearly engineered to be operational," Trummel said. "There's got to be a way to get it running, a pulley system, a power source, something." He tried all the octagonal buttons, but pushing them had no effect. "Maybe it requires a coded sequence like the gates." Trummel flipped through the diary and studied the inscriptions on the panels. "Harlan's codex doesn't help. None of these codes match the symbols in the book." He tossed it on the floor.

Imogen grabbed the journal and put it in her satchel. "Perhaps whoever built the lift abandoned it and took its power source."

"You're not helping." Trummel frantically pushed the buttons again. The panels remained lifeless. He slammed his fist against them and cursed.

At the back of the cube, Gosswick pried open double doors that were closest to the stone wall. "There's a ladder that runs up the shaft. Maybe we could climb it."

"We'd never make it," Dyfan said with certainty. "I can already see us falling to our deaths."

Gosswick kicked the wall. "Then this box is our coffin."

"Not necessarily," Dyfan said, sounding hopeful. "The *naturu* guide sent us to this lift for a reason. As I was walking away from her, she told me 'Across the bridge is our transport to take us up or down.'"

"Great," Trummel said. "Did she tell you how to power up the damn thing?"

"No. But I know it's possible. Imogen, I sense that you are the key to getting this running."

"Me? What do I know about operating lifts?"

"Forget trying to figure out how to make it work. Use your intuition. Mine tells me we'll get along faster if you help."

"I can barely even think straight after what just happened."

Dyfan put a gentle hand on her shoulder. "I'm devastated by Caleb's loss just as you, but we'll have to mourn him later. Right now, we need you."

Dyfan was right. Sitting on the floor and beating herself up wasn't getting them anywhere. She didn't come all this way to die in a box with this lot. She stood and helped the others search for a way to get the lift working.

* * *

Floating in a void amid plankton-covered skeletons, Caleb had yelled for so long his throat hurt. Nothing changed. He didn't suffocate and die. But the terror of being trapped in a confined space wouldn't leave him. He could feel madness setting in. He shook inside the suit. "Let me out! Let me out!" The movements caused the surrounding skeletons to crowd around him. His screams turned to tears and then to maniacal laughter until he fell silent and settled into a deep depression. He couldn't believe that after a life of praying to God and his faith that he'd been sentenced to suffer in his own personal hell.

"Our sins will eventually catch up with us," Dyfan had said.

Caleb stared out of his faceplate at the Greek divers. Nicolai and Christoph drifted quietly next to him in their dive suits. *Their deaths are my sins.*

He had hired them to teach him a single diving lesson in shallow water, then take him down into the Blue Hole. He had lied and told them he was diving to photograph coral fish. What he'd really been after was to capture photos of the Blue Hole's greater mystery – the floating skeletons he'd heard stories about. All that had mattered then was getting a feature story in the magazine. *My careless ambition pushed us all to dive too far down.*

The guilt he'd carried since that day constricted his chest until he couldn't breathe. He no longer had his St. Michael pendant to pray to. *You left it behind at the altar, thinking that would appease the higher power overseeing these realms.* He feared now that he may have honored the wrong deity. Was this underworld the devil's realm? Were the red nuns and the boatmen Satan's servants?

Through blind faith, Caleb had convinced himself he was following a soul's journey that would bring him closer to God and heaven. It turned out, it was a path to perdition.

Is this all that's left for me, God? Eternal suffering?

Closing his eyes, he focused on the archangel Michael's image and prayed for answers.

A long-forgotten childhood memory surfaced in his mind. While living in Chicago, ten-year-old Caleb had attended a private Catholic school. In the schoolyard, he had gotten into an argument with one of the boys, Lenny Gilroy. Caleb got so mad he pushed the boy down onto the ground and stepped on his glasses, breaking them. Lenny had cried and run to tell the nuns. Caleb had felt guilty afterward, angry at himself for allowing his temper to make him do something so mean. The school's headmaster, Father Victor, scorned him and lashed his palms with a ruler. The priest then told Caleb he would surely suffer in purgatory for his sins. "The devil's turning you wicked. If you don't repent now, you'll burn in hell for eternity."

Terrified, Caleb had run straight to Sister Maya, the one nun he'd grown close to. Whenever he had felt lost from God or confused about why there was so much evil in the world, Sister Maya always had the right words to say. He told her about the sin he'd committed against his classmate, and how badly he felt about hurting Lenny and destroying his glasses.

"Sister, I wish I could take it back, but I can't. Father Victor said I'm gonna burn in hell."

"Hmm," said Sister Maya. "Let's see if God has anything to say about that." Holding her rosary, she had prayed with young Caleb for several moments. Then she said, "The good Lord has offered me some insight. You are to tell that boy you are sorry and ask for forgiveness, and then – and this is important, Caleb – you are to forgive yourself and surrender your heart to God."

Remembering Sister Maya's words was a jolt to Caleb's brain. He had a sudden revelation. Ever since the accident, he had mentally tortured himself for the deaths of these two men, but never once had he asked for forgiveness. Shaking now, as he had the day he'd asked Lenny Gilroy to forgive him, Caleb faced Nicolai and Christoph. Their faces were hidden inside the darkness of their helmets. He imagined when the two men were alive, joking with each other in Greek, as they rode their boat out to the Blue Hole for a morning dive.

Caleb told them how badly he felt about what happened and asked them both to forgive him. The immense guilt of their deaths turned into a rush of tears. Over and over, he told them he was sorry. "Please forgive me." Something miraculous happened after that. The lights turned on inside their helmets. No longer skeletons, Nicolai and Christoph looked like the young men who'd been very much alive before the dive. There was peace in their eyes. Then both divers floated backward and faded into the void.

Caleb's eyes teared up as he looked upward and prayed to God for forgiveness; then he forgave himself and surrendered his soul to his Creator. A massive weight lifted from his heart. More cathartic tears streamed down his face. Next thing he knew, the air hose that tethered him to the boat began pulling him upward. He rose out of the floating cemetery, ascending to the surface. When his helmet and shoulders came out of the water, it was completely dark again, save for the light of a nearby boat. Arms of crewmen pulled him back onboard.

Laughing hysterically, Caleb had never felt so happy than to see the boatmen's faces. No longer did they resemble hideous demons from the deep. When Caleb saw their luminous eyes, he swore they were angels. One of them kneeled beside him and lowered his hood. Caleb's jaw dropped when he saw a familiar face.

Bakari smiled. "Welcome back, Caleb."

★　　★　　★

Inside the cube-shaped elevator, Imogen, Trummel, and Gosswick tried every switch, but still nothing powered up the lift.

Dyfan said my intuition is the key. Think, Imogen, think.

No, don't think – feel.

She closed her eyes and moved her attention to the center of her body. She couldn't shake the feeling the cube was waiting for them to solve its riddle. She slowly spun around, opened her eyes, and noticed a pattern on one of the walls.

"It's a puzzle."

"What's that?" Trummel asked.

"The pattern of the panels on this wall…they form a grid, but their designs are mismatched. The lines and dots look as if they should connect to form an image. And one square is missing. I think that's where the puzzle begins." It was like a tile puzzle game she used to play while sitting beside Grandfather in an aeroplane during long flights. Only now, she was standing in front of a wall-sized tile puzzle. She slid a panel toward an empty square. That made room to slide down another panel.

"Astounding," Trummel breathed. He helped her choose which panels to slide where. It became a game and they were both enjoying themselves, like the old days when they made discoveries together. Imogen began to have hope again. A half hour later, the wall's grid formed into a giant face made of circuit lines.

"A male god's face," Trummel said, sounding delighted by the find.

"One more piece to the puzzle," Imogen said. Moving the final panel into place revealed a secret compartment at the center of the face's forehead.

Imogen smiled at what was hidden inside.

"Another silver disk," Trummel said. From his satchel, he pulled out the disk he'd found in Nebenteru's sarcophagus and held it up. "A perfect match."

Imogen touched the center crystal. "I think it's a kind of energy source."

Trummel placed the disk toward the one fitted inside the wall. When the two center crystals got close, they began to glow brighter. Patterns on the disks lit up in a spiral sequence. Then the lift came to life with whirring machinery and blinking lights. The front and back double doors closed, securing them inside the cube. Each door had a small window. A single lever illuminated.

Trummel hugged Imogen. "Great work, Im. Sometimes you simply amaze me."

The rare compliment made her beam. Dyfan whispered into her ear, "I knew it would be you to get us moving again."

She smiled, feeling relieved that she had solved the cube's riddle.

Trummel pushed the lever up and the lift ascended soundlessly. As they rode toward some unknown level, Imogen's elation lasted only seconds before she was reminded that Caleb wouldn't be going the rest of the way. Trummel and Gosswick leaned back against a wall, watching the doors. Dyfan rested with his eyes closed. They traveled higher and higher. More than five minutes passed. Finally, the lift slowed and came to a stop with a soft hiss. The double doors nearest the wall opened to a stone platform.

Trummel exited first. Imogen gasped as she tilted her head back. They approached the base of a brick wall that rose so high it disappeared into the infinite black above. Giant stones had been masoned to fit together with perfect precision.

"Some sort of fortress," Trummel said.

Gosswick touched a brick that was taller than his six feet and longer than a car. "These stones must weigh several tons each. How do you suppose the builders stacked them?"

Trummel shook his head. "I've wondered the same about the pyramids."

"This feels like our final destination," Dyfan said. "We're very close now."

Other than the platform that led back to the elevator, there was no other way to go but through a colossal gate. Like many gates before it, the threshold was solid stone and required a code entered into a nearby panel. Imogen said, "We just have to figure out how to get inside."

⋆　⋆　⋆

The night boat carrying its crew of mariners trundled through dark waters. Caleb was grateful to finally be out of that dive suit. He felt different inside. Lighter. He'd faced his greatest fears and lived. He still couldn't explain the miracle that had given him another chance, only that Duat wasn't just a hellish landscape full of demons and ghosts.

God and his angels are present here too.

When Bakari returned from spouting orders to the crew, Caleb looked at him in amazement. "I watched you die."

Bakari smirked. "It will take more than a few *shemayu* to take me down."

"How did you escape?"

The guide pulled out a necklace that contained a small silver disk. "I can call upon a portal to my world whenever I need one." He turned and barked orders in another language. Two smaller boatmen came over. "Caleb, I'd like you to meet two of my sons, Toku and Benyi." Like their father, they had glowing blue symbols on their foreheads and beneath their eyes. One boy looked seventeen, the other around age twelve.

Caleb shook their hands. "Nice to meet you."

"I'm training them to be guides," Bakari said with a father's pride. Then he spoke in a commanding voice and the boys ran back to their duties.

"I don't understand," Caleb said. "Earlier your crew had hideous faces that looked like sea creatures. Their mouths were sewn shut with fishhooks."

"Sometimes my kind only appear to humans as reflections of their inner demons. That you can see us in our true form is a sign that you've healed a dark part of your soul."

"There's so much I don't understand about this underworld. Who's controlling the Dark Realm? Is it God or some other form of higher intelligence?"

Bakari shrugged. "Who created this world is a mystery to my kind as much as it is to yours."

The boat approached a high mountain wall that tapered off into the dark. Caleb recognized the ladder that ran up the elevator shaft. As the boat bumped against it, Bakari walked over to a panel and punched in a code. Moments passed as they waited.

Then, high up above, a cube outlined in lights began to descend. When it reached bottom and opened, Caleb was disappointed that the elevator was empty. He hoped he could find the others. Bakari helped him step inside and showed him how to work the lever. "Take the lift all the way to the top."

"Can you go with me?" Caleb asked.

"This is as far as I can go." Bakari held up his palm, a gesture of goodbye. "Best of luck on your journey, my friend."

The double doors closed. Caleb peered out a small window and watched Bakari's boat and crew growing smaller as the elevator carried him upward toward some unknown place.

PART FOUR
REVELATIONS

CHAPTER FIFTY-ONE

Working with the codex in Grandfather's diary, Imogen and the others made several attempts to open the colossal gate. She called out codes and Trummel pushed the buttons with symbols. The stubborn stone door refused to give them access.

Trummel cursed as he lost his patience. "Why won't it open?"

Imogen took a step back. Instead of a statue of a demon guardian, a stone relief of the all-seeing Eye of Horus seemed to study them. "I think the problem is we're trying to match the codes with a demon name."

"She's right," Dyfan said. "The vibration of this realm is much higher than in the demon realms."

Imogen searched through the diary, itself a crazy puzzle of drawings and symbols. There were mathematical equations here and there to make it all a confusing mess at first glance. The more she looked at it, the more she recognized patterns in the chaos. Codes on one page aligned with names on another. Even the illustrations began to link with the text. At last, she came across two side-by-side pages with the Eye of Horus drawn at the top of each. On the outside margin of the left page was a set of tiny symbols. Directly across to the far-right margin was a tiny phrase written in English. Imogen smiled. "Trummel, step aside. I think I've got it." She punched in the codes and called out, "Horus. All seeing, all knowing."

The stone door's surface changed to a tall reflective black pool that defied gravity.

"Good show, Im!" Again, Trummel got caught up in the spirit of their victory and put his arm around her. He waved his hand across the door, causing the pool to ripple with tiny black beads. Like at the previous mercurial gates, his arm crossed through it, submerging all the way to the elbow and came out dry. Trummel slapped his hands together, grinning. "I've lived my whole life for this moment."

His smile fell when lights reflected on the gate. In the watery mirror, Imogen saw the cube-shaped lift return to the top of the shaft. It clacked on the rails as it came to a stop. She whirled around to see the double doors sliding open. Caleb stepped onto the platform.

He smiled with relief. "Thank God, I found you."

"Caleb?" Disbelieving her eyes, Imogen ran to him. Without thinking, she hugged him, feeling his heart racing with hers. "You're alive? I thought we lost you."

"I thought so too," he said, holding her tight. "Did you miss me?"

She half laughed with tears in her eyes. "Very much." It was the first true miracle she had ever witnessed. The others came over and greeted Caleb.

Trummel's face was a mask of shock. "How on earth did you survive that fall?"

"For a while, I thought I'd died." Caleb told them about his descent into his own personal purgatory. How he used the power of his faith to rise out of it. He seemed lit up by the experience. His eyes were brighter. He had a vitality that Imogen could feel radiating off his body. If Caleb hadn't returned, she would have never believed it possible. She was overjoyed and relieved to learn that Bakari was alive, as well.

"I met his sons," Caleb said. "I owe much of my getting back to you to Bakari."

"Well, now I've seen it all," Gosswick joked, shaking his head. "You're one lucky bloke, Flash."

Dyfan shook Caleb's hand. "It's good to have you back, mate."

Trummel said, "I hate to spoil this grand reunion, but that gate won't stay open forever." He walked back to the gate and the others followed.

"Time to see what's on the other side." Trummel stepped through the portal. Gosswick and Dyfan followed.

When it was just Caleb and Imogen alone outside the gate, he took her hand. "Before we step inside, I need to share something with you. While we were separated, I missed you deeply. I feared I might never see you again. I know that right now you're not ready for a—"

Imogen pulled Caleb to her and kissed him, surprising them both. When again he kissed her with all his passion, this time she surrendered and kissed him with deep emotion. It was the most powerful connection she had ever felt with any man. The vulnerability she now felt was scary and exciting.

When they pulled apart, he said, "Ready for this next adventure?"

"I'm ready to find out what my grandfather discovered."

"Anything might be waiting for us on the other side."

"For some reason, I'm not afraid." She placed her hand on the giant brick wall, feeling its power. "This may sound funny, but I feel like I've been called to this place."

"I think we all were," Caleb said.

Imogen crossed through the portal. It was like stepping through a gentle waterfall of beads. On the other side, shafts of gray light filtered through a high vented ceiling. She could see far beyond the beams of their helmet lights. Before them stretched a vast chamber several hundred yards deep in all directions. The sheer size of this realm caught Imogen's breath. A grid of stone walkways networked between square hollows. Above each square floated a giant metal sphere. About three hundred yards away loomed a strange structure shrouded in gloom.

"Wow," Caleb said, taking it all in.

Dyfan stepped up beside them. "It appears with all this excitement, Dr. Trummel has abandoned me. Could I trouble you both to be my eyes?"

"Of course." Imogen explained what she was seeing – the infinite grid of bridges and square canyons, the spheres, the strange black structure that rose out of the grid's center. Then she placed Dyfan's hand on her shoulder. "Stay right behind me. The catwalks have no railing."

With Imogen leading, the three of them walked down the center walkway. The edges on either side dropped off into dark chasms that seemed bottomless. The danger of falling into one made her heart quicken.

This chamber seemed to defy the laws of physics. They passed between dozens of giant floating spheres that suspended over the squares without any signs of wires to connect them to the ceiling. Made of sleek black metal and pocked with holes that looked like eyes, the spheres silently turned, as if watching Imogen, Dyfan, and Caleb.

Light beams from two caving helmets cut the gray gloom ahead. Trummel and Gosswick were already at the massive structure. As Imogen, Dyfan, and Caleb reached the center of the chamber, Trummel cried out, "I've found it!"

Imogen stood in awe next to the others as their beams illuminated the dark stone steps of a giant pyramid.

★ ★ ★

The tomb's architecture, rising nine tiers to a flat apex, most resembled an Aztec pyramid, although the stone of this one was solid black and shimmered when their lights passed over it.

The revelation of discovering a strange, unknown pyramid hidden deep within an Egyptian mountain brought tears to Imogen's eyes. She had dreamed of discovering one since she'd been a young girl exploring tombs. She became overwhelmed with gratitude that Grandfather had invited her to seek this place for herself. She also felt sad that he couldn't be there to explore it with her.

She held Caleb's hand. "Have you ever seen anything so glorious?"

He shook his head in disbelief. "What is a pyramid doing inside Duat?"

"I don't know, but I can't wait to find out."

A moat of dark water bordered the wide base on which the pyramid sat. Another flat bridge led about thirty yards across to a stone platform on the other side of the moat.

Trummel hurried across the bridge. Gosswick followed. Together Imogen and Caleb walked Dyfan across the stone bridge. Like the walkways, there was no railing. A short drop led down to water so black it resembled tar. The surface was perfectly smooth. After walking thirty yards, they reached the other side, a wide plaza in front of the pyramid. Inlaid in the stone floor were peculiar metal designs. A blend of gold and platinum shined when light passed over them. The pyramid's front staircase ascended high above them. Trummel and Gosswick had already reached the sixth tier.

Caleb, Imogen, and Dyfan climbed the wide steps to the sixth level. They rested at a wide platform that had a walkway and another colossal door made of dark gray metal. Imogen helped the others search for a way to open the door. There were plenty of symbols around the threshold, but none matched the codes in the diary.

"There must be another way in." Trummel continued to lead the group up the steps to the ninth, smaller tier that made up the flat apex. The roof's architecture was like nothing Imogen had ever seen. Strange columns bordered the edges. The pillars resembled totem poles, with monstrous effigies and symbols etched into them.

Everyone spread out. Trummel turned in a circle, holding up his arms in reverence to the totems. "Years of searching…all those wasted expeditions…and now this."

★   ★   ★

Caleb stepped up to a column and studied the reliefs of the creatures' faces. He thought of the pyramids he'd visited in Egypt, the temples of ancient Sumer in Iraq. His mind found no match for any of the beasts etched into these ruins. Had they discovered a civilization that predated the Egyptians? Perhaps one even older than the Sumerians? The mythical lost city of Atlantis came to mind.

"Come have a look at this," Imogen called.

She was standing at the very center of the roof. Everyone gathered around her at a metal pylon that stood about waist high.

Imogen showed them a page from her grandfather's diary that had a sketch of the pylon. "He was here."

Trummel ran his hand along a round groove on the pylon's crest. "This has to be where the key goes." Trummel inserted the disk into the groove. It lit up.

A humming sound began to circle around the pyramid's roof. At each column, light glowed from within, flashing on and off. The strange glyphs illuminated the pillars with a sapphire glow. Even stranger, the patterns of the symbols changed each time they blinked on. As Caleb studied them, he began to see a sequence – dots, then lines, then crosses, then faces. Then the entire columns glowed with lines, crosses, dots and faces all at once. The hum changed notes with each pulse, making a sound that was almost musical.

The others stood, equally fascinated. Imogen looked Caleb's way, shaking her head in amazement. Trummel ran his hands up one of the columns. The musical notes and light patterns changed at his touch, as if he were playing a vertical xylophone.

"Incredible," Trummel said, grinning.

Caleb's gut knotted. He'd become overwhelmed with dread that activating the pyramid was wrong, a breach somehow of this mysterious fortress. Caleb couldn't shake his sense that whoever had built this underground pyramid still lived here.

Gosswick seemed anxious too. He walked the roof's perimeter, keeping his eye on the steps below.

"What's wrong?" Imogen asked Caleb.

"There's so much we don't know about this place," Caleb said. "Why is it here? Who built it?" He approached the edge of the roof to see if there might be anyone coming. He felt defenseless without his gun. Imogen stepped up beside him and placed her hand on his shoulder.

Something strange began happening below. The stone grid began to glow. It stretched like a giant net three hundred yards or more in all directions, ending at walls several stories high and constructed of those giant, perfectly matching bricks. The sophisticated masonry and network of lights made it clear that a civilization with advanced understanding of architecture and engineering had built this subterranean fortress.

But who were they?

This pyramid, a secret presumably kept by the pharaohs, must have been thousands of years old, built long before man had developed such advanced technology. Yet somehow the pyramid and grid were being powered by a source of energy.

The floating spheres came to life with bright white dots. Light beams from the orbs projected moving pictures onto the square pits between the walkways. Partially transparent, a hundred movies played at once. Caleb recognized himself in several – abseiling down a tube, trekking through a swamp, fighting men in deep-sea diver suits, kissing Imogen, and dozens more of his experiences in this realm. Other squares in the grid projected movies of Imogen, Trummel, Gosswick, and Dyfan.

"How can this be?" Caleb asked Imogen.

★   ★   ★

She shook her head, awestruck. There was nothing in her mind that could prepare her for what she was witnessing: scenes from surviving her burning house, studying a scroll with her grandfather, her journey through Duat. Seeing her experiences reflected inside the grid both amazed and frightened her.

Trummel stepped up beside them. The grid glowed in his eyes. "Absolutely brilliant. This realm is far more intelligent than I expected."

"You've been withholding information from us," Imogen said. "What do you know about this place?"

"This whole underworld, the reality you have come to understand, is an illusion."

She looked at him, confused. "What do you mean?"

"After your grandfather was committed to the asylum, I worked in secret with the doctors to try to make sense of the strange scars that covered his body. I visited Harlan and probed his mind for months. He would only speak coherently when he and I were alone. When he was most lucid, he remembered bits and pieces of what he had learned from his year spent inside Duat. The hospital never found out the truth, because Harlan only revealed his wisdom to me, and I kept what I learned to myself."

"You never involved me in any of this," Imogen said.

"That was a decision of the board's, although I agreed. You were too close to your grandfather to maintain a logical viewpoint. Harlan's mind was fragile. Had you been there during the inquiries, he might not have been able to recall what happened to his team."

She felt betrayed. Not only had Trummel kept this from her, but also the museum's board members had fed her lies, while appearing to sympathize with her loss.

Trummel was too enthralled by the grid to notice her devastation. "Harlan told me that Duat is a multidimensional realm of infinite possibilities. Our fears, our pasts, moment-to-moment decisions, conscious will, and our faith all affect how our soul's journey manifests. No two souls traveling through the Dark Realm have the same experience. And only a small fraction of explorers make it this far."

All the projected memories winked out. Row by row, the grid's squares went dark again.

Trummel said, "There's still much to discover," then returned to the center of the pyramid's roof where the silver disk radiated at the pylon.

Imogen's attention returned to the blinking columns, the lyrical hum they gave off with each pulsing heartbeat. Their vibration was growing stronger. "What have we activated by powering up the pyramid?"

Caleb shook his head, his eyes filled with worry.

The sequences of blinking patterns completed, and all the totem poles bordering the apex glowed with solid cobalt blue light. The pyramid vibrated. Imogen had the sensation the stone blocks beneath them were sliding apart and would fall, dropping everyone to their deaths.

The humming sound faded. The tremors slowed to a halt. The floor held together.

Imogen only had a second to release her breath before a series of clicks and clacks sent echoes through the fortress. On the roof's stone floor a large circular seal rose several inches and then rotated sideways, revealing an opening. The group circled around it and shone their helmet beams inside the pyramid. The interior was illuminated by its own light source.

Imogen gasped.

Ten feet below was a crypt with five giant coffins.

CHAPTER FIFTY-TWO

Trummel's mind was a frenzy of excitement as he and the others descended a staircase into the crypt. On all the walls and across the floor, blue light glowed from embedded veins that branched to a round hole in the floor. The five giant sarcophagi were placed around the hole, like spokes in a wheel, heads positioned inward, feet toward the walls.

Ever since Trummel had first traveled to Egypt, he had been curious about the history of early man and his gods. Here before him was a missing link to their past. The anthropoid coffins, made with gold and silver, were the largest he had ever seen. They appeared Egyptian in design, yet bore unknown markings too. The prone figures on top had the bodies of men and heads of animals – ram, jackal, crocodile, cow, and a bird with a long, curved beak, like an ibis. There was a crescent moon on the ibis's head. Trummel recognized that one as Thoth. The jackal, of course, was Anubis. The crocodile with a female body most likely represented the underworld goddess, Ammit. The ram god represented Khnum, and the cow goddess was Hathor. All gods known to have resided in the underworld, according to Egyptian scriptures.

Trummel had seen these figures countless times on papyrus scrolls and tomb walls. Standing before their coffins, he felt the same elation as he had as a young lad searching for treasure with his sister. That moment of discovering something important, something that expanded the mind to new heights and the heart to fullness…it was this elation, and the promise he'd made long ago to his sister's grave, that had driven him on his quest. How he wished Nell was there to share this moment with him. *I found this for us.* He sent the thought into the ether, hoping his sister's spirit might hear.

Everyone stood around the sarcophagi. Dyfan moved his hands over Ammit's crocodile face. He smiled, so emotional that he was almost in tears. "We found them."

"Yes, we did, old chap." Trummel ran his fingers over the intricate designs, marveling at the craftsmanship.

"What could be inside?" Imogen wondered aloud. "Giant mummies?"

"Let's open one and see," Trummel said.

They gathered around the sarcophagus with the jackal face. It took all of them to lift the lid and set it on the stone floor. Inside lay a giant corpse that must have once stood eight feet tall. It wasn't wrapped like a mummy. Its chest and abdomen were covered in armor that sculpted its muscular anatomy. The dark platinum armor was untarnished and the durable fabric that made up its mid-calf kilt had withstood centuries. The gray flesh of its exposed lower legs, arms, and neck had barely deteriorated. A metal, jackal-faced mask covered its head.

"A giant Egyptian warrior?" Caleb asked.

"Anubis, the god himself." Trummel removed its mask. The corpse's gray face beneath had a wide mouth with enormous teeth – just like the monstrous faces engraved into the columns on the roof. "What we are looking at is one of the Shining Ones." Trummel looked across the sarcophagus at Imogen. "Your grandfather told me that an explorer who makes it through the underworld gates and realms would arrive at a *shetayet* – a tomb of the gods."

"This is what he was searching for..." She shook her head, as if disbelieving her own eyes.

Trummel nodded. "Ever since he deciphered the missing piece of the Ani scroll. Harlan's team sacrificed their lives to pave the way for us."

Imogen stared silently at the corpse of Anubis.

Gosswick beamed. "This gold and silver must be worth a fortune. How do we get all this back to England?"

"We'll find a way."

"You actually plan to remove these?" Imogen asked.

"If we don't claim them, someone else will. Just imagine having the remains of actual ancient Egyptian gods on display at the British Museum. London will become a Mecca to the world." Trummel moved to the next sarcophagus and signaled the others to help. "Let's remove the other lids."

In each sarcophagus, a giant corpse had a skull and armor similar to the first. What distinguished the creatures were the different animal masks they wore and the emblems marking their chest plates.

Trummel picked up Thoth's bird mask. "We've found proof that the deities the Egyptians worshipped actually visited them in the flesh."

He thought of all the ridicule he had received from his university colleagues for his outlandish theories. Even Dr. Harlan Riley had remained a skeptic, trying to fit his understanding of the Egyptian gods inside a box limited by science and historical records. But Trummel, whose intellect far exceeded that of his colleagues, recognized that the mysteries of man lay far beyond the reaches of science, history, religion, and even the stars.

In a book Trummel published titled *Unexplained Mysteries of Ancient Egypt*, he theorized that a race of celestial giants helped the pharaohs design the pyramids and advance their civilization.

He had argued that mysterious giants were described in the texts of older civilizations. The beings that the Egyptians depicted in their art as gods connected to the Sumerian god-kings, the Anunnaki, who had reigned over ancient Sumer for thousands of years. The Middle East wasn't the only region where celestial giants supposedly walked the earth. The mythical yeti roamed the Himalayas to commune with Tibetan monks. The temples of Angkor in French Indochina depicted their own beastly creatures, as did the pyramids of Central and South America. The Mayas and Incas described underworlds similar to the Egyptians' Duat, all containing gods and demons.

Every primitive culture around the world that had radically advanced their civilization and constructed pyramids and giant statues of gods had been visited by an advanced race that, according to the stories of the ancient peoples, came down from the heavens. Or, as Trummel boldly stated in his book, "visited our planet when man still lived in caves. It was these celestial beings that civilized early man." Trummel's book had fueled the fires between the opposing theorists, including church leaders.

His lectures often evoked chuckles from the audience, sometimes outrage and heated debate. Not one colleague supported his theory. Now here, in this lost world hidden deep beneath an Egyptian tomb, lay compelling evidence that such a race existed. He couldn't wait to return with it to London and show the fools he had been right all along.

"Where did they come from?" Caleb asked.

"The stars, an alternate dimension. Perhaps these corpses will guide us to the answer," Trummel hypothesized. "The ancient Egyptians had a complex religious system and believed many gods lived here on earth among the people. The pharaoh acted as a mediator between men and a pantheon of gods. The Sumerians also recorded in their texts that they had communed with higher beings called the Shining Ones. Hopefully this discovery will shed light on the most enigmatic mysteries of ancient cultures."

Trummel grinned in the pyramid's interior light. "These beings that the Egyptians called gods must have died long ago. I'm after the relics they entombed here with their bodies." He stepped up to the hole in the floor. Below, at the core of the pyramid, glowed a narrow, vertical tube with honeycomb walls. Several feet down, the hexagonal cells contained large, disembodied hearts. Roughly the size of melons, each organ had a dark outer layer that swelled and contracted. Blue light glowed inside them. Thick, knotted arteries and veins branched across their outer skin and grew up the honeycomb walls like creeping ivy.

"How could a pyramid have beating hearts?" Imogen asked. "Is this tomb alive?"

Trummel noticed that the giant corpses' chest armor had paneled sections. He went to Thoth and pulled the center panel of its chest plate open like a door. The chest cavity was empty. Its anatomical design – part organic, part machine – fascinated Trummel. All along the interior of its rib cage networked rubber tubes that would connect to a heart. "The hearts of these creatures appear to be powering the pyramid."

Dyfan held his palms over the hole in the floor. "This is the source of the vibration that's been pulling us here."

"It is the divine power men have been searching for in these caves for centuries." Trummel breathed anxiously. He thought of all the skeletons of the ancient warriors in the bone maze. The web-enshrouded bones in the realm of spiders. The offerings of jewelry and trinkets left behind at the altars of the convent. So many had died on their quests to find this place. How many, besides Harlan, had actually made it to the pyramid? That Trummel had reached this tomb to find everything intact confirmed what he had always believed about himself: he was destined to solve the greatest mystery of the universe. What race of beings came before humans? And how did humans evolve from tribal cave people to architects of great civilizations?

He couldn't wait to see what amazing revelation he would learn next. "Imogen, climb down into the tube and pull out the hearts."

She looked at him with shock. "You don't mean that."

"Actually, I do."

"That's bad science and you know it," she said. "We should leave the hearts in place until we fully understand their function."

Trummel grew annoyed by her disobedience. "I didn't come all this way to leave the greatest archaeological discovery of all time." He pressed his face close to Imogen's. "Now stop wasting time and get down there."

Caleb charged Trummel. "That's no way to speak to her."

Gosswick intervened, pressing a firm hand against Caleb's chest.

"Stay out of this, Beckett." Trummel gave Caleb a piercing look, then turned to Imogen. "We're not here to follow standard protocols. We're here to bring these relics back to England."

"Why not climb down there yourself?" Caleb demanded.

"She's the only one small enough to fit inside that tube." Trummel pulled out his pistol. "Imogen, get a move on."

She stared at the barrel, then gave him a defiant smirk. "Put the gun down, Nathan, you're not a murderer."

"Maybe not me, but Goss won't hesitate to issue some pain."

"If you hurt me, you're not getting down there."

"You're not the one who will suffer." Trummel nodded at Goss. The soldier punched Caleb in the ribs and he fell to his knees. A chop to the back toppled him to the floor.

"No…" Imogen tried to go to Caleb, but Trummel stepped in front of her.

He gripped both of her arms. "I've traveled too far to get those relics. Now, get down that tube."

CHAPTER FIFTY-THREE

Imogen climbed into the hole. Her hands and feet followed grooves leading down into a tube so tight it pressed against her back and shoulders. The hearts beat loud, a synchronized *whump-whump, whump-whump*. The energy inside pushed warm air against her.

At the bottom of the tube, she reached another chamber that was bigger than the one above. Honeycombed walls stretched from floor to ceiling.

"What do you see?" Trummel asked from the hole in the ceiling.

"Dozens of hearts." Imogen explored deeper into the chamber. The honeycombed walls networked like a maze. In each hexagonal cell pumped a large beating heart that floated in clear liquid contained by a soft membrane.

Around each honeycomb glowed blinking glyphs. Conduits and cables snaked along the ceiling. The floor was a metal grid. Imogen shone her light down the small squares. The beam disappeared into a dark chasm below. She couldn't find any walls or floor. With each tier of the pyramid, she imagined the chambers got bigger and bigger.

As she weaved through the honeycombs, she passed two open doorways on either side that led into darkened passages. She followed one short hallway to the end where she almost lost her footing. A steep shaft cut in the floor went straight down. Vertigo caused her to teeter toward the edge. Imogen shone her flashlight into it, trying to find the bottom. The beam dimmed and winked out, the battery dead.

Relying on the pulsing ambient light, she returned to the labyrinth of glowing hearts. She found an exit at the farthest end and stepped into an enormous, warehouse-sized chamber. Thirty metal coffins lay evenly spaced apart on the chamber floor.

CHAPTER FIFTY-FOUR

Imogen walked among the coffins. They varied in sizes, some small and some longer than eight feet. Like the five in the tomb above, an animal mask covered the head of each sarcophagus. Two featured winged goddesses, Isis perhaps and her sister, Nephthys. Beyond them, elevated on a black slate platform, lay the largest sarcophagus, ten feet or longer. Imogen climbed several steps to the top of the platform. She recognized the face of Osiris on the coffin's lid.

The Egyptians had many myths about this god. He was an early king of Egypt, who had married his sister, Isis. His jealous brother, Set, eventually murdered Osiris and sent him down to the underworld, where Osiris became ruler of the dead and the demons of Duat.

Imogen had always believed that the deities in the myths were fictitious beings. With this discovery, the entire lineage of the pharaohs, dating all the way back to Osiris, rewrote itself in her mind. The revelation that gods had once walked the earth shook her to the core. It felt wrong to have climbed into their resting place.

"Imogen!" Trummel called impatiently. His echoing shouts startled her.

She made her way back through the maze and returned to the bottom of the tube. "I think we should leave at once," she urged.

Trummel was waiting at the top of the hole. "I'm not going round and round with you. Quit stalling and bring me one of the hearts."

Imogen hesitated. She didn't want to disrupt the pyramid's system. She debated whether to say anything about what she'd found in the far chamber. If Trummel knew more coffins were down here, he'd break through pyramid floors to reach the lower level. Fearing the consequences if he did, Imogen kept silent.

Trummel sighed. "Imogen, get on with it."

"No, I won't tamper with these. It feels all wrong."

"Then you give me no choice. Goss, send Imogen a message."

She heard Caleb's painful cry up above. Then Gosswick stepped up to the top of the hole. "A gift from your boyfriend." He dropped a bleeding severed finger down the tube. It landed beside Imogen's boot. An icy feeling swept through her. She stared up at Trummel and Gosswick in shock.

"Every precious minute you waste," Trummel said, "Goss will keep dropping down fingers."

Imogen gave Trummel a burning look of hatred. He stared back at her, cold. "Get on with it," he said.

She turned and faced the honeycombs. The hearts contained within looked like gestating larvae. She started to touch the seal of one cell, then pulled her hand away. The thought of sticking her hand in the cell made her stomach cramp with disgust. This beating organ had once been inside the chest of a god. Now it appeared to run the pyramid. She feared what would happen if she removed it.

"Ten seconds, Imogen, or Caleb loses another finger."

"No, I'll do it." Cringing, she slid her arms through a honeycomb's soft membrane and reached elbow-deep into warm fluid. The heart pumped faster as her hands gripped it. It had slick, organic skin with protruding veins. As she pulled the heart out, rubber tubes attached to the pulmonary veins and arteries popped off, leaking viscous liquid onto her legs and shoes.

The empty honeycomb turned black. The humming sound at the pyramid's core changed and the lights dimmed. In the surrounding honeycombs, all the other hearts pumped faster, their internal lights blinking.

Oh, God, what have we done?

The quick palpitations lasted only a moment before the floating hearts settled down. The lights brightened back to normal.

Feeling ashamed for violating the pyramid, Imogen came up the ladder with the glowing, swelling organ. As she stepped away from the hole, she cradled the heart as if it were a newborn. Its pulsations resonated inside the chamber: *whump-whump, whump-whump.*

"What does it feel like?" Dyfan asked.

"Alive. We're not dealing with just relics here; these are living organisms." Imogen offered it to Trummel.

"Hold on to it."

"I need to tend to Caleb."

He looked pale as he held his bleeding hand to his chest. "I'm fine. Stay where you are."

Trummel said to Imogen, "Do exactly what I tell you, or I'll let Goss choose what he cuts off next."

Behind Caleb, Gosswick held a bloodstained knife. "Maybe I'll go for an ear this time."

Imogen shook her head. "This isn't you, Nathan."

"I won't stand for anyone sabotaging my mission."

"I don't give a damn about your mission," Caleb said. "Imogen's safety is my concern."

"How chivalrous," Trummel said.

"Stop fighting," Imogen pleaded. "I've done what you asked."

Trummel offered Imogen his knife. "Your next task is to slice open the heart. What I want is *inside* it."

She met eyes with Caleb. He shook his head slightly. "Don't."

Her hand trembled as she grasped the knife's handle. The organ felt so vulnerable in her hands she felt as if Trummel was asking her to stab an embryo in its womb. As she started to bring the blade down, the heart pumped faster. She stopped short of cutting it. "I can't. Open it yourself."

Caleb cursed as Gosswick's knife nicked his ear.

Gosswick grinned at Imogen. "I can do this all day, sweetheart."

The fast-beating heart in her hands pumped against her chest until it synchronized with her own heartbeats. More than alive, the alien thing felt like a conscious life-form aware of being in danger. It nuzzled against her like a child seeking comfort in the bosom of its mother. Imogen felt its fear so strongly she dropped the knife.

Dyfan picked it up and stepped forward. "I'll open it. Please, give the heart to me."

"I don't think we should harm it," Imogen said. "I think it's aware of us."

"Give me that." Trummel snatched the organ from Imogen and gave it to Dyfan.

Imogen backed away, unsure of what was going to happen. Caleb rose to his feet, grimacing in pain. Gosswick drew his pistol and kept it trained on Caleb.

After taking a deep breath, Dyfan dragged the blade across the thick outer skin. The heart released a loud *hissss*. Purplish-blue liquid dribbled onto his hand. The organ opened like a juicy peach, revealing part of its hidden seed.

Trummel moved closer. "Ease it out, gently."

Gripping the dissected heart, Dyfan placed his thumbs into the slit and ripped it open wider. The thing inside pulsed. Its texture resembled metal infused with something organic. Trummel's torch illuminated the seed's many crevices.

Dyfan pulled the object free, letting the skin of the deflated heart drop to the floor. Neon blue fluid flowed along the stone floor to his shoes. The thing in his hands pulsated and writhed like a breathing, living organism. It was shaped like a sphere made of interwoven flesh with metal bands. Along the edges of the bands moved hundreds of tiny silver needles.

"What is that thing?" Imogen asked.

"According to your grandfather, inside the hearts of the gods is a codex made from their bodies," Trummel said. "It is the most advanced book man has ever discovered."

A fat vein coiled like a worm along one side of it. The book appeared to inhale and exhale.

Trummel's eyes gleamed. "It's breathing air for the first time. It has been here all these millennia, gestating since before the pharaohs reigned Egypt. The gods gave them books like this one to advance their civilization." He took the knife from Dyfan's hand, pointed the blade at the details of the book's skin. "Just look at the fine carvings of its surface, the life force that flows through its veins. No relic compares."

Imogen stepped forward for a closer look. Strange lettering curved and veined around the sphere. More needles and ribbed tubes crisscrossed in the design. A dark liquid oozed from numerous pores as the codex continued to swell and contract.

Imogen felt both enthralled and repulsed. "What else did Grandfather tell you?" she asked Trummel.

"This book was written by a race far superior to ours." He looked at the giant corpse with the ibis mask. "Thoth was the scribe and the keeper of the Books of All Knowing. These books contain the truth about all life, death, the universe, enlightenment, absolutely everything."

"Grandfather had been fascinated with Thoth," Imogen said. "Thought he was the key to ancient Egypt's mysteries."

Trummel nodded. "Thoth gave the Egyptians the Book of Two Ways, the Book of Gates, the Amduat, but there are countless more volumes stored in this pyramid." He motioned to the giant corpses in the open coffins. "The gods confined these books within their hearts. The knowledge of the cosmos was encoded in their genes. Through the ages, they sacrificed their bodies so primitive man could obtain their wisdom." Trummel began quoting theories from his book. "The early Egyptians seemed to be the most ready to receive this wisdom. After rising into a powerful empire, the pharaohs made these beings into deities. When the pharaohs stopped ruling Egypt, the truth died with them, buried in their tombs—" Trummel looked directly at Imogen, "—and lost to those who disbelieved the myths." He smiled proudly. "I intend to utilize this knowledge for the advancement of the human race."

"You're seriously out of your mind," Caleb said.

Trummel ignored this. He became animated like he did when he gave his lectures. "Imagine what the world will be like when we expose these books to the masses, the churches, other governments.... Thoth's collection of higher knowledge can answer every question ever imagined. Wars will end, religions will unify and finally preach the same gospel, because man will no longer quarrel over God or science. Man will know the whole truth."

"But what if we're not ready to receive the knowledge?" Imogen asked. "You can't foresee the consequences without knowing the contents of the books. The release of information beyond our present abilities to comprehend could easily unleash enough fear to be catastrophic on a global scale."

"You're being paranoid," Trummel said. "Our surviving the Duat and discovering this tomb proves that we're ready for the wisdom of the gods."

"Us, maybe, but we were drawn here. We've spent our careers searching for answers. That doesn't mean everybody else can handle learning that alien beings existed before us."

"Imogen's right." Dyfan's cataract gray eyes looked up from the book. "I'm getting a strong intuition that this knowledge won't bring power to the human race. It will only destroy us. I won't be a part of this." He walked toward the hole, his shoes squishing through the puddle.

"Goss, stop him!"

The soldier locked arms around Dyfan.

Trummel lifted the Scotsman's chin with the knife's blade. "Open the book, or I open you."

Gosswick released the blind man. Dyfan ran a hand across the sphere's bulging surface. Several needles pointed upward. They swayed with the movement of his hand like tiny sensors on an ocean-floor fish.

Imogen wished she could stop them, but Trummel and Gosswick looked insane enough to commit murder.

Dyfan placed his fingers into a groove. The thing released a squeal and attached itself to his chest. Spiked metal tubes shot out like tentacles. They swung around his arms and torso, making a *whoosh-whoosh-whoosh* sound.

Gosswick stood too close and one scratched his cheek, drawing blood. "Bugger!" The captain backed away.

Attached to the appendages were tiny hooked claws that carved into Dyfan's flesh, shredding his clothes as they moved. Blood poured from the wounds.

Dyfan cried out, his face a mix of pain and terror.

Imogen moved to help him, but Trummel grabbed her. She tried to shake his grip. "We have to do something! He'll die!"

Trummel smiled like a madman. "What is one sacrificed life, when we can enlighten millions?"

Dyfan fell to his knees, moaning. The thing clung to his chest like a sucking parasite. More metal tubes emerged from slits that opened in its flesh and coiled around his lower body. A silver needle-legged centipede slithered up his face and wrapped around his head like a thorny wreath, each of its needles boring into his scalp. Blood tears streamed down Dyfan's face. His shrieks echoed in the pyramid's chamber.

Imogen watched in horror as a thick appendage with a lamprey mouth rose behind his head and attached to the back of his skull. His eyes rolled back to whites as the tubes worked their way down his face.

After a moment of torture, the parasite fell off his chest. Dyfan's screaming finally stopped. He ripped off most of the tubes. His exposed red flesh revealed tiny scriptures carved on his entire face and body. He yanked the last tube from his cranium, now completely bald. His beard was gone too, every hair plucked. He remained on his knees, half naked, save for a few tubes.

Dyfan stared hard at Imogen and the others, his eyes focused as if he could now see them. His shredded lips bled. He spoke in a deep, reverberating voice that sounded like someone else. "I knew you all would come and right on schedule."

"Thoth?" Trummel asked.

"That is one of my names." Dyfan looked at the scars that mapped his arms and torso. "You seek to know the truth of all truths."

"I saw the codex on Dr. Harlan Riley's body," Trummel said. "He told me whoever opens the Books of Thoth will embody the knowledge of the gods."

Dyfan nodded. "Harlan spent a year as my apprentice. I filled him with as much wisdom as the human mind and body can hold. He helped me run the Dark Realm's matrix. He had one weakness, though, a part of his humanity he could not let go of." He turned to face Imogen. "He wanted to bring you here to be enlightened along with him."

Imogen's eyes teared up. "Did he suffer here?"

"Not while with me. He flourished in the Dark Realm. Once your grandfather left, he was vulnerable to a world that was light-years behind him."

"Except me," Trummel said. "I understood enough to lead us here. I come as an ambassador for the human race. We are ready to advance our evolution to the next level."

"Of course, you would think that," Thoth said through Dyfan's mouth. "You see yourself as chosen. The only modern-day messiah capable of bringing my knowledge to humankind."

Trummel nodded. "People around the world have become uncivilized. With your books, we can put human evolution on its rightful course." He gestured a hand toward Dyfan. "This body will be the next living codex to carry your message. *I* will become a pharaoh who communes with the gods and translates your divine knowledge to the masses."

"So this is about you gaining power," Imogen said.

"It's about enlightening an idiotic world," Trummel said. "It's about bringing us out of the dark ages of ignorance, war, and conflicting religious and scientific theories. I'm giving man absolute truth, Imogen.

It's time to advance people to a level of supreme intellect that only I have known. Therefore *I* must control the power of these books."

Thoth's resonating voice chuckled. "You've always wanted to be a god, haven't you, Nathan Trummel?" Blood and incandescent fluid ran down Dyfan's body as he got up on his feet and walked slowly toward the archaeologist. "Ever since you were a boy, you've considered yourself superior to those around you. Gifted with high intelligence, but no conscience, no ability to connect emotionally with others. Except for your twin sister. Nell was the closest you came to feeling love, the only person in the world who understood you, and then she was taken from you." Trummel shook his head as Thoth spoke. "Nell's murder still haunts your mind, doesn't it? The resentment that courses through you runs deep into your marrow. You could not stop Nell's suffering at the hands of a mentally disturbed child killer." Dyfan whistled a singsong note. "You blamed your parents for not paying attention, saw them as pathetic and weak-minded. With Nell gone, you felt abandoned in a world of idiots. You visited her grave and made a pact that you would fix this broken world."

Trummel's face trembled. "I never told anyone…"

"Everyone has a book inside them. Dark little secrets that they keep." Dyfan turned his red glistening face toward Imogen. "An orphan who feels abandoned, not only by her family, but by God. You contemplated suicide a number of times, because deep down you don't believe you deserve to be alive. A part of you wishes you would have died in that fire."

Imogen felt shame and looked away.

"Don't listen to him," Caleb said.

Dyfan faced Caleb. "You try so hard to be a saint, but when you go after something you want, you can be selfish to a fault. You missed your own father's funeral because you were on another continent chasing a story."

Imogen watched Caleb's tough exterior fracture. What guilt he'd kept submerged deep within him rose to the surface, filling his eyes with pain.

The angry being inside Dyfan was opening the darkness within them. "You all thought you had come here to steal relics from our tomb, enlighten your planet, become rich and powerful, when in fact you came into our world to confront your darkest wounds. Death is the only way to advance to the enlightened level you seek."

Gosswick glared at Trummel. "You promised to make me and my men rich. They all died for your bloody cause."

Dyfan grinned. "Aiden Gosswick, your book is the most sordid of all, isn't it? If people could read your pages, how sickened they would be. You've slaughtered dozens of innocent people for greed. You drink to numb yourself, but the guilt is like a swarm of flies crawling across your disturbed brain." Dyfan wriggled his fingers. "You're feeling the flies now, aren't you?"

Gosswick raised a shaky pistol. "Shut the hell up."

Dyfan walked toward him. "Those poor little orphans…. Killing their parents wasn't enough. You had to slaughter the children too."

"Shut up! Shut up!" Gosswick fired his gun, hitting Dyfan in the center of the chest. He gripped his wound with a look of shock on his face. Then he fell to the floor.

"Dyfan!" Imogen ran to him. His blank eyes stared at the ceiling. The psychic's death tore her heart to pieces.

"Christ, Goss, what have you done?" Trummel examined Dyfan's corpse. "You've destroyed this one."

Gosswick stood red-faced and shaking. He scratched at the back of his head.

For the first time, Imogen saw the scriptures up close. Inscribed on Dyfan's face were the holy cross, the Star of David, the ankh, mathematical equations…. "What in God's name?" she breathed.

Trummel said, "The codex could have answered so many questions."

CHAPTER FIFTY-FIVE

Imogen huddled with Caleb near a wall. Blood dripped from the cut on his right ear. She wrapped a torn piece of his shirt around his injured hand that was missing an index finger.

"I'm sorry," she whispered.

"Don't be," Caleb said. "They've both lost their minds."

Trummel paced, gripping his pistol. Gosswick knelt over Dyfan's corpse and mumbled something in Swahili. Then he dipped his hands in a pool of blood and painted his own face and bald head red. The whites of Gosswick's wild eyes shone bright against the face paint as he grinned at Imogen and Caleb.

"Goss, get over here," Trummel commanded.

The two men conversed heatedly at the far end of the room. They blocked the stairway that led up to the exit.

Imogen whispered in Caleb's ear, "We need to figure out how to escape."

"I'll distract them," he whispered back. "When I do, you run."

"I'm not leaving you."

"I don't see us both getting out of this. If you can get away—"

"Imogen, get over here." Trummel aimed his pistol and motioned her over.

She squeezed Caleb's hand and shook her head. *Don't do anything foolish,* she tried to tell him with her eyes.

As she approached, Trummel said, "Go back down into the tube. I want as many books as we can carry." He put a hand on her face, but there was no warmth to his touch. "Since Dyfan's book is destroyed, I've decided you will become my next codex."

Caleb charged Trummel. "You son of a bitch."

Gosswick's fist smacked Caleb's jaw and he fell to his knees. The soldier got behind Caleb and pressed the gun barrel to his temple. "Flash, you know what the Kikuyu natives called me in Kenya...*Shetani mekundu.* It means 'red devil'. They were smart to fear me."

Caleb didn't move. His eyes were intense, calculating the situation.

"Don't hurt him," Imogen pleaded.

Trummel grabbed her arm. "Do exactly what I tell you or I can't say what Goss will do to Caleb."

She looked into Trummel's eyes and searched for the kind man she'd loved once. That part of him was gone, replaced by a madman. "This is a mistake, Nathan. We should find our way to the surface and leave the gods to reveal what they wish in their own time."

He nodded toward the hole in the floor. "Quit stalling."

Imogen climbed back down into the tube. The organs swelled and contracted in their honeycomb cells. She handed up four hearts, near the vertical shaft.

"Get more from below," he insisted.

She walked back through the chamber where many more hearts floated in their hexagonal cells. This was Thoth's library filled with books that he had scribed. She couldn't fathom the vast knowledge they contained. She wondered if the human brain could even handle it all. She imagined Trummel attempting to enlighten nations around the globe and people panicking at the news that the god or gods they believed in were actually aliens. Worldwide chaos as religions collapsed. Mass suicides, enraged fanatics going on killing sprees, and more crazies on the streets than in asylums.

She saw a vision of herself marked head to toe with scars and living in some palace with Trummel, a pharaoh ruling like a tyrant. He would most likely treat her as less than human as he demanded information out of her. Would she even be conscious of being Imogen Riley, or would she be more like Grandfather, lucid some moments and completely absent most of the time?

She couldn't let Thoth's books reach the surface.

She came upon a set of beating hearts that glowed white in their shells. Their energy and color changed when she drew near. The heartbeats quickened as she reached for them with both hands. She wondered if the books within had a consciousness even as embryos in their wombs. And how connected was Thoth's awareness to his books? Could he see her now?

She imagined the honeycombs were like insect eyes seeing multiple versions of her. She got the sense the hearts were trying to communicate with her. She pressed her hands into two of the gelatin-filled hexagons and touched the hearts. "Thoth, I know you're aware of our presence here. Please tell me what to do. How can I stop Trummel?"

A strange energy entered her hands and coursed up her arms, making them tingle. Her mind filled with alien codes. They made no sense, but intuitively she knew what to do with them. She walked to one of the engraved metal walls and tapped several keys on a panel. The wall sections rearranged themselves, unfolding like a puzzle box and disappeared. What appeared behind the wall looked like a cramped cockpit with a single giant chair. The black stone had been carved at a tilt like an observatory chair. Another giant sat lifeless in the seat. Imogen knew by his markings and falcon mask that this was Horus, son of Osiris. A hundred tubes and wires flowed out of the surrounding cockpit's machinery and connected to Horus's body suit like he was a mechanical marionette.

Imogen didn't think, allowing the force that had entered her mind to take over. She stepped up to the cockpit's curved panel and touched the alien cuneiform. The glyphs lit up in a sequence of codes that began to beep and chirp rapidly. They glowed across the reflective metal falcon mask.

On the circular ceiling appeared complex mathematical calculations and fast-moving codes. A hundred transparent images began to float all around her. Amazed, she poked her fingers through them and the moving images projected onto her skin and clothes. They were God's-eye views of various realms within Duat – the bone maze, the river cliff dwellings, the haunted swamp, the realm of spiders, and many more chambers inhabited with horrors. In many domains, realm guides in various forms, from human-looking, like Bakari and the women in red robes, to glowing white orbs, moved through the shadowy caverns. *Is this array of floating images the all-seeing Eye of Horus?* she wondered.

Trummel began shouting for Imogen.

There was no time to marvel at the cockpit's technology. The strange force that had been inside her body went out of her hands and into the blinking panel. The lights inside the pyramid flickered. The humming sound died away. The chamber went completely dark for a tense moment. Then codes on the panel went haywire. Red pulsing floodlights turned on along the floor. An alarm went off, echoing throughout the pyramid.

What have I activated?

The falcon mask's eyes began to glow. The sleeping giant burst into life. Its arms flapped wildly, shaking all the wires and tubes. It rapidly tapped symbols on a panel. A hundred ghostly images floated around its head. One moving image enlarged and Imogen saw herself in it.

The falcon mask turned to face her and spoke in a strange language that sent Imogen running. Ahead sounded hisses of steam. Then loud metallic cranking, like a hundred chains banging the hull of a ship.

She hurried through the honeycomb maze. Red lights pulsed. She reached an exit and found herself back in the warehouse-sized burial chamber. She froze. The sarcophagus that sealed Osiris was illuminated by red symbols that blinked all along the coffin. One by one the other thirty-plus coffins began to light up. Steam hissed out from the vents around them.

The cranking came from all the heavy coffin lids slowly opening. On the platform above, a monstrous hand rose from the mist around Osiris's sarcophagus and gripped the edge.

Imogen backpedaled out of the chamber and sprinted through the honeycombs for the escape hatch. Steam filled the maze. The alarm rang in her ears. All the hearts pumped wildly in their cells. A dozen small machines with mechanical arms floated down from the ceiling. They pulled hearts from their gestation fluid. Imogen flattened against a wall as the machines flew past her, carrying hearts toward the coffin chamber.

The alarm and red lights turned off, returning to the dim glow from the honeycombs. The loud metal clanking continued to echo behind her.

Imogen kept running, dodging more machines holding the pumping hearts. She passed one empty honeycomb cell after another. Her boots splashed through amniotic fluids and iridescent blue blood that dampened the grid floor and filtered into the drain below.

Ahead, Trummel's light shined down the ladder. "Imogen, what's that noise coming from?"

The clanking stopped, replaced by damnable screams.

She started up the ladder toward Trummel. "We've awakened them! We must leave at once." Before she reached the top of the tube, the hole sealed shut.

CHAPTER FIFTY-SIX

"Imogen!" Caleb ran to the sealed hole in the floor. He could hear her pounding from below. "I'm going to find a way down to you," he called.

"Forget about Imogen. She's lost," Trummel said. "We have to leave."

"I'm not leaving without her." Caleb felt along the paneled walls.

Gosswick pointed the gun at him. "You heard the orders. Come grab a rucksack."

Caleb ignored him, half expecting a bullet to the back.

Trummel shouted, "Goss, help me with the books."

They stuffed the hearts that Imogen had brought up into two backpacks. Caleb continued to search the walls. There had to be another way into the next chamber.

Gibbering noises caused him to turn around. On the floor, Dyfan's eye sockets filled with light. His bloodstained body convulsed in a seizure.

"Bloody hell!" Gosswick backed away, his arm trembling as he held up his pistol.

Dyfan's reanimated corpse rose to his feet. His glowing eyes scanned the faces of the three men in the room.

Trummel stepped toward him cautiously. "Thoth, have you returned?"

The corpse stared down at the backpacks stuffed with hearts. The thing roared and backhanded Trummel. He flew across the room and slammed against a wall.

Gunshots fired, punching holes in the corpse's back. He turned his lethal gaze on Gosswick, who backed up, shooting Dyfan's body several times. Other shots struck the walls and coffins.

Caleb ducked behind a sarcophagus as bullets pinged the metal.

Yelling like a maniac, Gosswick unleashed his gun until it clicked empty. Then he fled up the steps.

Dyfan's corpse tapped a wall full of blinking lights, and the round hatch door on the pyramid's roof began to close. Gosswick barely made it out. The hatch grated shut, sealing Caleb and Trummel inside the tomb with the god that possessed Dyfan's corpse.

CHAPTER FIFTY-SEVEN

Gosswick hurried down the pyramid's steps. Fuck bringing back the relics and all the money promised. He just wanted out of this damned hell.

He ran across the bridge that stretched over the moat. In the tar-black water, small faces appeared. Children's voices called his name. Others pleaded for him to give them treats. From the dark pools, little black hands reached over the edges of the bridge, trying to grab his ankles.

Gosswick sprinted faster. At the end of the moat's bridge, he turned left down a crossway. The way the grid surrounded the pyramid, he felt like he was running atop a maze.

The giant floating spheres swiveled as he passed. Lights from their many glowing eyes beamed onto him. Moving patterns projected onto his body. Gosswick bolted faster, trying to avoid the spotlights. The metal orbs ahead rotated. Their beams illuminated a stone catwalk that stretched a hundred yards. At the edge of the grid, the horizontal crossways led to portals in the colossal wall. Most doors were solid as iron. The one straight in front of him whirled like roiling oil.

The exit!

From the darkness of each square bottomless pit he passed, children's giggles followed. He looked over his shoulder. Small shadows climbed out of the pits. They called after him, "*Mzungu! Mzungu! Muzungu!*" which meant 'white man' in their Bantu language.

Christ, they're coming after me.

He sprinted pell-mell the final thirty yards and charged through the liquid portal.

He found himself back inside the cave. "Yes!" he shouted.

He ran frantically through the tunnel. The beam of his helmet lamp bounced off jagged limestone walls that twisted and turned. Giggles reverberated off the walls. Gosswick's mind flashed to a crowd of Kikuyu children playing in the dirty street in front of an orphanage. Their smiling faces. Their greedy hands reaching for his bag of sweets.

Their running feet sounded right behind him. Gosswick ran faster. The passage opened into a chamber he'd seen before. Primitive cave paintings of slaughtered children.

The giggles echoed off the walls. Then came the staccato barrage of machine-gun fire. Children's screams.

Gosswick's body shook with terror. He felt along the walls for a way out. The only exits were a steep vertical shaft and the tunnel he'd come from.

More snickers from just beyond the entrance.

He panned his light across a crowd of children filling the chamber.

First, they were the Kenyan kids he'd shot down in cold blood. Then they shifted into undead things. They giggled as they surrounded him, pawing his body. "Treats, treats…"

Gosswick collapsed to his knees and wailed as the children dug their fingers into him.

CHAPTER FIFTY-EIGHT

The honeycomb library was only partially lit, much of it still cast in shadow. Symbols chirped as they blinked around the honeycombs. A few hearts, still floating in their cells, pumped with alarm. Imogen kept her helmet light off, relying on the ambient light as she made her way through the twisting maze. She wondered where to go. Every exit she could find had sealed. She was trapped inside the eighth tier of the pyramid. And she wasn't alone.

The metal grid floor began to shake. Ahead came the sound of heavy footsteps. Hollow voices spoke in a cryptic language.

Imogen veered off into a small vent clogged with black hanging tubes and cables. Hard and rubbery tubing bent as she squeezed through them. She hid within the mass of synthetic tentacles. She held her breath as the footsteps drew near.

A pair of giant shadows walked past her hiding place. Blue light beams passed over the tubes. Imogen tucked her head back and hid deeper, praying she wouldn't be found.

★   ★   ★

One level above, Caleb watched in horror as Dyfan's possessed corpse picked up one of the hearts and approached an open sarcophagus. "Anubis," he said in a deep voice, calling the jackal-headed god. The large heart pumped in Dyfan's hands as he placed it into the chest of a giant corpse. Then Dyfan's throat released a loud, guttural sound. It resonated off the walls, vibrated in Caleb's bones.

In the sarcophagus, the giant's body began to shake, the head moving fast, the arms flapping at its sides.

Dyfan picked up another heart and placed it into the corpse of the ram god. "Khnum…" Its body, too, began to fill with light and shake with violent tremors.

Dear God, he's resurrecting them.

While Dyfan had his back turned, Caleb eased away. A hand grabbed his ankle. He looked down at Trummel's bleeding face.

"Don't leave me," he pleaded.

"You deserve whatever happens to you." Caleb yanked his leg from Trummel's grip and went to the far end of the crypt. He cared about only two things now: finding Imogen and escaping Duat.

All around the chamber numbers and symbols lit up, falling down the walls in waterfalls of alien codes. The wall in front of him illuminated with the lines of the metal panels. Next to a panel was a slot with a lever. He pulled it down. A square in the metal floor slid open, revealing metal rungs leading down a very steep shaft. Scattered lights partially lit it all the way to the bottom, at least one hundred and fifty feet. Caleb crossed himself with a quick prayer and then began to climb down the ladder.

CHAPTER FIFTY-NINE

Trummel pulled himself up off the floor, feeling aches in his bruised body. He tasted blood in his mouth. He had one hell of a concussion and probably some broken ribs.

The crypt was a chaos of flashing lights. No sign of Gosswick or Caleb anywhere. *They abandoned me.*

Dyfan had his back turned and was placing a fat pumping heart inside a sarcophagus. "Ammit…"

Trummel drew his pistol and slowly approached Dyfan from behind. All of the scars on the psychic's head and body glowed from some phosphorescent light that came from within. The codex, with all of its cryptic knowledge, on full display.

In the open coffins, three of the giants convulsed.

Whatever entity had possessed Dyfan's corpse, it had to be stopped. Trummel cocked his pistol. Dyfan slowly turned his head, looking over his shoulder. He grinned and spoke in his normal Scottish accent. "You pompous fool. You thought these relics were for you?"

"What do you mean?" Trummel asked.

"I knew all along what destiny awaited me in this tomb. *The gods* called me here. You were nothing more than a means of transport. Jolly well done, old chap."

Trummel felt the sting of betrayal. He shot point-blank into Dyfan's skull. His head snapped back, and then he collapsed to the floor. Trummel put a couple more bullets in the psychic's brain. Dyfan remained limp. The light emanating from his body went dark.

In the coffins, blue light coursed through three of the giants' veins. Shafts of light beamed from their eyes and the gods began to moan.

Trummel shouldered his rucksack containing one of the heart-enshrouded books. He could feel the thing pumping frantically against his back. Holding his sore ribs, he walked to the steps that led up to the sealed door. He began hitting buttons on the wall. "Come on, open up!"

Behind him the resurrected gods howled.

He ran up the staircase. He tried to push the circular metal hatch open, but it remained locked.

A creature growled behind him. Ammit, the Devourer, crawled to the bottom of the steps and peered up at him with her crocodile head turned sideways. Saliva dripped from her sharp-toothed mouth.

Trummel tried to shoot the demon, but his pistol clicked empty. "Bugger!"

Anubis and Khnum, each wearing masks, chest armor, and kilts, stepped up behind Ammit. She crouched, ready to pounce. Anubis put his hand on her shoulder, holding her back.

Cornered, Trummel dropped the rucksack and did as humans have for millennia – he pled mercy from the gods.

CHAPTER SIXTY

Imogen stayed hidden in the dark vent filled with hanging tubes. Her heart beat so fast it felt like it would burst. Loud footfalls ran past her hiding place. Something just beyond her vision stopped and breathed heavy, long hiss-like breaths. Light filtered through the vent and created patterns on the black tubes beside her. She dared to inch her face around the edge of a ribbed pipe. She glimpsed part of a metal mask. Twin beams projecting from its eyes passed over the tubes to her left. Imogen jerked her head back, causing the tubing to shake and clack together.

The masked creature hissed. A hand with enormous claws lunged into the vent. Imogen ducked as it swiped at her. It tore off her caving helmet.

She dug her way through the pyramid's arteries, found an adjoining vent that stretched horizontally. An air duct. The elongated arm stretched through the tubes, reaching for her. Imogen crawled into the narrow passage. Claws scraped the back of her calf. Crying out, she moved as fast as she could on hands and knees. She followed conduits that ran along the sides of the cramped space. The air duct was mostly dark. Every ten feet, slats from a vent offered thin lines of light. As she passed the vents, she could see the honeycombed maze.

A shadowy creature followed her on the other side of the wall. It tore open a grate. Its hand grabbed her ankle as she crawled past. She kicked loose and kept crawling.

★   ★   ★

Caleb worked his way down the ladder, careful not to look at the hundred-foot drop below. At each tier of the pyramid, faint light glowed from a passage. His injured hand and cut ear constantly throbbed with pain. His sweat-slick palms made gripping the rungs difficult. There was nothing to support his back, no climbing rope to secure him to the ladder. One slip and he could fall, banging down the shaft walls to his death. The grim thought caused his foot to miss a rung. He gripped the ladder with all this strength, hugging the metal. He righted himself, placing his dangling foot back on a rung. He took a deep breath before continuing.

He stared straight ahead, lowering himself down one rung at a time. He thought of Imogen, alone somewhere inside the pyramid. *I have to find her.*

At last, he reached a hexagon-shaped tunnel that stretched through darkness toward a chamber with soft blue light.

Shrieks echoed from somewhere in the pyramid. The sounds of running feet seemed to come from a level below him. He remembered the last thing he'd heard Imogen say. *"We've awakened them!"*

He climbed into the tunnel and started running. He entered a maze of empty honeycombs dripping with fluids. He hurried through the curved passages. The chamber, which stored Thoth's books, appeared to be built like a spiral. It funneled Caleb into an enormous crypt filled with giant coffins. Their lids stood open. Every sarcophagus he walked past was empty.

Where was Imogen? He worried that whatever ancient beings they had awakened from hibernation had taken her. *She could be dead. No, don't think that. She's alive. You can still find her and escape.* Hope drove Caleb to keep searching. He would explore every level of this pyramid, if he had to.

He started toward one of the exits. Flapping sounds came from above. He looked up into a gloom partially lit by control panels. He made out the shape of a shadowy creature high up on a perch. It looked female. Wings flapped on its back. Its eyes glowed gas-flame blue. Its long fingers tapped a panel. At the chamber's four exits, metal doors grated as they began to come down.

Caleb raced through the coffins.

The winged creature swooped down.

Claws swiped, slicing his back. Caleb dashed left toward a closing door. He dove under it and rolled, pulling his legs in just as the door came down and sealed. Claws scraped the metal. What sounded like an angry woman howled on the other side.

The gashes on Caleb's back and shoulder burned and blood stained his torn shirt. He cursed as he pressed a hand on the wound.

Clanging metal and garbled voices echoed from the tunnel behind him. He got to his feet. At a junction, he turned right and ran through a dark tunnel.

CHAPTER SIXTY-ONE

Imogen somehow had eluded the creature chasing her. The air ducts were another maze that ran between the pyramid's walls. She followed one passage until it led to the outside. She was very high up, looking down the side of the pyramid that had no steps. She had an overhead view of one section of the grid, the spheres, and the fortress wall. That slanted drop to several stories below gave her vertigo. She couldn't find a way to climb down, so she backed up and took another passage.

Again she heard footfalls. She peered through a vent. When she saw who was approaching, her heart soared. "Caleb!" she whispered.

"Imogen?" he looked around, confused. "Where are you?"

"In the wall." She tapped on the vent.

He came to her and peered through the slats. "Thank God, I found you. Hang on." He felt along the grate and opened it. He pulled Imogen out and held her in his arms.

She clung to him. "I was sure I'd never see you again." She felt blood on his back. "You're wounded."

"It's just a scratch," he said, but she could tell he was in pain.

"Let me have a look." She pulled away the shredded flaps of his shirt. Five deep, red gashes ran from his shoulder down his upper back. "Quick, take off your shirt. I need to dress it."

"There's no time."

"You'll bleed to death."

"What if we came here to die? I'm not afraid of crossing over into heaven," he said. "And you shouldn't be either."

His weakening eyes and grim talk worried her. "Please, stay with me, Caleb."

She helped him remove his shirt. She soaked up as much blood as she could and wrapped the shirt around his shoulder and ribs, tight, making a tourniquet. He winced as she tied the knot. "There."

Caleb smiled. "Why didn't I meet you years ago? We would have made a fine couple."

Imogen put her hands on his face. "We're going to find a way out of these caves and back to Cairo." She tried not to think about how far they would have to journey to get proper treatment for his wound. If she could make it back to camp, there might still be some medical supplies there.

They quickly discussed a plan of escape. First, they had to get out of this pyramid.

"There's a door on the sixth level," Imogen remembered, having seen it from the outside.

"I found a passageway behind us that leads downward." Caleb took her hand. "Let's get moving."

They followed a twisting tunnel to another steep shaft that resembled the inside of a silo. They climbed down rungs attached to the wall. Imogen, going first, moved faster. Caleb groaned as he struggled his way down. "Keep going," he told her. "I'll catch up."

"No, we stick together." She waited until he caught up.

The sound of metal banging rose from below. Imogen looked down to see others on the ladder, about sixty feet down. Shadow shapes with glowing pinpoints for eyes climbed up toward them.

"Keep going," Imogen urged. "We're almost to Level Six." She continued down the rungs faster. The ladder vibrated from the creatures climbing it – three levels below now and moving upward with incredible speed.

She reached a horizontal tunnel and jumped into it. Caleb slipped down the ladder, skipping rungs, and then caught one just below the tunnel. Past his shoulder, Imogen saw the creatures were two levels down now. Their eye beams shined on Caleb. With a burst of adrenaline, he climbed up the rungs.

Imogen reached down. "Take my hand."

He gripped it. She pulled him into the tunnel beside her.

Running, they turned left and right through tunnel after tunnel. Steam hissed from vents. Strobe lights flashed on the walls. Their pursuers shrieked all around them. Tunnels they passed clattered with feet running on the metal floor.

Caleb, growing weaker, leaned on Imogen. "Stay with me," she pleaded.

They exited a tunnel into a foyer with a colossal platinum door. She studied the alien panel. "I don't recognize any of the glyphs." She no longer had Grandfather's diary to help crack the code.

Caleb felt along the threshold. "Maybe there's a lever."

Imogen tapped the symbols, hoping to find a sequence that opened the door.

Bright lights found them suddenly. Imogen turned as several giant shadows approached from the gloom. Before she or Caleb had time to react, nets shot out of the darkness and wrapped around them. They both fell to the floor. The next thing Imogen saw was a masked figure looming over her and stabbing a needle into her shoulder.

CHAPTER SIXTY-TWO

Imogen woke up lying on a cold stone floor, dizzy and disoriented. The heavy metal net that had ensnared her still lay on top of her. Blurry lights illuminated the darkness. An alien voice shouted in clicks. The net loosened and drifted upward, away from her body. A chill passed through her. She rubbed her arms. The seam of her shirt had torn at the shoulder where the needle had been injected. The drug began to wear off. She looked around for Caleb but couldn't see him anywhere.

"Rise!" a booming voice echoed.

She pushed herself up off the floor and stood. Her eyes adjusted to the surrounding gloom. She was at the center of a great rectangular hall with a high ceiling and black engraved walls. She figured she was now on the bottom level of the pyramid. A pantheon of giant beings, over forty of them, sat high upon thrones imbedded in the walls. Most of the creatures wore metal animal masks with glowing cobalt blue eyes.

A bright beam from above spotlighted Imogen. She turned in a slow circle, in awe of these beings. Not one of them made a sound as they stared down at her. The quiet was unnerving. Her body trembled.

One giant sat on a black spiked throne that rose from a pool of water. He wore no mask, only a white cone-shaped hat. He had an elongated cranium with a monstrous wrinkled face and long white chin beard. The elder had green skin and held a crook and a flail. *Osiris*. Behind him stood two female aliens with golden wings, who must have been his sisters, Isis and Nephthys. On a throne lower than his father's sat Horus, the cables and wires no longer attached to him. At the base of the king's and prince's thrones, on a stone lotus, stood four armored beings that Imogen thought must be the four sons of Horus.

She recognized this place from the Amduat's paintings. *I'm standing in the Judgment Hall of Ma'at*. To her left stood a tall set of golden scales.

In the legends, the souls of the Egyptians who made it through Duat had been brought to this hall. Osiris, as Judge of the Dead, decided which souls were permitted into his kingdom and who would suffer in the underworld. The Hall of Ma'at was for the dead.

I'm still alive, she thought. She feared what these creatures intended to do with her.

Cranking sounded from above. Two metal nets lowered from the ceiling and set Caleb and Trummel on the floor. The nets released them and lifted into the air. Both men looked disoriented, as if just waking up from the drug.

Imogen ran to Caleb and helped him to his feet. His face and chest were pale. The bleeding had stopped, but he was so weak he had to lean on her.

Trummel stood as well, craning his neck to look up at the underworld gods. Unlike Caleb and Imogen, Trummel showed no humility.

Osiris gazed down at the three of them, his expression unreadable. His closed, lipless mouth formed a straight line. He motioned with the flail.

Armored warriors appeared from the shadows, took hold of their three captives' arms, and separated them ten feet apart.

A metallic clacking echoed in the hall. A large trapdoor in the floor began to open in front of them, revealing a dark pit. Hellish cries and growls came from below.

Caleb looked across at Imogen. "Have faith," he told her. "No matter what happens."

The guard behind him pointed a golden staff at Caleb's back. A crystal tip glowed. An aura of light enveloped Caleb and he levitated off the floor. Imogen watched helplessly as he floated over the pit and hung there suspended. He looked down at the growling blackness, then closed his eyes. His lips moved in prayer.

On the other side of the pit, Anubis approached the edge and raised his long-fingered hand. Caleb cried out as a hole opened up in his chest. His red pumping heart flew out and into the jackal god's hand. Somehow Caleb remained alive as he watched Anubis carry his heart toward the scales. Thoth stood to the right, holding open a large book. The demon Ammit crouched to the left of the scale, her crocodile teeth glistening.

Thoth announced, "The ritual of the scales measures the soul's worthiness to join us in the kingdom Aaru."

Anubis placed a feather on one side of the scale and Caleb's heart on the other. Right away, the scale tipped. The side with the feather sank and his heart, being the lighter of the two, rose to the top of the scale.

Imogen let out a breath. "Your soul passed their test," she whispered.

Caleb's heart returned to his chest and the wound miraculously sealed. Osiris waved his crook. A swirling vortex opened high above Caleb, shining a bright white light down on him. His eyes went to Imogen and he smiled with a look of total surrender.

Tears ran down Imogen's cheeks. "Goodbye, Caleb," she whispered.

On a high perch, the goddess Ma'at stood and spread her broad wings. She glided down, scooped Caleb into her arms, and flew straight up into the vortex. It closed in a flash.

Imogen's grief turned to terror as a beam of energy struck her from behind, paralyzed her, and lifted her off her feet. Trummel levitated with her. Together they floated over the growling pit.

"Wait, no!" Trummel yelled as Anubis opened his chest and snatched his heart. Heavy as a stone, it sent the scale down to the floor with a *clack*. The scale with the feather swung at the top.

"No..." Trummel said. "I belong among the gods."

"Your misdeeds and selfish acts far outweigh any good you have done," Thoth said. "You belong among the damned."

Anubis tossed the heart into Ammit's sharp-toothed mouth and she devoured it.

Trummel fell screaming into the pit.

★   ★   ★

Down inside the deepest, darkest blackness, Trummel lay on a bed of nightmarish things that squirmed beneath him and crowded around him. Claws scratched his skin.

A beam of red light shined down on him, and the things that attacked him retreated into the darkness. They howled in protest of this intrusion of harsh light. Trummel squinted and followed the beam up to a robotic sphere with a dozen red eyes. One beam kept the horrors at bay, while a second beam illuminated a muddy path. It was well trodden with footprints. The sphere motioned toward him, then back to the path, as if telling him to follow, and then the machine glided ahead. Trummel got up and followed, doing his best to stay within the beam.

Just beyond the visible edges, shapes of creatures followed him. Some ran on two legs, others on four. He caught glimpses of zebra-striped skin. Curved horns. Hoofed feet. Some had hands and toes with black claws. The subterranean beasts reeked of shit and rotten carcasses. One four-legged thing had exposed bones and an open rib cage, as if it had been savagely eaten but refused to die.

Up ahead echoed cries of the damned.

Have I died? Trummel wondered. He felt his chest. The hole had sealed but he no longer had a heartbeat. The core of his chest felt cold. Still, he seemed very much alive. His lungs breathed foul air. His body felt pain from bruises and scratches. If anything, the sensitivity of his nerves had been heightened. His skin sweated from the balmy heat of this lower realm.

Where is this underworld guide taking me? As the machine glided forward, Trummel struggled to walk fast through mud that sucked at his boots. A third red beam shot out of the sphere. It spotlighted a horrific tableau off to Trummel's right. Men he recognized from his expedition – Ely, Sykes, Vickers, Quig, and several other soldiers and workers – were embedded in the walls by a black sticky substance. Their faces and portions of their bodies were exposed to hellish horrors that crawled over them and burrowed into their ravaged skin. The men continuously cried out in pain, a chorus of endless suffering.

The spotlight passed over Aiden Gosswick stuck to the wall. A crowd of child demons were peeling strips of muscle off his bones and eating him alive. Goss's flesh grew back instantly, only to be torn away again and devoured. He stretched out his arm, screaming for Trummel to save him.

Trummel looked away, terrified now of his own fate. "No, I don't deserve to suffer as these fools!" Trummel yelled, hoping the gods were listening. "I was led here by a higher cause, to bring enlightenment to the world. I made it past every obstacle you threw my way. I reached your pyramid. I should ascend or be sent back with your wisdom! If we're not ready for all of it, then let me return with something to raise man's knowledge."

The sphere moved faster, threatening to abandon him.

The ravenous herd behind him stayed close on his heels. Claws swiped at his back, ripped off a piece of his shirt.

Damn it, stay within the light. He picked up his pace. The muddy floor descended into shin-deep water. The sphere stopped and hovered over him. Its beams panned across a swamp with thorny trees. A giant tree with a crown of leafless branches loomed above the others.

No…anywhere but here.

The dark water moved with several black snakes. Some sat coiled in the trees. A serpent slithered past his leg and Trummel jumped.

The mechanical sphere rotated, its red eyes looking down on him in judgment. Then the lights turned off and left him in pitch darkness.

Screeching and clicking filled his ears. The creatures that had followed him closed in. They pinned him to the trunk of a tree. Thorny flesh and jutting bones poked into every inch of him. Their faces pressed against his skin and hissed, dripping thick cords of drool onto his face. Trummel fought to break free, his mind turning insane from terror. Razor-sharp hands braced his head and held down his wrists and ankles. They tore away his clothes. And then came the pricking pain of a hundred claws carving his skin.

★   ★   ★

Trummel's distant screams reached Imogen from the bottom of the pit. She couldn't bear to hear his cries. After several agonizing seconds, he went silent.

Is that what's in store for me? She thought of all the years she had turned her back on God. Memories of her misdeeds played out in her mind, the times when she had acted stubbornly and foolishly. She saw her younger self standing at the upstairs window of her family home, shooting her father's pistol at the angry protestors outside. How the ricocheted bullet that struck Geoffrey's leg had fueled the mob's murderous rage. She saw her near attempts at suicide. Had she done enough good in her life to spare her soul from being damned in the underworld?

She thought of Caleb, his faith in God and angels, the lightness of his heart, and she prayed for her soul.

Anubis stepped toward her. Even with her floating a few feet off the floor, he towered above her. With a broad, bare upper body and jackal-headed mask, he was an imposing beast. His hand stretched toward her chest. She felt only numbness as the hole opened and her heart shot out.

Anubis caught it and placed her still-pumping heart on the scales.

Imogen held her breath.

The heart began to sink, the feather rising.

She remembered the Book of the Dead offered forty-two declarations of innocence to be spoken in the form of negative confessions before Osiris. She called out as many as she could recall. "I am not deceitful. I have done no evil against any man. I have not stolen by my own accord…"

The scales tipped and bounced the other way, heart rising, feather falling. As she spoke a dozen negative confessions straight from the book that Thoth had written and given to mankind, the scales teetered back and forth. When her declarations were complete, she said, "I pray for mercy on my soul."

For several seconds the scales went up and down, slowing with each cycle, until they stopped. Her heart tipped the scales a half inch below the feather.

The beams from Thoth's eyes scanned the organ. Then he pointed at Imogen and yelled, "The guilt and shame you carry in your heart are too heavy. Descend!"

The light around her shut off. Then she felt the weight of gravity and fell through the trapdoor.

CHAPTER SIXTY-THREE

Imogen landed on soft carpet in a familiar den filled with elegant furniture and paintings. One was a melting family portrait of Mum and Dad with Imogen when she was six. Smoke filled the air. It stung her lungs, making her cough. Heat pressed against her skin. Screams echoed from above and below. Olga's baby wailed.

As Imogen walked through her burning house, she witnessed the memory of that dreadful night. Family members ran through the flames in slow motion.... Her father and Heinrich Müller fought the spreading fire in the study. Their clothes ignited like torches. Olga backed into a corner with the crying baby, penned in by a fence of fire. The maids, trapped upstairs, shouted for help as their hair and dresses caught flame, then fell over the railings to their deaths. Her nanny, Miss Emily, cried out Imogen's name as a blaze and beams collapsed on top of her.

Fire leapt and spread across the ceiling of a downstairs hallway. Imogen watched helplessly as her mum and younger self crawled on hands and knees toward a bathroom, where a tiny window offered escape for only one. The bathroom door closed.

Imogen beat on the door, feeling the flames scorching her back. She crouched, unable to handle the heat. Smoke clouded around her. She coughed in fits. She squeezed her eyes tight, awaiting the fire to consume her.

Then she was suddenly outside, the cool night air embracing her. Imogen opened her eyes. She was standing in the front circular driveway of the manor – now a looming fortress of flame and billowing smoke.

Her younger self cried, struggling to open the front door so her mother could escape. The chains shackling the door's handle to a post were so hot they burned the little girl's hands. She cried on the lawn. Imogen approached her younger self to comfort her, but the girl faded like a ghost and vanished.

"Immy..." called Mum's voice from inside the house.

The chains around the front door came loose and fell to the ground as the front door burned away. From a foyer consumed with hellfire, out walked a group of burning corpses. Her parents stepped onto the driveway. Next came the Müllers, her nanny, the servants…all gathered in front of the house. Heinrich's face was a blackened skull. All of Olga's beautiful hair had burnt away. The young mother cradled a small charred body.

Mum's and Dad's orange rippling forms stepped forward. Dad's skin floated up in cinders and ash. Flames draped Mum's body like a gown, as if she were dressed to attend a ball where devils and demons danced. She reached out her fiery arms. "Come to Mum and Daddy, Immy. It's time to go home."

All the grief and guilt that Imogen had suppressed gripped her heart. She couldn't help feeling responsible for her family's deaths. *If I hadn't shot the pistol at Geoffrey's mob and angered them more….* A part of her regretted not dying in the fire with her family. She had never understood why God had allowed her to survive and not them.

"Come be with us, ladybug," her father said. "We all miss you."

"I miss you too."

All the longing to be with her family again returned. To be home. Imogen began to reach for her parents' hands. Before they touched, she felt the painful heat and pulled away. She stared into her mum's eyes peering through a veil of rippling flame. It brought back the moment when Imogen was a little girl trapped with her mother in the bathroom as fire burned the door. Smoke had made them both cough. Mum had hurried to the small window and opened it. "You must go," she had said.

"I can't. I don't want to leave you." Young Imogen had wrapped her arms around her mother's waist and clung to her.

"I want you to live, my precious girl. Live and have a glorious life." Mum had hugged her tight, kissed her forehead. "Now, out you go." She'd ushered Imogen out the window.

A moment later, thick smoke billowed through the window and her mother's coughing and cries of pain went silent.

Now, standing with Mum and Dad brought tears to Imogen's eyes. "You helped me escape, so I could live."

Their ghosts nodded. "This was our destiny. It can be yours too. Come be with us again."

Her parents, all of their staff, and the Müllers started toward her.

Imogen backed away. She recalled what Caleb had said about the Duat projecting her darkest fears. It was trying to trick her into suffering an eternity with her guilt. "You're not real," she told them. "I won't go with you."

Everyone stopped and quietly watched her as the flames continued to burn skin off their bones. Soon they were nothing but skeletons glowing with fire. Only her parents still had faces.

"Goodbye, Mum and Dad. I love you."

They both nodded. The last thing her mother said to her was "What our enemies did to us wasn't your fault. It was ours."

Imogen wiped tears from her eyes as her parents' fiery ghosts burst into embers and were gone. The rest of her family vanished as well. The ruins of their three-story house caved in inside the crackling fire.

Imogen turned her back on it and continued walking through a dark tunnel. The surrounding darkness remained quiet. The more she walked, the more her grief, guilt, and shame left her body like ashes blowing away. A beam of light surrounded her. She floated up and found herself once again suspended in the Hall of Ma'at with all the gods watching. Her heart, back on the scale, moved up and down until it stopped in perfect balance with the feather.

A murmur of voices echoed around the pantheon.

Thoth stepped forward with his book and conversed with Osiris in their alien language.

Imogen, held suspended above the pit, wondered what was happening.

Osiris said something incoherent. Thoth read a few passages from his book, his voice reverberating around the great hall, and then he closed the book with an echo that made Imogen shudder. Anubis pulled her heart off the scale and sent it flying back into her chest. The hole closed up and she felt her heart beating rapidly against her breastbone. She floated toward the scale and was set down on her feet.

Thoth motioned with his hand. "Imogen, come forward."

Hearing the god speak her name humbled her. The spotlight followed her as she stepped before Thoth. The giant with the curved beak examined her with luminous eyes.

"You are one of the few who has balanced the scales," he said. "By the laws of the Supreme One, who is Highest of the Highest, we must give you a choice."

He held up his palm and two vortexes swirled open, one to Imogen's right. Inside it, a cave tunnel led straight to sunlight and the most beautiful blue sky. The second spinning vortex glowed directly above her. It glimmered with stars.

"You can go home or you can ascend to the next level," Thoth said. "Should you ascend, your time in the Earth Realm will be complete. To go to the kingdom Aaru, to learn every truth in the universe, you must shed this body for the next. Should you choose to go back to your world, you will forget all that you've experienced in the Dark Realm. What happened to the others on your expedition and knowledge of our existence will be erased from your mind. Now you must decide."

Imogen stared down the tunnel that offered escape. After all she'd been through, it was tempting to run to freedom and feel the sun on her face. But what was there to pull her home? Grandfather, the last of her family, was dead. She could continue working at the museum, piecing together the puzzles of ancient Egypt, never knowing that she had once come in contact with their gods or seen that Duat was a real place.

What she'd always wanted was to know the mysteries of the universe, see it in all its wondrous dimensions. The world she'd be leaving behind offered nothing but an endless search for answers. Her fear of dying melted away and she was left with a deep feeling of reverence. For the first time since she was a child, she had faith.

She looked up at Thoth. "I choose to ascend."

The god of knowledge nodded and raised his hands. A peaceful aura of blue light swirled around her. Both excited and curious as to what awaited her beyond this life, wondering if she might see Grandfather and Caleb again, Imogen floated upward into the swirling light.

EPILOGUE

Trummel woke to the sound of drumming and the feeling of a beetle crawling across his face. It burrowed into a wound on his cheek and nested there. Every inch of his body ached. The slightest movement felt like razor blades slicing his nerves.

Where the hell am I? His last memory was being judged by the gods, then falling into the pit. He'd thought the demons in the dark had torn him apart.

His eyes adjusted to rippling lights. Small green fires burned in altar bowls that hung from twisting, leafless branches. He had been tied to the top of a giant tree, with his arms strung above his head and his ankles crossed over each other. All around him stretched the black water swamp and its infinite maze of briars.

Thirty feet below, skeletal creatures with diseased pale skin worshipped him. A circle of them beat their hands on drums. Some danced with their arms raised, holding live snakes as they chanted. Others, on hands and knees in the mud, bowed repeatedly to the altar figure on the ancient tree.

They've made me an idol. Already he could sense the tedious nature of being held up as an object of worship. The sheer loneliness would drive him mad.

Trummel's eyes filled with tears as he spotted his sister walking among the leprous crowd. *Nell.* In her torn, muddied dress, she stopped and looked up at him with a faint smile. She put her hand on the back of one of the worshippers kneeling beside her. The man tilted his head, raising his bearded face. Trummel reeled as Göran Järvi stood and took Nell's hand. Trummel felt the pain of her loss a thousand times over. All he could do was stare into her killer's eyes and feel hate. Trummel fought against the ropes, causing more razor cuts of pain across his body. Blood leaked from freshly opened scabs. He screamed in agony, then collapsed in surrender. When he looked into his sister's eyes, he was surprised to see she was filled with peace. She smiled bigger and waved. Tears streamed down Trummel's cheeks.

A small ball of white light appeared on the dark horizon. It shot above the treetops. As the sphere drew closer, the worshippers below shouted in panic and scattered. Nell and Järvi took off with them, disappearing into the briars.

The sphere floated inches from Trummel's face, examining him. Then the ropes around his wrists and ankles unraveled. He feared he would fall, but as the bindings released him from the tree, Trummel floated down to the ground with the sphere. It expanded into a giant ball of bright white light, then burst into a thousand fireflies.

Standing before him was Thoth, wearing his bird mask and shiny armor.

Trummel stood weakly before the god and stared up at him with reverence.

Thoth waved his hand over the symbols that had been cut into every inch of Trummel's body. They glowed as the palm passed over them.

Thoth nodded as if he approved. "You are finally learning humility. Now, I will offer you a choice. You may stay in this realm as an idol to the damned or you may fulfill a mission for us. A great war is on the horizon, and the human race is devolving to the point they will destroy themselves. As a walking codex, you will deliver our message to those awake enough to find this place."

A portal opened beside them. Glorious sunlight glowed at the end of a tunnel.

"What choice will you make?" Thoth asked.

Moments later, Trummel emerged from a cave, squinting at the brightness of the sun.

ABOUT THE AUTHOR

Brian Moreland writes dark suspense, thrillers, and horror. His books include *Dead of Winter, Shadows in the Mist, The Witching House, The Devil's Woods, The Seekers*, and *Darkness Rising*. Several of his short stories have appeared in anthologies and horror fiction blogs. Brian loves hiking, world travel, and spending time with family. He lives in Tennessee where he is having fun writing new scary fiction.

Find Brian on Twitter @BrianMoreland or on Facebook: facebook.com/HorrorAuthorBrianMoreland. You can also find out more on his website: www.brianmoreland.com.

FLAME TREE PRESS
FICTION WITHOUT FRONTIERS
Award-Winning Authors & Original Voices

Flame Tree Press is the trade fiction imprint of Flame Tree Publishing, focusing on excellent writing in horror and the supernatural, crime and mystery, science fiction and fantasy. Our aim is to explore beyond the boundaries of the everyday, with tales from both award-winning authors and original voices.

•

You may also enjoy:
American Dreams by Kenneth Bromberg
Second Lives by P.D. Cacek
The City Among the Stars by Francis Carsac
Vulcan's Forge by Robert Mitchell Evans
The Widening Gyre by Michael R. Johnston
The Blood-Dimmed Tide by Michael R. Johnston
The Sky Woman by J.D. Moyer
The Guardian by J.D. Moyer
The Goblets Immortal by Beth Overmyer
Until Summer Comes Around by Glenn Rolfe
A Killing Fire by Faye Snowden
The Bad Neighbor by David Tallerman
A Savage Generation by David Tallerman
Ten Thousand Thunders by Brian Trent
Two Lives: Tales of Life, Love & Crime by A Yi

Horror titles available include:
Snowball by Gregory Bastianelli
Thirteen Days by Sunset Beach by Ramsey Campbell
The Influence by Ramsey Campbell
The Wise Friend by Ramsey Campbell
The Haunting of Henderson Close by Catherine Cavendish
The Garden of Bewitchment by Catherine Cavendish
Boy in the Box by Marc E. Fitch
Black Wings by Megan Hart
Will Haunt You by Brian Kirk
We Are Monsters by Brian Kirk
Hearthstone Cottage by Frazer Lee
Those Who Came Before by J.H. Moncrieff
Stoker's Wilde by Steven Hopstaken & Melissa Prusi
They Kill by Tim Waggoner
The Forever House by Tim Waggoner

•

Join our mailing list for free short stories, new release details, news about our authors and special promotions:

flametreepress.com